THE EVENING WOLVES

IRON ON IRON

BOOK FOUR

GREGORY ASHE

H&B

This is a work of fiction. Names, characters, places, and incidents either are the product of the author's imagination or are used fictitiously, and any resemblance to actual persons, living or dead, business establishments, events, or locales is entirely coincidental.

The Evening Wolves

Published by Hodgkin & Blount
https://www.hodgkinandblount.com/
contact@hodgkinandblount.com

Published 2024
Printed in the United States of America

Version 1.05

Trade Paperback ISBN: 978-1-63621-071-1
eBook ISBN: 978-1-63621-070-4

1

A broken jaw of Christmas lights sagged ahead of Emery Hazard, and he stepped gingerly over a fallen strand. Leaves, wet and slimy, made the sidewalk treacherous underfoot. A siren in the distance. A door slamming. The wind a wolf at his heels. Not a night for a private detective to be out in the cold, much less a nineteen-year-old girl.

Ahead, the dark funnel of the street ran until it dissolved. It was barely half past six, and he was in a city with millions. But it was winter, and on this block, half of the streetlights were dead. Maybe one house in three showed a scrap of yellow where curtains failed to seal a window adequately. It was late for this kind of work, which was better done in the daylight—among other reasons, because people in the camps tended to go to sleep once the sun went down. But he wanted to finish the job and go home, and so he kept walking. Not for the first time, he checked the revolver holstered under his arm.

The homeless encampment took shape gradually: a jumbled geometry of shadows at first, and then, by degrees, discrete shapes. A pallet leaning at a drunken angle. Plastic tarps rustling when a winter wind moved through them and made them billow. Armchairs lashed together with bungee cords. One improvised wall had been made from a pair of bifold doors. Cardboard, of course, the flattened boxes bending with moisture.

Encampment was a grandiose word, Emery decided, for a space that couldn't have held more than a dozen people. The camp was on an empty lot in one of the inner Kansas City neighborhoods. On the next street, strip malls held massage parlors and tattoo artists and payday loan stores. Go a block in the other direction and you'd find tire yards and a Dollar General and a walk-in clinic with security grating over the windows and about a million signs that said WE DO NOT HAVE OPIOIDS. A hundred years ago, the Italianate brick homes here, with their mansard roofs and redbrick walls, had held the city's well-to-do. Fifty years ago, they'd been less desirable as people with money fled to subdivisions and developments farther out. Thirty years ago, they'd been slated for urban renovation, only the money had mysteriously disappeared. Emery stepped over a used condom and thought maybe they should just clear everyone out and light a match. At least then people would be warm.

Huddled amidst the makeshift structures of the camp were a few tents, and at the curb, a Ford E-350, thirty years old minimum, with powder blue stripes and flat tires. Many of the camps Emery had visited over the day had been similar—a mixture of types of shelter. Like everyone else, people who were homeless had a pecking order. He ignored the van for now and turned toward the cluster of tents and shanties.

Pushing back his coat, he cleared the Blackhawk under his arm. The cold pressed against his chest. He called in a low voice, "Deanna?"

In some ways, Deanna Vance might have been considered lucky—or, at least, luckier than many people. She was alive, for one reason. For another, she had a family who cared for her. Parents who, until recently, sent her money. The last time, to a Western Union fifteen blocks from here. They'd known about her drug use. They hadn't known where she was staying. When Emery had asked, her mother had said, *With a friend*, the way some people talked about Santa Claus.

As he moved into the encampment, he left the sidewalk behind. Instead of leaves, he now had to navigate a path trampled into the snow, which had melted and frozen again, and he went slowly to keep his balance. The stink of smoke met him—an acrid, unclean smell that suggested whatever they'd been burning had been soaked in chemicals. Pressure-treated lumber, maybe. Or some sort of synthetic. When the breeze bellied the tarps again, plastic rustling, he caught a whiff of soiled bodies, a hint of shit. Among the shanties, the darkness thickened, and he worked a flashlight out of his pocket and turned it on. "Deanna?"

"Fuck off!" a man's voice barked back at him from a jumble of fruit crates.

Emery kept moving. The beam from his flashlight showed him the garbage littering the snow: flattened foam cups, an airplane bottle of Fireball, an empty pack of USA Gold, its cellophane unspooling to catch the light.

The wind picked up again. Emery's ears stung. The tip of his nose. He blinked his eyes clear. How cold was it? The weather had been predicted to be in the 20s for tonight, but when the wind picked up…

"Deanna," he called as he stepped over a lone, detached bicycle wheel.

The sound of a zipper came, and Emery shot his light in that direction. A man poked his head out of a tent. He had to be in his fifties, his face lined and puffy under graying stubble, and unless Emery missed his guess, his glasses were bifocals. He wore a Bass Pro hat, and then a hood pulled up over the hat. He stared at Emery for a long moment. Then he pointed in the direction Emery had been going and said, "She's at the end."

Emery nodded.

The man stared a little longer. Maybe it was a threat or a warning. Maybe it was simply curiosity. Maybe he'd been hitting his substance of choice.

When nothing more came, Emery continued in the direction he'd been walking. He glanced back once and, even in the dark, could make out the man's head as a silhouette against the dark.

The tent at the end of the row was striped red and gray, and the beam of the flashlight penetrated the thin shell enough to suggest shadows on the other side. A two-tier shopping cart was tied to one tentpole, the top basket filled with a carry-on roller bag, the lower basket jammed with loose clothing. Plastic totes were stacked next to the cart; the topmost's lid was broken, and inside lay what appeared to be nothing more than junk: wadded-up newspaper, a clear vinyl toiletry bag, a coaxial cable, more bungee cords.

Emery stood to one side of the tent's flap and asked, "Deanna?"

No reply.

He shifted a little farther to the side and called again. After thirty seconds, he gripped one of the poles and jostled the tent. In a louder voice, he said, "I'm looking for Deanna Vance."

"Shut up," the first man called from far off, "or I'm going to shut you up!"

Emery counted to thirty again. He unzipped the tent, and the sound seemed unnaturally loud in the stillness. He braced himself for sudden movement, for outraged shouts, for drug-fueled confusion and rage. But nothing came.

She was too pale, dirty hair spilling over one cloudy eye, blueness at her lips. Then he registered the dirty water bottles piled around her, the improvised pallet of clothing, a sleeping bag twisted around her waist. The smell of loose bowels was stronger here, enough to make him rear back, draw in a lungful of the relatively cleaner air, the sharpness of it catching in his throat.

Before anything else, he drew on a pair of disposable gloves. Then he checked her pulse. Nothing. She was cold, and rigor had set in. Or perhaps, in this weather, her body was literally frozen. He would leave that to a forensic pathologist.

He found her purse, a glossy black thing that reminded him of patent leather shoes his mother had bought for him when he'd been a child. For church. It was split on one side, and the clasp had broken. No license. No ID of any kind. No cash. A tampon, a clump of dirty tissues, a stub of lipstick that she hadn't used recently, if she had used it at all. A nearly empty bottle of hand sanitizer. He returned it all to the purse and set it next to her. Scabs marked one side of her face. No bruising that he could see. No visible wounds. No petechiae to indicate strangulation, although again, that would be a decision for the pathologist. No needles, no empty baggies. She was nineteen, and he thought she had died from the cold, alone, in the dark. He noticed distantly that the sirens had stopped.

The sound of a zipper came from behind Emery, then heavy breathing, footsteps. When he turned, it was the man in the Bass Pro hat. Over the hoodie, he wore a satin Royals jacket, and where his jeans rode up, Emery saw at least two layers of socks. He looked past Emery into the tent and shivered, his shoulders riding up.

"Did you know her?" Emery asked.

The man shrugged.

"Did you hear anything tonight? See anything?"

The man shook his head.

Emery nodded and took out his phone to call emergency services.

"You the friend?" the man asked.

As Emery raised the phone to his ear, one of the streetlights sparked and went out. "She didn't have any friends."

2

"It's a simple request, Nico." Emery pushed the pen and paper across the kitchen counter. "Print legibly, please."

Nico sighed and looked at John. "Where are Noah and Rebeca? Why isn't anyone bailing me out?"

It was the Sunday before Christmas, and in theory, everyone was still buoyed up with holiday cheer. That was probably because most of them hadn't spent the previous day wading through clusters of human misery. Emery tried to focus on the present. The house was warm and full of light, with holiday decorations and the Christmas tree in pride of place (Colt had taken charge of decorating it), and sweet with the smell of baking cookies. Colt had been determined to frost sugar cookies, and now he stood watching the oven, turning the light on and off in thirty-second intervals, muttering to himself about the color of the Christmas tree-shaped cookies Evie and Lana had helped cut out. He'd set two timers. In between checking the cookies, he also spent a fair amount of time touching his hair, which had gotten long over the last few months, and which he was clearly dying for Nico to comment on. Biscuit waited patiently next to him, clearly under the belief that she would eventually be rewarded, either by accident or design.

"Out of town," John said with a laugh. "You're on your own."

"He's your husband."

"Is it Chase again?" Emery asked.

Nico scowled. He was, in a turn of events that was becoming more and more common, dressed something like an adult: slim chinos, a wine-colored sweater, his shaggy hair longer than Emery remembered and spilling over his collar. "Shouldn't you have him trained? Shouldn't he know all his commands by now? Sit, stay, quiet."

"We've been working on sit," John-Henry said.

"Did you know you have to train a dog to speak before you can train it to be quiet?" Colt asked without looking away from the oven.

Groaning, Nico sank down onto the stool. "God, never mind."

"You're all hilarious," Emery said, bumping Nico with the pen and paper. "Now write."

"Is Nico telling you about his date?" Auggie asked as he came into the kitchen. His dark hair was dusted with snow, and he was shrugging out of a jacket that managed to look both expensive and understated at the same time. It went with the rest of the package: the soft brown of Auggie's skin, the stunner smile, the fact that, even though he was shorter than average, he was ridiculously good-looking. A few months before, a killer had cut his face with a knife. Although the scar was still red and raised as it healed, thanks to a good plastic surgeon, it was only a fine line that ran straight down his cheek. When it healed completely, Emery guessed, it would barely be visible. Emery didn't particularly care about that, though; he was looking forward to Auggie's thirties, particularly to the first time Auggie saw a wrinkle.

At the words, Nico sat up, horror streaking across his face.

"It's a date?" John asked.

"You said it was coffee," Emery said.

This, apparently, was enough to break Colt's attention—if only for a moment. He looked surprisingly hurt as he glanced at Nico and asked, "How old is he?"

Emery looked at his son.

Colt blushed, mumbled, "Hi, Mr. Lopez," and turned his stare back to the oven.

"If necessary," Emery said, "I can find his Social on my own, but I'll need a first and last name. Date of birth would be ideal."

"It's not a date," Nico said.

"I thought you were staying at his—" Admittedly a bit late, Auggie managed to stop. He put a hand to his neck as color rushed into his face, and then he said, "Um."

Nico set his glare to murderous.

"You're staying at his place?" Emery asked.

"Thank you, Auggie."

"I thought they knew!"

"Just because he's staying at his place," Colt said, darting another big-eyed glance at Nico, "it doesn't mean anything. Like, he could just sleep on the couch. Nico could sleep on the couch here, and it wouldn't mean anything."

Emery looked at his son a little longer this time. Face on fire, Colt took out his phone, apparently to set a third timer.

"I appreciate the concern—"

"It's not concern. I simply don't want to have to hire another administrative assistant and teach him how to file."

"—but you're not my boyfriend, and you're not my brother, and you're not my dad."

"You don't talk to your brother," Emery said. "And for someone who's not your dad, I spent a lot of time figuring out that ridiculous health insurance you have through the college."

"Ok, yes, that was really cool of you. And I appreciate it. But Emery—and I mean this with a lot of love—it isn't any of your business. You're my—" He stopped, and the unfinished sentence hung in the air.

"Ex?" Emery said drily.

"Ree," John murmured.

"Boss?"

"A little help," Nico said to Auggie.

"Kind of like a general in an army, only you used to have sex with him. Oh, a sex general."

Emery cut his gaze to Auggie.

A huge smirk spread across Auggie's face. "I'll go check on Theo and Lana."

"Excellent idea, August."

For whatever reason, that only made Auggie's smile grow as he left the room. He even did a little jump at the end and slapped the top of the opening to the living room. It reminded Emery of something his son would have done. Or, for that matter, his husband.

"You're my friend," Nico said. "And I hope you know how much you mean to me. But I'm an adult, and when I'm ready for you to meet—"

"The word is interrogate," John said.

"—someone I'm interested in, I'll introduce you. Like an adult. Not because you were skulking outside his window and when he got a little aggressive, you started tapping on the window and saying, 'Hey, you!'"

"Oh my God," Colt muttered.

"He peed himself."

John gaped at Emery.

"Don't act so shocked." Emery settled himself at the counter again. "Very well, Nico. If you refuse to tell me, I can't force you."

"And I don't want you following me."

Emery snorted.

"Promise."

"Why would I follow you?"

"Emery Hazard."

For a moment, Emery considered a lie. Then outrage won out. "For heaven's sake, Nico, it's for your own good. The one in July was running a meth lab and had three restraining orders filed against him!"

Nico shoved the pen and paper across the counter. A blush swam under his coppery skin, but his jaw was set. "Promise."

"Fine. If you're going to be a fool, I can't stop you."

"I want to hear the words."

"I. Promise."

The kitchen seemed hotter than it had a few minutes ago, and Emery threw the blank sheet of paper in the recycling and tossed the pen back into the junk drawer.

"I appreciate it, Em," Nico said in a quieter voice. "Really."

Emery made a noncommittal noise.

"What are you guys doing?" John asked, breaking the quiet that followed. "Dinner?"

The look of strain on Nico's face almost made Emery take pity on him. When he spoke, he directed the words toward the floor. "He said it's a surprise."

John gave Emery a warning look, and he put his hands up in surrender.

Another silence stretched out between them. Then Nico said, with a little too much enthusiasm, "What about you, Colt? How are things with Ashley?"

Colt shrugged and turned on the light in the oven.

"Is that a good shrug or a bad shrug?"

Nico got another shrug in reply, but then Colt said, "Good, I guess."

"It seems like they're going really good," John said. "They exchanged their gifts early, and Ash got Colt a necklace for Christmas."

A smile transfigured Colt's face, and he forgot about the oven. "It's real gold," he said, fishing it out from under his shirt. "And it's exactly like the one I wanted, and he didn't even ask me or anything."

Nico inspected the chain, smiling. "These are really in right now. Ash did a good job."

Colt was blushing now—and some of that, Emery had to admit, was the proximity to Nico, the undiluted attention—and he nodded. When Nico released the chain, he tucked it back under the borrowed (stolen) Blues sweatshirt that had once been John's.

"And what did you get Ashley?"

"This stupid fishing reel. He'd been talking about it for months, and I thought that's what he wanted."

"He did want it," John said. "He loved it."

"I should have gotten him something else."

"I caught Ashley practicing casts in the backyard," Emery said. "In the snow. For the love of God, he didn't even have any line on it. I'd say he was pleased with your gift."

Colt shrugged.

"It sounds like it was a perfect gift," Nico said. "Not everyone wants jewelry, Colt. What matters in a gift is that it shows you know that person, that you care about them."

It took Emery a moment to realize that the strange way Colt was holding his head was an attempt to keep both of his dads out of his line of sight as he said, "But it's not, like, romantic."

"That's why you've got Valentine's," Nico said, the crook of a smile forming.

"Holy shit."

"Language," Emery said.

But Colt was smiling to himself as he checked the cookies again.

"You two looked very cute together at GLAM the other day," Nico added.

Colt's smile grew, and his blush deepened. The Gay and Lesbian Alliance of Mid-Missouri had opened recently, occupying a glorified storefront in a strip mall on the northeast side of town, and once football had ended, Colt and Ashley had started going one or two afternoons every week.

"Are you volunteering there too?" John asked.

"Just dropping off a donation. I thought I saw you guys carrying chairs."

"They help run the afternoon programming," Emery said.

"We just put out chairs, snacks, that kind of thing." Colt chewed on the sweatshirt's cuff for a moment, and then he blurted. "Did you know almost a third of LGBTQ kids experience homelessness or housing instability at some point?"

Nobody said what they were thinking: that not too long ago, Colt had been one of those kids.

"I didn't know that," Nico said, which Emery assumed was a lie.

"And over forty percent of them seriously consider attempting suicide every year?"

Nico shook his head. "Is it really that high?"

"It's even higher for trans kids."

"Colt's really passionate about helping other LGBTQ kids," John said, scruffing their son's hair. "He raised donations at school for GLAM."

"Ash is the one who's really good at it. Everybody likes Ash."

Emery couldn't help the noise that escaped him, but when his husband shot him a look, he did manage to tamp down the volume.

"And they all talk to him. They tell him everything, even kids who won't talk to anyone else. He can just, like, smile at someone, you know? And he gets really quiet and listens. And even though he's super funny, he doesn't clown around or anything, so kids feel safe with him. Like, you know, they can relax with him. Be themselves." Colt bit savagely at the cuff again and mumbled, "Or whatever."

"That sounds very nice," Nico said. "I bet Ash feels that way about you too."

Colt shrugged, but happiness radiated from him so intensely that, for a moment, Emery found it almost painful. He was surprised to feel John bump against him, slide an arm around his waist, and lean his head into Emery's. Emery tightened his arm around John in answer.

"I never see you post about GLAM. How long have you been doing that?"

The fact that Nico followed him on social media clearly wasn't news to Colt, but by the way his face lit up, the possibility that Nico actually paid attention to his posts was life changing. "Oh, um, Koby won't let us. That's the rule at GLAM. No phones. He says he has enough trouble keeping us from—" He stopped, his face coloring as he actively did not look at his dads again. "—getting in trouble," he finished lamely. "Jessica says it's a privacy thing, like, what if a kid isn't out?"

"For those playing along at home," Emery said, "Koby is the head of GLAM, and Jessica is a girl Colt made friends with there."

"She's so nice. The one time I saw her get mad was when Ty kept trying to livestream even after Koby told him to put away his phone." Colt shook his head. "Jessica helps with everything; she's really passionate. Koby couldn't do half the stuff he does if he didn't have people like Jessica and Farah and Jamir."

"And people like Ash and Colt," John said with a smile.

Colt shrugged. "Plus," he said with the tone of someone casually passing along important information, "Ash and I both play football, so we're in charge of making sure nobody causes trouble. Jessica tries to keep them in line, but, like, some of these kids don't know how to act, you know?"

Nico did an adequate job of hiding his amusement as he nodded and said, "Good thing they've got you guys. And I bet your dads have taught you some self-defense."

"Oh yeah," Colt said, and in that instant, he sounded like every teenage boy everywhere experiencing a surge of testosterone. "I showed Ash some moves."

"Some moves," Emery said under his breath.

John elbowed him.

"Speaking of which," Emery said, "how are your self-defense classes going, Nico?"

"Nope. This topic is off-limits."

"Don't be ridiculous. You told me you were going to enroll because, quote, 'I'll do better if my instructor isn't my ex-boyfriend shouting at me to make my fist better, whatever that means,' end quote. Which, by the way, I showed you what I meant—"

"And that's a wrap," Nico said.

"Let it go, love," John said.

"Hypothetical scenario: he becomes physical when you attempt to leave after dinner, because you've realized the foolishness of spending the night in another city with a complete stranger and no weapons in your possession—"

Nico made a buzzing noise.

Emery tried a different tack. "As your evening progresses, he refuses to take no for an answer—"

Another buzz.

"You find yourself in some sort of sexual encounter in which an imbalance of power exists. For the sake of this example, let's say a bondage scenario with some degree of consent—"

This time, Colt's three timers went off simultaneously.

"That's a no," Nico said.

"No, there was no consent, or no—"

"Colt?" John asked.

Colt was staring at Nico, his cheeks aflame, as three timers chirped and chimed and flashed. Then he must have heard John because he started, his eyes widening as he took in the three adults staring at him, and the color in his cheeks deepened until it was almost purple. He sprinted to the oven, yanked the door open, and at the last moment remembered the oven mitts.

"Good Christ," Emery said.

"Be nice," John said. "It's cute."

"It'll be less cute when a set of handcuffs goes missing."

John shushed him.

"I swear to God, if I find Ashley trussed up like a summer ham, I'll shoot myself."

John shushed him again.

Colt was making a production out of inspecting the cookies, doubtless buying himself time before he had to face the other men in the room. Nico, of all people, gave Emery a dirty look and grabbed a bowl and hand mixer. "Come on, Colt. We'll make the frosting in the dining room and get everything set up for the girls."

Theo and Auggie came into the room as Colt bolted after Nico, and Auggie made a soft *aww*-ing sound.

"He was practically riding his ass," Emery said. "What's cute about that?"

"He's got a crush," Auggie said. "I mean, it's not in the same league as his crush on No—"

Theo's discreet nudge had not been quite discreet enough.

"Boy," John said, "you're really having a night, aren't you?"

"It's not my fault!"

"As his crush on whom?" Emery asked.

"On nobody," Theo said. Emery opened his mouth to press the question, but Theo was saved by his daughter rushing into the room to grab his hand. Lana was ten, small for her age, and her voice had an affectless quality that had to do with the lingering effects of the car accident she'd been in as a child.

"Evie needs a cookie," she said.

"Evie does, huh?" Theo asked.

Lana turned big, dark eyes on Auggie.

"Maybe they could split one—" Auggie began.

"Oh no," Theo said with a laugh. He turned Lana back toward the living room. "You and Evie can play for a while. When the cookies are ready to frost, Colt's going to help you. Then you can eat the cookies."

That seemed to satisfy Lana, and she took off at a wild run, apparently completely oblivious to the brace on her leg.

Theo pushed back his bro flow of strawberry-blond hair as he sat at the counter. He wore a sweater that Auggie had obviously picked for him—a Christmas green, with reindeer stitched across the front. One of the reasons Auggie had clearly been the one to buy it was the fact that it accented Theo's broad shoulders and solid physique. Another reason was that the reindeer were made of sequins.

They made small talk for a few minutes, catching up. Theo and Auggie had been part of Emery and John's lives for a long time now. John had known them first, from his time as a detective, when Theo and Auggie had become involved in a series of strange disappearances and deaths connected to the college. Emery had met them later, but he hadn't really known them until Theo had been Colt's teacher the year before.

What had really brought them together, though, was what had happened over the summer. An escalating series of events had forced them to work together as they tried to uncover a criminal organization operating out of a place called the Cottonmouth Club. That investigation had collapsed after the deaths—murders—of two key witnesses and, in the process, Sheriff Engels.

Auggie, of course, was the one to break the flow of easy chatter. "Any luck?"

Emery shook his head.

Theo's expression tightened. Auggie said, "God damn it. For real?"

Since August, Emery and John had been doing their best to continue the investigation into the people operating in—or through—the Cottonmouth Club. The reality, though, was that they had few avenues to pursue. They had sussed out a connection between a local politician, Eric Brey, and the Cottonmouth Club, although the extent and nature of that connection wasn't clear, and Brey wasn't cooperating. The opposite, in fact; he'd lawyered up and refused to talk, and after Emery had tried to press him for answers, Brey had threatened him with a restraining order, a harassment lawsuit, and a complaint with the state board.

"I finally thought we were on to something," Auggie said. "I can't believe this."

"What happened?" Theo asked.

The break in the case had come a few weeks ago, when John had made an important connection. Earlier that year, Gray Dulac—one of John's detectives with the Wahredua PD and, Emery was forced to admit grudgingly, one of their friends—had stumbled upon a van full of people being trafficked. Women and children, fourteen of them. And Dulac's bust had come only because he'd spotted the van's expired tags. It had been proof that, his personality aside, Dulac was a good cop. It had also been his last big case before he had been injured while trying to rescue Ashley from a killer. Those injuries had removed him from active duty until recently. And, in many ways, had also removed him from Emery and John's life, with the rare exception of when they bumped into him.

"What happened is," Emery said, "she was dead."

Auggie let out a breath and rubbed his eyes.

"How?" Theo asked.

"Exposure. I heard from my contact today. Death by accident is the medical examiner's ruling."

"Are they sure?" Auggie asked.

"I don't know, Auggie," Emery said, "would you like to talk to my contact yourself?"

Theo shot Emery a warning look, but all he said was "That's awful."

"It is awful," John agreed. "She'd been through a lot, and she was young, and it shouldn't have happened to her."

Emery didn't say what he suspected most of them were thinking: it shouldn't have happened, but it wasn't uncommon either. John's idea had been a good one—to track down the women and children Dulac had rescued and see if they could provide some sort of information that might lead back to the Cottonmouth Club or to the organization hiding behind it. It seemed unlikely, to say the least, that multiple trafficking organizations would be operating in the same rural area, and when John had made the connection and suggested the course of action, Emery had been optimistic. Hell, he'd been excited.

But the reality was that many of the victims of human trafficking—most, in fact—were marginalized people with weak social networks and very little in the way of safety nets. That was the whole point, of course. People who were unhoused, people abusing drugs, teenagers and children in foster care or group homes, and, of course, LGBTQ youth. Anyone, in other words, who was vulnerable. Anyone who could go missing without anyone noticing. Or, if they noticed, without caring.

Those same people, even after they were rescued, didn't seem to be doing any better. Although the women and children rescued by Dulac had been offered some support and assistance, the reality was that the children had ended up in foster care, and the adults, after a short period, had disappeared again. To a degree, that was to be expected. They hadn't come to Wahredua by choice, after all. But the problem was that these were still the same people they'd been before they'd been taken—and the same problems had hounded them.

The children in foster care, when John and Emery approached them under the umbrella of the Wahredua PD, had refused to disclose anything helpful. Perhaps they hadn't known anything helpful. But more than one had seemed terrified by the questions, and it didn't matter what promises Emery and John had made—the children refused to talk, and that seemed to be the end of it.

The adults—well, Deanna Vance had been the first one Emery had actually managed to find. And look how that had turned out.

"This is ridiculous," Auggie said. "One of those women has got to be around here still. They can't all have moved away."

Theo nodded and settled one hand on the back of Auggie's neck.

"Maybe," John-Henry said. "In the meantime, we'll keep doing what we've been doing: we'll check every massage parlor, every motel, every strip joint. In the state, if we have to. Eventually, somebody's going to slip up."

Frustration twisted Auggie's face, but he nodded. Theo said, "They can't get away with this forever."

"People do," Emery said. "All the time."

An outraged "What?" came from the dining room, and a moment later, Nico appeared in the opening. A smudge of green frosting ran across one cheekbone, and to judge from the giggling, Evie and Lana had, at some point, become fully invested in the frosting creation process.

"It's cute," Auggie said, "but it's not really your color."

"Huh?" Nico thumbed away the frosting and wrinkled his nose. Then he pointed at Emery. "What are you thinking? This is an awesome opportunity for Colt."

Behind him, Colt hovered, defiance and pleading mingling in his features.

"Jesus Christ," Emery said.

"No, no, no," Nico said. "This is an all-expenses paid trip."

"It's not a vacation," Emery said.

"No," Colt shot back, but his voice was low. "It's just something that would look amazing on a college application."

"Excuse me?" Emery asked. "Do you have something to say?"

Colt shrank back, glowering, and Nico said, "He's right. This would be fantastic on a college application. On top of that, it's a service opportunity, and it's a really good one."

"It's a day in St. Louis, Nico. Working in a shelter. He's not curing cancer."

"You never cured cancer," came Colt's quiet volley.

When Emery looked past Nico, Colt took another step back.

"This is exactly what I was talking about. I understand that you're protective, but—"

"It's not exactly the same, Nico. It's quite different, as a matter of fact. I'm Colt's father. It's my opinion that this trip isn't a good idea. What if they get stranded? They're coming back Christmas Eve; he'd miss Christmas."

"And it's my opinion that it is a good idea," Colt muttered. "And we're not going to get stranded."

"We've already had this conversation, Colt. Nico's not going to change my mind."

"Ash's parents said he could go!"

"It's a great opportunity, Emery—"

"Ash's parents are not your parents. Nico, you are not his parent. John and I have discussed this, and the matter is closed."

"I don't care!" But the pitchiness of his voice, and the thickness of the words gave him away. "I'm not even going to college anyway!"

Colt's heavy steps carried him out of sight, and a moment later, treads groaned, and his bedroom door slammed shut upstairs.

Nico lips were parted, his arms folded, his gaze not quite meeting Emery's.

"Thank you so much."

"I'm sorry, I didn't mean to—"

The doorbell rang, and John said, "Do you want to get that?"

"I do not."

John sighed and headed toward the front of the house. Nico was still standing there, shifting his weight, not looking at anyone.

"I think the cookies are cool enough to frost," Theo said quietly.

"I can help." Auggie slipped past Emery to grab the tray, and on his way to the dining room, he chivvied Nico ahead of him. As they left the kitchen, he said in a low voice, "He's not mad at you, not really. Everyone knows you're just trying to help."

Whatever Nico said back, it sounded broken and small.

"I suppose you have some brilliant advice for dealing with teenagers?" Emery said to Theo.

Theo's laughter was rich and full, and Emery's first spike of outrage at the reaction melted into a kind of resigned amusement. He rolled his shoulders and took a deep breath.

"I guess I should go fix this."

Theo nodded. "You're a great dad, Emery. The problem is it's an impossible job."

"Somehow, that doesn't make me feel any better."

"But you still need to hear it every once in a while."

On his way through the living room toward the stairs, Emery stopped. John had stepped out onto the porch. His hands were open at his sides, almost like he was displaying them. And facing him, still in uniform, were Neecie Weiss and Roy Peterson. Weiss was a sheriff's deputy, and acting sheriff at least until the special election in April. Peterson was the day watch lieutenant and, as things went in a department as small as the Wahredua PD, John's second-in-command.

Emery rerouted to the front door. As he opened it, Peterson was saying, "—nothing personal."

"I know," John said. Something was wrong with his voice. It was flat, almost affectless, a parody of his usual good humor. And there was a burr in it that, on someone else, Emery might have called anger.

Weiss's gaze snapped to Emery as the door opened, and she said, "Mr. Hazard, please step outside slowly and show me your hands."

"What's going on?" Weiss looked tired, the weariness bone-deep and seeping through her mask of resolve. Peterson met Emery's gaze, but only for a heartbeat, and then his eyes slid away. "What is this? John, what's happening?"

"I'm under arrest," John said, and the way he said it, it sounded like he was trying to make a joke.

"What are you talking about?" The wind sent old snow skittering. "Somebody give me some fucking answers."

"Em, is everything ok?" Nico asked from the entry hall.

"Girls, why don't we take some of these cookies to Theo?" Auggie said.

Still no one had answered Emery's question. Facts, he thought. Focus on facts. "Under arrest? On what charge?"

Weiss dropped her eyes to the ground. Peterson blew out a long, white breath.

"Child pornography," John said, turning to face Emery. He looked sallow in the porch light, his eyes wide and unseeing. "They're arresting me for possession of child porn."

3

In the interview room at the county jail, after being booked, John-Henry waited for his lawyer, and he tried not to think the thing he wanted to think.

He sat in one of the metal chairs, his hands hanging between his legs below the battered steel table. He wasn't cuffed anymore, and that was something. He used his knees to brace his hands. He was still trembling a little.

The handcuffs on his front porch. The frisk as he stood there, where his neighbors could see the whole thing taking place. The Miranda warning. Peterson had stopped once to clear his throat, and Weiss had suggested he start over, so John had heard it again. The drive in the back of Weiss's cruiser, the cage separating them, looking out the window and waiting to see a familiar face, for someone to spot him in the back. That had been bad enough.

The booking process had been worse. The casual indignities of being printed, of the mug shots, of men and women he'd known and worked with for most of his life—some of them, all his life—staring at him, disgust contorting their expressions. And then worse yet. Being forced to strip. His pubic hair combed for lice. The full-body search, fingers pressing inside him. A part of him tried to remain detached, to be a professional, to think about the sheriff's department's process, about its effect, to consider everything in that clinical light because it would give him useful insight into the procedures of his own department. But his mind wandered. *I'm done* was the numb thought that kept coming back to him. I'm done. I can never work in this town again.

And now, in jailhouse slides and jailhouse scrubs, his hands locked between his knees to keep them steady, he focused on controlling his breathing, building a wall between himself and the tempest of emotions: rage, humiliation, and simplest of all, the childlike desire to burst into tears.

One trick was to focus on sensory details. The cinderblock room smelled tomatoey, vinegary, with a processed-fat smell like margarine. He'd reviewed enough institutional meals to guess sloppy joes, instant mashed potatoes, some sort of vegetable boiled until it was about to dissolve. The same kind of thing he'd be eating tomorrow. And the day after that. And the day after that. A door slammed somewhere, and John-Henry startled in the seat before catching himself. The silence that came after was worse. The fluorescents buzzed. His head throbbed. He had to be careful not to look around the room, to see the figure in the mirror connected to the observation room. Cameras watched him, and he knew that, no matter what Weiss tried, the footage would be in a hundred different hands by the morning. The chief of police in custody. Be cool, he told himself. Be cool.

Emery would fix this. That was his hope to cling to. Emery wouldn't stand for this. On the porch, in the aftermath of saying those words, of being forced to say those words about himself, John had watched the fury rise in Emery's face, and then the iron control as he took hold again. Emery had asked to see the arrest warrant, but Weiss and Peterson had refused. John-Henry couldn't blame them; if he'd been in their position, he would have refused as well. Emery had simply grown colder. He would drive separately, he'd told John. He'd call a lawyer. And John, who should have been saying something, doing something, figuring out how this terrible mistake had been made, had simply stood there and nodded. Emery would fix this.

How?

That was the question he didn't want to look in the eyes. The part of him that had been a police officer for close to twenty years, the part of him that knew how the system worked—that part of him knew this kind of thing, the arrest of any law enforcement officer, much less the chief of police, wasn't something that happened quickly. Someone had been working on this for a long time. Someone had been laying the groundwork. A grand jury had been empaneled. Witnesses had been called. Evidence produced. An indictment had been handed down, and the presiding judge had issued an arrest warrant.

For child pornography. John-Henry felt a moment of dissociation, like his head had separated from his body. And then the need to vomit gripped him, cold sweat breaking out across his body as he rode it out.

A buzzer sounded, and the door opposite John-Henry opened. He glimpsed the hallway beyond, the deputy standing guard—a self-important dud named Glover, who was probably loving this—and then Aniya Thompson stepped into the room.

She was Black, her hair in short, beaded braids, and wearing a neat gray suit. Over the years, Aniya had helped John-Henry and Emery with the occasional legal trouble, and seeing her now—a familiar face, someone who was here to help—John-Henry felt a rush of affection and gratitude disproportionate to his actual relationship with Aniya. He smiled as he stood, almost grinning.

"Aniya, thank God. I mean, thank you. Thank you for coming."

She nodded. A reflexive smile appeared and then was tucked out of sight again, never touching her eyes. Motioning for John-Henry to sit, she took the chair opposite him. "How are you doing?" she asked.

"Fine. I mean—" He laughed and heard the unhinged sound of it. "—horrible. This is a nightmare. But I'll survive."

"Yes, you will. And you're going to need to keep telling yourself that because this is going to be long and ugly, and I want you to know that from the start." She watched him, her braids clicking as she moved her head. "If it's not the worst thing you'll ever go through, it might be close. But we're going to beat it, and you're going to come out the other side."

She waited long enough that John-Henry realized a response was required so he nodded. "These charges are bullshit. I've never—and I mean never, Aniya—come anywhere near—" He stopped, fighting another of those fraying laughs. "I can't even say it. Jesus, I'm going to throw up."

Raising an eyebrow, she made like she might get the guard, but John-Henry waved her back into her seat.

"Never," he said. "Not a video. Not a picture. I would never touch that stuff. I would never go anywhere near it. For fuck's sake, I know how bad it is, what they do to those kids. I have a son and a daughter. I would never—" He'd heard this all from the other side of the table: the repetition, the cycling, someone stuck in a loop. He forced himself to corral his thoughts. "I would never look at that stuff." He firmed up his voice. "Much less have it."

Aniya nodded. John-Henry wasn't sure what he'd been expecting—assurances, conviction, a passionate declaration of her belief in him—but in the wake of that single nod, all he could do was sit back as confusion and disappointment bled together.

"You'll be arraigned tomorrow," Aniya said, the words clipped and professional. "I imagine Diana will ask for you to be held without bail, but that's not going to happen. She'll talk about your pattern of avoiding arrest, and that's not going to help you, but we'll focus on your long service to this community, your roots here, your family."

"My father," John-Henry said. The grin on his face felt dead. A rictus. That was the word.

"That might hurt us, actually. We'll see what Diana does and play it by ear."

That sense of disorientation came again at hearing Diana referred to so casually, at understanding—in a way his brain had avoided until now—that the county attorney he'd worked with on hundreds of cases was now actively involved in prosecuting him. Another realization came on the heels of that one.

"My father," he said again. "He's got to be furious."

"That's one way of putting it. I passed him in the lobby; he was tearing strips off Neecie Weiss, and I bet he was about five minutes away from getting himself arrested."

"Did Emery—" John-Henry didn't know how to finish that question.

"Believe it or not, he was being the reasonable one."

A laugh escaped John-Henry. Then his eyes stung, and he rubbed them and blinked, trying to rein himself in.

"You'll be out on bail by the end of the day tomorrow. You'll be suspended, of course, so you'll need to find a way to occupy yourself. I wasn't exaggerating when I said this is going to be long and hard, and you're going to need to find a way to keep yourself healthy and stable throughout the process. In a couple of weeks, we'll have the first set of discovery materials, and we can start figuring out our defense."

"In a couple of weeks?"

Aniya hesitated a beat too long.

"You know something," John said. "You know what they've got on me."

"Right now, you need to be thinking about tonight and tomorrow. You need to sleep if you can—they'll put you in the isolation unit to keep you safe—"

"And look how well that worked for Dalton Weber."

He hadn't meant the words to be loud, but they bounced back from the cinderblock walls. The dead man's name echoed between them.

"You need to sleep if you can. Because tomorrow, you need to look like a solid citizen who's been wrongly accused, and you can't do that if you're a wreck."

She wasn't meeting his eyes. And John-Henry thought about how long it had taken her to arrive. Even after he'd spent all that time being booked and processed into jail, he'd still waited—how long? An hour? Longer? And it wasn't like Wahredua was busy on a Sunday night.

"What is it?" John-Henry asked.

Aniya opened her mouth and shut it again.

"I don't care how bad it is. And I don't particularly care how you got it. I want to know what they've got on me." She opened her mouth again, and he said, "Even if you're not sure, I want to know what someone told you. I'm your client. I'm telling you to tell me."

Her shoulders sagged. "It's important that you understand that my information might not be correct."

"What do they have?"

The only sound was her breathing, the soft whisper of wool as she shifted in her suit and her jacket rubbed against her. "They have a man who claims you tried to buy child pornography from him."

"That's a lie." He held up a hand. "Sorry. I—sorry."

"He seems like a solid witness. He's ex-military, a few medals." She brushed at her skirt. "He works with an anti-trafficking organization."

John-Henry shook his head, but he managed to clamp down on the words.

"He played a recording for the grand jury. It was...convincing."

"And a bunch of people sitting in a room thought it sounded like me? You've got to be kidding me. That's their case? If I'd taken something like that to Diana, she would have served me my ass."

Aniya drew a deep breath. "No, that's not all. The Wahredua PD's IT department conducted a search of your computer. And yes, a warrant was served, John-Henry."

He grappled with what that meant. With the people who had known about this and said nothing. With the fury that no one had told him, no one had even hinted, and, at the same time, his awareness that they had been doing their job, doing what they thought was right, doing what the court had ordered.

"They found images and videos, John-Henry. Over ten thousand of them." She sounded weary as she said, "I'm so sorry."

Somewhere far off in the jail, a door slammed again, and a man screamed. Jailhouse sounds. Inmates screamed all the time. Shouted. Cried out. At times, John-Henry knew, it sounded like a madhouse. "They aren't mine."

Aniya nodded.

"I didn't—those aren't mine."

She nodded again. "Let's wait for discovery and see what they have."

He couldn't bring himself to answer. She said something else, another reminder about trying to sleep, but he barely heard her. She said something after that, and something else, and he knew he was responding, knew he was keeping up his part. And then it was over, and she left, and he was still sitting there, alone. He noticed now, like someone waking up, the blue-ink graffiti on the steel table: Bart Simpson strapped into an electric chair.

He had grown up with parents who had bulldozed his every wrongdoing. He had paid a steep price to learn he wasn't perfect, that perhaps he wasn't even a particularly good person. And since then, he had struggled not to be the boy his parents had raised. He knew that he was being framed. He knew it had something to do with the Cottonmouth Club, with his search for whoever was hiding in the shadows. He knew that someone was doing this because he was a threat, and because he had to be neutralized, and in one stroke, they had removed him from the game completely. He knew all of that.

But in the silence of that cinderblock room, his willpower faltered, and for one hot, vicious moment, he thought the thing he had trained himself not to think: How fucking dare they?

4

Emery did another lap of the house.

Monday evening, dark came early, shuttering the house in the cold glitter of snow and stars. The house itself was full of light and warmth and bodies, but Emery was only distantly aware of it all. His mind was out there, in the darkness beyond the ice, and his body moved mechanically: entry hall to living room, living room to kitchen, kitchen to dining room, dining room to entry hall.

"Don't you want a slice of pizza?" Auggie tried.

Theo murmured something that made Auggie drop his head.

"We're having pizza, Dee," Evie told him as he moved through the kitchen again.

"He's busy," Colt said, stroking her hair. His amber eyes followed Emery, though, and Emery was grateful when he passed into the dining room again.

Pacing was a waste of time and energy; Emery knew that. But in the last twenty-four hours since John's arrest, he'd managed to accomplish absolutely nothing, so it wasn't much of a change. Even the initial, panicked calls—first to John's father, and then to Aniya Thompson—were things someone else could have done. Things John could have done for himself, as a matter of fact. After that, Emery had been useless. No one would talk to him at the sheriff's station. Nobody in the police department would answer his calls except Dulac, John's former partner, and the detective knew less than Emery. All the contacts he had made, all the inroads, the entire network he'd crafted both as a detective with the Wahredua PD and as a private investigator—it had all been worth nothing.

That night had been worse. Theo and Auggie had offered to stay over and keep an eye on Colt and Evie, but Emery had sent them home. He was aware that it had been an old response, instinctual, his desire for solitude the way injured animals holed up in their dens. He had seen the need in Colt's eyes, the silent plea for reassurance, and the best Emery had been able to give him had been a hug, stiff and unfamiliar, as though they were strangers, before asking him to go to bed.

Then he had lain in bed, and the room had seemed unfairly bright. He had made the mistake of looking at his phone, at the notifications piling up on different social media platforms. Then he had deleted the apps and lain there, staring up into that too bright room. Ambient light reflecting off the snow on the ground, perhaps. More likely, nothing but his imagination. So much light that it was impossible not to see the emptiness of the bed.

He had not cried. He had lain there, and thought, and planned, a cat's cradle game he was trying to play one-handed. Over and over again, the same phrase breaking through the storm: They're doing it again.

Then, the madness of the arraignment, the farce of Judge Platter reading out the charges, the nightmare unreality of John in cuffs as he entered his plea, the courtroom packed with people who wanted to see John-Henry Somerset brought low after a lifetime as the town's golden child. And coming home to find the empty cans of spray paint—

Now, the sound of steps on the porch made him stop his pacing, and a moment later, the door swung open. John stood there, dressed in jeans and a sweater, eyes smudged with fatigue. He smiled when he saw Emery and said, "Thank God."

It was John's smile. It was John's voice.

Emery reached him in two steps and wrapped him in his arms. John hugged him back. He smelled like cheap soap and day-old clothes, but also like John. His body was John's, fitting to Emery's the way it was supposed to. He was breathing slowly and deeply, pressing his head hard against Emery's, his fingers knotting Emery's shirt.

Movement came again, and John stepped aside as his parents came through the door. Glennworth Somerset had opted for a sweater and loafers under his winter coat, instead of the suit he usually wore as part of his mayoral image. Grace Elaine wore a button-up and black pumps. If seeing their only son arrested and charged with one of the most disgusting crimes imaginable had affected them, it showed in different ways. Glenn looked hollow with exhaustion. Grace Elaine, on the other hand—Grace Elaine looked like Grace Elaine, and Emery wished he knew what that meant.

"I thought you'd be home hours ago," Emery said.

"We met with Ms. Thompson," Glenn said.

Grace Elaine smiled as she shrugged out of her coat. "We didn't want to bother you, Emery."

Emery opened his mouth to reply, but John shook his head, mouth twisting. "I'm sorry," he said in a low voice. "I tried."

It was harder than Emery expected to let that go, but finally he nodded. "Have you eaten? There's pizza—"

"J-H?" Colt appeared in the entry hall, glanced around, and then charged. His feet slapped the floor, and then he crashed into John. John hugged him, and almost as quickly as it had happened, Colt disentangled himself, pulling up his shirt to wipe his face. Biscuit came after him, but her pace slowed when she saw Glenn and Grace Elaine, and she slunk across the remaining distance to greet John—clearly reluctant to get too close to his parents. One of them, Emery suspected, in particular, even if fur coats weren't in style any longer.

"Look who's home!" That was Cora, John's ex-wife and Evie's mother. She smiled at them and pushed back dark curls as she nudged Evie into the entry hall.

"Daddy," Evie informed him, "Mommy says we're having pizza, and all my friends are here!"

She raced back toward the kitchen, and Cora gave a small laugh. "I tried." Her face changed, and she asked, "Are you ok?"

"I'm here," John said, bussing her cheek. "That's better than ok. Thank you for coming."

"I'm totally useless, it turns out. Evie's obsessed with—"

"John-Henry?" Shaw passed through the opening from the living room. His auburn hair was up in its bun, and he wore a snowsuit (blue, with cartoon flames crawling up the arms and legs) that rustled as he ran toward them. His crash sounded only slightly less enthusiastic than Colt's, and the hug went on significantly longer. When Shaw finally stepped back, he whispered, "We were so worried."

"Hey," John said in that tone so many people used with Shaw. "You're here."

"We're all here," North said, one arm braced across the opening. He held a can of Four Hands, and his blond brows were knitted together as he assessed John. Whatever he saw must have reassured him—to a degree, anyway—because the look on his face passed and he said, "It's a fucking nightmare."

"What do you mean—"

"Yo," Jem said as he squirmed under North's outstretched arm. "You're alive!"

John gave a laugh and cut his eyes toward Emery. "Am I awake?"

"Auggie called them," Emery said. "They flew out on a red-eye."

"Not us," Shaw said. "We drove. Well, North drove. I offered to drive, but North said he'd rather have a—" He glanced around, spotted Grace Elaine, and mouthed—directly at her—*finger* "—in his—" He mouthed *butt.* "Only he didn't say finger. Oh! And he didn't say butt either."

"Will you stop talking?" North asked, clamping a hand over Shaw's mouth. "They're trying to have a heartfelt family reunion, and you're over here being fucking Pudd'nhead Wilson."

Another day, another time, Emery would have relished the look on Grace Elaine's face.

"Hi, John-Henry," Tean said from behind North and Shaw's wrestling. His hair was wilder than Emery remembered, and he wondered if he had missed something. "Are you all right?"

"Just a little tired."

"His hair looks like that because North was giving him noogies," Jem said. "It's one of the top ten cutest things I've ever seen in my life, like that time Scipio sneezed."

"It wasn't cute," Tean said. "I feel like it's important for everyone to know that."

"It's because the doc never had any big brothers to mess with him," North explained as he grappled with Shaw. Then he shouted, "Don't grab my dick, you pervert!" A moment later, he and Shaw stumbled into the closet door.

"You need to send these people home," Glenn said to Emery, his voice low.

"Oh, we are home—" Shaw cut off with a squeak as North began shaking him inside the snowsuit.

"Emery said we could stay here," Jem said. "Well, actually, Colt did, but he's mini-Emery, so it counts."

"Everybody go back to the living room," Emery said. "North, knock it off."

Because North was constitutionally incapable of acting like an adult, he did stop wrestling with Shaw—but only after he shoved Shaw into the coat closet and locked the door. The others drifted back into the living room.

"I'd like a moment alone with my husband," Emery said.

Grace Elaine waited a moment, long enough to make it clear that it was her decision to leave and not Emery's request. Then she and Glenn headed deeper into the house.

Emery studied John: the dark rings around his eyes, the poor color that even John's golden complexion couldn't hide, the hint of tension in his jaw. John met his gaze for a moment and then looked away.

Touching his cheek, Emery said, "You're home."

John nodded.

A million things jostled to come next: *I was so worried,* and *I can't believe this is happening,* and *Are you ok,* which was quite possibly the stupidest question ever, and *I'm sorry,* and *I love you.*

Before Emery could say any of those things, John took his hand and moved it away from his face. His fingers squeezed Emery's for an instant. Then he let go, and the air felt cool on Emery's skin where John had touched him.

"Pizza sounds good," John said.

Emery blinked. He opened his mouth to say—what? Then he shut it again.

John smiled again and started toward the kitchen. "I guess I should hope Colt left me some pepperoni."

Emery followed.

Auggie and Theo sat at the counter, and as John plated a slice of pepperoni, Auggie said, "John-Henry, we're so sorry."

John nodded and smiled. "I appreciate that."

"Nobody is going to believe this," Theo said. "Anybody with half a brain will know this is made up."

"Thank you for saying that." John took a can of Four Hands out of the fridge and popped the top. He sipped foam from his knuckles. "But somebody did believe it, Theo. Lots of people, it turns out, believe it. A grand jury. A prosecutor. Men and women I've worked with for my entire adult life." He smiled again. "But I appreciate you saying that."

Theo looked like he'd been slapped. Tears filled Auggie's eyes, and he tried unsuccessfully to brush them away.

"John," Emery said.

John lifted the can of Four Hands and took a long drink. Emery remembered how he looked with a beer—he remembered, more or less, everything about his husband. It was the curse of being in love, knowing the shape of him, the space he filled, the geometry of his body, no matter where he was or what he was doing. It had been a long time since he'd seen John with a beer, but in that moment, it didn't seem long at all. It seemed like yesterday.

When John lowered the can, he ran the back of his hand across his mouth and met Emery's eyes, his gaze cool and flat.

Emery looked away first. "You should eat something."

John took a bite of the pizza. He chewed. Swallowed. The sounds seemed magnified, even with the chaos in the living room filling the house.

Auggie slid off the stool, the legs screeching against the floor, and said, "Excuse me," as he hurried out of the room.

Theo cleared his throat. "Why don't I—"

"What's that?"

Emery glanced over and saw, too late, the pile of rags and bottle of acetone he'd left by the back door.

Theo pushed back his stool and stopped.

"What is that?" John asked again.

"It's nothing," Emery said.

John threw down the slice of pizza. He grabbed a napkin and cleaned his hands. "What does it say?"

"You don't need to worry about it."

Shaking his head, John started toward the door. Emery tried to block him, but John shouldered past him and strode out into the cold.

PEDOPHILE. Emery could see it in his mind: huge red letters across the side of their garage.

He watched from the door as John made his way to the end of the house and then stared at the side of the garage; the light didn't reach far, but he must have been able to see it, must have been able to read enough to know what it said.

Brittle, refrozen ice snapped under John's steps as he came back. It was harder for Emery to see him now through the storm door, the glass foggy as condensation gathered. Then the door swung open. His cheeks were red. The tip of his nose. He angled his body past Emery to grab the acetone and a handful of rags.

"I got sidetracked," Emery said.

"It's fine."

"I'll take care of it. I didn't want you to see it."

"It's fine, Ree."

He was already slipping out the door again.

"John, come sit down. Eat something. I'll do it in the morning." Please don't do this was what he wanted to say, but something in John's face stopped him.

"Close the door." Ice broke under his steps. "It's freezing out here."

Heat prickled in Emery's face. He was aware of Theo's gaze, the weight of his attention. He fumbled with the latch on the storm door, his knuckles bumping the glass to streak the condensation. It was already freezing, and it furred the backs of his fingers as it scraped away.

A hand caught Emery's arm.

"Close the door," Theo said quietly.

Emery shook his head. He didn't trust himself to say anything.

"He's not angry at you. He's hurting, and he's humiliated, and he doesn't know what to do."

"Let go of my arm."

Theo sighed. But he didn't let go.

"I'll talk to him," Jem said.

Emery glanced back. Jem wore an unreadable expression. Today, his outfit was a flannel over a T-shirt that showed a joint curved into the shape of the Nike swoosh. JUST DOOB IT. Jeans, Roos. Not warm enough for a night like this one. But then, John was only wearing a sweater.

Jem laid a hand on Emery's back as he passed him, and a moment later, the storm door was rattling shut behind him. Emery had a glimpse of John rising from a crouch, already shaking his head, but Jem said something too low for Emery to hear, and then Theo reached past him and shut the door.

"You probably won't believe this," Theo said, "but speaking from experience, sometimes it's better coming from someone else."

Emery nodded. He made himself think the words until he knew he could say them clearly. "Excuse me."

"Emery—"

But Theo let go when Emery took a step toward the stairs, and he didn't follow.

The basement lights were on. Luggage rested at the bottom of the steps—a Reebok duffle next to a Louis Vuitton roller bag. North and Shaw, of course. Emery made his way to the weight bench. He leaned against it. The steel felt oiled under his palm, like his hand would slide right off it. Something tightened around his chest, and he couldn't breathe. John in handcuffs on their porch. The look on Colt's face. The empty bed awash in the light coming off the snow. The arraignment, every jibe, every snigger. John's face half-paneled in light as he read that word marking their home.

The noise screwdrivered out of him, and he stepped back and kicked the bench. It rocked. He kicked it again, and again, and the bench passed its tipping point and began to fall. He kept kicking it as it went over, the bar crashing against the floor first, then the bench. He kicked until black spots swam in his vision. Those steel bands around his chest contracted, and he could hear his own sick, panting breaths as he slumped against the overturned bench.

He wasn't sure how long he sat there before he noticed Tean. The vet sat on the bottommost step, arms wrapped around his knees, watching.

Emery warred with himself before he finally managed, "I'd like to be alone."

Tean nodded.

As Emery's heartbeat faded from his ears, he realized the house had fallen silent. He rested his head in his hands for only a moment. Then he said, "How bad was it?"

"Not bad." Then, as though hearing the unasked question, he added, "I'm not sure Evie and Lana even heard."

"But Colt did."

"He's worried about you, but we agreed it might be better if you had a chance to talk to someone else first."

"So I could scream at someone who wasn't my son, you mean."

What might have been a smile laced Tean's voice. "If it makes you feel any better, Shaw volunteered himself as tribute. Theo and North seemed to think you'd be less reactive if it were me, though."

"North didn't say reactive."

The amusement was definitely there. "I believe his word was 'murderous.'"

A smile cut the corner of Emery's mouth, but it faded quickly. He listened to the silence for what felt like a long time. "John?"

"He'll be alright, Emery. Jem is—I don't know how much Jem has told you, and I don't want to speak out of turn. But Jem knows what it's like. A little, anyway. He'll know what to say."

Emery listened to the words, heard them. A part of him wanted to follow that thread about Jem. But another part of him felt exhausted as his adrenaline ebbed and the last twenty-four hours caught up with him. And yet another part of him was remembering what it had felt like, all those years ago after he'd come out. The whispers when he walked into a room. Or, worse, sudden silence. And he remembered, today, the arraignment. The way people he knew had turned their faces away. They're doing it again, he thought. They're doing it to John.

The thought galvanized him. He got to his feet, cleared the bar, and grabbed the bench. He didn't hear Tean cross the basement, but he was there, taking the other end and helping Emery set it upright. Emery got the bar, the knurled steel familiar under his hands, and Tean gathered the fallen plates. It took them a few minutes to restore everything to order. It was always like that. The damage done in an instant, he thought through the fog, might take a lifetime to repair. Or might not ever be fixed, not completely.

"I'm sorry, Emery," Tean said. "For all of this. It's horrible, and it's not fair, and it's wrong, and I'm so sorry."

Emery nodded. His eyes followed the light wrapping itself around the steel.

"It's going to be ok." Tean closed the last few feet between them and hugged him.

It was the first time that the tears had threatened to come, and it took a surprisingly long time to fight them down.

When he was sure of his voice again, Emery asked, "How awful is this for you?"

"Only moderately."

John's voice came from the stairs. "Am I interrupting?"

"Of course not," Emery said, squeezing Tean's shoulder as he stepped back. He took a moment to consider his husband: the same shadows around his eyes, the same pallor that the golden complexion couldn't hide. But something was different.

"Tean, could I speak to Emery for a moment?"

Tean smiled for some reason as he passed John on the stairs.

Then they were alone.

"How are you—" Emery stopped, his mouth twisting. "Do you know, I believe I have an above-average vocabulary, but I'm having a difficult time asking how you are without phrasing it in a way you've probably heard a hundred times already today."

Laughing quietly, John came down the stairs. He crossed toward Emery, and for an instant, Emery was a boy again, watching this creature of beauty and grace orbit him, always within sight, forever out of reach. It had been torture, in its own way. Wanting him. Not being able to have him. Worse than any of the cruelties John and his friends had dreamed up. Wanting him in spite of the bullying. Unable to separate, in the tangle of feelings, hatred and desire. And then, one day, they had collided. No more orbiting—no more distance. And the real John, it had turned out, was quite different from the one who had haunted Emery's boyhood.

John smirked as he got closer.

Well, Emery thought, perhaps some traits had stayed the same.

"I know that look," John said, and he stepped into Emery's embrace and turned his head up to kiss him. "I missed you too."

"It's a good thing they had you in solitary, or I imagine you would have had a great deal of unwanted attention."

"Who said it would have been unwanted?"

Emery kissed him again, and this time he pulled John's hair until John made a soft whimper against his mouth. But John didn't pull away, and Emery didn't let up, not until he thought he had made his point.

When the kiss broke, John pressed his forehead to Emery's shoulder, heavy in the circle of Emery's arms, as though that were the only thing holding him up. Emery kissed the side of his face and tasted that unfamiliar soap. He kissed his ear. He soothed the patch of hair he had pulled. He was hard, and John was hard, and the rage that had been cycling through him for a full day had taken on a different, sharper edge.

"Later," John said, a laugh buried in the word. He raised his head and met Emery's eyes and said, "I'm sorry."

"What in the world are you sorry for?"

For whatever reason, that cracked open a smile. "I don't know, dummy. How I acted when I got home, let's start with that."

Emery smoothed blond hair away from John's forehead. "You were understandably upset."

"I didn't need to take it out on you."

"Believe it or not, John, I can handle it."

That stole some of the light from John's face.

"That's not what I meant."

"I know." He gave a tiny shrug inside Emery's embrace. "I'm sorry for letting this happen, Ree. That's what I'm sorry for."

"For letting it happen? What in the world are you talking about?"

"This is my fault. If I'd been halfway decent at my job, we wouldn't still be chasing our tails looking for these guys, and they wouldn't have been able to set up something like this. Not to mention my own department, somebody getting to my computer—"

"What do you mean your department? What about your computer?"

Rubbing his eyes, John freed himself and sat on the couch. Emery sat next to him and listened as John laid out the evidence against him—the witness, the audio recording, the files on his computer.

"Fuck me," Emery said. He got up, paced a few times across the room, and gave the weight bench another kick. "You fucking idiot."

"I know—"

"Not you, John. Me. What the fuck was I thinking? Of course there'd be a grand jury. Of course there'd be evidence. I should have been doing something productive, finding out what had led to these charges, instead of—"

"Taking care of our children? Holding our life together? Getting me an attorney?"

"Feeling sorry for myself."

John's smile was unexpectedly relaxed, almost loopy. It changed his whole face, washed away years. He held out one hand and beckoned with his fingers.

"I'm not done," Emery said and kicked the weight bench again.

That made him laugh. He twiddled his fingers again.

Eventually Emery made his way over to the couch. John took his hand, drew him down next to him, and cupped his cheek. "You do have a talent for being hard on yourself. Have I ever mentioned that?"

"I believe there have been passing references."

"The flat tire."

"I should have checked the pressure before we left."

"We picked up a nail."

"I should have bought the drive-flat."

"The t-shirt."

"It said clearly on the label that the dye might transfer. I knew I was taking a risk."

John laughed again, the sound fuller now.

"I ruined an entire load of laundry, including some of those ridiculously expensive undershirts you prefer. I'm not sure what's so amusing."

"My love," John whispered, pulling Emery's forehead to his. "My one true love. How about we make a deal? No beating ourselves up about this. I'll keep an eye on you. You keep an eye on me."

"You have no cause to beat yourself up. I, on the other hand—"

"Deal or no deal?"

"It's a simple question of responsibility—"

"Deal or no deal, Ree?"

"You sound like that idiotic TV show."

John bonked him softly with his head. "Dummy."

It took a while, but Emery finally managed to growl, "Deal."

"Thank you."

"I make no promises about my internal monologue, though."

"I'm not worried about your internal monologue. I'm going to have Tean keep an eye on your internal monologue, and the instant he tells me you're going somewhere dark, I'll send you and Shaw on a vacation together."

"Tean doesn't know what I'm thinking." But there was a bit of bravado in the words because the vet did have a worrying tendency to seem to know what was on Emery's mind. "Wait, a vacation? Where?"

"How does a nude beach strike you?"

Emery thought about that for a moment. "You know, I think that would drive North crazy."

"Oh my God," John murmured.

"I'd wear a swimsuit, John. But, of course, North wouldn't know that. We'd stage the pictures."

"This whole thing you two have going on, it's a bit much. You realize that, right?"

"If he saw me putting sunscreen on Shaw, he'd lose his mind."

"Ok," John said. "Never mind."

"It was your idea, John. I'm not at fault for seeing the advantages."

From upstairs came a crash, and then a swell of laughter mixed with screams of surprise.

"What are those numbskulls doing?"

"I imagine North is at the center of it."

John made a noise that could have meant anything.

"He's probably giving Tean an atomic wedgie or something along those lines. You realize someone needs to put him in his place again? He's been away for months, and he and Shaw will be completely out of control again."

"I guess we have to deal with them sooner or later." Tugging Emery to his feet, John set off for the stairs. In a contemplative voice, he said, "Maybe if you kissed him. Just once."

"Shaw already tried to kiss me, remember? He said it was his name day, whatever that's supposed to mean."

"Not who I was talking about."

Upstairs, North knelt at the coffee table, arm propped up on one elbow. Theo knelt opposite him, shirtsleeve rolled up.

"I'm going to take it easy on you, Gramps."

"Uh-huh," Theo said.

Auggie already had his phone out and was recording. "Please make this epic, Theo."

"Epic."

"You know, crush him. Destroy him. Obliterate every fiber of self-confidence."

A grin slashed across North's face. "Yeah, Paw-Paw. Obliterate my self-confidence."

"This is very childish," Theo said. "Tean, back me up."

"Oh no, Auggie's right," Tean said. "This needs to be a massacre, or he's going to be impossible to live with."

If anything, that made North grin harder.

"Say something about alpha males," Jem said. "Oh! Say something about mounting."

"Yes!" Shaw was bouncing on his toes. "Say something about mounting!"

On the far side of the room, Glenn and Grace Elaine looked like they'd wandered into a nightmare, and Cora was laughing into her sleeve. To judge by the barking, Lana and Evie were playing with Biscuit in the front room. And Colt, Emery's only son, was staring at North McKinney with something approaching awe.

"Are you kidding me?" Emery asked.

"Emery—" Theo began, and he turned around.

North grabbed his hand and slapped it down against the table. "Boom!" he shouted, raising his hands in triumph. "Take that, Grandpa!"

"He wasn't ready," Auggie protested. "You cheated!"

"Suck it!"

At which point, North stood, cupped his crotch, and began humping the air in Theo's direction.

"Are you out of your mind?" Emery asked, clapping his hands once. North stopped moving. "There are children in this house, not to mention people to whom I have a societal need to show a reasonable amount of respect. This isn't the back room of the Manhole, you horse's ass."

North spun toward Shaw, stabbing a finger at him. "I told you! I told you he did backroom stuff at the Manhole when he lived in St. Louis!"

"I did not—" Emery began.

"That place is filthy!"

"I don't know," Shaw said. "I think he's faking it. I've never seen anybody arm wrestling in the back room. Oh, one time I did see this guy with his arms tied behind his back, and—"

Emery clapped again. It was all he could manage, since he was, quite literally, choking with rage.

"Bubs," John said with what sounded like a suppressed laugh, "we've got to talk to these guys. Can you keep an eye on the girls?"

"That's not fair," Colt said. "I'm old enough—"

"Go watch the girls, you walking boner," North said.

Emery waited for the explosion.

Instead, though, an enormous, goofy grin spread across Colt's face. He glanced at North and jogged toward the front room.

"Who said being a parent was hard?"

Emery opened his mouth.

"Not right now," John murmured.

"Later."

"Oh, definitely later."

That was good enough for Emery.

The first few minutes, John spent greeting everyone properly—hugs, slaps on the back, squeezing shoulders. North actually gripped him by the arms and shook him a few times, which only made John laugh, and Jem's hug turned into a quick grapple as John tried to recover his wallet. Shaw whispered something in John's ear that made his shoulders soften, and Tean's hug, although reserved, made John swallow and grow still for a moment. Emery had watched a documentary on the restoration of old paintings, and it was something like that—like the real John was emerging, moment by moment, from where the pale, exhausted man had stood before.

Finally, John stood at Emery's side again, holding his hand. When he spoke, everyone fell silent.

"Thank you all for coming. I couldn't have imagined anyone doing this for me. Thank God Auggie had his phone, and, as usual, was much smarter than the old men in the room." A laugh rippled through the room, and Theo hugged Auggie to him as a flush lit up Auggie's face. "We love you all so much, and we're so grateful you came."

"We love you too," Shaw said, and Tean nodded.

"I know you gave up a lot to be here, and I'm so thankful for your support. But the reality is, the best thing you can do now is go home. This is going to be a long process. It's going to be hard." A grim smile shadowed his face. "It's going to be awful, I imagine. But I'm innocent, and all we can do is let the justice system take its course. I hate to ask you to go home after you just got here, and I don't want to seem ungrateful. I'm always going to remember that you came like this, to show your support. Thank you. I don't think I can say that enough. Thank you so much for doing this."

In the silence that followed, Colt's voice came from the living room, "No, bite Lana! Bite Lana, you dumb dog!" And Lana and Evie giggled helplessly.

"John, may I talk with you privately?" Emery said.

"What happened?" North asked. "Did they do that thing in prison where they put all the bunks in a circle and bang your brains out?"

"If anybody's going to bang his brains out," Shaw said, "it's Emery, only Emery hasn't had a chance unless they were banging in the basement."

"They weren't," Jem said. "Tean would have told me."

"Jem!"

"What? You would have. Oh, you know what it is? It's probably because he hasn't had any real food and his brain is low on—Tean, what's that thing when I get McDonald's brain because I haven't had a McGriddle or anything delicious?"

"There's no such thing as McDonald's brain."

"Glucose. His brain probably doesn't have any glucose. He needs a Big Mac, minimum, supersize fries."

"They don't do supersize anymore. There was a movie. Someone died."

"Nobody died. Well, maybe. But if you make friends with the fry lady, and then you come up with 'supersize' as a code word—"

"John-Henry," Theo said, "you've been through a lot. Why don't we talk about this in the morning?"

"I appreciate that you all want to help," John said, "but I believe in this town, and I believe in our justice system, and—"

"For heaven's sake, John-Henry, don't be a fool."

The words came from Grace Elaine. She had drawn herself up, her pale eyes fixed on her son.

"Mother—"

Glenn spoke over him. "Your mother is right."

"Again, I appreciate that you want to make sure I'm alright, but I'm not a child, and I don't need or want my parents to bail me out." He must have heard his own words, though, because a pained smile crossed his face. "I take that back since you literally bailed me out, but I think you know what I mean."

"John," Emery said, pitching his voice low and squeezing his hand. "The situation is complicated—"

"Do you have any idea what this will do to you?" Grace Elaine said. "Do you have any idea how the world works? You're a grown man, John-Henry. Don't be naïve. As far as this town is concerned, you're already guilty."

"That's enough," Emery said.

"It's not enough, and we don't have time for you to coddle him. The people in this town are like people everywhere, John-Henry. They're pack animals, and they're vicious, and at the first sign of weakness, they'll go for your belly. This is their opportunity. And since no one else will do you the service of being frank with you, I will. Every day this charge hangs over your head, it grows closer to being permanent. It doesn't matter if they clear you. It doesn't matter if you're acquitted. What people in this town will remember—what they'll think every time they hear your name—is that you did these things and got away with them. Have no delusions about that."

"Jesus," Auggie whispered.

Some of the color had leached from John's face. He was clutching Emery's hand so tightly that his nails bit into the flesh, but the pain registered only distantly.

When Emery opened his mouth, though, Grace Elaine said, "Am I wrong?"

Emery finally had to shut his mouth because he had nothing to say.

John gave a tiny, dazed shake of his head. Emery watched him. I'm sorry, he wanted to say. I'm sorry I couldn't tell you first, without everyone here to see it. I'm sorry I couldn't spare you this. I'm sorry that she's right. I'm sorry that I can't stop your world from collapsing.

"I don't—" John gave a rubbery laugh. "I didn't think about that."

"Son," Glenn said, "there's more to it than the court of public opinion. Someone has engineered these events, and they've done so in a way that suggests an undue influence. They've fabricated evidence—and, in the process, accessed and tampered with a police computer. They arranged for the grand jury to be empaneled and for an indictment to be handed down, and I never caught a whiff of it. And neither did you. That should tell you something about what we're facing. Whoever is behind this will not hesitate to manufacture more evidence if it's necessary, to bring that influence to bear on whoever might be useful in furthering their designs. You cannot count on your colleagues to do their jobs. You cannot count on the courts to be impartial. Emery, for God's sake, say something."

The hollows around John's eyes looked worse. A faint tremor showed in his jaw before he turned to look at Emery.

I'm sorry, Emery wanted to say.

But instead, he said, "There are logistical complications to investigating. The conflict of interest, of course, and the fact that whatever we find will be perceived as biased. If we don't do everything exactly right, a prosecutor will make mincemeat out of it, and that's not to mention the possibility of additional criminal charges like witness tampering, interference with an ongoing investigation, and obstruction of justice." He took a breath. "But, at the same time, the defense is entitled to an investigation too, and I don't think there's anyone better suited to do this. I see two primary approaches: one, identify this witness and learn everything we can about him so that we can discredit him and his bogus recording; and two, prove that the material on your computer was planted. We'll have to be careful. And we'll have to be smart. But most of all, we'll have to be fast. Whatever is happening, I believe it's time sensitive. The kind of influence being brought to bear, and the quality of this evidence—at some point, scrutiny from state or federal officials will unravel the whole mess. But, John, that might be six months from now. Or a year. Longer. We can't wait for that." He shook his head. "I won't wait for that."

"If we're not going to wait," North said, "then we'd better fucking do something."

Jem nodded. "We should hit the Cottonmouth Club. Tonight. Get in there hard and fast, before they can stop us."

"Sounds like your dating profile," North said. "But he's not wrong."

"Also, I want to propose as a backup plan that Tean should make a lion eat them."

"You know what we're going to do? We're going to get a baby gate, and we're going to put him and Shaw and the fucking dogs on the other side of it."

"The Cottonmouth Club is a dead end," Emery said. "Whoever was or is operating out of it, they've left nothing in the club itself that might give them away."

"You don't know that."

"Actually, I do. I've been in there three times since August."

"The last time, he tripped their new security system," John said.

"I should have anticipated that they'd upgrade it. The point, however, is that there's nothing in the Cottonmouth Club to help us. I'm not sure we'll ever know how deeply the club was involved in their organization, but whatever they were using the space for, they've since shifted their operations elsewhere."

"Where?" Tean asked.

John shook his head. "We don't know."

When Shaw spoke, his voice was subdued. "They prey on people who are helpless. People who can disappear, and no one will care. In St. Louis, they were using a homeless shelter like a feeding trough."

"Kids, too," Theo said. "It happens all the time. Kids who don't have a responsible adult in their lives, or kids whose parents just don't care what happens to them. They meet someone. That person pretends to care about them. It doesn't take long before they trust that person. That's maybe the most messed-up part of a lot of trafficking; the victims go along willingly, either because they trust their trafficker, or because they think it's their chance at a better life."

Auggie was rubbing Theo's back, studying his fiancé. When he spoke, though, the words were for everyone. "There's a lot of rural poverty out here. A lot of people—kids and adults—who could disappear, and nobody would ask too many questions."

"And that's why we're not going to let them get away with this," Emery said. "They think they can get rid of John and keep doing what they've always done. We're going to make sure that doesn't happen."

"I'll reach out to my contacts again," Tean said. "I didn't have any luck when we were here before, but someone has to know something about the wildlife trafficking side of their organization."

"The drugs, too," Theo said. Something flickered on Auggie's face—something Emery couldn't read, but that seemed to make sense to Theo. He closed a hand around Auggie's, but he didn't look at him as he said, "I should have thought about that earlier. It's not just people and animals; organizations like this, they usually have ties to drug cartels. I might know someone. And I'll see if I can pick up anything at school, ask about kids who've withdrawn or been truant."

"This jabroni who fingered John-Henry," North said.

"His name is Emery," Shaw said. "He's right there."

Red darkened North's cheeks as he rounded on Shaw.

Emery couldn't have sworn to it, but he thought, just maybe, Shaw winked at him.

"I know what his name is, you knob. And that's not what I meant."

"Well, I'm sorry. You'll have to be more specific."

"I don't need to be more specific. I need not to have a pansy-assed jamoke permanently glued to my dick-cheese—"

"North," John said with a kind of strangled desperation.

Grace Elaine was watching North with something approaching interest. Glenn, of course, was on his phone. Cora's eyes were huge.

More red rushed into North's face, and, sounding like he was choking on the words, "This clown tool and I will look for him, see if we can figure out who's paying him to lie."

"Oh, that guy who fingered John-Henry. I thought you meant—"

North got a hand over Shaw's mouth, and Shaw dissolved into giggles as the two of them began to wrestle.

Emery was surprised to see a smile—a real one—cross John's face.

"I'm going to come up with some uniforms for us," Jem said. "They're going to be fire. One thousand percent spandex, super tight around the junk, probably some sort of bubble-butt extender for you, Emery, oh, and they'll definitely show off our abs."

"Nothing can be one thousand percent," Emery said, "and you don't have abs. I've seen you without a shirt."

Jem turned an outraged look on Tean.

"You're very handsome," Tean said in what Emery thought was supposed to be a reassuring tone. "And strong."

"Well, yeah, but my six-pack."

"Of hash browns," Auggie murmured.

"Auggie!"

Auggie grinned, chewing on the collar of his shirt—and, in the process, exposing his ultradefined stomach.

"I stood up for you when North wanted to ship you back to Twink Island."

"What is Twink Island?" Theo asked.

"Wouldn't you like to know?" Shaw said.

"Jesus, Gramps," North said breathily as he continued grappling with Shaw. "Excited much?"

"Did you notice how he didn't even miss a beat?"

"I could hear his ancient boner creaking to full mast all the way over here."

"It must be really loud then because ever since the ravages of time robbed you of your hearing—" Shaw cut off with a squeal as North attempted to twist his balls off. The thick padding of the snowsuit was the only thing that saved him.

"I'm not making anyone a uniform except Theo," Jem said. "Because everybody's mean to us."

"You're not making any uniforms," Emery said. "You're coming with me because—and I honestly cannot believe I'm about to say this—I need you."

5

It was past midnight, and the night had a frozen-solid quality, as though the darkness and the cold were something tangible—all razor edges that caught in Emery's throat every time he took a breath. The Wahredua police station hunkered under the wash of sodium lights. The orangish glow seeped across the snow, an island of dirty light in the gloom. Nothing moved inside the redbrick building, as far as Emery could tell—nothing had moved in the last hour. The windows were dark except for the emergency lights. There were a handful of cars in the parking lot, but he didn't recognize any of them. Someone would be on dispatch. A handful of other officers would be on the night shift, out patrolling or handling the calls that inevitably came in—domestic violence, noise complaints, shoplifting, vandalism. Emery guessed, though, it would be quiet. The worst nights were in the spring.

"How many people are in there?" Jem asked.

"I don't know. Fewer than five, I expect. But if we're lucky, only one—whoever is on dispatch."

"One?" Jem sounded faintly disappointed. He scratched under one arm, pulling at the Pizza Hut polo.

"Would you prefer more?"

"Well, no, but—I mean, on TV, there's always a million people there day and night, and they're always shouting at each other, and the fax machine is screeching, oh, and Sipowicz says, 'Put him in the tank.'"

"I have no idea what you're talking about."

Jem's grin flashed in the darkness. "I know. I actually love that about you. You don't even care, do you?"

"Not particularly."

"That's so friggin' dope. Tean's the exact same way. He kept asking who the flight attendant on TV was, and I honestly didn't have the heart to tell him it was Taylor Swift."

"Who?"

Jem dropped back against the seat, shaking his head. "I can't. I'm dead. Not two of you." He sat up so abruptly that Emery glanced around to see what had alerted him, but all Jem said was "Wait, have you seen *Buffy*?"

"I was a gay boy growing up in the '90s," Emery said with disgust. "Have I seen *Buffy*?"

"Ok, you can't tell Tean, but I'm pretty sure we need to kiss now."

"Sure, we can do that. And then I'll murder you, and I'll have to spend the rest of the night hiding your body."

"Or I could do, um, my thing. I guess."

"Sure," Emery said again. "How about we do that?"

Jem climbed out of the Odyssey and jogged around the block.

It was partially his own fault, Emery thought, for playing along. But, in his own defense, he probably wouldn't have known who Taylor Swift was if not for John and Colt.

Emery counted to sixty. Then he got out of the minivan, checked the lot once more, and loped toward the station. He was halfway there when Jem came around the corner in his rental, a silver Malibu with Florida plates. Emery let Jem's approach register only peripherally; he kept his focus on the building in front of him.

Breaking into the station was perhaps not, Emery had to admit, his best idea. Although he wouldn't have gone as far as John, who, when they had discussed it again in their bedroom, had called it *the stupidest fucking thing I've ever heard*. There were logistical challenges, of course, even though Emery had less confidence in the station's security than his husband. And there was always the possibility that Emery would be arrested for trespassing. But the reality was that they had little time and few options, none of them good. Someone had framed John using his work computer, and at the very least, Emery had to see if he could turn anything up. The alternative would have been more of what he'd been doing for the last few months—chasing old leads that took him nowhere, finding himself in one blind alley after another.

The silver Malibu rolled down the street. Then, as Jem approached the station, it began to drift toward the shoulder. The car jerked, as though Jem had caught himself drifting and overcorrected, and brake lights flashed. Predictably, the Malibu fishtailed, the rear end swinging out as the sedan slid into the thick snow at the side of the road. Jem spun the wheels for good effect, throwing up snow until the tires were sliding on ice. He turned on the hazards and got out of the car, and in the process, he even got himself tangled in the seat belt. It was, Emery had to admit, a masterful performance. He also decided he would have to keep a closer eye on any interaction Jem had with his son.

Emery's line of sight to Jem was cut off as he approached the side of the station. Next to a steel door, a bucket of sand was peppered with cigarette butts. Technically, the no-smoking policy included the parking lot, but in practice, too many officers and civilian employees smoked to make the policy realistic—at least, that was what people told Emery. As a result, this door saw a fair amount of use during the day shift. It also meant that the snow here was trampled and packed, and that Emery would leave no sign of his approach.

At the front of the building, Jem hammered on the security glass and called, "Hello? Hi, hello? Is anybody in there?"

Emery fished out a key. John, of course, had been required to surrender his keys while he was suspended from duty, and Emery had turned in his official set when he'd resigned. The reality of a small town and an equally small police department, where no-smoking policies weren't enforced and other, similar regulations saw equal disregard, was that a lot of things never got recorded. A spare key, for example, if you left yours at home one day. And Emery hadn't bothered to return that one, on the off chance it would be useful. Until now, it hadn't mattered—John had keys to everything. But tonight—well, tonight, Emery was grateful for that little bureaucratic incompetence.

"Oh my God, thank you," Jem said. "This cat ran out of nowhere."

He even sounded upset. Maybe, Emery thought, he should send Colt to boarding school while Uncle Jem was in town.

The key slid into the lock, but when Emery tried to turn it, the lock didn't budge. He stared at the key for a moment. Then common sense asserted itself. He tried the key again, making sure it slid all the way home, and jiggled it. This time, the lock turned, and Emery slipped inside.

Warm air, full of the scent of toner and wet winter clothing and the station's old furnace, met him in a darkened hallway. An emergency light hung a pale cone farther down; from above Emery, the red wash of an exit sign fell over him. Distantly, he could hear someone talking—the voice sounded like it was coming from the front of the building, and it sounded like the person was annoyed, which meant Jem was doing his job.

Emery moved quickly down the hallway. His first stop would be John's office, which meant—most likely—picking the lock. It would also require him to cross the bullpen, where he'd be exposed. It would be the most vulnerable moment of the operation—

The lights came on, and for the first moment, they were blinding. Emery blinked as his eyes adjusted, trying to make out the shape standing in front of him.

"God fucking damn it. Are you kidding me?"

"Dulac?"

The lights went off, and once again, Emery was blind. He waited, listening as steps moved down the hall toward him.

In the shadows, Gray Dulac was an outline: average height, slim build, the lines of his clothing suggesting a suit. He smelled like something medicinal—a liniment, maybe—and like unwashed hair and a chemical fruitiness. The latter was explained when he produced a vape, hit it, and jetted a thin stream from the side of his mouth visible only in the vape's LED glow.

"What the fuck," he asked, "are you doing?"

"What are you doing? Isn't it a bit late for you?"

"I was asleep at my desk until some jerkwad started pounding on the doors. Jesus, that was you too, wasn't it?" Dulac hit the vape again, and the artificial smell filled the space between them. "This is some kind of joke, right? You're not serious with this shit, are you?"

After Emery had resigned from the department, Dulac had been John's partner. He was, in spite of his natural fuckboy tendencies, a competent detective. Or had been. Half a year earlier, a killer had left a light bulb trap, and Dulac had activated it. Shards of glass had damaged his face and one eye, and his recovery had been slow and uneven. He was back on active duty, which Emery considered a mistake—Dulac might be physically fit for duty, but the emotional and psychological damage were still a long way from being healed.

"I was just picking up some of John's stuff."

Dulac pocketed the vape. He rubbed his face. "That's what you were going to tell someone?"

"John is entitled to his personal property, but I thought it would be easier if I came—"

"And broke into the station from the smoke pad?"

"In other scenarios," Emery said, "whoever found me would not have known how I entered."

The red light from the exit sign seemed to vibrate.

"Bad luck," Dulac said.

"Admittedly poor planning. I haven't slept much. And I'm emotionally dysregulated."

Dulac laughed. "I bet that's making you fucking crazy."

"More or less."

"What about the cameras?"

"Why would someone have reason to review the security cameras?"

"Ok. What about John-Henry's computer?"

Emery said nothing. He could taste the artificial flavoring of the vapor on every breath. He thought he could feel it, like a film that the vape had left on his face.

"How is he?" Dulac asked.

Somewhere in the building, a radio crackled with static.

"How do you think?"

In the darkness, it was impossible to make out the expression on Dulac's face. And maybe it wasn't even an expression. Maybe it was a shadow.

"Poor John-Henry," Dulac said softly. "His perfect little world in smithereens."

The shadow was there again. A trick of the light. Or, as it were, a trick of the dark. The warmth of the station seemed oppressive now, Emery's coat too heavy, his shirt clumping under his arms.

"And how are you?" Dulac asked.

"Busy."

Dulac craned his head, considering Emery from a new angle. It brought a sliver of his face into the light: a triangle of brow and nose and cheek. The scars were red and raised, his injured eye shot through with blood, even all these months later. He was smiling, and it made Emery think of ridiculous comparisons, the kind of overblown descriptions in the novels John favored. A cat and a mouse. His voice lilted mockingly as he said, "Emery."

One moment, and then another. Dulac didn't move. He didn't draw a gun. He didn't shout. He didn't do anything but stand there, smiling, that panel of thin, pale light cutting a triangle out of his face. But Emery found his mind racing, mapping possibilities, probabilities. If he takes a swing. If he tries to draw. Hand on his wrist, foot behind his ankle. The odds were good that Emery was faster than Dulac; he was certainly bigger, and the advantage of strength in a close encounter was significant. But all it would take was a single noise to bring someone else running, and then it would be over.

"It is...difficult."

"You can do better than that."

His heart beat louder, the sound trapped inside his head. He wanted to press a hand against his chest, to bear down on the pain there. But he kept his hands at his side, and he kept his voice on a tightrope. "You know John.

This is an attack on who he is, and even though he's trying not to let it get to him, he's struggling. To be shoved out of your place in the universe. To be cut off, alone. To have everyone look at you like you're worse than nothing, like you're less than human. To learn that all the things you relied on are smoke."

"I'm not asking about him. I'm asking about you."

And I'm telling you, Emery thought, a hint of disorientation, as though somehow one of them had slipped into a foreign language. Confused because it was obvious. And a sense, too, that perhaps he was the one who was confused. I'm telling you because it's happening to me, he thought with that same dazed uncertainty. Because they already did it to me.

Then the moment passed, and the shadowed length of the hallway resolved in his vision. Dulac was still waiting, one blood-dark eye fixed on him.

"How is it? I want to take my family away from here and burn this fucking town to the ground."

The corner of Dulac's mouth canted into an unfamiliar smile. "How about that?"

"Gray, I don't have time for this. The clock's running, and you've got a decision to make. Are you going to help John? Or are you going to sit back and let these people destroy him?"

Dulac settled back on his heels. Darkness covered his face again like a caul. That hooked smile might have still been there. Or not. But finally he said, "What are you looking for?"

"Anything. You know how it works. It's the first rule of an investigation: every contact leaves a trace. Someone managed to plant those files on John's computer, and I'm willing to bet they had to do it from inside the station. That means someone was here, in this building. Contact. Multiple points of contact. So, I'm going to look. And I'm going to keep looking until I find a trace that leads me back to these sons of bitches."

"Or until the night watch rolls in and finds you digging through their lockers. Why not file an official request? Get whatever you want the right way."

"Because things are moving quickly, and because whatever I want, I think there's a good chance it will disappear if I file an official request." Emery paused. "I understand your bitterness. And I understand your anger. But I don't understand how you could let someone do this to John. He's always been your friend."

"He's always everyone's friend! That's the whole problem!"

The words weren't a shout—they were too low for that. But they were furious, and filled with an intensity that broke them into syllables.

"Never mind," Emery said, angling his body to twist past Dulac.

Dulac's hand snaked out and caught his arm. For a moment, Dulac seemed to be struggling with something—like he couldn't catch his breath, like maybe he was having a panic attack, and his body was telling his brain he couldn't get enough air. And then, for one horrible moment, Emery thought he was laughing. Dulac's fingers tightened until they bit into Emery's biceps. And then, slowly, Dulac seemed to take control of himself. He released Emery, shifted to let him pass, and then, when Emery took another step, said, "Peterson changed the codes."

Emery stopped. He had counted on institutional inertia. He had counted on small-town laziness.

"Didn't think about that, did you?" Dulac didn't sound gleeful or amused, though. He sounded tired. "Come on."

They crossed the bullpen with only the sound of their steps for company. If Jem was still buying time, Emery knew it wouldn't last much longer—if the problem dragged on for too long, officers would be called back to assist, and that was the opposite of what they wanted. Dulac stopped in front of the unmarked door that led to the station's small security room, thumbed a code into the ancient push-button lock, and opened the door.

Emery had only ever visited the security room a handful of times; it doubled as a kind of catch-all storage for electronics, and the metal shelves lining the walls held old TVs, dusty radio sets, rotary phones, point-and-shoot 35mms. One wall was taken up by displays, where footage from the station's security cameras rotated at regular intervals. On one screen, the silver Malibu was pulling back onto the street, leaving behind it the patch of kitty litter and sand that had been thrown down to provide traction. The air smelled like Funyuns and, even more strongly, the hot-dust odor of the furnace. A single rolling chair with pilled upholstery waited at the desk.

Dulac dropped into the seat, clicked through several screens, and began scrolling through a list of time-stamped recordings.

"What are you looking for?"

"I had an idea." And then, the words wary with something that was a cross between defensiveness and an apology, "I wouldn't hang him out to dry on this, you know."

Emery said nothing, and Dulac continued scrolling. He took out his phone, opened an email app, and began cross-referencing. Finally, he pulled up a video. The timestamp said it was from Thursday, November 26. Thanksgiving night.

The recording began to play, and Emery only paid partial attention as Dulac scrubbed forward. Thanksgiving. When the station would have held only a skeleton crew, like tonight. Because everyone wanted to be home with their families. Even the people at the station would have been tired, or tipsy, or sleepy from too much tryptophan, or simply lulled by the fact that it was a quiet night, and a holiday to boot.

"Gotcha," Dulac said and smacked the keyboard, freezing the video.

In the frame, the security camera from the lobby showed a young man standing in the doorway. Shorter than average, muscular build visible even under the dark pea coat, he had skin the color of boiled leather and his hair buzzed down to dark fuzz. He was carrying a laptop bag over one shoulder, and in the other, he held what looked like a Gameboy—or whatever they were called today. As Emery watched, the man approached the desk, spoke with the officer on duty—Andrea Ehlers—and produced some kind of ID. He signed the log, which meant putting down his Gameboy, and then, Gameboy in hand again, he followed Ehlers off-camera.

"God fucking damn it," Dulac said to himself.

He cued up several more videos, and they spliced together the man's passage through the station: Ehlers led him down the hall, past the bullpen, and into the utility closet where, among other things, the station's dedicated internet line, server, and other network equipment was located. Ehlers appeared to ask the man something, and he shook his head. He looked even younger with a smile on his face; Emery wouldn't have put him at much older than Auggie. And then, without any apparent concern, Ehlers turned her back on the man and left. He stepped into the utility closet and shut the door.

Shaking his head, Dulac moved the mouse to close the video, but Emery said, "Wait."

Dulac scrubbed forward, and less than five minutes later, the door opened, and the man emerged. They switched video feeds and watched him return to the bullpen and, without any seeming sense of hurry, open the door to John's office and step inside. He shut the blinds on John's windows. The lights stayed off. Maybe, if someone had walked past, they would have wondered if the blinds had been open or closed the last time they'd passed the room. But it was a moot consideration; no one came into the bullpen, and twenty-seven minutes later, the man opened the blinds again and emerged from John's office. He took a step as though heading back to the utility closet. Then he stopped and looked up, straight into the camera. He smiled a huge, shit-eating grin and flipped the camera off with both hands.

For the first time, the angle of the camera revealed a scar on the side of his neck.

"Motherfucker," Dulac breathed.

The rest of the video was less interesting. The man returned to the utility closet and, four hours later, he left. Ehlers checked on him once. Emery tried to pay attention, but his mind raced with consideration, questions, possible explanations. Ehlers being corrupt seemed laughable—or was it? If she was, why have the man sign the log? Why parade the man around on camera? Why not choose a route with fewer opportunities to be spotted—

Dulac was on his phone again. "Jesus Christ." He tossed it onto the desk and reached up like he was going to rub his face, but he stopped short, hands still inches away from the red ridges of scars.

"What the fuck was that?" Emery asked. "He walked right in here."

"Sure, why not?" Dulac gestured at his phone. "He was right on schedule."

"Gray, what the fuck is going on?"

"Server upgrade. Or network upgrade. Or whatever those tech boners called it. Over Thanksgiving weekend, they upgraded a lot of the department's computer equipment."

Emery stared at the display where the video, now paused, still showed the man. A fan whirred to life in the CCTV's DVR, the small sound filling the silence. Pieces began to tumble into place.

"They put it out for bid," Emery said. "They told people what they were doing. Jesus Christ, whoever got the contract, it would have been public record."

"Network Solutions of Mid-Missouri," Dulac said, pointing at his phone again. "They were doing everything over Thanksgiving weekend." His mouth slanted in that unfamiliar smile. "Not, by the way, Thanksgiving night. But how hard could it have been? This guy figures out who's supposed to be doing the job. Hell, he probably even has the dates from the contract. He calls up, says he's with Network Solutions of Mid-Missouri, sorry for the inconvenience but he's got to do some preliminary work the night of Thanksgiving, will anybody be around?"

"Fifteen minutes with a color printer and a laminator, and he has his fucking corporate ID. Jesus Christ. How'd he get the files on John's computer? It's password protected."

"You mean, if the department's IT guys didn't just hand him all the login information when he called?"

The fan's high-pitched whine filled Emery's head.

Finally, he said, "You have got to be fucking kidding me."

"I kept thinking about it and thinking about it. I kept thinking it's impossible, no way, how did someone hack him after we just had that big security upgrade." For the first time all night, the old Dulac smile flashed out again, cocky and wry and all too self-aware. "Only took me twelve hours before I finally heard what I was thinking."

"You've got to talk to Diana about this. If she sees this, she'll throw the whole thing out."

Dulac's silence went on a moment too long. "Emery."

"Fine. I'll tell her—"

"Jesus, bro. Listen to yourself, will you? I'll tell Diana. And for that matter, I'll tell Aniya Thompson. And I'll make a copy of this before we go, and I'll send a copy to my boy, and I'll send a copy to you, and I'll send a copy to the President of the fucking United States if you want. But get your head on straight, man. He walks into John's office. He closes the blinds. He comes out again. That's all you've got."

"Network Solutions will say they didn't send anyone on Thanksgiving night."

"Yeah. And that's something. But unless you get your hands on this guy, you might as well have a handful of shit."

"Digital forensics will show when those files were loaded."

"Maybe. Eventually."

Emery tented his hands over his nose. He breathed in slowly. The stink of rancid Funyuns made his stomach roll.

"Bro, I'm not trying to dump on you. I'm just saying, this isn't a silver bullet."

Emery nodded. The rage was there, the cold fire of it, burning away everything else: his helplessness, his frustration, the hopelessness choking him. He walked deeper into that anger, until the cold froze his marrow, until he ached with it. Someone did this to John, he thought, fanning that icy fury. Someone is doing this to John. Someone is doing this to my family. It was like an ice plunge, his head shoved into winter water. One moment, the pain seemed like too much. And then, relief. He didn't feel anything, really. Just the monumental cold of his anger.

"I'll talk to Aniya," Emery said, dropping his hands. "She'll be able to have someone examine the computer. The video would be useful if you're willing to give us a copy."

"Of course, dude."

"The emails would be helpful too, although I understand that might compromise you. No, never mind; it should be enough to request the bids and the final contract for the network upgrade." In his mind, he saw again the man staring up into the camera, the cruelty of the smile on his face, the double eagles shot at whoever was watching. The rage was like wind and snow, a black blizzard inside Emery's head. The sound of it was like something rushing through a vast, empty dark. "He knew. He knew someone would eventually look at the footage. He knew someone would see that he planted those files on John's computer. He knew, and he didn't care. Like—like it was a game to him. You saw him; he was having fun."

Dulac's voice was troubled. "Why would he do that? He's fucking up his own frame."

Emery shook his head.

"Let me get you a copy of the log," Dulac said. He even sounded like Dulac again, the stranger's voice gone. When he stood, he wore uncertainty behind the freckles that dusted his cheeks and nose. The blood-dark eye seemed to have trouble tracking Emery. Dulac raised a hand, hesitated, and then touched Emery's arm. "Bro, I'm sorry. I am. I—will you tell him?" He looked like he wanted to stop, but his voice broke when he added, "I can't. I just can't. Not yet."

Emery nodded.

He waited in the bullpen while Dulac tracked down the sign-in log. The photocopy he brought back showed the sign-in for 11:07pm on Thursday, November 26. Kyle McCall. The name was bullshit, of course. But you never knew. Sometimes, in a case, the strangest things ended up being important.

Dulac let him out onto the smoke pad, and the wind hissed in Emery's face. He started across the lot toward the Odyssey. He tried to think about what he would tell John. Enough. Not too much. Not so that he'd start blaming himself again. He had learned, later than he should have, that John was much harder on himself than people realized. Confident, yes. Even cocky. To a degree, perhaps, that Emery knew better than anyone. But always so sensitive to the gap he perceived between himself and Emery. Always wanting to be better. Always pushing himself, because John was used to being the best, and because so often, it came to him naturally. And this, Emery thought, this he would have to touch lightly, perhaps not at all, not until John had some time and distance. Because John wouldn't be able to see that it wasn't his fault. John would only say that he was chief, and it was his department, and in the end, it was his responsibility. And responsibility, for John-Henry, was the lifeline he'd given himself.

Emery's burner phone buzzed as he reached the van—that had been a precaution they all agreed on, along with taking back roads and avoiding traffic cameras. Until this was over, they couldn't afford to leave a trail. North's name flashed on the screen.

"We found him," North said.

For a moment, Emery's only point of reference was the man from the video, and he tried to make sense of the impossibility. Then he remembered their plan from earlier, North and Shaw's offer to track down the witness who had testified against John. Only hours ago, but it felt like days.

"What? How?"

"Because unlike some people, we don't sit around mooning because our one true love is in trouble, plus we're actually good at our jobs—Jesus Christ, Shaw, you tore out part of my scalp!" Silence came. And then, "No, I'm not telling him your willie is a divining rod or—no! Sit your ass—"

But something scraped the phone's receiver, and then Shaw's voice came across the call. "Emery, my willie actually is a divining rod! But that's not how we found this guy. Well, not this time. Well, not entirely. I mean, it did give a twitch—"

The sounds of struggle came again, and then North, breathing a little harder, said, "You will not believe the tiddlywinks shit in this town. One of the butt-lords from the grand jury was holding court in a bar. Mac's something. We literally walked in on the conversation, didn't even have to ask. He was going to keep talking as long as people were buying him drinks."

"My divining rod—"

"He threw wood when this frat boy bent over to tie his shoes. What kind of fucking divining rod is that?"

"But we found him, didn't we? And Emery, you should have seen this guy! Imagine two ham hocks—wait, are they hocks, or are they loins?"

"Where is he?" Emery snapped. "Who is he?"

"I don't know his name, but I could definitely identify him by his, um, derriere—"

"Not him, you—" Words failed him. "You butt-lord!"

A vacuum opened on the other end of the call.

"This is the single greatest moment of my life," North said.

"Thank you, Emery," Shaw said. "I'm flattered."

"Of course, you're flattered, you horse's ass. You don't even know what a butt-lord is."

"I know what a butt-lord is! It's like a power bottom, but in chain mail—"

"I swear to Christ," Emery said, "I will murder both of you if you don't start talking."

"His name's Jace Vermilya," North said. "And he looks like a walking, talking argument for autofellatio."

Shaw sounded inordinately proud of himself as he began, "We followed him to these trailers—"

The staccato of gunfire broke through his words.

Then silence.

"Motherfucker," North breathed.

"Are you okay?"

"Yeah, yeah. It was in the compound. We're good."

"Send me the address," Emery said. "And don't go in there."

6

When headlights appeared, John-Henry tensed inside the Mustang. His breath had long since stopped steaming, and the air was arctic; he'd kept the windows cracked so that his breath wouldn't fog the glass. Not that he could see much—a hundred yards, give or take, of rutted dirt road. Around the car rose tall weeds and prairie grasses, brittle and brown from winterkill. When the air moved, they brushed the side of the Mustang. The sound was alien: feathering and soft, but also metallic.

The headlights drew closer, and John-Henry focused on controlling his breath as he picked up his Glock. By degrees, the shape of the vehicle resolved into the familiar outline of the Odyssey. The van slowed. Then it stopped. The headlights went off, and Emery got out. For a moment, the weak yellow of the van's interior light glazed the side of his face. The hard line of his jaw, and John-Henry's memory of how it fit his hand. The angle of cheekbone, and John-Henry's body knowing how it fit against his shoulder. The dark hair that was a little too long, pulled by the wind, glinting like sable.

Tired. That was John-Henry's first thought: Emery looked tired. But there was something else, too. A hardness that John-Henry remembered. He hadn't seen that look in a long time. In years, actually. The set of his mouth. The scarecrow eyes. Every inch of him armored against a world he refused to give ground to. It was the way Emery had looked when he'd come back to Wahredua, ready for a fight. It was the way he'd looked as a boy. And John-Henry was shocked, in the first moment, to see the stranger in front of him. And maybe it was the fact that he knew Emery better than he knew just about anyone by this point. Or maybe it was that he knew himself, as he ought to have known himself all those years ago. Maybe it was simply that they were both older now. But with his next heartbeat, John-Henry was shocked again to see how all that armor only revealed how vulnerable Emery was.

The van door shut with a quiet thud. Steps clipped the frozen dirt. When the wind blew, the winterkill grasses shuddered sideways. Emery crouched at the Mustang's passenger window, looking in, and he looked like Emery again—the question scrawled in the tilt of his eyebrows, the poor attempt to master his impatience. To his own surprise, John-Henry grinned, the feeling something like relief, and got out of the car.

"I see you're in a better mood," Emery said.

"Not really. Happy to see you, I guess."

That smoothed out Emery's brow. Then he scowled again. "Do you want to explain yourself?"

"I'm not going to sit on my ass, Ree."

"That's exactly what you're going to do. Your involvement endangers you—"

John-Henry smoothed Emery's hair back. Sable. And holding flecks of starlight like it had a static charge. "We do things together."

It was around his mouth. At his eyes. John-Henry wondered how, for all those years, he hadn't seen it, how easily Emery could be hurt.

Then Emery grunted. "That'll be a wonderful way to tell people we're going to prison together."

Laughing quietly, John-Henry pointed down the dirt road. "North and Shaw are that way."

They made their way down the narrow break in the prairie grass. The ground was slick and hard and rutted, and more than once, they steadied each other as they made their way through the darkness. After a couple of hundred yards, a darker shadow coalesced in the darkness ahead of them. A dark gray Impala, no frills. Apparently North and Shaw had learned a lesson about driving showy cars.

As John-Henry and Emery approached, the St. Louis detectives got out of the sedan. North was hugging himself, chafing his arms. Shaw, still dressed in the snowsuit and quilted booties, looked remarkably comfortable, although he did make a lot of rustling noise when he moved.

"It's colder than Frosty's balls out here," North said. "What the fuck took you so long?"

"It's approximately twenty minutes from—" Emery began.

John-Henry laid a hand on his arm. "What happened?"

"We followed him out here," North indicated farther down the road with his chin, "and we called you. We were going to check out his goat orgy, but the shooting started."

"I didn't need to see the goat orgy because I've been to one before," Shaw said.

"Go on," North said, squaring up with Emery. "Ask him."

"Honestly, I didn't care for it. So much hair. Wait, is it fur? North, is it fur?"

"It's blow my fucking brains out."

"And one of the goats bit me right on the hinus." In a rush, Shaw added, "And not in a sexual way."

"Breathe, love," John-Henry said, stroking Emery's arm.

North glared at him, of all people. "It was a petting zoo, since you're absolutely fucking dying to know. And it wasn't an orgy, it was a feeding stampede. And we're banned for life, thanks oh so fucking much."

The starlight robbed the world of color, but it looked like Emery's face was a startling shade of red. "And then?"

"Oh, I wasn't really in the mood after I got bit," Shaw said. "Which was a shame, because they really did seem to be having a good time—"

"I meant after the shooting," Emery snapped. He managed to control his volume, but only barely.

"Nothing," North said.

"Nothing?" John-Henry asked.

North shook his head. "Not one fucking thing." He shifted his weight. "Do you want us to call this in? Anonymously, I mean. Whatever happened in there, it's going to be bad."

"He's still in there," John-Henry said. "Vermilya, or whatever his real name is. You said nobody left, so he's still there. But if we leave and call the police, he might disappear again."

"Fantastic," Emery muttered. He drew a deep breath, squeezed John-Henry's shoulder, and started down the road. "If you fall in that fucking snowsuit," he shot back, "I'm not helping you up."

"Those goats didn't help me up either," Shaw said as he hurried after him. "Oh! Wait! Unless the one who bit my, um, fanny was trying to help me up. Emery, slow down. Did you hear my breakthrough?"

"Lots of big trees," North said, looking around. "Should be real easy to hang myself."

They quieted as they moved down the road. When they followed another bend, light shattered the darkness ahead of them: bright, white, and high in the trees. It outlined the bare winter branches and threw shadows across the rutted dirt. Behind the screen of old-growth oaks, John-Henry could make out the straight lines of man-made structures. A metal gate stood open, and parked in front of it was an old, battered Jeep.

Emery was the first to draw his gun. John-Henry was second. North got a handful of Shaw's snowsuit and yanked him backward, the fabric rustling, and produced a handgun of his own. Discomfort flickered inside John-Henry; it was dangerous enough conducting any sort of tactical operation with men and women who had trained together, who knew what they were supposed to do—and, as importantly, what they weren't supposed to do. North and Shaw were more than competent as private investigators, but John-Henry doubted they'd had any training on how to work with a group to enter and clear a structure.

"I want you two to hang back," he told North. "Nobody comes in. Nobody goes out."

North's grin was surprisingly knowing. "Plus you don't want me blasting your tits off."

"That would be ideal, yeah."

"Don't say tits," Shaw whispered from behind them.

North scowled over his shoulder, but he spoke to John-Henry. "All right. The big, bad cops can do the hard work. I'll just sit back and—"

He cut off, and his face filled with something that, on someone else, John-Henry would have called guilt. Or, at the least, fear.

"What are you going to do while you're waiting?" Shaw asked a little too innocently.

"Read the Bible."

"In this light? With your eyes?"

Perhaps the universe was taking mercy on John-Henry because by that point, they had reached the gate. John-Henry waved North and Shaw back, and their low, restless squabbling faded into the background. The wind picked up again. Branches creaked, clacking against each other, and shadows danced across the road. The gate shivered, the hinges moaning. It lifted some of Emery's hair, but if it bothered him, he gave no notice; his eyes moved constantly, assessing the darkness around them, and John-Henry did the same.

After the gate, the final stretch of road led them around a line of bare oaks. At the center of the compound, a repurposed telephone pole stood with a pair of security lights mounted on it, filling the clearing with light. The structures John-Henry had seen from a distance took on familiar forms: a forty-foot shipping container, a trailer home with crumbling plywood skirting and cinderblock pilings, an Econoline campervan that had to date back to the first Bush, a pole barn made out of corrugated steel panels. The smell of gunpowder hung in the air, and beneath it, the chill of leaf mold, and a stink like paint thinner that told John-Henry this place was what he had expected: a meth lab.

At the edge of the trees, Emery stopped. John-Henry listened. The wind died. The branches settled. His pulse drummed in his ears now, and his face felt hot. He couldn't hear anything from the compound ahead of them. Emery pointed across the clearing: two pickups were parked next to the pole barn. One looked like the kind Colt dreamed about—an F-150 with a luxury trim. The other was a Ram, older, paint chipped around the wheel wells, the bumper tied on with baling twine.

At least three, John-Henry thought. Three. And you always add one more.

He realized, with a distant surprise, that Emery was waiting. So much for all that talk about hanging back. John-Henry assessed the compound again. Thin curtains hung in the windows of the trailer, but they did nothing to hide the light inside. The Econoline was dark, in contrast. As was the pole barn. The shipping container had chains across the doors, and John-Henry marked that one as last. He nodded at the trailer and took the lead.

Up close, the plywood skirting around the base of the trailer looked even worse, and where the sheets had crumpled—or, in a few cases collapsed—the cinderblock piers were exposed, and the deeper darkness beyond. Calling the structure unstable didn't really do it justice; a couple of weeks before, Ashley and Colt had broken a chair while they were wrestling. If they'd been here, they would have done some Godzilla-level damage.

The treads of the stairs that led up to the trailer were soft and spongy underfoot, and John-Henry kept to the outer edge as much as possible, where the wood felt more solid. He stopped at the top of the stairs and listened again. Then he glanced over his shoulder. Emery had his back, of course. Old times, he thought. And then he shouldered the door open and moved into the trailer.

They still worked well together; he'd known they would. They didn't need to speak. They moved quickly through the trailer, clearing each room. They found the bodies in the kitchen.

Two men and a woman, all three of them dead and still warm. Less than an hour, he thought; rigor still hadn't set in. That lined up with the shooting North and Shaw had heard. The two men were both white, and both looked rough. One was bigger, with a snarled beard and long, frizzy hair. The other was skinny, young, with peach fuzz and a prominent Adam's apple. The woman was white too, her blond hair short and gelled back, in a coverall and boots. She'd fallen when she'd been shot, and somehow, her trucker hat had stayed on. It showed a cartoon rendering of a vulva and then, in bold pink letters, EAT UP. Next to her lay a big old Glock. Blood pooled on the linoleum; more blood spattered the walls. Mixed now with the gunpowder was the stink of bodies torn open.

Emery crouched and snapped photos of their faces. Then he moved back, snapping more photos of the bodies in situ. When he'd finished, he tapped the screen on his burner a few times. A moment later, it buzzed.

"North says none of these are Vermilya."

The phone buzzed again. Emery locked it and dropped it in his pocket.

"Shaw?" John-Henry asked.

"Don't ask."

It was a crime scene. Three people had been murdered. And, for all they knew, they were still in danger. But John-Henry laughed—the sound quick and keen and startling even him. His blood was up, adrenaline still burning like jellied gasoline. Later, he'd feel sick. Later, he'd have nightmares. He'd been through it enough times to know how it all worked. But for now, it was almost like being drunk.

Wiping his mouth on his sleeve, John-Henry nodded at the back door. "The van?"

"It's a fucking shooting gallery. Perfect setup, just wait for somebody to poke their head in."

John-Henry nodded again. "The barn?"

"Fuck me," Emery said, but he nodded.

They drew on disposable gloves—Emery Hazard, always prepared—and kept moving. The trailer's back door led onto a small deck. A jumble of junk cluttered the space: work boots, a bag of fertilizer that had split and stank of ammonia, a post-hole digger, a five-gallon bucket filled with plastic dinosaurs, another bucket with the roaches of joints and the flattened discs of beer cans, a child's sled, a snow shovel, ice melt, and bag after bag of garbage.

They moved down the steps, away from the rotting plywood skirting and the rickety cinderblock piers, and John-Henry took the lead toward the pole barn. He approached from the side, keeping an eye on the Econoline in case someone was hiding in the van, and then pushed into the barn.

Fluorescent panels made the large, open space as bright as day, and the paint thinner smell was overpowering here. A large cook setup filled the barn, spread out across folding tables. This wasn't a *Breaking Bad*-style operation, with genuine lab equipment. This was Ozark Volunteers-level stuff: pressure cookers, Mason jars, empty plastic two-liters of Coke and Fanta, turkey basters, Hamilton Beach blenders, ten-cent funnels, Great

Value aluminum foil. John-Henry and Emery divided the room and began moving through it, but aside from the lab, it was empty. No one hiding under the tables. No bodies.

"North and Shaw followed him here," John-Henry said. "Unless he walked out, he's still here."

"He didn't walk," Emery said.

"So, he's still here. The van?"

"Fan-fucking-tastic."

Before approaching the van, though, Emery checked the shipping container. The chains rattled, and a padlock rang out when he let it fall back against the metal. The time for silence was over; anyone living knew they were here, and now it was time to minimize the remaining risks.

Together, they closed in on the Econoline. It reminded John-Henry of a traffic stop. The reason traffic stops were so dangerous—part of the reason, anyway—was that you had no idea what someone was doing inside a car. No clear line of sight. Lots of opportunities for concealment. It was true for a sedan, where someone could have a gun hidden between their seat and the door, and you wouldn't see them draw it until it was too late. It was even more true of a campervan—the only windows not blacked out with curtains were the ones in the front. Depending on the configuration of the seats, someone hiding in the back could have a built-in barricade. And, of course, there was the over-cabin loft where a shooter could lie in wait.

They picked a spot diagonal to the rear of the van, where someone hiding inside wouldn't have a clear line on them. Then Emery said, "Jace Vermilya, if you're in the van, you need to come out slowly, and with your hands up."

The wind answered, soughing through the stripped branches of the oaks.

"If anyone's inside the van," John-Henry said, "you need to come out right now."

A screech owl cried. John-Henry wasn't a jumper, and he didn't flinch at the sound. His heart, on the other hand, shot somewhere into the thousand-beats-per-minute range, and as the owl's cry faded, the fresh infusion of adrenaline made blood sing in his ears.

"Mother of fuck," Emery said under his breath. A little more loudly, he said, "I'm going to open the back. Cover me."

"Ree, no. I'll do it."

"Like hell. You're the one with the pension and health insurance."

John-Henry didn't have a response to that, actually, and by the time he'd realized he couldn't wrap his head around that logic, Emery was already moving. As he approached the van's cargo doors, John-Henry steadied the Glock. In a crouch, Emery closed the last few feet to the van. He waited for a three count, and John-Henry could feel it, the clockwork of their bodies.

When Emery yanked the door open, John-Henry already had the Glock up and ready.

His brain predicted: muzzle flash, the clap of a gunshot.

Nothing. The cargo doors opened onto a black well inside the van.

"Jesus fucking Christ," Emery said, slumped against the side of the van. The hand holding his big old cowboy revolver, though, looked steady. "I need an EKG after this."

"Light."

Emery produced a flashlight from one pocket of his coat. He braced himself against the van and then directed the beam inside.

More nothing: the van's rear bench was folded down into a bed. The over-cabin loft was empty. John-Henry inched closer, and he confirmed what his gut had already told him: the van was empty.

"Well, what the actual fuck?"

John-Henry took out his burner and called North.

"Let me guess," North said. "You fucked up."

"You're sure nobody left?"

"It's a valid question, North. Your failing vision—" Shaw cut off with a squawk.

"Am I sure?" North asked.

"Right." John-Henry took a deep breath. "If Vermilya isn't one of the victims, then where the hell is he?"

Emery was already holstering his revolver. He jerked his head at the trailer and said, "Come on."

"We'll check the Jeep," North said. And then, before the call disconnected, "Quit dinking your dork through that snowsuit, or I'm going to cut it off."

"I think I have a rash—"

John-Henry pocketed the phone. The earlier rush, the adrenaline-fueled high spirits, it had all worn off, and now he felt tired, his body aching from thirty-six hours of no rest, high emotions, and constant demands. The light seemed too bright, the darkness too deep, the world slippery—like if he turned his head too fast, everything might slide away.

Their steps rang out on the old, packed snow, and the security lights high overhead sent their shadows sprinting in front of them. They went back inside the trailer, being careful to avoid disturbing the crime scene as best they could, even though at this point, John-Henry knew the damage had been done. If whoever processed this scene was careful and attentive, they'd see that someone had been here. Not all blood spatter was visible, for one reason, and between the two of them, Emery and John-Henry had doubtless trampled through some of it.

In that way he had, Emery said, "We're going to have to get rid of these shoes."

John-Henry couldn't help the quiet laugh, but when Emery looked at him, eyebrows arched in a question, he shook his head.

They moved more carefully through the trailer this time. In their haste to clear it, with adrenaline hammering at his nerves, John-Henry's first impression had been of space and color: rooms with dingy gray walls and soiled carpet. Now, moving through the space like a detective, he saw what he'd missed on his first pass: the hole in the bathroom where the toilet should have been, dropping into the darkness below the trailer; the water stains spreading across one bedroom wall, greenish brown and shaped like angel wings; the beach towels stuffed around ill-fitting windows. They were decorated with cartoon characters—one of them was Woody Woodpecker. Stained twin mattresses lay on the floor in one room. In another, a camp stove, a jumble of dirty pots, and several cardboard boxes of canned and dehydrated food suggested how the meth cooks had lived while they were out here. Jugs of water filled the tub in the bathroom, although it didn't look like either man had spent a lot of time on personal hygiene. In what must have been considered the living room, an old Dynex TV was duct-taped to a stand, the screen canting at a slight angle. A stack of DVDs next to the TV suggested how they'd passed the time.

"They really liked Asian women," John-Henry said, eyebrows raised at the pictures on the covers. "Do you think they knew what ladyboys are?"

"The name pretty much tells you, John. It's not rocket science. Where the fuck is he?"

John shook his head.

"I'm going to check the trucks we saw near the barn. Then the perimeter."

"Wait, you think he did walk out of here?"

"He'd have to be off his ass, but I don't know what the other option is. He didn't lock himself inside that shipping container."

"Maybe someone else locked him in there."

"And left how? North and Shaw were watching the only road."

"I don't know, Ree. I'm suggesting possibilities."

Emery opened his mouth to say something, and then one of those tiny, Emery Hazard smiles cut across his face.

"Oh my God," John-Henry said with a grin.

"Does this feel familiar?"

"I'm having flashbacks. Go ahead and check the trucks. Let me know when you want to check the shipping container; we should do that one together."

"What are you going to do?"

"Something felt weird about those bodies. I'm going to take another look."

"Something felt weird."

"I'm definitely having flashbacks. Go check the trucks."

Emery left, and John-Henry moved back to the trailer's kitchen. The smell seemed worse now, and he pulled his sweatshirt up to cover his nose and mouth. The two men lay near the center of the kitchen. The woman was farther back, near the door that led out of the trailer. John-Henry tried to play out the sequence of events. The most obvious scenario seemed to be that Vermilya had arrived, parked at the gate, and proceeded on foot. Most likely, John-Henry thought, to avoid being heard. He'd entered the trailer, found the men and woman in the kitchen, and shot them. He must have known this place, been familiar with it. If John-Henry were going out on a ledge, he'd guess that Vermilya had been trusted by these people.

He studied the bodies, and then the blood, looking for clues that might supplement or contradict the narrative he was constructing. The two men had been shot in the head. The spray of blood and brain covered the wall and door behind them. The woman, in contrast, had been shot twice in the chest. Unlike the men, she looked like she'd taken care of herself, her blond hair—what he could see of it under the trucker hat—clean, the hat and coverall immaculate except, of course, for where she'd been shot—

That thought brought him up short. Because it didn't make sense for the hat and coverall to be free of spatter, not if she'd been standing behind these men when they'd been shot. Some of the spatter would have shown—on her clothes, her skin, or her hair. Most likely, on all three. On the other hand, her appearance made perfect sense if she'd heard the shots and come running, rushed through the back door, and arrived after the fact.

John-Henry turned in place, examining the walls of the kitchen and the trailer's narrow hallways beyond it. Blood spatter covered these walls too. No void. He shook his head and loosed a few choice swears inside his head. Then he retraced his steps to the front of the trailer, inspecting the carpet and the walls more carefully. He didn't see any blood, so he retraced his steps.

The fact that there wasn't a void was significant. John-Henry didn't consider himself an expert by any means, but he knew enough to know that a void in blood spatter suggested something had blocked the spray of droplets. Voids could indicate that something had been removed from the scene after the incident. Or, in the same vein, where the shooter had been standing. This blood spatter was behind where the shooter would have been standing. In theory, if the blood had come from the victims, then there should have been a void.

But there wasn't.

Which means, John-Henry thought with a surge of the old excitement, someone else got shot.

He crossed the kitchen again and let himself out onto the crowded deck. Unlike Emery, he didn't lug an entire forensic laboratory with him everywhere he went, so he used the flashlight on his phone to inspect the deck. It didn't take him long to find the drops of blood: on the plastic dinosaurs, on the bag of fertilizer, on the sun-faded boards of the deck itself. A bloody transfer pattern suggested where someone had grabbed the rail.

And then the trail ended.

"John?" Emery called from across the compound.

"I think I've got something. Had something. I don't know."

Emery came jogging back. John-Henry showed him the spatter and then the blood on the deck.

"Fuck me."

"You would have seen it too."

Emery snorted. "I didn't see it, John. There's no need to be generous." His high-powered flashlight did a much better job of illuminating the deck and the stairs down, but even with both of them looking, they couldn't find where the trail of blood picked up again. It seemed like it ended here. "Where the fuck did this shitweasel go?"

"There's no way he went back through the trailer," John-Henry said. "Not bleeding like this. I checked."

The only response was a grunt. John-Henry understood his husband's frustration; it was like someone had scooped up Vermilya and carried him away—with a nice, convenient plastic tarp underneath to catch all the blood.

John-Henry's eyes went back to the junk on the deck. To the plastic sled propped up in the corner.

Emery's head came up. Those scarecrow eyes glowed when the light caught them—a flicker of winter fire. "You're shitting me."

This time, John-Henry's laugh felt like it loosened something in him. "Why not? Set it on the deck, sit, slide down the steps. The ground's covered in ice; it wouldn't take much to drag yourself along."

"We're talking about someone who was shot."

"And motivated," John-Henry said. "And, if this is the same person we've been dealing with for the last half a year, intelligent and disciplined and careful. Aniya told me he's ex-military. He must have been going into shock, but he held it together and got out of here."

"No, not quite. He got out of the trailer. But he's still here."

Before John-Henry could reply, Emery took the steps down. He ran the flashlight over the ground. The packed ice didn't take impressions easily, not the way snow would, and John-Henry couldn't see any tracks that indicated where the sled had passed. But it was easy to guess which way Vermilya—disoriented, injured, and rapidly losing strength—would have gone: down, following the gentle slope of the ground.

Emery ran the beam of light in that direction.

A sheet of the trailer's plywood skirting stood cattywampus, one corner sticking out.

They approached together. Emery kicked the sheet, and it toppled over. He sent the light into the crawlspace.

The man was blond, big, and his face was white and slack, and he lay on top of a plastic sled. John-Henry looked for some trace, anything that suggested he had met this man before, but he found nothing. For a moment, John-Henry thought he was dead, and then he heard faint, labored breathing.

"Well," Emery said, "shit."

7

The next morning, after Colt left for basketball practice, the eight of them met in the kitchen. The silence had a brooding quality, lingering over the house all morning. Now and then, Evie and Lana's laughter from upstairs took some of the edge off. John-Henry tried to focus on that, on the taste of the peppermint creamer he'd poured into his coffee, on the familiar rhythms of their home in winter. If he tried hard enough, he could pretend he'd taken a day off work. That this was a vacation.

"I'm not trying to be a downer," Tean said. He sat at the table, a mug of tea wrapped in his hands. Jem stood behind him, a hand on Tean's shoulder. "But are you sure no one saw you?"

"It's ok," Shaw said. "You don't even have to try to be a downer. It comes to you naturally."

"Uh."

"It's a compliment," Jem said.

"I'm not sure—"

"It's definitely a compliment." Shaw nodded along eagerly with his words. "It's one of your five sexiest traits."

"I really don't think—"

But Jem said over him, "Top three, I think."

"Five sexiest traits," North said. "I'm standing right here."

"Oh, you're a downer too. I mean, not in the same sexy, my-hair-is-wild-and-my-eyes-are-the-deepest-softest-brown-and-I've-stared-into-the-black-cold-heart-of-the-universe way like Tean."

"Damn, that's spot on," Jem said.

Tean twisted around. "Jem!"

"What? I never thought about the universe's black, cold heart."

"You," Shaw said, "are more of a downer in the where-did-this-credit-card-bill-come-from-and-did-you-just-buy-those-shoes-and-I-thought-we-talked-about-this way."

"Because we had talked about it."

"It's more of a boner killer than a boner, uh, enhancer? Inducer? Auggie, help me out here."

"Engorger," Auggie said without looking up from his phone.

Theo gave him a look.

"What?" Auggie murmured. "I'm being helpful."

"He's being very helpful," Shaw agreed. "In fact, helpfulness is one of Auggie's top ten sexiest traits—"

"I'm right fucking here!"

"Everyone stop talking," Emery barked. He gave a kind of universal glare, and then, in a more controlled voice, said, "We were as careful as possible." And he gave John-Henry a look that left no doubt how he felt about what that sentence actually meant.

North had scored the STILL GAY mug, beating Jem to it by a hair, and he picked it up now to take a noisy swallow of coffee—the words on the mug pointed in Jem's direction—before saying, "And Shaw and I cleaned up their mess."

"Hardly."

But it was, technically, true. After finding the man known as Jace Vermilya under the trailer, John-Henry and Emery had, well, run. Their options had been limited at that point, and the risks had increased tremendously. North and Shaw had stayed to do a quick pass, making sure no obvious sign of their presence had been left behind before calling in the shooting from a burner. Emery had taken John-Henry's shoes before he'd gotten in the Mustang, to dispose of the shoes and gloves where an inconvenient search wouldn't turn them up. Then, in stockinged feet, John-Henry had driven home. The night that followed had felt impossibly long, given the few hours remaining. His sleep had been fractured, his dreams full of jagged edges, and he'd woken sandy eyed, his whole body a pain point.

Tean squirmed a little. "But there are traffic lights and security cameras and neighbors, and it's a small town, and people know each other—"

Jem squeezed Tean's shoulder, and he cut off, unhappiness creasing his forehead.

"Talk about a boner killer," North muttered into the mug.

"Got something to say?" Jem asked.

North took another long—and loud—drink of coffee as he scratched his temple with his middle finger.

"This is uncharted territory," Emery began.

"Everyone's trying to be kind," John-Henry said. "But we all know Tean's right. Last night, we took a huge risk." Tiny ripples spread through the peppermint coffee, so he released the mug and folded his arms to hide his hands. "I want you to know that if things go wrong, I'm going to take full responsibility. I want you to keep your mouths shut and let me—"

"Good Christ," North said. "Does he always act like this?"

"He has an overdeveloped sense of responsibility," Emery said drily.

"How do you fuck?"

Jem burst out laughing.

John-Henry's arms tightened across his chest. "I appreciate that you—"

"It's a legitimate question," North said over him. "He's so fucking righteous and respectable and shit, how do you ever push his face into the mattress and dick him down?"

Tean's eyes were huge. Shaw had melted off the chair in giggles. Auggie appeared to be hyperventilating into Theo's shirt, and Theo, stroking Auggie's back, was covering his mouth with one hand.

Even Emery was smiling—crooked, maybe even a bit wry. "We take turns."

"Emery Hazard!"

The rest of the jackasses cracked up even harder.

"What?"

John-Henry couldn't help the disbelieving laugh that broke free. He swatted Emery's arm. Then again. Emery warded him off, chuckling.

"What?" he asked again.

"What are you—how can you—shut up!"

Emery's grin spread. Somehow, all that swatting turned into John-Henry tucked under Emery's arm. Emery kissed his hair. John-Henry wasn't sure the last time he'd blushed, but he felt fifteen years old all over again.

When the collective dumbasses had regained a semblance of control, John-Henry realized they were waiting for him to say something. He shot North a dirty look, and then said, "I don't want anything bad to happen to you. To any of you. I love you guys. This is my—"

"Five bucks he says responsibility," Jem said.

Tean slapped his hand, and a grin exploded across Jem's face.

"Five bucks Emery gets a stiffy," North muttered.

John-Henry grappled for what he wanted to say, but finally he said, "I don't know what I want to say."

The words were meant for Emery, but of course, the peanut gallery had to chime in.

"You don't have to say anything," Theo said.

"We love you too," Shaw said. "That's why we're here."

"After," Auggie said, "when this is all over, you can buy us a beer and say thanks. That's all you've got to say."

John-Henry shook his head. He was surprised how thick his voice felt, how difficult it was to say, "Thank you."

Emery kissed his hair again, drawing John-Henry tight against him. Then he said, "This is all well and good, but it doesn't address the fact that my grocery bill has quadrupled, or the fact that there's not one fucking corner of this house where I can get five seconds of privacy."

"What fucking grocery bill?" North said. "Buy some fucking tortilla chips. Buy some fucking cheese." He turned to the other men. "You know what he's got in the fridge? A bag of pre-shredded, store-brand cheddar."

"No," Jem murmured in what John-Henry hoped was mock outrage.

"Yeah," North said. "It's a fucking debacle."

"I'm not sure now is the best time—" Tean began.

"I've been checking the local news all morning," Auggie said, "but there's nothing about anybody called Jace Vermilya—holy shit." He sat up straight and turned his phone to show the others. "Is this him?"

The photo showed a blond, blue-eyed man receiving an award at some kind of ceremony. The suit didn't hide the fact that he was a big guy, and he had the neck and shoulders of an action hero. When John-Henry had seen him the night before, his lips had been blue with the cold.

The room quieted.

"I know that dude," Jem said. "I've seen him before."

"He was at the Cottonmouth Club," Auggie said. "I saw him arguing with Gid the night I went there. Him and Eric—remember, I told you I'd seen Eric there?"

"We remember, pint-size," North said, but his voice was subdued. "You're sure?"

Auggie nodded, but it was Jem who spoke: "It's totally him. He was there the night I met up with DeVoy."

"Well, that's something," Emery said. "Now we know there's a connection. Whoever this guy is, he's not a good citizen who's made a terrible mistake, and he's not a pawn who's been coerced or manipulated into perjuring himself. He's part of this."

"So, what happened last night?" Tean asked.

Auggie made a beckoning motion. "Let me see the other ones."

Emery produced his burner phone and displayed the close-ups of the shooting victims from the meth lab. Auggie shook his head, his mouth curling into a moue as he studied first the smaller man, then the bigger one. When he swiped to the woman, though, he said, "That's her!"

"That's who—" Jem began, and then he said, "No fucking way. She was at the club too. Real hard-ass vibe. She had a bunch of guys hanging around."

"Her name's Ingra—I don't know, Ingra something. I looked her up when we were trying to find Shaniyah. Theo, remember?"

Theo nodded slowly. "I remember seeing her. I don't remember the charges, but I remember thinking she looked like she was Ozark Volunteers. Or maybe a motorcycle club—didn't we talk about that?"

But Auggie only stared at the phone and said again, "Holy shit."

"Something's wrong," Shaw said.

"You can say that again," North muttered.

"What does this mean?" Tean said. "Why would they shoot each other?"

"An excellent question," Emery said, cutting his eyes to John-Henry.

"It could be a lot of reasons." John-Henry spread empty hands. "They had some sort of deal, and it went wrong. Or they were tweaking, and things got out of control."

Emery made a noise of dissent and shook his head. "Occam's razor."

"See," North said, "he's finally starting to get all growly and bad ass, and then he opens his mouth and something like that dribbles out."

Jem asked, "For those of us who don't know, probably just me, what is Occam's razor? And is it better than my Wahl?"

Emery gave him a flat look to show what he thought of the second question, and then he said, "Occam's razor: all things being equal, the simplest explanation is usually the correct one. In this case, John is positing that a man known to be connected to the Cottonmouth Club, who was involved in a shooting that involved a woman connected to the Cottonmouth Club, had some separate criminal activity going on unrelated to this attempt to frame John. That means multiplying all sorts of factors. Instead, it's simpler—and more likely—that everything is connected."

"Ree—"

"Why wouldn't it be? Since the beginning, we've known that whoever was behind this operation, they were involved in a range of criminal activities. We knew that they had a wildlife trafficking operation. Jem also found controlled substances, legal documents, jewelry. Criminal organizations involved in human trafficking don't usually limit themselves to moving people illegally from place to place. Drugs, sex work, and yes, animals. It's all connected. In this case, we're seeing the drug angle—the Ozark Volunteers are one of the major producers and distributors of methamphetamine in the state."

Jem raised his hand.

"Yes?" Emery said.

Jem pointed at Tean.

Tean shifted in his seat, shrugged, and said, "I don't know if this means anything, but—but when I reached out to some colleagues this morning, they told me they've had a lot of strange reports."

"Strange how?"

"Well, someone found a tiger cub in a dumpster."

Shaw opened his mouth, and Jem rushed to say, "It was fine. Someone found it before it froze to death."

"A python in a woman's pantry," Tean said. "A macaw flew right into this old man's window. It's not unheard of for people to release exotic animals once they realize that they don't have the means or knowledge to adequately care for them. Every once in a while, you'll hear about someone spotting a lion walking across their yard, something crazy like that. But this has been…a lot."

Everyone was silent for a moment.

"What does that mean?" Theo asked.

Tean shrugged. "Whatever it is, it seems like something has changed."

Emery opened his mouth, but John-Henry spoke first. "I understand your point, Ree. We've discussed this before; I agree that the drugs and the wildlife trafficking, they're all tied together with what's going on. But I'm trying to say there are a lot of possibilities, and we shouldn't jump to conclusions."

"And I'm saying that it's ineffectual to pretend we don't know the most likely possible explanation for what happened last night."

"What's the most likely explanation?" Auggie asked.

"Jace Vermilya either did something stupid," Theo said, "or was no longer useful."

North made a noise of disgust.

Emery gestured and said, "Exactly."

"They didn't need him anymore?" Tean asked. "But the case won't go to trial for months."

"He's a witness," Jem said. "His name is all over legal paperwork now. He's in the system because he's tied up in this shit with John-Henry. He was a liability, and more importantly, they didn't need him anymore—they would have known, beforehand, they'd have to cut him loose at some point."

"Or he asked for more money," Shaw said. "Or he thought he could score for free. Or he threatened to recant if he didn't get whatever he wanted."

"I don't know," John-Henry said. "It looked like he got the jump on those guys before that woman, Ingra, took him down."

Emery shook his head. "That doesn't mean anything one way or another. He might have suspected they were about to turn on him. They might have been arguing. We have no idea what happened."

"He did something stupid," North said, "like Theo said."

"Shouldn't we have heard something about him being shot?" Jem asked. "Maybe the police don't know who he is."

"Silence doesn't necessarily mean anything," John-Henry said. "The police could be withholding information while they try to figure out what happened. They could be watching us right now, waiting for us to make a mistake. Even if Vermilya's prints aren't in the system, they could have identified him based on his ID, credit cards in his wallet, that kind of thing."

North and Shaw traded a long look.

"About that..." North said.

Emery was the first to respond. "You're shitting me."

"It's not as bad as it seems—" Shaw tried.

But Emery cut him off. "Really? Because it seems like you took the personal property of a shooting victim and brought it into my home, creating a direct link between last night's shooting and my husband, which was the very fucking thing we were trying to avoid!"

The sentence ended in a shout.

"You're thinking about it the wrong way," Jem said. "You're thinking about keeping him safe."

Emery opened his mouth, but Tean spoke first, "What he means is, you're worried about John-Henry, and you're thinking about how you can protect him. But I think Jem's right. I think that might not be the best way to think about this, not right now. Right now, we need to think about the next step. How do we prove this man, Vermilya, was lying? More importantly, how do we prove it if he dies?"

"It's more than that," North said, "If last night was an accident, then whoever's behind this, they're going to have to change their plans. They're going to have to act. We're sitting ducks if we don't do anything."

When John-Henry looked over, Emery's usual reserve flickered, and for a moment, his face was full of fear. Then it was gone, and he gave a reluctant nod.

John-Henry wanted to dig in his heels. He wanted to fight about it. What about other people, he wanted to ask. What about people who don't know what we know, people who don't have friends with these skills, people who get railroaded or framed? How is this fair to them? His father taking the high school coaching staff to lunch. His mother meeting with the principal. A quiet conversation with a judge about a speeding ticket. His face was hot. He wiped his hands on his pants and then didn't know what to do with them. It wasn't the same. He knew that. He thought he did, anyway.

"All right," he said. "What are we supposed to do?"

Emery was the one who answered. "Let's start by figuring out who Jace Vermilya really is."

8

They gathered around the table, and North produced a plastic bag. He shook the contents out across the table: a wallet, a set of keys, a watch, a phone, and a cascade of loose paper—to Emery, they looked mostly like receipts, but several larger pieces were mixed in.

Emery handed around disposable gloves. "He had all this on him?"

Shaw shook his head. "We took some of it from the Jeep."

Auggie was already separating the receipts, and he glanced up and said, "Tean, want to take a look at this with me?"

Tean moved over to join him while Jem picked up the watch. "Thirty bucks," he said. "Walmart."

"You know that just from looking at it?" Theo asked.

"Sure. You used to be able to boost them—" Jem cut off.

North muttered, "Nice save."

Emery took the wallet and began laying out its contents: a driver's license, two Visas issued by Wells Fargo, a hundred and sixty-seven dollars in cash, a loyalty card for Super Subs with four of the ten sub-sandwich silhouettes punched out, and an expired condom. Jem picked up the cash and began riffling through it.

"I counted that," Emery said.

Tean shifted in his seat like he might say something, but Jem just laughed.

The driver's license was the obvious place to start. Emery examined it, checked the security features, and grunted. Then he handed it to John. After a moment, John shrugged.

"It wouldn't be hard to acquire an ID," Emery said. "Jem said he saw Social Security cards and driver's licenses in that van. Vermilya could have gotten the necessary documents without much difficulty."

"Your turn or mine?" North asked.

"Yours," Shaw said.

"Bullshit."

Shaw gave him a lopsided grin and jogged toward the front of the house.

"Let me see that," North said, plucking the license from John's hand.

"You said you heard someone identify him in a bar," Emery said. "You left out some rather pertinent details, such as how you found him and how you ended up following him out to that meth lab."

"Yeah, well, I got kind of busy when someone started shooting at me."

"Nobody was shooting at you—"

"Boys," John said.

"Have you ever thought about letting them kiss?" Auggie asked without looking up from the papers. "Just once. So they can get it out of their system."

Theo started laughing so hard he had to walk out of the room.

"Funny you should ask," John murmured.

"Bunch of fucking comedians," Emery said.

That was when Shaw came back carrying a laptop. He set it up on the counter, and he and North bent over it together, quibbling for a few seconds until Shaw said, "I know how to do it, North!"

Grumbling, North drifted a few feet away.

Tean whispered something in Auggie's ear, and Auggie broke down giggling. Jem had a huge smile on his face.

"What is so fucking funny?" Emery asked.

"You know what?" Jem said. "You wouldn't get it."

"You all are a real fucking cluster of ass-nuts, you know that?" North said. "He's got a little house on the east side of town. All the utilities in his name. It took me one search. We got there, sat around for a while, and then he walked out of the house and got in that fucking Jeep. We decided to see where he was going."

Emery frowned. "He didn't notice you tailing him?"

North snorted.

"North, Jem take some of these," Auggie said, pushing two piles of receipts across the table. "Jem, start a shared map and drop pins. North, make a spreadsheet and log them chronologically."

"Easy there, Captain Crunch."

"Fine. Emery—"

"I didn't say I wouldn't do it," North said as he swept up the receipts.

"What do you want me to do?" Theo asked.

"Supervise North."

"Hardy-har, chuckle-fuck," North said. "Theo, get your ass over here and help me."

Emery was examining Vermilya's phone when he glanced up and caught an unfamiliar expression on John's face.

When he noticed Emery's attention, John's face smoothed out, and he gave a short laugh. "This is so frustrating. Normally—I mean, you know what it's like, Ree. If I want to know who somebody is, I get his fingerprints, I get aliases, I run search after search until NCIC is about to explode, I get a warrant for his phone." He raked fingers through his hair. "And now I don't have any of that, and I'm useless."

"You're certainly not useless." Emery cocked his head. "What else would you do?"

John gave him a crooked smile. "That's very sweet."

"I'm serious. Fingerprints are out unless we can get somebody inside the department to help us."

"I don't want to do that. That's asking them to compromise their professional ethics, and even if they're doing it to help me, what am I supposed to do when this is over? I don't want anyone who would do that working in my department."

"For those of us not on the soapbox," North asked, "what's it like up there?"

"Does the altitude keep you from getting a boner?" Jem asked. "It seems like it would."

They shared a smirk, which vanished when Emery directed a glower at them.

Turning his attention back to John, Emery nodded, which was—in his opinion—less of an outright lie. After all, a nod could simply mean acknowledgment. And there was no point in mentioning his run-in with Dulac, not yet. "What else?"

"Traffic cameras—"

"Not the things you can't do. What else?"

John reached for his mug of coffee, but he didn't drink; he just held it, hands wrapped around the ceramic, the hint of mint rising on the air. In a different voice, he said, "If I had a photo, I'd show it around locations that were significant—the crime scene for starters."

"We've got pictures," Auggie said. "He's on the internet."

"I'd check his social media."

"Go ahead," Tean said. "I can finish."

"On it," Auggie said, whipping out his phone.

"What else?" Emery asked.

"If he had any identifying physical characteristics, those get entered into—"

"John."

A smile, a real one, bloomed.

"What?" Emery asked flatly.

"Good God," John said to himself. Then, smile growing, he said, "Thank you."

"Thank me later. What else?"

"Even without database access, identifying physical characteristics could be helpful. I didn't see any, but that doesn't necessarily mean anything."

"We didn't strip him to his skivvies," North said, "if that's what you're asking."

"I didn't see anything," Emery said. "What else?"

John shook his head. "Dental records, DNA—"

Emery made an annoyed grumble.

"Well, I don't know, Ree. If it's a murder victim, you examine their personal possessions, try to reconstruct whatever you can—a geographic area, a timeline—"

Emery let a tiny smile slip out, and John stopped.

"And if we have some photos and a starting place," John said slowly, "we work backward, and we try to build out every angle of this guy's life."

"That sounds like surprisingly good police work for someone who doesn't have access to a single database."

"How long does it take before you stop hearing the snark and just recognize how adorable he is?" Jem asked.

"About a week," Tean said.

"A week," John said in a tone that might have meant anything, his eyebrows crooked, the lines around his eyes deepening.

"He's got some utilities in his name," Shaw said, "all of them for the address on the license. But there's not much else—an account at Wahredua Savings and Trust. No loans."

"Because it's a cover," North said. "It's not his real name. You're not going to be able to dig up anything useful on there. Meanwhile, I made this kickass spreadsheet—"

Theo scratched his beard and, in that annoying way teachers had, found a way to make his silence pointed.

"—that shows half a dozen stops our boy made yesterday afternoon. And we're just getting started."

"We should start with his house," John said, "before the police—"

Emery shook his head. "You were right about one thing: last night exposed you in a way that's not acceptable. We have to be smarter, particularly because things are only going to get more dangerous from this point. North?"

"On it. Come on, spunk musket."

Something must have happened on the way to the front door because Shaw started giggling uncontrollably. When the door shut off the sound, Theo let out a long slow breath and gave Auggie a look.

"One year, they made Theo teach freshmen," Auggie said.

"Thank you, Auggie."

"And every day he came home looking like that."

Theo scratched his beard again.

"We went through a lot of beer."

"You two are good with working the social media angle?"

Auggie nodded, and the relief on Theo's face was transparent.

"We can keep an eye on Evie and Colt," Tean said. "We can't forget about that other guy, the one who's come after us before."

"And I want to dig into this anti-trafficking organization Vermilya supposedly runs." Jem frowned. "It stinks, and I want to know what's really going on."

Emery nodded and glanced at John. "Here we go."

9

They spent the morning crossing off each place Vermilya had visited the day before, working their way backwards through the list Theo and North had compiled.

They went to Reasonable Grounds, a coffee shop not far from the police station, where a barista recognized Vermilya, even remembered that he'd tipped, but couldn't tell them anything about him. He came in sometimes. He seemed nice. They tried the Kum & Go. They got lucky at first—the clerk on duty had worked the afternoon shift the day before—but their luck ran out. If Vermilya had come into the convenience store, the clerk didn't recognize him. They hit a dry spell after that: a stub for an unmanned parking lot on Jefferson Street; a Super Lube, where a dead-eyed technician stared at them until John-Henry had to drag Emery away to prevent a murder; the Piggly-Wiggly, where they finally found a red-headed woman cleaning her nose with her apron, who remembered Vermilya.

"He tips the bag boys," she said. "Don't you think he should tip the checkers too?"

The day was clear and cold, so crisp that John-Henry thought he could hear it crackle when he got out of the Mustang, and an enameled blue like the inside of a bowl. The snow was dirty. When he wasn't getting the cutting edge of the wind, the air smelled like car exhaust. By noon, his feet were wet, and two hard nights meant his head was starting to pound. He was surprised, as they got into the car after the Piggly-Wiggly, when Emery's hand came to rest on the back of his neck, and he began to massage the stiffness there.

John-Henry groaned. "Give me two Tylenol, and I'll do anything you want."

Emery laughed quietly. "Why don't you go home, get some sleep?"

"Because five minutes after I lie down, I'll be ready to bang my head against a wall again."

They sat like that for a while. John-Henry arched his back. Emery's thumb scraped over the short hairs on his nape. He was painfully aware that they were in public, the pale winter light filling the car, and that what he wanted, right then, was to be touched and held. It felt like it had been years instead of days. The last person who had touched him had been the deputy who processed him into the jail, and the violation lingered in his body at a level below words.

John-Henry spread his legs until his knee bumped the shifter. Then he said, "Maybe a quick nap."

Another of those quiet laughs. Emery's fingers tightened, and he gave John-Henry a tiny shake.

"Is that a yes?"

"I'll drop you off."

"That's not what I had in mind."

"John—"

"I know, I know." He started the car. Warm air began to pump out of the vents, carrying the smell of the car's heater. "I'm just being needy."

Emery's thumb traced his nape again, came to rest on the vertebra there. The whisper of the vents had swallowed up the sound of his breathing.

John-Henry checked the spreadsheet, marked the address for their next stop, and pulled out of the parking lot. They drove in silence, the only sounds the tires hissing over ice, the occasional crunch of refrozen snow collapsing. The town was busier than it would have been on a Tuesday. Winter break, he reminded himself. No school. A gaggle of boys was horsing around in the Olive Garden parking lot—grabbing chunks of ice and chucking them at each other as hard as they could. The dummies were in shorts and t-shirts, of course. One kid kept having to haul his shorts back up, and they were all red-cheeked and laughing. Two women stood outside Morgan's Music, waving their arms wildly—apparently giving directions to the men who were wheeling an upright piano out of the store. At the next red light, John-Henry glanced over at the minivan next to them. The man driving had unbuckled his seat belt and crawled halfway into the passenger seat. When he sat back, John-Henry saw the portable DVD player balanced on a cooler in the passenger seat. You know, so he could watch it while he drove. Something began to play, and as the light turned green, John-Henry saw just enough to hope desperately that he had misunderstood.

"Was that vintage Christmas-themed pornography?" Emery asked.

The minivan pulled ahead. It had a YOUR STICK-FIGURE FAMILY WAS DELICIOUS sticker on the back, and it showed a dinosaur eating stick-figures, of course.

"I've never seen Mrs. Claus depicted with crotchless panties before," Emery said in what sounded like a thoughtful tone.

John-Henry decided to turn on some music.

They made their way north and east, the city bleeding out around them as they headed toward the older part of Wahredua. This section had been built years ago to serve the old MP line, and, as travel shifted away from trains, it had decayed into a never-quite-renovated mixture of commercial and light industrial. Traffic thinned. The buildings crowded together on narrow lots, tall enough to cast deep shadows, the old frame structures sagging under the weight of all those years. A Pepsi Max bottle rolled under the Mustang and popped when one of the tires went over it. The sound was like a gunshot.

John-Henry turned off Emmylou Harris. "I'm sorry about that."

"Hm?"

"Back there, at the Piggly-Wiggly."

Emery was looking at his phone. "What?"

"And at home, I guess. The other day."

Lowering the phone, Emery seemed to take John-Henry in. "What are you talking about?"

"I know I've been...off."

"I don't think—"

"So, I'm sorry. For, you know, losing it. A little bit."

It was easier to focus on turning into the strip mall than look at Emery's face.

"John, you've been through a tremendous amount of upheaval in the last few days. You were arrested and charged with a terrible crime. You discovered someone has framed you and, somehow, managed to outmaneuver your father and your other allies in local government. You stumbled onto a shooting last night. You're exhausted, and your world has been turned upside down, and you still managed to make Colt pancakes this morning and get him to smile about that ridiculous game you both play. I'm not sure what you consider 'losing it a little bit,' but from what I see, you're holding things together better than anyone has a right to expect."

John-Henry eased the Mustang into a parking stall. He stared out at the stuccoed strip mall: the Foot Locker retail outlet (closed), Masouda's Missouri Mafrum, and a U-Haul dealership housed in what appeared to have been, at one time, a garden center. Masouda's had a wall of windows where tasseled curtains hung. A neon sign glowed OPEN.

"Right. That's kind of you." He swallowed. "Thank you."

"I'm not being kind—"

"But the last few days, that's not how the chief of police should act. It's not how your husband should act."

It's not, he thought—and the thought swam in a blizzard of other thoughts, like he was shaking a snow globe—how John-Henry Somerset was supposed to act.

"John, what in the world—"

"Nothing." He opened the door and got out. "I don't know. Never mind."

He thought Emery might have said more, but he shut the door first.

By the time Emery got out of the car, John-Henry was already walking into the restaurant. A mezuzah was affixed to the jamb, which wasn't something he saw often in this part of the world, and a wall of damp heat steamed against him. Condensation beaded on the inside of the glass, and as he watched, a too heavy drop gave in to gravity and streaked down the window. The smells of hot oil, cumin, coriander, and the bright acidity of tomatoes filled the air. Inside, the dining room was small—two booths with laminate tops chipped at the corners, a counter, and a battered door marked EMPLOYEES ONLY. An illuminated sign above the counter displayed a handful of dining options, and a chalkboard menu announced the day's sides: chershi and mseyer, whatever those were. A green-and-silver Wroxall Wildcats banner nestled among plastic-covered photos on the wall, and an unobtrusive sign announced that concealed carry was permitted in the restaurant. Behind the counter, a curtain wall allowed only a glimpse of the kitchen's stainless steel and white tile. A bell rang overhead, and a moment later, a woman stepped behind the counter.

She was short, stocky, with graying brown hair and dark eyes. If the heat bothered her, it hadn't kept her from wearing a Wahredua High sweatshirt and jeans. She assessed him for a moment and then, as John-Henry waited for Emery, wrapped a napkin around a set of plasticware and placed it in a tub.

The bell rang again as Emery stepped inside, and John-Henry approached the counter. The woman looked up as she continued to wrap the plasticware sets.

"Hi," he said with a smile. "I'm sorry to bother you, but I've got kind of a strange question." He produced his phone, pulled up a photo of

Vermilya that Auggie had sent him, and displayed it. "This man was in here yesterday, and I was wondering if you recognize him."

She didn't look at the phone. Her eyes came up to John-Henry's face, and she asked, "Do you have a warrant?"

"Why would he—" Emery began.

But John-Henry made a small motion with one hand, and Emery cut off. He studied the woman and said, "You recognize me."

"It's a small town."

"I'm sorry, but I don't think we've met."

This time, she smiled—a small, dry expression that was gone as soon as it came. "It's not that small."

"Why don't we start over? You already know me, but I'd like to introduce myself: I'm John-Henry Somerset."

"And he's your husband. And I'm Masouda. And you're the chief of police."

The words felt like bait, but John-Henry wasn't sure what kind. His whole life, he'd been good at reading people, at easing through the shifting currents of social interactions. He thought about that smile, the fleeting one, and he went for wry. "Suspended, actually. But I get the feeling you know that."

"Which is why I asked for a warrant."

"He doesn't need a warrant," Emery said. "He's not requiring you to turn over evidence or testify. He's asking questions. As a private citizen."

She made a considering noise. When she finished wrapping the next set of plasticware, she glanced at Emery, and then her gaze slid to John-Henry again.

And then John-Henry felt it—the tug, the flow, everything in him shifting as he caught the direction of the current and oriented himself. "I need help," he said. "Actually, I'm desperate. I'm hoping you can help me."

"Sit."

Without waiting for a reply, she stepped into the kitchen, and she called out something John-Henry couldn't make out, the words distorted by the curtain wall.

"Maybe she's getting her concealed carry," Emery said.

"Be nice."

John-Henry sat, and Emery slid into the booth next to him. They'd barely gotten settled when Masouda returned. She was carrying two plates heaped with couscous and...balls. At first, John-Henry took them for meatballs because of the thick, red sauce covering them, but when she got closer, he could see that the shape wasn't quite right, and the smell of cumin and coriander was even stronger. She set the food in front of them, brought two bottles of Mexican Coke back from the cooler, and drew a bottle opener from her apron. The Cokes hissed as she popped the caps, and in the warm, humid air, vapor drifted above the cold bottles.

"Eat."

"What is it?" Emery asked.

John-Henry picked up a fork and used the side to cut open one of the balls. Ground meat, like he'd expected. But it was sandwiched between slices of creamy potato. He made sure to get a little of everything—meat, potatoes, couscous, tomato sauce. The flavors exploded in his mouth, savory and rich, acidic and smoky. He made a noise that, to judge by Emery's expression, might not have been appropriate and went for a second bite. He hadn't realized how hungry he was—couldn't remember, in fact, when he'd eaten. Before jail? That seemed impossible, but since then, all he remembered was coffee.

"This is a public restaurant," Emery said as he forked up his first bite. "Could you try not to sound like you're in a bordello—" Through a mouthful of food, he said, "Jesus Christ, that's amazing."

Masouda's tiny smile came and went again. "Mafrum."

"Why have we not eaten this before?" Emery went for more of the mafrum. "When did you open this restaurant? And what kind of advertising have you done?"

"A few months ago. And not much." The brown of her eyes was smooth and deep. "You looked like you needed to eat."

John-Henry managed to pull himself back from the food long enough to wipe his mouth. "It's delicious. Thank you."

"Eat," Masouda said with a laugh. "I'll talk, and then you can ask your police questions after you've finished."

"You've seen that man? The one from the photo?"

Masouda nodded. "He was in here yesterday. But I think you knew that."

"You remember him?" Emery asked.

"It's so hard. I have so many customers."

To John-Henry's disbelief, a tiny, Emery Hazard smile curled the corner of his mouth.

"I asked you about a warrant because I want to know if I'm breaking the law by telling you this."

"The information isn't privileged." Emery paused, his fork poised above the plate. "Why would it be illegal?"

"I didn't say it was. Is it?"

"Of course not—"

"Ree," John-Henry said. He set his fork down—ignoring his stomach's outraged grumble—and took the Coke. He traced his thumb down the side of the glass, gathering the condensation and leaving a clear line down the bottle. "You're not breaking the law. And I'm not planning anything illegal, so you're not going to be an accomplice, even unknowingly."

"That's what someone would say," Masouda said, "if they were going to break the law."

"I suppose it is." John-Henry took a swallow of Coke. "And I'm not sure it helps if I say that I'm not acting as a police officer, just to be clear, and you're under no obligation to answer my questions. But it's a standard part of a criminal defense to investigate witnesses. Any good defense team would want to know as much as they could before a trial."

"To figure out if a witness is lying, in the first place," Emery said. "And, even if they're telling the truth, to look for evidence of bias, to determine how credible they might appear to the judge and jurors, to shake loose details or inconsistencies, and, of course, to uncover new evidence. The last thing anyone wants in a trial is a surprise."

Masouda brushed a hand down the front of her apron, straightening it.

"But," John-Henry said, "that's what somebody would say if they were going to break the law."

"Chief Somerset—"

"John-Henry, please. I'm suspended, and I'm not here as the chief of police."

She shrugged. "It seems like it would be hard to keep your personal investigation separate from your official role. Besides, I imagine most defense attorneys employ an independent investigator. I have a hard time believing they send their clients out in search of witnesses."

Emery's voice grew dry. "We're an unusual case."

"I can't prove to you that I'm not doing anything illegal," John-Henry said. "And I can't force you to tell me what you know. And I'd be grateful if you could help me. I don't know what to say except that I didn't do what they say I did. Someone is trying to frame me. Someone wants to hurt my family. And I don't know how to prove I'm innocent except try to run down every lead I possibly can. If you can't help me, I'll respect your decision. I appreciate the food, and we'll pay for it, of course. We'll leave and stop bothering you."

In the silence that followed, faint music filtered in from the kitchen—it sounded like pop, but in a language John-Henry didn't recognize.

Without a word, Masouda collected their plates and carried them back to the kitchen.

John-Henry waited until her steps had faded to rest his head in his hand.

Emery's hand found his back, rubbed against the tightness between his shoulders. "It's ok. We'll check the U-Haul dealership; they'll have cameras all over the place. Maybe they got Vermilya on tape—"

"And what, Ree? We already know what kind of car he drives. He walks in. He walks out. What are we going to see?"

Emery flattened the napkin against the chipped laminate. "I don't know."

You asshole, John-Henry thought. You stupid asshole. "I'm sorry."

"No, you're right—"

"I'm not right. It's a good idea. We'll ask—"

The tread of Masouda's kitchen shoes made John-Henry glance over his shoulder. She was carrying a laptop under one arm as she came around the counter, and when she met John-Henry's gaze, her eyebrows went up. She sat, opened the laptop, and angled the screen to show them. A video was already cued up, and it only took a moment for John-Henry to understand what he was seeing: footage from a security camera that looked down on the restaurant's dining room. He shot a look up, spotted the camera, and returned his attention to the video. Masouda began to play it.

"No audio. It's an old system; it was already installed."

John-Henry barely registered the words because on the screen, the man who called himself Jace Vermilya strode into view. The picture on the screen was grainy, but it was unmistakably him. It felt unreal, watching the confident, controlled movements of a man whom, later that day, John-Henry would find bleeding out under a meth trailer. Vermilya was big and muscular, and the way he moved suggested he knew how to carry himself. He approached the counter, said something to Masouda, and took out his wallet.

"He was very polite. He asked if he could leave a tip."

Emery opened his mouth like he had something to say about that, but before he could speak, another man came on screen. This one, John-Henry recognized immediately—Eric Brey was a state representative for a town called Auburn, and a few months before, he'd been a suspect in a double murder. Brey was still a free man, but that had more to do with a good team of lawyers and knowing when to keep his mouth shut than anything else. On camera, Brey moved up behind Vermilya. The two men exchanged words, and Vermilya's response—even though John-Henry couldn't hear the words—had a kind of contained anger that made John-Henry straighten in his seat.

Masouda was already shaking her head when he looked up. "I didn't hear what he said; I was making change. But the other man looked like he might be sick."

Even from the high angle of the security camera, John-Henry could tell Brey didn't look his best. The state rep went to sit in a booth, his movements jerky, his body taut. Vermilya finished his transaction with Masouda and joined Brey at the booth. Brey said something, but Vermilya cut him off and began to speak, bending over the table, a finger drilling into the laminate to emphasize his words.

"Doesn't exactly look like a naïve innocent or a victim of coercion, does he?" Emery murmured.

If anything, John-Henry thought, Vermilya looked like he was the one doing the coercing. One of the things they'd learned about Brey while investigating months ago was that, among other things, Brey liked to tie women up and hurt them. There was a sexual component to it that went beyond kink and play. That thought flickered at the back of John-Henry's mind now as he watched Brey shrink into the booth, making himself smaller and smaller as Vermilya tore his hide off. The men quieted when Masouda brought Vermilya's food, but the conversation picked up again almost immediately. Twice, Brey tried to interject, and both times, Vermilya slapped him back down—not literally, but whatever he said made Brey curl his shoulders and drop his eyes. Abruptly, Vermilya made a dismissing gesture, and Brey slunk out of the booth.

"Why meet here?" Emery asked. "Why not anywhere else—an empty stretch of road, for heaven's sake? For that matter, why meet at all?"

"I don't suppose you heard anything when you brought the food?" John-Henry asked.

Masouda shook her head. "I stayed in the kitchen after I took them their food. I kept thinking he was going to do something. I kept thinking I should tell them to leave."

Do something, John-Henry thought. Like hurt Brey. Maybe kill him.

"Can you send us a copy of this?" Emery asked. "And make a second copy for yourself."

Masouda raised her eyebrows again.

"I imagine at some point, law enforcement is going to ask for this. It'd be nice to know that you have a backup in case it gets 'lost'."

Frown lines deepened on Masouda's forehead, but she nodded.

When Emery followed Masouda to the counter to pay, John-Henry rubbed his head and tried to think. As his body went to work digesting the food, exhaustion swamped him; he'd burned through his final reserves, and now it felt like all he could do to keep his head off the table. He tried to make sense of what he'd seen: Vermilya and Brey, the pantomimed argument, Brey's fear. They had already known that Brey and Vermilya were each individually connected to the Cottonmouth Club. Now, they had something linking them together. Like the woman from the meth lab, John-Henry thought. She'd been at the Cottonmouth Club too—Auggie and Jem had both seen her. And they had a link between Vermilya and her as well, now. Three people with ties to the Cottonmouth Club. One was dead, and one was seriously injured. That meant they needed to talk to Eric Brey.

Lost in his thoughts, John-Henry didn't catch the timbre of Emery's voice until alarm bells started going off. As he dragged his mind back to the present, he realized two things: Emery was talking on the phone, and angry red slashes marked his cheekbones.

"We'll be right there," Emery said and disconnected.

"What happened? What's wrong?"

"Colt." Emery stormed toward the door. "Vandalism, destruction of school property, and trespass."

10

Wahredua High School was a sprawl of low buildings and athletic fields, evidence of the construction and growth that had happened in stages over the years. Blank-faced cement walls. Narrow windows. Covered walkways joined some of the buildings, where—before vaping—students and staff had gone to sneak a smoke. The school's colors, red and gold, provided the only adornment to all the institutional gray. As John pulled into the parking lot, Emery was remembering the senior prank the year before he'd graduated. The jackasses had trashed the building—literally. They'd brought in garbage over the weekend and left it everywhere. They'd urinated on the walls. They'd taken a sledgehammer to the newly refinished gym floor. One gem of a human being had dropped a deuce on the principal's desk. And they'd done it all on camera.

"Breathe, please," John said as he shifted into park.

"I'll breathe after I murder him."

"Emery Hazard, stop and take a breath."

Emery shook his head and reached for the door handle.

John caught his arm.

Neither of them said anything; their bodies said all of it, the firmness of John's grip, Emery's balancing act between yanking free and settling back into his seat. Then Emery shook off John's grip and dropped his head back. A moment later, John's hand returned to rub his leg.

"What the fuck was he thinking?"

"I don't know. Before we jump to any conclusions, why don't we go inside and see what happened?"

"What happened is he got himself arrested by the police, John. What happened is that while I'm trying to keep my husband out of jail, my son has apparently decided to get himself locked up instead."

He could only see John out of the corner of his eye, but he saw the way John shifted his weight, the way he drew back.

"That came out wrong."

John's laugh was surprisingly bitter. "No, I think you pretty much nailed it."

"John."

"Forget it." For a moment, it seemed like John might say more—like he was on the cusp of it. Then he shook his head. "Come on."

Officer Samuel Yarmark was waiting by the door. He was winter pale, his dark hair mussed in what Emery had decided, over the last year, fell somewhere between adorable and insane in its imitation of John's. He filled out his uniform in a way he hadn't when he'd been hired. Some of that was Yarmark's 'coincidental' timing at the gym; John had eventually given up and started helping the younger man with a workout plan. But some of it had to do with how Yarmark carried himself: shoulders back, chest out, head high. It helped, Emery thought a little uncharitably, that Yarmark was also less of a pimply-faced goon these days.

"Chief Somerset." He nodded. "Hello, Mr. Hazard."

"Why don't we go with John-Henry today?"

Holding the door for them, Yarmark shook his head. "Sorry, Chief. As far as I'm concerned, you're still chief until they fire you. Um, not that they're going to. Fire you, I mean."

"What if he orders you, as chief, not to call him chief until the suspension is lifted?" Emery asked.

Yarmark's forehead furrowed. Then he brightened. "It wouldn't count because he can't give orders while he's suspended."

"Touché," Emery said as he passed into the school. He shot a look at John, hoping to see something there—the familiar mixture of amusement and exasperation would have been nice, but he would have settled for annoyance, even anger. Instead, he got emptiness, everything in John's face shut down and closed off. The worst part was how natural it looked—if you didn't know him well, you'd see the perfect symmetry of his face, the lack of expression there, and you might believe he was just thinking about something else.

As though sensing Emery's attention, John brought his eyes up. The tropical blue skimmed toward Emery and then away. The only sign, if it was a sign, was that the set of his shoulders hardened.

Yarmark led them through the school, their steps loud on the linoleum, the smell of floor wax and new rubber filling the air. After the first few minutes, as his body adjusted to the temperature, Emery realized the building was rather cool. Warm compared to the frozen clarity outside, but not by much. Saving money, he decided, while school wasn't in session.

The farther they moved into the school, the more Emery narrowed the range of possibilities. They were leaving the classrooms behind and approaching the athletic facilities. The gym, he thought. The gym was a favorite target because there was so much room to work. Or the locker rooms; for whatever reason, generations of boys had found the locker rooms the ideal spot for fuckery. He thought, like touching a live wire, about that day all those years ago: John-Henry Somerset standing naked in front of him, steam swirling up from golden skin, the brush of dry lips, the hot and cold of his own body like he had a fever.

The sound of Yarmark clearing his throat drew Emery back to the present. The younger officer did a whiplash check of John's expression and said, "I'm really sorry about this, Chief."

"Thank you, Sam."

"Nobody believes it."

All John said was "Thanks."

After a quick glance around, Yarmark lowered his voice. "Chief, someone shot that guy. The one who pretended to, you know, know stuff about you." His voice dropped even lower. "They're talking about you. I think they want to pin that on you too."

"Do you know if they have any evidence?" Emery asked.

Yarmark only gave a tight shake of his head. He might have said more, but when they took the next corner, the scene of the crime came into view. This hallway was lined with trophy cases, photos, framed equipment and jerseys. Light warped and ran along the brass plating. More light sparked against the shards of glass strewn across the floor, and when Emery looked again, he saw that the front of one of the trophy cases had been broken. Overhead, the banners celebrating Wahredua High's few state wins hung where shadows thickened. Colt stood near the broken trophy case, cradling one hand with the other. Even after months of watching—and hearing about—the process, Emery still wasn't used to Colt's longer hair. It had a wave to it, and between Jem and Auggie, he'd learned to style it in a way that fit his face. For an instant—because of the strangeness of this encounter, maybe, or the fact that only a handful of the fluorescent panels were lit, or the disorientation of the last few days—Emery didn't recognize his son, and he thought, Who is that man?

Next to Colt stood a pair of familiar faces. One was Officer—Lieutenant—Peterson, who must have taken the call personally because of the stakes. His face was set in professional neutrality. The other was Drew

Klein. In high school, he'd been one of John-Henry's friends. He'd fallen in teenage Emery Hazard's rather broad category of people labeled *assholes*. Not because Drew was particularly aggressive in seeking out and tormenting Emery (not like John and Mikey and a handful of others). But because Drew was a pack animal, and because whenever the teasing and bullying and harassment began, he was quick to join in. Now, an adult, he had acquired a paunch that strained against the Wahredua Wildcats polo, and he looked jowly under a day's worth of stubble. He didn't smile when he saw them, or nod, or anything, and Emery remembered, vaguely, John mentioning some sort of trouble with Drew. Something about a speeding ticket for his son, special treatment.

"Good luck," Yarmark whispered as he retreated toward the front of the building.

"Hello, Lieutenant," John said when they reached the trio. "Colt."

Colt looked up, eyes rimmed with red and full of tears waiting to fall.

"Are you all right?" Emery asked.

The boy nodded, but he moved his hands, one still holding the other.

"What happened to your hand?"

"He broke into the trophy case," Drew said. "What does it look like?"

"Mr. Klein," Peterson said in his even voice, "we talked about this."

"He desecrated this place."

"Desecrated a bunch of Pee-Wee trophies?" Emery asked.

John gave him a look. "Ree."

"That's a pretty big word, Drew. Did you pick it up from a pack of chewing gum?"

"Hey, just because you were a butt-fuck nobody in high school—" Drew began.

Colt's face transformed: eyes widening, lips peeling back, features hardening. He angled his body toward Drew, settled his weight on the balls of his feet, one arm dropping as he brought the other back.

"Colt," Emery snapped.

Colt wavered.

"Get over here."

Drew opened his mouth.

"Now!"

Colt slunk over to him. He was breathing hard, but after a moment, he cradled his hand again and stared at the floor. Emery settled a hand on his neck and squeezed once; the muscles there were tight.

"You see—" Drew began.

"Mr. Klein," Peterson said, "don't talk unless I ask you a direct question. Do you understand?"

Klein's puffy cheeks colored, but after a moment, he gave a jerky nod.

"Mr. Hazard, I don't want to have to ask you to leave. Do you hear me?"

"Yes," Emery bit out.

John gave a considering look at the trophy case and began to ask, "What happened—" Then he stopped.

Emery followed his gaze.

He knew what would be in there. He'd always known what was in that case. The trophies from their senior year were held there. Plaques. Photos. That was the year John-Henry Somerset and the rest of the football team had won state for their division. There was a team photo, and then an individual one of the star quarterback: John-Henry Somerset blond and tousled, golden and perfect. Skinnier, then, because he hadn't grown into all that lean muscle. The hair slightly different before he'd changed how he wore it as an adult. But it was still John, the John of Emery's boyhood dreams, frozen forever in a perfect moment.

And now, spray-painted across both photos—and, for that matter, the plaque that celebrated their win at state—were the words KIDDIE DIDDLER.

"Ah." Someone who didn't know John, someone who didn't love him, wouldn't have heard the slight unsteadiness of that sound. "I see."

"There's more," Peterson said.

John laughed, and the sound seemed too big for this moment. "Jeez, do I want to know?"

"Your jersey got torn down." Peterson indicated the gym, where jerseys with retired numbers hung. "It was also vandalized."

"They pissed on it," Colt said.

"Who?" Emery asked.

But Colt shook his head and wiped his eyes on his shoulder.

"Jesus," John-Henry said, and he laughed again. "Ok, I didn't expect that. So, what's the problem? Am I supposed to file a complaint?"

Emery opened his mouth and shut it again.

"Mr. Klein says he caught Colt spray-painting the trophies."

John turned, and for a moment, the hurt was visible in his face. Emery didn't have to hear his thoughts; he knew. When Colt had come to them, at the beginning, he'd resented John. Hated him might be closer to the truth. And much of where he'd focused that emotion had to do with the John-Henry Somerset from high school.

"That's a lie," Colt said.

Drew had recovered some of his smugness. "He had the can in his hand, and he tried to hide it when he saw me."

"I didn't do anything! He's lying!"

Emery tightened his hand on Colt's nape and, in a low voice, said, "Enough."

Colt blinked rapidly and then gave up, surrendering again to wipe his eyes on his shoulder.

"Did you see him using the spray paint?" John asked. "Or just holding the can?"

Drew shifted his weight. "He was the only one here—"

One of the more remarkable things about John, in Emery's opinion, was how easily, how naturally he controlled social situations. And, since becoming an adult, for the most part, John used that ability for good. It made him a good cop. It made him a good host. It made him a good friend. And, off the record, it made him a remarkable lover—attentive, insightful, able to predict what Emery might want or need, sometimes before Emery even knew it himself. But right then, Emery watched as John used the other side of that skill.

He stopped Drew without even opening his mouth. Without doing anything, really, except angling his body slightly toward Peterson, the new stance cutting Drew out of the conversation. When John did speak, his tone did the same work: the collegiality of two men who had walked a beat, neatly pushing Drew even farther out of the conversation.

"I don't suppose anyone else saw anything?"

"Mr. Klein says the boys were moving through the building, doing conditioning at different stations."

"So, the gym was empty. And anybody could have pulled that jersey down at any time. And anybody could have broken that case and had a can of spray paint waiting. And Drew wouldn't know, because he had kids all over the place."

"I know—" Drew began.

But Peterson spoke as though he wasn't there. "That's more or less it."

"Are you going to charge Colt?"

"Not right now."

"Hold on," Drew said. "Hey, wait. I want to say my piece too."

Peterson's glance was bemused, almost as though he were surprised Drew were still there. "You already gave your statement, Mr. Klein."

"Hey, I'm not finished." He glanced from Peterson to John and back to Peterson. "Can't you make him wait outside? He should have to wait outside. There are kids in this building."

John turned his head to look at Drew, and Drew took a step back.

Colt gave a choked, snotty laugh.

"That's a great idea," Emery said. "Let's go outside, Drew."

Maybe it was the familiar setting, the old high school days coming back to Drew, because when he turned his attention to Emery, he seemed to gain back some of his confidence. His chest puffed out, and he dragged himself to his full height. "What are you going to do? You're not a cop."

"I'm not going to do anything. So, why don't we go outside?"

"You'd like that, wouldn't you?"

"I don't know if I'd like it. I think it might be satisfying."

"Are you hearing this?" Drew directed the words to Peterson. "He's threatening me."

Peterson spoke instead to John. "Colt refused to answer any questions."

"What?" Emery squeezed Colt's neck again. "Why?"

Colt stared at the floor.

"Any information he can provide would be helpful."

"He's not answering any questions," Drew said, "because he's the one who did it!"

"How about this?" Peterson gave Drew a look and then turned his attention to Emery and his family again. "You go on and take Colt home. I'd like to talk to him again when he's ready."

John nodded. "Thank you."

"Are you kidding me?" Drew waved one arm at the trophy case. "I caught him red-handed. Are you serious right now?"

"Mr. Klein, lower your voice."

"Fine. If you won't do anything, I will. You're off the team."

Colt's shoulders hitched, but he kept his gaze on the floor.

"And your butt-buddy too—"

John moved like silk unfurling on a breeze. The punch connected with Drew's mouth, and Drew's head snapped back. His body followed as he stumbled and then caught himself against one of the undamaged cases. His eyes were huge as he stared at John. Then his fingers came up and touched his split lip, the scarlet welling there.

"You hit me!"

"Talk to my son like that again, and I'll do more than give you a fat lip."

"You can't do that!"

For a moment, it looked like John was going to follow up on the punch. Then his shoulders slumped. He rubbed his face and sent Emery a look full of self-recrimination. Turning to Peterson, he said, "That was a mistake."

Peterson was silent for several long moments. Then he said, "Why don't you take Colt home?"

"Are you fucking kidding me?" Drew screamed.

"I'm going to have a conversation with Mr. Klein," Peterson said. "Explain the pros and cons of pressing charges in a situation like this one. If he decides to press charges, I'll swing by your house."

"Of course I want to press charges! He punched me!"

Peterson nodded, but his eyes stayed on John.

John wiped his face again, the movement full of exhaustion, and then he said, "Thanks."

"I'm going to have your badge for this! You stood there and watched!"

John turned, and Emery steered Colt with him. They walked in silence. The new rubber smell was giving Emery a headache, and he knew he was holding Colt too tightly, his fingers biting into the sensitive flesh of his nape. He managed to relax his fingers by degrees, but he didn't let go of his son. He couldn't. Not yet.

When they got in the Mustang, Emery said, "What happened?"

Colt sniffled and wiped his nose with his shirt.

Emery twisted to look over the seat. "I asked you a question."

Colt's head came up. He set his jaw, and amber eyes met Emery's. They were full of tears. But they were full of fire, too.

"Do you know how much trouble you're in?"

Dropping his eyes again, Colt mumbled something.

"Excuse me?"

"I don't care!"

"Don't raise your voice to me!"

"Ree," John said, his voice tight. "Not right now."

Emery wrestled with himself for what felt like a long time. Finally, he managed to nod, and he dropped back against the seat. John started the car, and they drove away from the school.

It was a short drive. In nice weather, the school was close enough to walk to, although now that Colt had the truck, walking was out of the question. Walking was for underclassmen. And now that Emery thought about it, he realized he wasn't sure if the truck was at school or if Colt had gotten a ride to practice with Ashley. If they'd left it, they'd have to go back later today and get it. No point letting some eager officer ticket it. Although maybe that would be for the best. Maybe they'd tow it, and then Colt could pay the impound lot fee himself, and he could see what life was like without a truck for a month. He could walk to school. Like all those fucking underclassmen.

When John pulled into the garage, Emery realized his husband had been talking during the drive, the tone and cadence suggesting that the words needed no response.

"—ridiculous, really. I mean, that's what they decided? To trash some old stuff at the school? It's kind of funny, actually."

When Emery glanced at his husband, he saw a too bright smile there. It made him think of movies. Of old incandescent bulbs flickering in a power surge, the light fading and rising until all of a sudden, the bulb exploded.

He turned his attention to the back seat again. "You're going to tell me what happened today."

Colt glared back at him.

"Do you hear me?"

Colt looked away.

"Did you—"

"I heard you!"

Emery took a deep breath. He got out of the car and went inside.

Afternoon sunlight filled the kitchen, and the air smelled like butter and toasted bread. A skillet on the stove still held a few crumbs, suggesting either Tean or Jem—let's be honest, Jem—had decided to eat grilled cheese for lunch. The house was quiet. For about ten seconds.

"Honestly," John said as he came into the house. That power-surge smile was still there. It didn't match his eyes. "Honestly, they did me a favor, you know? Somebody should have cleaned that stuff out a long time ago."

"What are you talking about?"

Colt stormed past them, every step shaking the house.

"Get back here," Emery said.

Somehow, his son managed to stomp harder as he continued toward the stairs.

"Colt, God damn it!" Emery threw the skillet into the sink, where it clanged against the stainless steel. He pushed his hands through his hair and looked at John. "That school has got to have security cameras. It's twenty-fucking-twenty. I want to know who did this."

"Ree." John laughed. "Relax. We've got bigger things to worry about."

A door slammed upstairs. Biscuit's distant bark sounded startled.

"Oh no you fucking don't," Emery said.

When he got to Colt's room, though, the door was locked, of course. Emery hammered on it. "Open this door right now!"

"Go away!" Colt screamed. His voice was raw, and it sounded like he was crying.

"Colt, I swear to Christ!"

"Just leave me alone!"

John passed Emery in the hallway, headed toward their bedroom. Emery gave the door a frustrated slap and then followed.

He paced as John opened their closet and began sliding clothes along the hang rod.

"That son of a bitch was behind this," Emery said. "Drew. You know he had something to do with this bullshit."

"High school trophies," John said. "Come on."

"What is he? The JV coach? Probably not even that. Probably some kind of assistant. And he just happens to be the only adult in the building today when this shit goes down. He just happens to split up the kids, spread them out all over the place, and that's supposed to be a coincidence? No fucking way."

"I mean, I'm an adult. I'm a grown man. I'm not some washed-up jock clinging to my glory days." Hangers made a shimmering sound against the rod. John threw something to the floor, and in the indirect light through the windows, it took a moment for Emery to make it out. His old letterman jacket, still in a garment bag. "What do I care about that stuff? I hated being that kid."

"John, what are you—"

A battered Wahredua Wildcats hat hit the floor next. Then a windbreaker. Then a hoodie. Joggers. He bent, rummaged through the shoes on the floor of the closet, and pitched first one sneaker and then another. They were custom, white leather with accents in Wahredua Wildcats colors: red and gold. They'd sparked a moderately serious argument about discretionary spending. Emery stared as the pile grew. The hat and the letterman jacket were the only pieces that dated back to their time in high school; John had acquired the rest recently, always with an explanation that it was a fundraiser for Colt's team, or he'd wear it to Colt's games. Sometimes it was Colt who made the argument for him. They'd bought two pairs of the sneakers.

Emery tried again. "What's happening right now?"

John scooped up the pile of clothing and started for the door.

Emery went after him. All he could see was the back of John: the set of his shoulders, the stiffness of his spine. He took the steps two at a time with an energy that Emery couldn't decipher. In his head, he pictured that smile growing brighter and brighter, the bulb exploding.

"Slow down," Emery said.

If John heard him, though, he didn't stop.

As they passed through the kitchen, Emery's phone buzzed. Reflexively, he drew it out. An email from Drew Klein showed in the notifications, and the preview showed the subject line: RETURNING COLT'S EQUIPMENT.

"You have got to be fucking kidding me."

"What?" John asked as he shouldered open the door and stepped out. The winter sunlight fell over him like a thin, white shawl. It bleached the gold from his cheek. It turned his hair the color of bone. Only for an instant, though, and then he was pressing outside, the hard smell of winter—a mineral iciness—met Emery as he followed him out into the afternoon.

"Drew, that piece of shit. He didn't waste a single fucking second. You know what I should do? I should make him tell me what happened today. Fucking overcompensating dad-bod fuckbait with a fucking micropenis. How tough do you think he's going to be when he's not terrorizing a child? I bet I wouldn't even have to touch him. The big fuck would probably wet himself."

John shook his head. Somehow, the motion conveyed amusement, with a trace of annoyance.

"Are you listening to this? He's kicking Colt off the basketball team."

Ice crunched under John's steps as he headed toward the trash cans against the fence. "Ok."

"Ok? It's not ok, John. It's about as far from ok as it can be. Do you understand how Colt's going to feel? Not to mention that something seriously fucked up happened today, and he won't talk about it. He won't even look me in the eye. And instead of helping us, like a responsible adult, Drew's being a petty-ass bitch because he's still got his butt hurt because you wouldn't waive his kid's speeding ticket."

When John reached the trash cans, he juggled the load of clothes for a moment before getting the lid off. Then dumped everything into the can. He wiped his hands, considered the inside of the can, and replaced the lid. When he turned around, he must have seen something on Emery's face because his own eyebrows went up. In a surprisingly smooth voice, he said, "Actually, Ree, I think it really is ok."

"What are you doing?"

"Oh shit. Does it need to be in a bag?"

"John." For a moment, Emery was speechless. All he could come up with was "Your jacket."

The brilliance of the answering grin nearly blinded Emery. John's steps clipped across the ice. "Like I said, I should have gotten rid of that stuff a long time ago."

He tried to pass Emery, but Emery put a hand on John's chest. The cold stung the tips of his ears. His cheeks felt hot, and under his fingers, John's chest rose and fell rapidly, and Emery thought of a bird, the delicate, hollow bones that broke so easily. "I don't understand what's happening right now, but that's yours. That's your stuff." What he wanted to say was *It's important*. But those words seemed like a chasm, so he heard himself say again, "It's yours."

"Great. I don't want it anymore. Ree, Colt's going to be fine. In fact, I think it's a good thing that he's not going to be playing basketball. It'll make it easier when he transfers to a new school." He slid past Emery; Emery's fingers caught on his sleeve, and then John was past him, moving into the house as he said, "God, it's cold out here."

In the kitchen, John was looking at his phone. It dinged, and Emery recognized the sound of a notification from one of John's many social media apps.

"Turn those off," he said. "Whatever they're saying about you, it's only going to make you feel worse."

John didn't raise his head.

"Do you want to repeat that last bit?" Emery asked as he shut the door. It shut out the apron of winter sunlight as well, and then the kitchen seemed too dark. "About Colt?"

"Hm?"

Emery closed the distance between them and pushed John's phone down.

"I was reading that."

Emery's hand felt far away. "Go over that part again."

"It's pretty simple, I think. Either we let him go to school with kids who are bullying him, or we find him another school. Why? Is there something I'm missing?" The corner of his eye twitched. "I thought it was obvious."

"You thought it was obvious," Emery echoed.

Seconds ticked past. Tilting one shoulder in some incomprehensible attempt at body language, John lifted the phone again.

Emery pushed it back down.

"What is going on here?" John asked.

"That's what I want to know. Send him to another school? Are you kidding me?"

For the first time since they'd gotten home, the smile flaked away, and the John who looked out at Emery had cold, hard eyes the color of a winter sky. "Why would I be kidding?"

"Because I'm already freaking the fuck out that any minute now, Ramona is going to call and tell us they're taking Colt. How about that?"

"They're not going to take him. Even if I get convicted, they won't take him. You're a fine, upstanding citizen. They'll let him stay with you."

"Then how about because he shouldn't have to leave school because of some jackass kids. Do you have any idea how hard transitions are for him? He can't just pick up and start over, John. It's taken a lot of work for him to put down roots here. In a way, it's a miracle, because he's thriving. He has friends. He's doing well in school. He has a boyfriend."

"Thriving? That's what you call it? Did you notice he can't stand up straight? Did you think about why that might be? What about his hand, Ree, did you notice that?"

The magnitude of what John seemed to be suggesting went beyond what Emery felt capable of handling. It lurked at the edge of words, something he wasn't quite ready to say to himself. And, instead—like a coward—he found himself grappling for something he could deal with. "Your hand—"

When Emery reached for John's hand, though, John moved it away. "I'm fine. I know how to throw a punch, thanks. Unlike our son." With what seemed like an effort, he tamped down the heat in his voice. "I do not want Colt going to that school anymore. It's not going to get better. In fact, it's going to get worse. You know that trip he's been begging to go on? The service trip to St. Louis? That's a great idea. We'll let him go, and when he gets back, we'll tell him that we're pulling him out of school until we figure out where to send him. It's not like we have a ton of options, so we should start applying and interviewing as soon as we can."

Emery stared at him, and John met his gaze.

"I honestly can't believe what I'm hearing."

"It's not that complicated, Ree."

"You're going to rip his life down to the studs—again, John—because of a few dumbasses. And, incidentally, in the process you're going to teach him to run away from his problems."

"So, what? You think he should stay, and we'll let these kids torture him for the next year and a half? Fuck that, Ree. I'm not letting him go through that."

Maybe it was the word *torture*. Maybe it was the way John cut his eyes to the side, and the red in his cheeks didn't look like it was from the cold.

"I did it," Emery said.

"That's not what this is about."

"You know what, John? I think it is."

To Emery's surprise, John's lip trembled. But when he spoke, his voice had a buckled-down control. "Why the fuck would I keep that fucking shit, Ree? I hated that kid. I hated being that kid. I hated that fucking kid." He shook his head, the way sometimes guys shook off a punch. "I will not let that happen to our son."

"John, I understand—"

"You don't, Ree. You really don't. So do me a favor and don't pretend that you do."

Emery reached for John, but John took a step back and shook his head again. He tried to think of what to say, the right thing to say. *It's ok* wasn't the truth. *It'll be ok* didn't seem like solid ground either. *He's our son, and we can give him so much more than either of us had growing up* came close. And so did *We don't have to let them win*. But what Emery heard himself say with cool, measured finality was "We're not pulling him out of school."

"Yes, we are. And you want to know why, Ree? Because I wish they'd done it for you. Because if you'd been my child, I would have done it for you. I will not let it happen to Colt, do you understand me?"

"John—"

"No!" The word was wild, a shout, and it rang out in the stillness of the house. John looked feverish: cheeks flushed, eyes shining.

The creak of a joist made both of them glance at the opening to the living room. Jem stood there, arms folded, appraising them. "Everything ok?"

"Fine," Emery said. "We need a minute."

"No," John said, "we don't. And no, it isn't."

Before Emery could say anything, John stepped past him. A moment later, he was out in the garage, and then the door was rattling up, and the growl of the Mustang came.

As the sound of the Mustang faded, Emery realized with a distant clarity what he'd been trying to say. What the right thing had been to say.

I love you.

11

It felt like a long time before Emery could look at Jem. The blond man leaned in the opening, arms still folded. He wore a *Mighty Ducks* t-shirt, washed so many times the crossed hockey sticks were starting to flake away. The sweatpants had the words HARLEY-DAVIDSON running down one leg. On the other, a lightning bolt was striking a motorcycle.

"Tean?" Jem called quietly toward the stairs.

Emery shook his head, held up a hand, and headed for Colt's room. He passed Tean on the stairs. The vet was running both hands through his dark storm of hair, and he pressed himself up against the wall to let Emery pass, soft eyes following him.

When he reached the door, Emery rapped lightly.

Silence. If Colt was still crying, he'd passed the sobbing stage.

"Colt," Emery said. "I need to—" He stopped. His throat was tight, and he found himself struggling to master the wave of emotion threatening to swamp him. "Could we talk? Please?"

Ten seconds. Fifteen. And then shuffling steps came on the other side of the door. The lock turned, and then the shuffling steps moved away. Emery gave him the grace of a handful of seconds before stepping into the room.

Colt's room looked the way it always did: joggers and sweatshirts carpeting the floor, shoes—many of them once belonging to John—everywhere, water bottles abandoned on every available surface. A faint funk hung in the air—laundry that needed washing, and a teenage boy who had come straight from basketball practice. Colt lay facedown on the bed, a pillow pulled halfway over his head. His breathing sounded thick. One sock, improbably, had come halfway off.

Emery shut the door. He sat on the bed. He tried to float above his thoughts. Ground effect, was that what it was? When the plane flew close to a flat surface and the wings generated more lift and less drag. Like gravity didn't exist and you could just rush along forever, inches above reality. He reached over and pulled Colt's sock into place.

Colt made an unfamiliar noise and then spoke into the mattress. "You are so weird."

Emery saw John's face again. He felt the old helplessness, not knowing what to say when it would have been obvious to anyone else.

Colt saved him by rolling onto his back and pulling the pillow to his chest. He didn't meet Emery's eyes when he said, "Are you and J-H fighting?"

"I don't know."

Somehow, even snotty and red eyed, Colt managed to snort.

Emery let out a tiny, broken laugh. "I suppose we are."

"About me?"

"No."

Disbelief painted Colt's face.

"No, Colt. Not about you. This is about a lot of things, I think. Things I didn't know John felt. Or still felt. We both said things we probably shouldn't have."

"So, you should apologize."

Emery nodded.

"J-H too."

"He will. He's much better at it than I am."

Colt tightened his arms around the pillow. "I'm not going to talk about it." And then, like a challenge, "If that's why you came up here."

Emery nodded again. "Let me see your hand."

It took a lot of squirming and wriggling, and, in Emery's mind, it would have taken a lot less effort for Colt just to sit up, but eventually the boy wormed his way across the bed and held out his hand. The knuckles were swollen, and when Emery took his hand, Colt let out a harsh breath.

"How much does it hurt?"

The boy shrugged.

Emery palpated the hand.

"Stop."

"Is that a 'stop' because you're being a baby or because there's a sharp pain?"

To his surprise, a lopsided grin appeared on Colt's face. "Being a baby."

"That's all right then," Emery said, letting go of his hand. "We'll have Tean take a look. I bet he'll tell us to ice it and see how it looks in the morning."

Less than a minute passed before the boy blurted, "I didn't do that stuff. The spray paint. I wouldn't do that."

Emery raised an eyebrow.

Snuffling into the pillow, Colt mumbled, "Well, I don't know. You get pretty mad sometimes."

"Who hurt you?"

It was the way Colt stiffened that answered the question—his body tight with fear that his secret had been exposed.

But he said, "Nobody hurt me."

"Colt—"

"Nothing happened."

"If you got in a fight, I won't be mad. But I'd like to talk to you about self-defense."

"Pops, nothing happened." He didn't add *please* at the end, but Emery could hear the begging in his voice.

The house creaked. It was an ordinary sound, a familiar sound. Something contracting in the winter cold, the afternoon already growing long and dark. A rafter, maybe.

"I understand that I can't make you talk about it. But I also want you to know that if someone is hurting you, it's my responsibility to keep you safe. I won't let anyone hurt you, Colt. Whatever it takes, I'll keep you safe." And even as he said the words, Emery heard the emptiness of his promise. Because his child was almost a man now, and he moved in the world in ways that Emery couldn't monitor, couldn't control. High school was just the proving grounds, a slightly expanded universe for Colt to stand on his own two feet before stepping into a larger, more dangerous world. There were so many hours every day when Emery couldn't keep his son safe, and the hurt of that threatened to collapse his chest.

Colt was silent for what felt like a long time. Then he said into the pillow, "I'm fine."

Emery nodded—not because he agreed, but because he wanted Colt to know he'd been heard. "John didn't do those things."

"I know."

"I want you to hear me say it. He did not do what they're saying, Colt. And whatever you hear at school, this is the truth: John did not do anything wrong."

Another nod. Colt squirmed around some more until his head was at the edge of the bed. It let him look up at Emery. His hair spilled down the side of the mattress, and Emery couldn't help himself: he combed his fingers through it, and he smiled when Colt rolled his eyes.

"You say he loads the dishwasher wrong."

Emery's smile widened. "The cups go on the top rack."

"Even Evie knows that. She busted him a couple of weeks ago."

The laugh erupted before Emery even realized it was coming. He ran his fingers through Colt's hair once more, and then he did a quick scrub to mess it all up.

"Pops!"

Laughing again as Colt pulled away, Emery considered his son. "Please tell me," he finally said, "if it gets too bad. I can't do everything. But I can do something."

A shadow lay over Colt's face. He shrugged and looked away. In a low voice, he asked, "Am I grounded?"

"I don't think it would be fair to ground you for something that's not your fault."

"You grounded me when Ash shut my door."

"That's because you knew exactly why Ashley shut the door and you were perfectly happy with it."

Colt rolled his eyes, a hint of a blush in his cheeks. "Pops," he said in a different tone, "this service trip is going to be so dope."

"Colt."

"Please, it's going to be epic. And everybody from GLAM is going, and Ash's parents said he can go if I can go, and it would be so fucking fire if you said yes."

"Language."

"Please?"

Emery hesitated.

"Please, please, please?"

"Maybe it would be a good idea for you to get away for a few days."

"Oh my God, yes. Thank you."

"I didn't say you could go; I have to talk to John about it."

"Pops, thank you! Thank you, thank you, thank you!"

Colt scrambled upright and launched a hug at Emery. Laughing, Emery patted his back. "I didn't say yes, Colt. Slow your roll."

Pulling back, Colt made a face.

"Auggie taught me that."

"Don't ever say that again."

"Honestly, Colt."

"I'm serious. That was the grossest thing of my entire life. Um, Pops?"

"This sounds like you're about to ask for something that you know I'll say no to."

"No, like—I know I shouldn't have, uh, whatever today."

"That's an extremely vague account of what you shouldn't have done."

"Gotten into trouble."

"Much better."

Colt flashed that crooked grin. "But, like, can I still go to GLAM this afternoon?"

"I don't know—"

"Pops, please. I promised I would, and they're counting on me. They've got this huge truck to load with all the donations for the service project, and Koby says Ash and I do twice as much work as anybody else, and if they don't get it all loaded tonight, they're not going to be able to leave on time, and you always say you can't let other people affect your decisions—"

"Jesus Christ, are you quoting me to myself?"

Head lolling, smile broadening, Colt said, "Language."

Emery gave him a pat on the cheek and said, "If Dr. Leon says your hand is ok."

"He will. It's fine; it doesn't even hurt anymore."

"I want you to ice it. I want you to take ibuprofen."

"I will."

"I'm going to teach you how to throw a punch so this doesn't happen again."

"I didn't—"

Emery held up a hand. "We've been doing so well. Don't insult me by lying."

Colt gave an unsure nod.

"And I don't want you overdoing it."

"I won't. Ash always helps me lift the heavy stuff."

"Good Lord. Come on; let's see what Tean has to say."

12

At first, John-Henry just drove. He had to get out of the house. He had to get away from Emery, from the anger boiling up inside him. For a single, satisfying moment, he had a vision of driving straight out of Wahredua and never looking back. Emery and Colt and Evie could come join him wherever he ended up. Just not here. Anywhere but here.

Then, as he made his way down Market Street, he had to stop and wait at a crosswalk while people bundled in winter gear made the most of winter break. The street was lined with restaurants, with local shops, with bakeries and coffee shops. It was Wahredua's historic downtown, running along the Grand Rivere, and people came for weekend trips and for a nice dinner and for a night out, hitting one of the bars. Snow dusted redbrick buildings, turning an already charming street into a gingerbread village. Everybody shopping and laughing, faces chapped with the cold, everybody happy. And you didn't know, unless you lived here, that Barbie Hail, who owned the cookie decorating store, had put one of her kids in the hospital with a garden hose, or Aidan Sheppard, who played barista at River Coffee, had been driving drunk once and gone right through the wall of his own house, killing his wife in the process. You didn't know Art Whitaker had gone up for molesting his nieces, and when he'd gotten out, his wife's brothers had knocked every tooth out of his head. The heat from the vents was too much, and the world swam. John-Henry looked past the neatly kept storefronts and the antiquated signage, trying to find the horizon. Right then, with the sun already dropping, the river looked like an oil slick: black except where red and orange curled along the surface.

The crosswalk cleared. A horn blared behind him. John-Henry startled in the seat, sweat breaking out all over him, and his eyes fell on St. Taffy's: just another redbrick building on Market Street, but this one with neon signs in the windows. The one that mattered—the only one that mattered—was the blue-and-red one announcing that the cop bar was open.

Slide onto a stool. Smile at the waitress. Start with a flight of tequila because today wasn't about fucking around. Today was about fucking up. He could feel it, the instantaneous need as every cell in his body started screaming for it, his nerve endings ablaze.

And then the horn blared again, and John-Henry took his foot off the brake. The Mustang rolled forward. The heat from the vents baked him, made his skin feel dry to the point of cracking, but he was also aware of the flop sweat soaking him, the chill damp under his arms and across his back, dimpling his chest so that his shirt clung to him. He drifted past Festive Offerings, where two kids were tying each other up in garland. He braked on autopilot as a woman jaywalked, her terrier lunging at the end of its leash. The apartment he had shared with Emery, what seemed like forever ago, loomed on the right. And then the worst of it was over, the sudden pressing need. He could turn around. He could go back to St. Taffy's, or to the Mill House, or he could pull a classic John-Henry and hit the Jack Flash, load up, and get blasted in the bleachers at the high school. That was part of his legacy too, wasn't it? Partying. Getting wasted. Anything, back then, not to be who he was. But the need had passed, and what remained was mostly self-pity, so he kept driving. It was safer to keep driving, to get away.

His phone buzzed. He turned it off and kept driving.

Wahredua shrank behind him. Streets lined with houses gave way to the town's fringes, the lots larger, homes and businesses jumbled side by side, barns and sheds, a single ancient corn crib from when this had been an agricultural community. Then all of that contracted, and John-Henry was driving through thick stands of hickory and oak, alongside clumps of pine, weaving his way over the rolling limestone hills. In places, when they'd built these roads, they'd blasted straight through the rock, and the raw face of the limestone was yellow as the sun fell lower.

He came around a turn, and the sun hit him in the face, and for a moment, he remembered another set of lights, their brightness hitting him, the intensity like standing in a spotlight. The smell of torn-up turf, of cleats heavy with dirt, of his own body warm and loose and alive, of the hot October day, when everyone had been hoping it would have been cool by then. His jersey chafed under his arms, soaked with sweat and pulled crooked from running, from tackles, from guys who grabbed him when they thought they could get away with it. The certainty of the knowledge that Emery was up in the stands, watching him, even though he couldn't say to himself why it mattered, not back then. He remembered the feeling, although it had been later—much later—before he could put it into words. That this was his. Not his mother's, who worried about injuries and accidents and anything that might damage the perfect toy she occasionally liked to take out to play with. Not his father's, who couldn't be bothered coming to games, not unless he needed to show off his son to a prospective client. This was his, John-Henry's. He had worked for it. Fought for it. Poured every ounce of confusion and frustration and fear and self-loathing into it. It was, in a way, the first thing that was John-Henry and not the cocktail of commands and conditioning and expectations from his parents. And he remembered the determination that it would not be the last. That he would be his own person. That one day, he would be whoever he wanted to be.

The broken glass. The spray paint. At least, he thought with something approaching a laugh, I didn't have to see the jersey.

It didn't matter; he knew that. Things didn't matter. People mattered. His son, who was hurt and scared, mattered. His husband, who was terrified, mattered. At the front of his brain, where reason lived, John-Henry knew those things. The same way he knew he should turn back, go home, and start the work of patching things up.

But that part of his brain wasn't in charge anymore. Another part was. An animal part. A part that remembered the feeling of Emery's chest under his hand as he pushed and sent Emery falling down the stairs. A part that conflated that memory, blurring the lines, so that it was the same feeling as the thinness of Emery's shoulder under his hand when he'd touched him in the locker room, when everything he'd fought against for so long threatened to slip free. He remembered the hatred. And the guilt that was so much worse—unbearable, and because it was unbearable, it was easier to retreat into hatred again. That was the same boy who had stood under stadium lights and promised himself he'd be whoever he wanted to be. The boy who had been so scared of what other people thought that he'd tried to kill a part of himself. And, when he couldn't do that, he'd wanted to kill the boy who was like a living mirror, everywhere John-Henry turned, showing him himself in all his ugliness. The boy who had stood under the stadium lights, proud in that adolescent fantasy of independence, was the same one who had gone running to his parents every time it looked like there might be consequences for his cruelty, because he was John-Henry Somerset, which meant life always fell in his favor.

That's not how life works, he thought. Life isn't fair. Everyone has ups and downs. You've had your share of setbacks.

And another part of him, the rabid part of him, thought, How fucking dare they?

The clock on the dash had passed five when John reached Auburn. The sun had disappeared below the horizon, leaving only a blister of red that was shrinking steadily as he watched. He looked around and felt like he was waking up. He hadn't meant to come here, not consciously. But here he was. Streetlights pushed back pockets of darkness. Strip malls shone like islands—a Walmart, a tattoo parlor, a Dollar Tree with its sign on the fritz, an empty anchor store at one end that had clearly, years before, been a Blockbuster. Even in the car, even with the heat going, he could smell the Chinese buffet—ginger and garlic and the sodium explosion of soy sauce. He passed the Epiphany of Light campus where, earlier that year, the search for a killer had ended in yet another tragedy. The campus was dark, and he wondered in an absent way if it had closed permanently.

I should turn around, he thought again. He wiped his mouth. He looked at his phone on the seat next to him, powered off, its screen dark. I should go home.

But at the next light, he turned onto a side street. He knew where he was going.

The homes were large and old, built long before the Lake of the Ozarks had been imagined, back when Auburn had been a farming community on the Osage River. Back then, the hot spot for Auburn's wealthy families had been the bluffs that looked over the city's high street and, beyond it, the river. And so he followed the road up into the bluffs, past big, old Victorian and Tudor homes. In the dark, with the streetlights spaced out and the porch lights too small to push back the gloom, the asymmetrical faces of the houses crowded around him, their dim yellow eyes following him.

Eric Brey—state representative, potential murderer, and sadist—lived in what had been the family home. He ran what had been the family business, a farm and tractor supply store. Old money, in other words. John-Henry had seen the house before, back when he'd been trying to get Brey on the hook for the double murder in the county jail. But it was one thing to have researched Brey, to have seen photos of the home, to have come here during daylight hours as an officer of the law. And it was another thing now to be a man out on bail, skulking through the frozen night, unarmed. He didn't even have a pocketknife. Not that a pocketknife would have helped, since John-Henry had no idea what he was trying to accomplish.

Watch, he told himself. That's all. Observe. The video that Masouda had shown them connected Brey to Vermilya. Maybe John-Henry would knock on the door. Maybe he'd see if Brey wanted to talk. Vermilya had been shot, and Ingra was dead. Another man who had once been connected to the Cottonmouth Club, Gideon Moss, had died by his own hand because he'd been so terrified of retribution. So, maybe Brey was feeling the pinch too. Maybe, watching his partners drop one by one, he'd be ready to talk. But for now, John-Henry would simply watch. That was all.

He parked half a block down from the house, where he had a good line of sight. The Brey family home was a Tudor—not quite a mansion, but close enough that you might miss the difference. It had half-timbering complemented by brick and stone, with a steeply gabled roof and the kind of tall, narrow leadlights that must have been hell on the heating bill. The trees were old and bare. The hedges were sprinkled with snow. There was even a row of perfect icicles hanging from the gutter. People probably stopped and took pictures.

Upstairs, light showed in several windows. On the ground floor, the windows looked dark, but with the curtains open, John-Henry occasionally caught a glimmer of a light from deeper in the house—the kind of blue-gray flash that suggested a TV. He turned off the car, settled into his seat, and immediately began remembering all the logistical realities involved in a stakeout, the kind of thing that—if he'd been acting rationally—he would have considered. Not freezing his fingers off, for example. And the fact that he hadn't eaten since Masouda's. And he needed to pee. And, maybe most importantly, that this was stupid. This whole thing was stupid, coming out here like this, with no plan, not even really thinking about it.

What am I doing, he asked himself as he reached for the keys. He'd call Emery on the way back—

A gust of wind made the night shudder. That's what it looked like, at least—as though everything were moving: stars, sky, branches, the darkness itself. And the front door of the Brey house shimmied open. When the breeze died, the door rocked back into place until, once again, it appeared to be shut.

John-Henry watched, one hand on the steering wheel.

It could have been anything. It was an old house. It was an old door. He and Emery lived in an old house, and one of the realities of old houses was that, as the house settled, things quickly shifted out of true. Floors became uneven. Windows stuck. Doors that might have closed easily when they'd first been hung now became impossible to open—or wouldn't shut at all, not unless you really laid into them. Brey had come home. He'd been careless. The latch hadn't caught. That was all.

Once more the night seemed to ripple, branches creaking, granules of snow rattling against the side of the Mustang, a strong current running through the river of darkness. The door inched open again, a wedge of light fattening on the porch. And then the door drifted shut again.

Or someone else, John-Henry thought with a detached clarity. Someone who didn't know the house, didn't know old doors sometimes didn't close as easily as you thought.

He grabbed his phone and got out of the car.

The wind rose again, raking his hair, a cold hand pressing against his cheek. He hurried across the icy street. He could smell the cold dark and something like dog piss and his own breath. Little clouds of vapor trailed him. The night was so still, he thought the first sound would crack it.

When he reached the house, another breeze forced open the door, and John-Henry found himself staring inside: a foyer, dark timbers, dark tile, a switchback staircase, a rug. It was impossible to make out anything else without more light. He listened. TV voices, too low for him to make out the words, came from an archway to his left, and he caught those glimmers of bluish-gray light again. A smell wafted out to him, unpleasant but too faint for him to be able to tell what it was. He told himself to call out, to announce himself. But he didn't.

He'd been police for a long time—at this point, he'd been police longer than he'd been anything else. And right then, instincts honed over the years were screaming at him, telling him to get back to the car, call this in, and next time, pack a fucking gun. But he didn't do that either. This was Auburn, and the chief of police in Auburn was Jonas Cassidy. Cassidy's past was problematic enough—the short version was that he'd been Emery's partner and then, when Emery had exposed his corruption, Cassidy had been saved by his father, a captain in the Metropolitan Police, and Emery had found himself ejected from the force. On top of that, though, Cassidy was somehow tied into whatever organization was operating out of the Cottonmouth Club. If something was happening here tonight, calling Cassidy would be like bringing in reinforcements for the bad guys.

He might have turned back. He might have gotten in the Mustang and driven away. But a sound stopped him—a phone buzzing. John-Henry shoved a hand into his pocket to silence it, cursing his stupidity and bad luck. But his phone wasn't vibrating, and a moment later, he realized the sound had a different quality. A dim glow showed him where a phone lay on the floor next to the stairs. The screen went dark, and the phone's buzzing stopped.

Nobody left their phone on the floor, John-Henry thought. Not unless they had a good reason. Not in the entry hall. It would have been another thing if it had been somewhere else—on the floor in the living room, say, where it might have gotten knocked off the arm of the recliner and overlooked. But here? Something had happened. And it had happened right here.

John-Henry stepped inside and shut the door, leaning against it to close it firmly. No prints, he thought. Absolutely no fingerprints.

He started off at a quick walk and, the next heartbeat, almost ended up on his ass. The rug slid underfoot, and because he'd been walking so quickly, it had almost taken him out. He recovered his balance and took a deep breath; he could feel his heartbeat in his fingertips. His first thought, mingling disbelief and outrage, was that Emery never would have let something like that happen. He would have bought one of those rug backers, the no-slip kind. And the thought, how immediate it had been, made John-Henry want to burst out laughing. He recognized the laughter, too, as an overflow of adrenaline, and he managed to swallow it as he moved deeper into the house.

When he cleared the rug, his sneakers made a soft squeak on the tile—the rubber, wet from the snow and ice, and it squeaked again on his next step. He moved more slowly, trying to minimize the noise, hoping the sound of the TV would cover it.

He started with the archway on his left. It connected with a hallway, and the first opening in the hallway led into what must have been called a great room or a family room or a gathering room. A massive television hung on one wall, faced by an ancient Chesterfield sofa and a much more modern-looking recliner, with gleaming leather and chrome. An updated wet bar, with a lot of expensive-looking glassware, took up the wall opposite the TV. A large opening connected with a kitchen, where the only light came from under the microwave. The television displayed the Netflix home page, and as John-Henry stood there, it cycled through the preview clip for what appeared to be a Christmas-action-horror movie called *Just Clause*. A bare-chested and ridiculously buff Santa was carrying a waifish (and mostly naked) girl over his shoulder. He had positioned her just right so she didn't get in the way of the assault rifle strapped across his muscular back.

"We've got to get out!" the girl screamed.

"The only way out," Santa answered, "is up."

Since they were approaching the fireplace, John-Henry decided that meant going up the chimney. He also decided that if he survived the next few days and didn't spend the majority of the next decade or two in prison, he and Colt were definitely going to have to watch that movie.

The Netflix trailer reached its end. Silence swallowed the house again. Then something beeped, breaking the quiet, and John-Henry started. His gaze moved to the kitchen. The microwave's display flashed. The Netflix trailer began again, but now that John-Henry was listening for it, he could hear the microwave's reminder beep when it came again. He passed into the kitchen.

The stink that had met him in the entry hall was stronger now. Burned popcorn. The microwave flashed the word DONE at him and beeped again. John-Henry's mind began to assemble a narrative: Brey had been ready to call it a night. He'd turned off the lights. Popped a bag of popcorn. Started scrolling through Netflix, looking for something to watch. And—

A gap opened in the story. Something had happened. Something that had left the front door swinging in the breeze.

John-Henry retraced his steps through the great room, out into the hallway. Without the glow from the TV, the darkness seemed even thicker, but he didn't want to use the flashlight on his phone because it would reveal his position, announcing his presence to anyone still in the house. He moved slowly, each step coming down carefully on the tile, straining to hear. The next door opened onto an office—he could make out the shape of the desk, the computer, the filing cabinets—and the one after that appeared to be a guest room, with a bed and dresser, but pristine and smelling slightly musty, with no personal effects to suggest anyone used the room regularly.

The hallway turned, and the final door was bolted. After a moment's hesitation, he covered his hand with his sleeve and threw back the bolt. When he opened the door, he found the garage. Cold air washed over him, making him shiver. A single car occupied the garage. The gloom made it impossible to make out details, but he guessed the shadows clumped up against the walls were the usual junk that accumulated in a garage. He shut the door, wiped down everything he'd touched, and retraced his steps to the entry hall.

He found a dining room with big windows that looked out on the street. Light filtered into the room and gleamed on a table and chairs and china hutch. Next, a formal living room, with more of those big windows. Another old-fashioned sofa and chairs, a piano with its lid open, the steel and bronze inside glittering like teeth. Someone had left a copy of *Country Living* on the coffee table, and even though there wasn't enough light to read the date, it looked like it might have been older than John-Henry.

The only other door off the entry hall led into a bedroom. John-Henry knew at once it was the master or the primary or whatever you were supposed to call it these days. The size was one clue—the room was much bigger than the guest room he'd seen earlier. Heavy wooden furniture made bulky shadows in the weak light. He caught a faded, floral scent that reminded him of the sachets his grandmother used to keep in dresser drawers, but it mingled with a musty smell that reminded him of the guest room. John-Henry debated exploring the room further. Curiosity made him want to check the closets, the walk-in bath, the bedding. Why hadn't Brey moved into this room after his parents died? What might John-Henry find if he poked around? He had a Hitchcock-induced vision of finding a mummified Mother Brey wrapped in a nightgown and propped up in an old-fashioned wheelchair. Honestly, he thought as he eased the door shut and retreated, at this point, *Psycho* would be a relief compared to what he was dealing with.

The only place left was up, and John-Henry fought the urge to whisper to himself, *The only way out is up*. He didn't, of course. In part because his instincts were still screaming at him. And in part because he knew the goofiness was a result of the hormones rushing through his body, making it hard to think clearly. But mostly because he knew that Emery would have killed him if he'd been here.

He was on the landing of the switchback stairs when a thud came from above him, and then a muffled grunt. John-Henry stopped. His heart raced, the sound of its drumming filling his ears. He thought, for a moment, it was too loud for him to hear anything else. But then the microwave beeped downstairs. He waited. On the walls, generations of Breys stared down at him, their eyes silver in the weak light that filtered in through the windows. No more noises came from above. After a minute, he started up the stairs again, testing each tread to see if it would creak before he trusted his weight to it.

Why didn't you bring a gun, he asked himself.

Because I'm an idiot, he told himself. Because I was making a point.

What that point might have been, though, was lost to him. It had been a long time since he'd run away from a fight—even a fight with Emery. And he was aware, under the roil of emotions, that he'd acted like a child, and that even Colt had probably rolled his eyes at that display of emotional maturity.

He drew himself back to the present moment as he reached the top of the stairs. The argument didn't matter, not right now. What mattered was that he was here, alone, without backup and without even the option of calling the local police. And he didn't have a gun. And someone was here. Maybe it was only Brey, but someone was in this house.

A door stood immediately to the right of the stairs, but no light showed inside the room. He kept going. The hallway continued, the shadows thickening as it stretched away from the windows facing the street. John-

Henry thought he could make out a pair of double doors. He filed the other details—the console table with a vase and flowers; the dull gleam of the wainscotting; the smell of wax and polish and pine; oil paintings that showed pale-faced men and women in antiquated clothing—all the way at the back of his brain.

The double doors opened onto what he would have called a trophy room or a game room—he could make out the animal heads mounted on the wall, the shape of the furniture filling the space. It was the kind of thing that didn't really exist anymore, but here it was, existing. He could smell it, an animal smell, dry and dusty and unpleasant. He shut the doors and kept going.

When the hall turned, he stopped. Ahead, light spilled from a partially open doorway, cutting an arc out of the darkness. For what seemed like an eternity, he heard nothing. And then the rustle of clothing came, strained breathing. He inched forward.

The door stood open far enough for John-Henry to see into the room, and he registered some of the details instantaneously: the unmade bed, the dresser cluttered with the usual wallet and keys and loose change, the familiar smell of a space heater. Like the great room and the kitchen, this was a lived-in space—one of the few in the old Brey house. The sound of movement came again, then it stopped, and someone exhaled in frustration. John-Henry moved closer, tested the door for squeaky hinges, and then pushed. It swung open another handsbreadth.

Two men were on the bed, one straddling the other, and for a single moment, embarrassment washed over John-Henry. Then he took in the rest of the picture. Both men were fully dressed. Eric Brey sat propped against the headboard, a belt looped around his neck and between the headboard's spindles. His head hung loose on his neck, and he didn't appear to be breathing.

The other man wore dark jeans and a dark coat, and the coat rustled when he moved. John-Henry did the automatic catalogue: possibly Hispanic; dark hair buzzed; muscular but not big—a whipcord kind of strength. John-Henry guessed that if the man were standing, he'd probably be Auggie's height, maybe even a little shorter. The raised tissue of an old scar ran along the side of his neck.

With a satisfied noise, the man yanked the belt tight. Then he shimmied back until he was clear of Brey's body. He undid Brey's jeans and yanked them down to his ankles. Brey's peppermint-striped boxers went next. The man sat back on his heels, inspecting the picture. And then his whole body stiffened, and his head snapped toward the door.

Dark eyes locked with John-Henry's. Then he cut them to the left. The man didn't cry out. He didn't demand to know what John-Henry was doing there. He rolled off the bed, the movement liquid, and landed easily on his feet. Then he lunged toward something out of sight.

Instinct took over. John-Henry hit the door with his shoulder as he barreled into the room, and he was moving at full speed when he jumped. He caught the shorter man in a flying tackle, and they both went down. They hit the floor hard, the impact sending a shock through John-Henry's shoulder. It was like heat. Like a flower of heat opening inside his shoulder. A bad tackle, a small part of his brain thought. Coach would have his ass.

But those thoughts were happening in a far-off place as he rolled across the floor. The smaller man was trying to get free, twisting and bucking, and John-Henry grappled with him, trying to hold on. It was harder than he expected—the coat was some sort of synthetic, the material slipping out of his grip, and the man was strong. Much stronger than he looked. They crashed into the dresser, and something toppled. Glass broke. A sweet, citrus smell filled the air, and that far-off part of John-Henry's brain said, *Cologne*. When the man planted his feet and tried to rise, he dragged John-Henry into a sitting position.

That was when John-Henry saw the knife and gun resting on a chair near the door.

He only had a moment to process the threat before the man tried to headbutt him. John-Henry avoided a blow that would have broken his nose and, quite probably, left him unconscious, but only by letting go of the man's coat and dropping back. The man twisted like a snake, taking advantage of the sudden freedom to break toward the gun and knife.

John-Henry scissored his legs, trapping the man's ankles. The man's own momentum worked against him, and he crashed to the floor again. The whole house seemed to shake under the impact.

Seconds, John-Henry thought in that far-off place. It would be over in seconds, not minutes. He wasn't a brawler like Theo. He didn't know how to fight dirty like Jem. He lacked Emery's mass and strength.

But even as those thoughts spilled out, years of training, years of being a cop, were already activating: lines of defense going up inside his brain, conditioning taking over. You fight to win. That was the first and final rule of any engagement. You will win. They called it the winning mind. You fight until you win. The one who keeps fighting, the one who doesn't give up, that's the one who wins.

He crawled toward the smaller man, grabbing his leg, the waistband of his jeans, one flailing arm, and dragging him back. The smaller man must have given up on reaching the weapons, at least temporarily, because he flopped onto his back, obviously having decided he had to deal with John-Henry right then. But John-Henry had already closed the gap, and he was ready.

John-Henry's first punch caught the smaller man in the face, and his head rocked back and clipped the floor. John moved into the blow, following it up by clubbing the man on the side of the head, and then again. He stuck with his right hand; his left shoulder, where he'd fallen, was still a white-hot bloom of pain, and the most he could manage was to keep those fingers hooked in the smaller man's belt loop, securing him as John-Henry rained down blows. The smaller man's face was a mess of gore, and the third time his head rebounded from the old boards, John-Henry felt a flicker of hope.

Then, faster than John-Henry could believe, the man sat up, grabbed John-Henry in a bear hug, and rolled. They came down on the floor together again, and John-Henry let out a cry of pain when his shoulder took the fall. They rolled again. And again. Suddenly teeth were at John-Henry's throat, and animal instinct took over: panic. All he wanted to do was get away from those teeth, the sharp threat seeking his jugular. He threw an elbow with his good arm, twisted, whipped his head from side to side. The teeth withdrew, but too late, John-Henry realized he'd given his opponent exactly what he wanted: an opening. And then fingers were at his injured shoulder, as though the man had a sixth sense for weakness, biting down.

John-Henry's world exploded. He screamed. He couldn't fight; he couldn't think. But he thrashed, a frenzy of uncoordinated blows, and something must have connected because the pain stopped, and a choking, gurgling sound reached him from what seemed like a long way off.

Somehow, he scrambled to his feet. The smaller man was on his hands and knees, choking and gagging. John-Henry stumbled back. They'd gotten turned around. He was closest to the door now. The chair, where the gun and knife had been, had gotten knocked over in the fight, and the weapons had disappeared. Under the bed, maybe. Or under the dresser. Or—

The man spat blood and wiped his mouth on his coat sleeve. His head came up. His nose was broken, that much was obvious. Blood was caked around nostrils already beginning to swell. More blood ran around his mouth. It looked like a clown's heavy makeup, John-Henry thought. Like some grotesque lipstick.

"I'm going to cut your cock off and stuff it in your mouth," the man said. The words were hard, but he sounded younger than he looked. "That big fuck of a husband too. I'm going to leave you in your kids' beds. I'm going to let them find you. And tonight, before I kill you, I'm going to tell you everything I'm going to do to them before I finally, eventually, let them die."

John-Henry had heard a lot of hard men make threats. He'd heard a lot of bravado. A lot of bluster. And he'd heard the real thing, too. People who said what they meant. People who did things other people couldn't fathom. A matter-of-factness to the words. The conviction—

Cover and concealment.

The old cop part of his brain was still alive, still running tactics.

Decision, advantage, adapt.

Why talk? Why take the time to say anything unless—

The smaller man dropped to his belly, his hand shooting out toward something under the bed.

John-Henry ran.

A gunshot clapped behind him.

Cover, his brain said again. Concealment. Situational awareness. Situational awareness. What's around you, and how can you use it. What are the threats. What are the tactical advantages.

Those thoughts took place in a sub-layer of his brain, not even quite words, but a combination of instinct and training and the flash fires of adrenaline. His steps hammered on the wooden floorboards. His blood sang in his ear. He was distantly aware of the rest of his body: the breath whooshing in his lungs, the stinging citrus of that cologne lingering in his nostrils, the slow white scream of his shoulder.

Another gunshot rang out. Ahead of John-Henry, a piece of the railing at the top of the stairs blew apart. Splinters flew to strike the glass with a soft, rattling noise like rain. Steps came after him, and John-Henry risked a glance back. The smaller man sprinted down the hall, and if his injuries slowed him, John-Henry didn't see any sign of it.

He turned his attention forward and realized, with a flash of horror, how stupid he'd been. He was running full speed when he went off the top of the stairs. The old animal horror of falling made his stomach weightless. Then he came down, and it was luck as much as his natural athleticism that kept him upright even as the shock zinged from his heels up to his knees. One more stride carried him to the landing, and he swung around the switchback staircase to launch himself down the next flight. For a moment, he and the smaller man were facing each other. The man didn't break stride as he raised the gun to fire again, and John-Henry launched himself down the stairs. The shot cracked the air. The bullet must have come close; John-

Henry felt it like an angry whisper, the air so sharp it felt like it stung his cheek.

He hit the bottom of the stairs and tried to crank on the speed. He was in excellent condition. Better than most guys his age. Better, for that matter, than most guys ten years younger. But the smaller man looked like he could have been half John-Henry's age, at that time in his life when energy seemed endless, when the body rebounded from everything, when eye and hand were most tightly fused. If I can get to the car, John-Henry thought. If I can get to the car. He sucked in air as he sprinted toward the front of the house. Just get outside. Just get across the entry hall, open the door, get outside—

Situational awareness.

The rug.

At the last moment, John-Henry jumped. He'd never been a track kid, and running had always been a means to something else—kicking ass in football, at first, and then, as an adult, as a way of being a better police officer. Having Emery in his life had taken that to the next level. The decision happened between one footfall and the next, and John-Henry jumped. He cleared the rug, landed hard at the front door, and checked the wall with his bad shoulder. Pain moved the world back a few inches, but he kept moving. He managed to remember to keep his sleeve over his hand as he got the door open. A wordless shout came from behind him, and then the door jerked in his hand as though someone had kicked it. Gunfire thundered again.

But John-Henry threw the door open and darted outside. The wind was a knife against his cheeks. Frozen concrete and asphalt threatened to make him slip with every step. The branches were moving again, or maybe that was just the blood rushing in his ears. Half a block. He had to make it half a block out in the open, with the streetlights making him an easy target.

Even over the hammering of his blood, he heard the thud and cry from within Brey's house. The rug. He wanted to laugh, but something else was surging up inside him—the anger that he hadn't felt until now because he'd been too busy staying alive. Anger at this man who had tried to kill him. Anger at yet another dead end in the investigation. Anger—a thick, seeping black rage—at the universe, the world, this town for allowing this to happen to him. It ballooned inside him until it felt like it took up all the available space inside his body, until it felt so big that he didn't think he could breathe.

His hip bumped the Mustang as he fumbled the keys out of his pocket. He risked a glance. The man stood framed in Brey's doorway, looking up and down the street. The way he held himself suggested that when he'd fallen on the loose rug, it had been a bad one. Or maybe the blows that John-Henry had gotten in were finally catching up. Maybe both.

John-Henry wasn't going to wait around to find out. He got in the car, cut a sharp U-turn, and sped into the night.

13

The restaurant was called The Nifty Fifties, and from the road, it looked like the perfect spot: an hour away from Auburn on a state highway that, on an ordinary night, couldn't have seen more than a hundred cars. A lone security light in the parking lot sent a gleam warping along the plexiglass window and picked out the fuzzy algae growing on the side of the frame building. A handful of cars suggested other people, real people—which meant the Nifty Fifties felt like an oasis of light and warmth and normalcy in this nightmare.

John-Henry parked behind the restaurant, between an overflowing dumpster and a Port-a-Potty. At least it's winter, he thought. He tried not to imagine summer.

His hands were shaking so badly his finger missed the first time he tried to call Emery.

"Where are you?"

"Hi. I'm fine."

"Good. Where are you?"

In spite of himself, John-Henry smiled. "The Nifty Fifties."

Silence. Then, "Have you been drinking?"

"Not yet. It's the name of a restaurant out on—Jesus, I don't even remember. It's on the way to Auburn. I had to stop, so I just wanted you to know I was here. I'll be home, I don't know, in an hour or two."

"Why are you out there?"

John-Henry heard the real question, though. The one that Emery had already asked once: *Have you been drinking?*

Then Emery said, "Wait, Auburn?"

"It's a long story."

"What happened?"

"Well, I was going to tell you about that. It's more of an in-person conversation. As soon as I'm good to drive, I'll be home." John-Henry heard how that must have sounded, so he rushed to add, "I swear to God, I haven't had a drop. I'm just a little shaken up."

More of that silence. John-Henry could almost hear the calculations.

"Are you safe?"

"Yeah, of course."

"Are you hurt?"

"Nothing serious."

"Jesus fucking Christ."

"I know." John-Henry had to wet his lips; they were cracked, and they stung after his tongue passed over them. "I'm sorry."

"What the fuck are you sorry for?" Emery asked. "All you did was run off and nearly get yourself killed."

The call disconnected.

John-Henry let his head fall back. The adrenaline rush from the fight was fading, and in the aftermath, his body was exhausted, and the shakes were only part of it. He felt sick to his stomach, his skin clammy. Moments from the fight flashed at him: that first, bad tumble; pain flowering in his shoulder; the realization that he might lose this fight, and the struggle to hold on to the belief that he could win.

He tried to steer his thoughts onto new tracks. He was too tired to process Emery's anger, and anyway, even if he hadn't been, he was too angry himself for it to have much of an impact. Angry at himself. For the childlike outburst. For how quickly it had escalated into a fight, when he and Emery had been doing so much better. For the fact that he couldn't explain, not in any coherent way—couldn't even put into words—why it felt so important to pull Colt and put him into another school. Because they did it to you. That was part of it. Because they're doing it to me. That was part of it too. Because they'll do it to him, and it doesn't matter what we say or do, we can't protect him from that. That was part of it as well. But it was so much more. It was this newfound sense of helplessness. And it was the anger.

The anger ran so deep. The injustice of it all. The unfairness of it. He could hear the childlike petulance of his thoughts. And he summoned the old mantra: *I will not be that boy. I will be who I want to be.* For a long time, willpower had been enough. He had resolved not to be what his parents wanted him to be: entitled, selfish, spoiled in the truest sense of the word—his emotional maturity forever stunted, his capacity for love and compassion and understanding ruined, and ultimately, his independence and personhood and individuality crippled. It had taken him a long time to put into words why he had thrown away what his parents and so many other people had considered a perfect life, but he had understood even as a teenager, in a way below words, that he was being poisoned. That he was, in fact, poisoning himself. And it was making him sick, even though he couldn't have told anyone the particular symptoms, or explained what was wrong, or what he wanted to be different. He only knew that there was something different out there. Something more. He had tasted it that night on the football field, the stadium lights like mercury on his face.

So: BJs with his dormmate; the police academy instead of law school; then Emery; and then coming out, whatever that meant at his age, when you were already spending twenty-three-hours a day with the person you loved most in the world. And all of it had cost him something; he wasn't a fool, and he wasn't blind. He'd known every time he broke the rules that he was going to pay for it. But the price had always been worth it because what he got in exchange had been so much better. He'd learned to be responsible, to think for himself, to choose kindness and integrity over importance and celebrity, to be himself. That last most of all. With Emery, in a way that might not have been possible with anyone else, he could be himself. Goofy. Smart. Messed-up.

But this—this wasn't the same. This was someone hacking at the foundations of his life, and all the resolve John-Henry had mustered in the past was crumbling. Because it wasn't fair. Because he was a good person, and he deserved a good life, and the price he was being asked to pay didn't lead to a better, more enriching life. It led only to—what? He couldn't picture it, refused to let himself. He closed his eyes. He thought of how the night had rippled outside Brey's house, the whole world shuddering, the clack of the branches like dry bones.

He must have dozed because the rap on the window made him jolt upright in the seat. The distant security light was still enough for him to make out a familiar silhouette.

"Ree?"

In answer, Emery tried the door. It was locked, and John-Henry, still waking up and not quite sure if this was a dream, fumbled to unlock it. Emery opened the door on the next try and crouched so they were at eye level. Then he pulled out a flashlight and shone it in John-Henry's face.

"What is happening right now?" John-Henry asked, shielding his eyes with one hand.

"I'm inspecting you." Emery took John-Henry's free hand. It jostled his injured shoulder, and John-Henry hissed. Emery passed over the flashlight and directed John-Henry to hold it steady as he palpated John-Henry's hand. "Who?"

"I don't know his name."

Emery grunted. He must have been satisfied with whatever he found because he released John-Henry's hand, and the movement made John-Henry gasp again. Emery's dark brows drew together. "What?"

"It's—"

Emery didn't wait for the answer. He got hold of John-Henry, turned him in the seat, and began pressing on his shoulder.

"Jesus Christ!"

"Don't be a baby."

"Ah, shit, Ree! I think I separated my shoulder. What are you doing?"

"I'm sublimating my rage by determining the extent of your injuries."

"Oh good, because for a minute there I thought maybe you were torturing—" He cut off with a wordless shout. His eyes watered.

Emery released him with another of those wordless grunts. It was, to be fair, almost a shove, the force of the release rocking John-Henry in the seat. Emery took back the flashlight and shone it in John-Henry's face again. The reek of the Port-a-Potty filtered through the night—faint because the air was too cold to carry the smell, but even a whiff was unmistakable.

"Describe him."

John-Henry held his hand up again to block the light. "No."

"Excuse me?"

"This isn't an interrogation. And I'm thrilled to learn you've found a new way to avoid dealing with your feelings, but I'm tired, and I'm hurt, and I don't want to fight with you tonight. So, knock it off. I need my husband right now, not the ex-cop out for revenge."

The sound of tires on asphalt came from a long way off. The security light hummed.

"Sublimation isn't necessarily an unhealthy way of dealing with strong emotions."

"Jesus Christ."

"Would you prefer I went with my first option?"

John-Henry grinned even though he knew he shouldn't. "Frying pan through the wall?"

"Tire iron to the Mustang. Extensively."

"Ah. No, I wouldn't prefer that."

"Then show some fucking gratitude for that *Psychology Today* article I read."

It was hard to tell in the dark, hard to tell with that hard, uninflected voice. But John-Henry thought if the light were a little better, he'd see one of those tiny, Emery Hazard smiles. A moment later, Emery's hand cupped the side of his face. John-Henry leaned into the touch. Then, swinging his legs out of the car, he moved to lean against Emery, his face pressed into his side. Emery's hand slid around to cradle the back of his head. He was warm and solid and real, and he smelled like the ridiculous body spray Colt had gotten him for Christmas, and his fingers worked against the back of John-Henry's head in silent expression of all the pain and fear he was struggling to master.

John-Henry pulled back. He got out of the car, stood, and met Emery's eyes. "I'm sorry."

"I'm sorry too."

"I don't feel like that conversation about Colt is resolved, but I'd like to finish it another time."

Maybe it was the change in position, giving him a better look at his husband, but this time John-Henry could make out the almost invisible smile. "Like not standing near a plastic bucket full of frozen human waste?"

"That would be ideal. And another time like when I'm not—not so worked up."

"I think that's reasonable."

"I shouldn't have run off."

"You're allowed to need time and space to yourself."

"Yeah, but—wait, why are you being so nice?"

"I'm always nice." Before John-Henry had to reply to that, Emery added, "Also, you requested your husband, who is loving and supportive. I'll tell you later, at length, what the non-husband part of me thinks about your decisions."

"Shouldn't all of you be my husband? Like, a hundred percent of you?"

"That would be ideal, wouldn't it?"

A car door closed, and voices rang out in the night.

"I'm not saying you can't talk about penises however much you want and with whatever language you want. Dongs. Dingalings. Dingos. Dorks. Prongs. Puds. Prawns."

That, of course, was Shaw.

North said, "Nobody has ever called it a prawn, dumbass."

"Really? It kind of looks like one. Especially when yours gets really red—"

"It doesn't look like a prawn! It doesn't look like any kind of shellfish!"

"Well, not to argue, but it does. And anyway, that's not really the point. The point is that when you use words like sausage to talk about, er, dingalings, you're participating in the long Western tradition that values and prioritizes the production and consumption of meat, which is intrinsically tied to the inhumane treatment of innocent animals."

"So, what? I can't call them sausages without being part of Big Meat?"

"Well, ideally, I'd like you not to refer to them as any kind of particle meat. Hot dog. Bratwurst. Weisswurst. Leberwurst. Any kind of wurst at all, actually—North, no!"

Shaw's outcry came moments before a loud crash.

"All that talk about leberwurst," North said contemplatively, "but you really should have been watching where you were walking."

Shaw started up again almost immediately, but John-Henry tuned him out. It was hard to tell in the shadows, but he thought Emery might be blushing.

"It's that stupid car," Emery said. "He insisted on racing me."

More car doors slammed shut.

"But you'd look so handsome," Jem said.

"I wouldn't feel handsome," Tean said. "I'd feel like I was participating in cultural appropriation."

"What culture?"

Tean's hesitation lasted a moment too long. "*Saved by the Bell*?"

"Oh my God! You weren't even listening to me?"

Emery rubbed his eyes. "Don't say anything." He was quiet for a moment and then, his voice verging on despair, he said, "They're never going to leave, so we're just going to have to move. That's our only option at this point."

The bell on the restaurant's door jingled, and the voices cut off.

"Theo and Auggie?"

"With Evie, Lana, and Colt."

John-Henry considered the situation for a moment. It was one thing that Emery had driven out here to find him—admittedly, yes, in part to pick a fight, but mostly because he was worried. It was something else entirely for the other guys to come too, and the rush of emotion left him struggling to speak for a moment. Finally he managed, "I guess we're going inside."

"Do we have to?"

When they stepped inside, the first thing out of Emery's mouth was "You've got to be fucking kidding me."

John-Henry almost didn't hear the words. Part of that was the music—an Elvis song played at eardrum-shattering volume. And part of it was the sensory overload. The air was warm, smelling like fried onions with an undernote of sour yeastiness. Instead of ceiling lights, the restaurant was only dimly lit by wall sconces shaped like old convertibles painted a light green blue. The tables and booths were covered in vinyl checkerboard tablecloths, and although distance made it hard to be sure, John-Henry was fairly sure the salt and pepper shakers were meant to look like Dwight and Mamie Eisenhower.

A woman with a shag of shoe-polish-black hair swept toward them, laminated menus in her arm, but then North stood from behind a pony wall and waved at them. John-Henry smiled at the waitress, pointed, and started across the room.

The four men sat at a round table. Shaw had laid the salt and pepper shakers on the table and was trying to look inside Dwight Eisenhower's head. As John-Henry and Emery sat, Emery opened his mouth, but North spoke first.

"Don't get me started. I've already had to listen to donkey-tits here tell me he had a dream about this place."

"A sex dream," Shaw corrected and then added, "And don't say tits."

"I had a sex dream too," Jem said, struggling with a grin.

"No," Tean said, "he didn't."

"Oh, did it have that guy from *I Dream of Jeannie*?" Shaw asked, his inspection of Dwight Eisenhower forgotten as he straightened in his seat. "The equestrian? He used his spurs on Tony, and Tony was screaming and screaming, but you could tell he liked it?"

North threw up his hands "It's been four months. Four fucking months. And every fucking time, every fucking one of you makes it so fucking easy for him."

"I don't know what you're talking about," Jem said, the grin slipping free now.

"Yes, he does," Tean said.

"Nobody ever knows what North is talking about," Shaw said, beginning his inspection of Mamie now. "Cheese this, boots that. It's exhausting."

"You don't know what I'm talking about? Really? Because you seemed to understand really fucking clearly when I said we should go to bed early—"

"John-Henry," Tean said, "why don't you—"

"Because that was part of my sex dream," Shaw said. "Of course I understood it."

Even in the restaurant's dim light, John-Henry could tell North had gone a murderous shade of red. Before North could respond, he said, "I need to tell you about tonight."

"Hold on," Jem said as he took out his phone.

North groaned. "You were serious?"

"Auggie made him promise," Tean said, half-apology, half-defense. "And they deserve to know what's going on."

Jem placed the call, and a moment later, Auggie's voice came over the speaker. "Yo, yo, yo! Auggie in the house!"

Silence, except for Elvis in the background. He was singing about just what, exactly, made his whole kissin' cousin situation alright.

"What the fuck was that?" Emery asked.

"I was joking!"

"See, even when he's literally pocket sized," North said, "he's absolutely fucking unbearable."

"I thought it was cool, Auggie," Tean said. "You sounded like Arsenio Hall."

Theo's laugh came across the line. It went on and on until it cut off with a muffled grunt.

"I don't know who that is," Auggie said when he came back on the call.

Emery opened his mouth.

"And don't tell me! You know this is a curse, right? People my age think I'm cool."

"People your age," North said. "He's a couple of years younger, and he acts like he's a Gen Z sex doll."

"I think you're cool," Shaw said absently as he positioned the Eisenhowers in various poses of carnal knowledge. "Just like Casino Hall."

"Definitely like that," Jem said, nodding vigorously.

Tean muttered something that sounded threatening, and it only made Jem's grin bigger.

"John-Henry?" Theo said. "Before I have to put the children to bed, please? And I mean all the children."

Another grunt came across the line.

Before John-Henry could begin, though, the waitress with the shoe-polish hair came over. She took their orders, which included a four-and-a-half-minute fight between North and Shaw about the morality of cheese on a cheeseburger, and Jem, meanwhile, asking the woman about everyone in every picture hung on the walls. Every single one of them. When the waitress finally left, Emery had a tiny tic near the corner of his eye.

"A lot has happened tonight," John-Henry said before anyone could get started again. And then he told them about arriving at Brey's house, the door that wouldn't latch, and finding the man upstairs.

"What did he look like?" Emery interrupted.

"Around Auggie's height. Muscular. Dark hair, but he had it buzzed."

"Oh," North said, "so, like a walking jizz stain. Got it."

"It's not fair when I'm not there," Auggie said. "Because I can't beat him up."

"Hold your water, sweet cheeks."

"He does have sweet cheeks, doesn't he?" Shaw asked. "Very pert."

Emery, though, had fixed a look on John-Henry. "Did he have a scar?"

"On his neck, yeah. Wait, how did you know that?"

Grimacing, Emery took out his phone. It took him a moment to bring up the video, and then it began to play. John-Henry recognized the scene: it was part of the Wahredua police station, in the bullpen outside his office. The man he had fought earlier that evening was standing in front of the office, grinning up at the camera as he flipped them off.

"What is this? And how did you get it?"

"I have a source," Emery said. "It's probably better if you don't know."

"So, Gray. But how did you—" His gaze slid to Jem, who shrugged, face bland, and buffed his nails on his sweater—brown-and-gray squares in a geometric pattern, obviously from the '90s grunge collection. "Ok. How many laws did you break?"

"I didn't break any laws," Jem said with a trace of outrage. "That would have been cheating."

John-Henry looked at his husband.

"You're missing the point," Emery said. "This man planted that evidence on your computer. He murdered Eric Brey tonight. We're getting closer, John."

"Let me see." North took the phone and frowned at it. He took a screenshot, opened the messages, and typed something out.

"That's my phone," Emery said.

"I know."

The sound of a message being sent came. Then it came again. And then North passed Emery's phone to Jem.

"Got it," Auggie said.

Face bright, Shaw held up his phone. "Me too. And I love you too, Emery. Thank you for taking the time to send me such a thoughtful message."

"I didn't. My phone, please."

Jem shook his head. "I don't recognize him."

"I do," Auggie said, his voice tight with excitement. "When Theo and I went to the Cottonmouth Club, he was there. Remember how I told you about Gid realizing he'd said too much? Well, he went over and talked to this guy, and it was him. This guy you got on camera, I mean."

"There it is," Emery said to himself, voice low and satisfied.

Theo said something too quiet for the microphone to pick up, and something rustled on the other end of the call. Then he said, "Jem, he's about the right size, don't you think?"

Jem stared at the phone. "Oh shit."

"The right size for what?" John-Henry asked.

"It could be him," Tean said. "The man who broke into Theo and Auggie's home."

"It is him," Jem said.

"How could you possibly know that?" Emery asked.

"I don't know, but I'd bet you a gajillion dollars it's him. He's got the right look, and—" Jem's head came up. "You said you guys got into it tonight?"

John-Henry nodded.

"Was he good?"

He nodded again. And then, reluctantly, he added, "Better than me."

North snorted. "That's because you're a cop."

"Excuse me?" Emery asked.

"North probably forgot you used to be a cop too," Shaw said.

"Yeah, that was it. I forgot." He plucked the phone from Jem and gave it a closer examination. Finally, he grunted. "It could be him."

"Let me look."

"What are you going to see? You were buried under flaming rubble."

"Oh, North, that could be the title of our sex tape!"

"Sounds appropriate," Emery muttered. He took back his phone and considered the man on the screen. "This is the guy who gave all of you so much trouble?"

"Fuck off," North said.

Theo said, "Really, Emery?"

Auggie booed.

"I would have been fine if I'd had a gun," Jem said.

"Obviously," Emery said. "Anyone would have been fine if they'd had a gun."

"Yeah?" North said. "You try facing down a maniac with a scythe and see how calm and collected you are."

"It wasn't a scythe."

"I was there. I think I know a fucking scythe when I see one."

"Apparently you don't, since a scythe, by its design, has a handle anywhere from four to five and a half feet long."

"Oh!" Shaw said. "Cheese curds!"

John-Henry opened his mouth to ask what he meant—or, more likely, to ask him to be quiet—but this time, Shaw wasn't hallucinating or tripping or under the influence of any kind of psychedelic, because at that moment the waitress set a basket of cheese curds on the table. North dragged them toward him, shielding them with one arm and giving Jem, of all people, a dirty look. Once everyone had their food and drinks, the waitress retreated again, and everyone began to eat.

John-Henry discovered he had ordered a burger—he barely even remembered looking at the menu, and he didn't feel particularly hungry. He took a bite, though, and was instantly ravenous. The burger was juicy, the cheese sharp and perfectly melted, and some genius had buttered and toasted the bun. He forced himself to slow down when he realized he'd already pounded half the burger, and he grabbed a napkin to clean his face and hands.

"The point," he said after a drink of Pepsi, "is this guy is dangerous, whoever he is. North's not wrong; I know how to handle myself well enough, but this guy's in another league."

"He's not just in another league," Jem said in a subdued voice. "He's unreal. It's like he lives for this stuff. I swear to God, he enjoyed it."

North paused with a cheese curd halfway to his mouth, made a face, and nodded.

"And fearless," Theo said. He sounded thoughtful. "He didn't hesitate, didn't slow down. Part of that is training. But part of that is being totally uninhibited. It's an advantage."

What he didn't say was what John-Henry was thinking: an advantage the rest of them didn't have, because they had people they loved, people depending on them, and having something to lose meant a reason to be afraid.

"It's an advantage until it isn't," Emery said. "He's already gotten overconfident. He wasn't wearing his cat-burglar getup tonight, was he? And John saw him and lived to tell about it."

"Because I ran away. Let's be real about that."

"Jem and I couldn't take him down together," Theo said. "John-Henry, he was winning until Tean saved us."

Tean blushed and bent his head over his food.

Shaw elbowed North.

It seemed to cost North to say, "This guy's good."

"Plus he beat North up," Shaw said.

"He didn't beat me up, you badgerfucker. It was a draw."

"It didn't look like a draw. It looked like he was about to kill you, and you were trying to run away, only you couldn't run away, and possibly it was because of those boots. Only then I saved you because I shot him."

"You didn't shoot him. You shot at him. And you missed, by the way."

"He's already made mistakes," Emery said again. "He'll make one again."

"I think we made a mistake," Tean said. He looked up from his food, brow furrowed. "I think we were wrong."

Emery opened his mouth, and then chagrin filled his face. "God damn it."

"Wrong about what?" Auggie asked.

"About what's happening," Tean said. "About what these people want, or what they're doing, or however you want to say it."

John-Henry picked up his burger and put it down again. His hands felt greasy, and he fought the urge to wipe them on his jeans. "What do you mean?"

"He means," Emery said, "that what we saw at the meth lab doesn't line up with what happened tonight. It made sense at the time to believe that Vermilya had some sort of connection to the criminal organization working out of the Cottonmouth Club, which explained why he put himself forward as a witness to testify against you, John. And it made sense to believe that he was either a liability or that he had done something stupid, and in the process, the shooting had begun."

"But it doesn't explain why someone would kill this guy Brey," Jem said.

The burger turned, greasy and heavy, in John-Henry's stomach. "It wasn't just about framing me or about getting rid of Vermilya. Somebody's cleaning house."

"Why?" Shaw asked.

Emery shook his head. "That's an excellent question."

"So, who is it? This little rug rat who likes to dress in black?" North frowned. "I don't know. He's definitely the muscle behind this operation, but who's running things?"

"Cassidy?" Theo asked.

Emery blew out an amused breath. "Cassidy would be flattered, but no, he's not smart enough to pull off something like this—certainly not to this degree of sophistication. Although he must be involved at some level, even if he's simply being paid to turn a blind eye."

"What about this guy Vermilya?" Jem asked. "Somebody tried to kill him, and I bet they'll try to finish the job. Don't you think he'd be ready to talk?"

"He's still in the hospital in Columbia, as far as I know," Emery said, "and good luck getting past the police who are guarding him."

"I bet the IRS could get past them," Jem said. "They're probably dying to talk to him about that totally bogus anti-trafficking organization."

"It's fake?" John-Henry said.

Tean nodded. "There's no nonprofit—well, no business entity at all—registered under that name. And when Jem tracked down some of the donors, they ranged from confused to pissed. Some of them had legitimately donated money and then never heard anything else. Others just wanted to talk about identity theft."

"I knew there was something weird about this guy," Auggie said. "I spent all day trying to dig up something on Jace Vermilya. He's a very pretty cardboard cutout, but he's not a real person."

"What does that mean?" Tean asked. "He's got a stolen identity?"

"I'd say pretty much definitely. His socials are carefully curated. His web presence too. At first glance, it looks like there's a lot—the kind of stuff you'd see if you were digging into a real person's life. It probably holds up pretty well, even to moderate scrutiny. But it's too controlled, too...limited, I guess you could say. His history only goes back a few years. Where was he before that?"

"We've run into something like that before," North said with a glance at Shaw. "I think Lil' Bits is right."

"Still don't love that nickname."

That made North smile, but it faded as he continued, "This guy is bogus. Shaw and I checked out his place, and it's—it's like Lil' Bits said. It looks like a real person lives there. Hell, a real person does live there. But it's like he's in a hotel, or something. Nothing that's truly personal. No clutter. None of the junk people collect, like your boyfriend's boxes and boxes of 'art'—" He drew the air quotes with his fingers. "—and more boxes and boxes of 'dildos'."

"Why did you put dildos in air quotes?" Jem asked.

"Come over sometime," North said in a dead voice. "Take a look."

"It's important to represent the full spectrum of penises," Shaw said.

"Where does the one that looks like a jellyfish fall on the spectrum?"

"Oh, that's a great question for Tean—"

"I don't know," Tean blurted.

"I bet he actually does know," Jem said. "I'll ask him later."

"Vermilya is out of reach for right now," John-Henry said. He glanced at Emery. "If Emery's source is able to ask him some questions, that might be an option, but even that seems like a stretch."

"God damn it." North spun the empty paper tray that had held his cheese curds. "What are we talking about, then? Another dead end?"

"Did you get anything from Brey?" Tean asked. "His wallet or phone or laptop?"

"What about a car you could connect to the killer?" Jem asked.

"Security cameras on the other houses?" Theo said. "Maybe a neighbor saw something?"

"The last thing we want is a neighbor with a camera," Emery said. "John was in that house. And sooner or later, the police are going to learn Brey is dead, and they're going to start asking questions."

"His phone," John-Henry said. The memory seemed like a half-formed thing: the phone at the bottom of the stairs, buzzing as the screen lit up. Like it had fallen there. "I think he must have tried to call someone. Maybe he did call someone. Brey, I mean. It looked like he'd either dropped his phone or had it taken from him."

Shaw glanced at North.

"God fucking damn it," North said as he took out his phone. "Do I have to do everything?"

As North put the phone to his ear, his face souring, Shaw said, "I could have done it, but it's good for his self-confidence—"

North pinched him, and Shaw squealed. Then North spoke into the phone. "Hey, Park. No, that must have been on your end."

John-Henry hid a smile as Shaw massaged his arm. A few months before, while pursuing an escaped killer, North and Shaw had bumped into an old friend who happened to be working for Eric Brey's re-election campaign. Parker Rhodes had helped them once, and it looked like North was willing to try again.

"Listen, I need a favor: can you still get on Eric's computer? Uh huh. Uh huh. I'm actually still with Shaw, Parker. That's not why I called. Yes, I did call you because I wanted to make you drive across town in the freezing cold in the middle of the—his phone records. Because he's a shady shit and something bad is going down. Is that good enough for you?" North grinned. "Yeah, you sneaky fuck. That'd be fine." He lowered the phone long enough to say to the men at the table, "He can access his phone records from home, so he's checking them now."

"How can he access them from home?" Emery asked.

"Brey gave him access to his computer at the campaign office. It looks like Parker got bored and started snooping." North raised the phone to his ear again and said, "Uh huh. Uh huh. You're sure? He didn't make any other calls? Got it. You're a lifesaver. Yes, Park, I'm sure I'm still with Shaw. I've got to go." Dropping the phone on the table, North said, "He called 911 at four-fifty-seven today, and the call lasted three minutes."

"Jesus," Theo said.

"So, what happened?" Jem asked. "Where were the cops?"

"Excellent question," Emery said.

John-Henry shook his head. "I didn't see anyone. And I got to the house, I don't know, less than half an hour after that call. It's possible a patrol car came and did a walk-around, but—"

"But it's also possible they didn't."

Shaw pushed some of the lettuce around in his salad. "You think Chief Cassidy helped?"

"It certainly looks that way."

"Good luck proving it." Jem sat back, arms folded across his chest. "What are you going to do? Ask him, 'Hey, Chief, did you let Eric Brey get murdered? Ok, thanks.'"

"Do you find it helpful to be facetious?" Emery asked.

Jem grinned. "I mean, it doesn't hurt."

"But let's say someone did get that call-out," Tean said, "and went out and checked the house, and they didn't see anything, and then Brey was murdered. If Cassidy didn't have something to do with his death, do you think he's in danger too? If our theory is right, I mean, and someone is—how did you put it? Cleaning house?"

"Someone might kill Jonas Cassidy," Emery said. "What a shame."

"Do you find it helpful to be facetious?" Jem asked.

"Not at all. But it is, occasionally, tremendously satisfying."

"Why don't you ask?" Shaw said.

"For some reason, I doubt Jonas is eager to tell us if he was an accomplice to murder."

"Not Cassidy. I mean, not that Cassidy. Because North's middle name—"

"Then what the fuck did you mean?" North asked.

"The dispatcher."

No one said anything.

"I mean, someone had to answer that call," John-Henry said slowly. "But they've probably got a few people who do that job, and we don't know who they are or which one was on tonight."

"Give me a minute," Jem said, pushing back from the table. He took out a phone and tapped furiously at the screen as he walked away.

"What's he doing?" Theo asked.

"Being a squeaky-assed sneak," North said. A hint of color came into his cheeks, and he mumbled toward Tean, "No offense."

Tean smiled, eyes bright behind his glasses. "Actually, I think he'd love that."

"What does that even mean?" Shaw asked. "The squeaky-assed part?"

Fortunately, the waitress came back, preventing North from explaining. She began the process of handing out the check holders and collecting dishes. John-Henry was surprised to realize that, at some point in the conversation, he'd finished his meal. He was warm. He was full of greasy carbs. And he was exhausted.

"These are Chevy Bel Airs," North said, reaching up to tap one of the wall sconces. "Jesus Christ, they even got the color right. Somebody has a serious boner for the 1950s."

"I think that's fairly common," Tean said. "Lots of people are nostalgic for the post-war years. It's ironic because very few of them are the ones who actually lived through that period." He ducked his head. "Sorry. That sounded pretentious."

"It's also ironic," Theo said, "because the 1950s weren't all that ideal. There were so many problems. So much displacement and social upheaval. It's just that people have this memory of that time—only it's not even a memory because they didn't live through it, like you said. It's a mélange of cultural icons that have shaped how people think about that time. TV shows, in particular, make it seem idyllic."

"Now that sounded pretentious," North said. "Lil' Bits, can't you give him something else to do with his mouth?"

Shaw said something about how little the bits were, and Auggie, laughing, tried to defend himself, but John-Henry barely heard it. He looked at the Chevy Bel Air wall sconces, the fan of yellow light above them, the checkerboard tablecloths, the salt and pepper shakers. Elvis was still crooning in the background, but now it was about a dream—much less disturbing than the kissin' cousins song. He thought about that day in the locker room, the ridge of Emery's shoulder under his hand, the sensation that his skin was like paper and his hand was a match. The stadium lights against his face so strong that he thought he could feel their weight. On and on like that. We all do it, he thought through the haze of fatigue. We all find a place and a time, and we tell ourselves that, at least in some ways, things were better.

"John?" Emery asked in a low voice.

"Because how's he going to measure it, numbnuts," North was shouting at Shaw, "with a fucking electron microscope?"

Rising out of his seat, voice triumphant, Shaw shouted back, "That doesn't make any sense because you don't measure anything with an electron microscope! You look at it!"

"Braxton Campbell," Jem said as he dropped into his seat.

The argument cut off.

"On it," Auggie said.

"Tell me what you said," Emery said, "and explain why it was effective."

Jem smirked.

"I'm waiting."

"It really wasn't anything," Jem said. "Just a little, you know, razzle dazzle."

"That doesn't make any sense."

"He's teasing you," John-Henry said, putting a hand on Emery's arm.

"Got him," Auggie said. "He's—oh, he's cute."

"Excuse me?" Theo said.

"Just, you know, objectively."

Silence.

"Obviously he's way too young for me."

"Was that supposed to be a save?"

North cleared his throat. "While we're all enjoying front-row seats to the cuck-fest currently happening, maybe Pint Size could grace us with some more information before Daddy sends him to bed?"

"Uh, he lives in Auburn, and it looks like he has a sailboat."

"Does he prefer beach vacations or mountains? What color are his eyes?"

"Go ahead, Auggie," Theo said. "What color are his eyes?"

"You know what?" Auggie said. "I'll send you guys some screenshots." A moment later, phones around the table began to buzz. "On Instagram, he's got a post practically every day of him working on his boat, and he geotagged the storage facility. Oh look, his dinghy!"

"Let me see," Shaw said.

"Not that kind of dinghy," North snapped. "Wait, Ponyboy, is it that kind of dinghy?"

"His boat!"

"I'm going to hang up now," Theo said, "unless you need anything else before I murder my fiancé."

"Thanks, Theo," John-Henry said. "Thank you, Auggie."

"We can dig up a home address," North offered.

"Oh, Tean and I can snoop," Jem offered.

"No, we can't," Tean said. "Last time, you pushed me into that closet, and a bra almost jugulated me."

"But the important part of that sentence is almost."

"The important part of that sentence is bra," Emery said. "What the hell kind of bra was it?"

"Uh—"

"Bralette? Strapless? Bustier?"

"What's the one that had the secret Illuminati message in *The Da Vinci Code*?" Shaw asked.

North set his jaw and looked at Jem. "Go ahead. Open the fucking door for him."

Jem laughed so hard he almost slid out of his chair.

In a matter of minutes, they were all headed out into the night, the cold popping against John-Henry's cheeks as he stepped out of the restaurant. North, Shaw, Tean, and Jem crossed the lot toward their parked cars. Jem was asking about a wizard's eye while Shaw quivered with his eagerness to answer, and North looked like one of those cartoon characters with steam about to come out of their ears.

Emery lingered by the door. The lone security light threw stark shadows across his face. One scarecrow eye glittered in a ribbon of light. He took John-Henry's hand. "Are you ok to drive?"

John-Henry nodded. The night fell still as the other men got into their cars and conversations cut off, and for a moment, he almost knew what he wanted to say. Then North started his car, the engine roaring, and the moment broke.

"I'll follow you home," Emery said.

He walked John-Henry to his car. He shut the door for him like it was the end of a date, and suddenly, for some reason, John-Henry wanted to cry. He drove home, thinking about wall sconces shaped like Chevy Bel Airs and Dwight and Mamie Eisenhower and a boy who had trembled under his touch. The night was a long, dark tunnel through the ice.

14

When they arrived at Auburn's small harbor the next afternoon, the day was overcast, and the light was a dirty yellow that made the clouds look like cigarette smoke, but Emery felt like a new man. Part of that was the night's sleep. And part of that was knowing that his daughter was safe with her mother, and his son was safe with Ashley's parents (who were under strict orders not to let the boys share a room), and his husband looked—well, like John again. The color was back in his cheeks. His eyes were no longer bloodshot. He'd slept almost twelve hours, and then, while Emery worked from home during the day—making phone calls, primarily, trying to turn up anything he could on Vermilya or the other recent victims—John had napped another handful of hours. The only interruption had been a phone call from John's lawyer, Aniya Thompson, who had informed them of Brey's death and suggested, in a roundabout way, that various law enforcement agencies would be asking where they had been the night before.

Now, as they parked in the harbor's small lot, John could have been any other man in this part of the world: his mussed hair tucked under a Cardinals cap, a dark coat, dark jeans, Adidas. Then Emery reassessed that statement; his husband was simply too attractive to pass for anyone else.

John checked the sky, which was already darkening, and frowned. "We should have come earlier."

"He would have been sleeping, John. He works second shift."

"We could have asked around about him. Found out what people knew."

"If we need to, we will."

"You didn't have to spend all day pretending to make phone calls so I could sleep."

"Do you feel the pressing need for an argument?"

John's grin was quicksilver. "You know what? I don't."

"Fantastic."

They followed the boardwalk past the marina shop, toward a storage facility at the end of the harbor. Ice crusted the rocks along the shore, glinted on ropes and pilings, and had been trampled into a dull, compact layer on the docks. A breeze stirred the gray water into shark's teeth, disturbing the petroleum sheen left by fuel and motor oil. It sent an old Dairy Queen cup bobbing toward the shore. That same breeze, when it reached land, cut through Emery's coat as though it weren't there, and he pushed his fists deeper into his pockets.

He hadn't spent much time in harbors and marinas; most of what he knew, he knew from reading. Only a few boats bobbed in the water. The majority would be drydocked until the spring. The marina shop flew a miserable-looking American flag, its windows crowded with fishing poles. A single orange-and-black sign said WE RENT. They passed a fish-cleaning station, and Emery caught a whiff of the reek and was grateful for winter. Farther down—past the storage facility—he could see the fuel pumps, and next to them, a pile of life jackets under a skin of ice.

The storage facility was a post-frame building with steel panels for walls and an orange metal roof. A ramp led down into the harbor, presumably for people who needed or preferred to load and unload their boats here. John took the lead, heading toward a service door set into the side of the building. When he tried it, the handle didn't turn, but he gave it a tug and it opened. Someone had taped the latch to keep it from setting—the small-town preference for convenience over security.

Inside, the air was warmer, and the steel panels made a soft humming sound as they caught the wind. Fluorescent panels provided steady light. They began their search. The layout of the structure was straightforward enough: it had been built in a U, with the shortest side facing the harbor. On either side of the hallway were storage units that could be accessed through roll-up doors. Occasionally, one of the doors had been left standing open to expose a vacant unit. Each unit, Emery discovered, had a second door that connected directly to the outside of the building. It made sense, he decided, for a facility designed to store boats—once the boat was on a trailer, it could be moved directly into one of the units.

They heard the music first—pop that, as they grew closer, resolved into what sounded like Harry Styles. Then a long scraping noise came, followed by a soft swish-swish. They followed the sounds until they stood outside one of the roll-up doors. Light showed in the gaps, now they could hear singing along with the music.

"He sounds like a cat in heat," Emery said.

John grinned and rapped on the door. The metal shivered, and the singing cut off. A moment later, the music quieted, and a man said, "Uh, hello?"

"Braxton Campbell?"

The pause was longer this time. "Can I help you?"

"We were hoping you had a minute to talk."

Often, it was enough to leave it at that—most people were accommodating, to greater or lesser degrees, and even more so, most people were curious. Sure enough, the latch drew back, and the door rattled up.

Braxton Campbell was a nice-looking kid, solidly built, with tousled brown hair that was a little too long in back like he'd missed a haircut. A pencil was stuck behind one ear. He wore an insulated winter jacket and work pants with waterproof leather boots, and although the gear all looked quality—and, therefore, expensive—it also looked well worn. In one hand, he held what looked to Emery like a putty knife. The other hand opened and closed restlessly against one leg.

"Hey," John said, smiling again as he extended a hand. "John-Henry Somerset."

Braxton fumbled the putty knife to his other hand, dried his fingers, and clasped John's. He smiled as they shook—that was a natural response, Emery had found, to interacting with John. "Braxton, but I guess you already knew that."

"Well, more like I was hoping. This is Emery."

Braxton wanted to shake again, so Emery obliged. The young man's hand was callused—not soft and smooth like what Emery would expect from someone who did a night shift on dispatch. But then again, he liked to sail, and even though it was winter, his skin held a trace of color that suggested plenty of time outdoors.

"Sorry," Braxton said, jerking his head behind him. "Do you want to come in? We're letting the heat out."

Emery followed John into the unit, and Braxton lowered the door. True to his word, it was warmer inside—a space heater in the corner raised the temperature until it was almost comfortable. It made a soft hissing noise and left a hint of kerosene in the air. The only light came from several bare bulbs hanging overhead, but they brightened the space considerably. Most of the unit was taken up by a sailboat that, while probably on the small end as such things went, nevertheless seemed quite large to Emery. Next to the boat was a bucket of sudsy water and a scrub brush, which Emery guessed was responsible for some of the sounds he'd heard earlier.

"You're washing your boat?"

Braxton followed Emery's gaze and laughed. "Well, yeah. I guess it does sound kind of silly when you put it like that. But that's part of the process, you know? Get all the gunk off it." He held up the putty knife. "You wouldn't believe the kind of goop that gets stuck on there. Once I've got it clean, I can inspect the hull. This is the best time to find any problems—once it's in the water, it's too late."

His voice trailed off at the end, and his gaze shifted from Emery to John. John broke the moment by saying, "My dad would kill for me to take an interest in sailing. It wasn't something he cared about while I was growing up, or I'm sure he would have found a way to rope me into it. A lot of people start when they're young, right?"

"Oh sure, but you can pick it up later if you want. I did. I'd never touched a sail until I was in my twenties, but I had to get out on the water again." He must have read the question on their faces because he touched his shoulder and said, "I rowed in college until, well." He shrugged. "Blew it out."

"Ah," John said, and it was the kind of sound one athlete makes for another—exactly the right amount of knowing and commiseration and manly buck-up-and-bear-it. It made Emery want to roll his eyes.

Braxton shrugged as he set down the putty knife and grabbed an insulated tumbler. When he opened the top, the fragrance of good coffee wafted out. "After a few surgeries, I kind of accepted it." He took a sip. "I'm guessing you guys aren't here to talk about the boat or about my shoulder."

"No," Emery said, "we're not."

"We're here because we need your help," John said.

No one spoke. The kerosene heater hissed in the silence. After several long seconds, Braxton said, "Ok."

"Did you take a call from Eric Brey when you were working last night?"

Braxton's face shut down. "Look, man, I don't know who you are—"

"I know. And I'm not trying to jam you up or get you in trouble or anything like that. It's just a question. You know those calls are public record. You know I can find out the answer another way if I have to."

"Then that's what you should do. Call the station. Ask for the records. Not show up at my storage unit—"

"That's going to take too long," Emery said.

"Ree."

"No, he needs to understand. This is important, and we don't have time to wait for some bureaucrat to get his thumb out of his ass long enough to look at a Sunshine Law request. Things are happening right now, important things, life-and-death things, and every minute he dicks us around, we're losing ground. It's an easy question, and it's not one that costs you anything, so answer him."

Braxton's jaw tightened, his fingers curling and uncurling around the tumbler.

"He meant to say please," John said. "But he's right, Braxton. This is important, and we don't have time to wait for official channels."

The hardness in Braxton's face cracked. "Who are you, though?"

"Private investigators," Emery answered.

"I'm a police officer," John said.

"John."

"And I'm suspended, and that means I can't do what I'm best at, and it's driving me out of my fucking mind. I think you know what that's like, Braxton. And I think you've got a good sense for people, a good sense for bullshit. You spend your nights listening to people and making decisions about what they tell you. Well, listen to me right now: lives are on the line, and I need you to help me."

Somewhere distant in the facility, metal flexed and boomed, the sound echoing down the concrete corridor. Braxton rolled his shoulder once—the bad one, Emery thought.

"Mr. Brey called a little before five."

"You know Brey?" Emery asked. "The way you said that, it sounds like you recognized his name."

"Well, yeah. I mean, it's a small town. Everybody knows him."

"All right," John said. "What did he say?"

"He wanted an officer to come out right away."

"Did he say why?"

"He said he thought he saw a prowler." Braxton frowned. "I asked him what he'd seen, you know, details, but he got agitated and started demanding I send someone over."

"And?"

"And I sent Bonilla to check it out."

"Did Brey stay on the line?"

"No, he said he wasn't going to wait on the phone, then he disconnected."

Emery frowned. "Is that unusual?"

"I don't know. Not necessarily, I guess."

"But?"

Braxton reached for his coffee again, but this time, he didn't drink. "I don't know," he said again. "He sounded scared. I told him to stay on the call until an officer showed up, but he didn't want to. So maybe it was a little weird, yeah."

"What happened when Bonilla showed up?" John asked.

"Oh, she didn't. She had just gotten out of a domestic, and the chief got on the air and said he'd handle it."

"Cassidy?" Emery said.

Braxton nodded.

"Why would he do that?" John asked.

"Well, you know how it is. It's a small town, Brey's a big deal, the chief likes the personal touch. Plus like I said, Bonilla was just getting out of a domestic. The chief must have been in the area and figured he'd pick up the call."

Emery grimaced and saw some of the same frustration on John's face. What Braxton was describing wasn't unheard of—in Wahredua, for example, when Cravens had been chief, she'd been known to take a call if she wanted to make a point or if she thought it needed special handling. And Wahredua was bigger than Auburn by a fair margin, which meant in a town this size, with an even smaller force, it might even be common for the chief to pitch in when the other officers were unavailable or were getting run off their feet. None of that changed the fact, though, that Brey had called 911 for help, Cassidy had jumped in to take the call, and now Brey was dead.

"But he didn't say why?" Emery asked. "He didn't explain why he was taking it?"

Braxton gave a little laugh, eyes crinkling. "Well, no. But does your chief always explain everything he does?"

John must have seen something on Emery's face because he rolled his eyes. "No," he said, "I guess he doesn't. Did Cassidy radio back after he checked out the property?"

"Sure. He told me to close it; false alarm."

Emery thought he could hear, far off, the water in the harbor: the open-and-close of those gray shark's teeth.

"What?" Braxton asked. "Is something wrong?"

"No," John said. "That's what we needed to know. You didn't hear from Mr. Brey again last night?"

"No," Braxton said slowly. "Honestly, I didn't even think about him. We got another call, a girl who died from carbon monoxide poisoning, and after that—hey, what's going on? I'm getting a seriously weird vibe about this."

"I'm not sure yet," John said. "You've been a big help, Braxton. Thank you."

"Yeah? It doesn't feel like I helped. I feel like I screwed something up."

John shook his head. "You did your job. And you helped us. Listen, we might have additional questions. Could we get your number just in case?"

With a miserable nod, Braxton said, "You're going to talk to the chief about this, aren't you?"

"It might come to that. We won't tell him that you talked to us—"

Braxton shook his head. His hand was tight around the tumbler, and he shifted his weight. "He's gone."

"What?"

"The chief. He said he was taking some personal time. A vacation." He stared at them, like maybe they weren't getting it. "Chief Cassidy left Auburn this morning."

15

They drove back to Wahredua, and when they got home, the house was dark. Up and down the block, other houses were bright with holiday lights, windows aglow. Cars lined the streets. Across from them, silhouettes moved inside Mr. Tomlinson's house. It was the holiday season, after all, and everyone else in the world was living their normal lives, gathering and celebrating.

Emery waited until the garage door had rattled down. John still had his hands wrapped around the steering wheel. The only light came from the bulb in the garage door opener, and the glow it shed was dim and yellow, but the skin across John's knuckles looked tight.

"It's not the end of the road," Emery said.

John shook his head and barked a tiny laugh. "He's not coming back, Ree."

"We don't know that."

"We don't?"

Emery didn't have an answer for that.

When John released the steering wheel, it creaked, and the sound felt loud in the stillness. He rubbed his face.

"Tomorrow," Emery tried, "we'll—"

"This alleged witness, Vermilya, who is somehow tied to all these other pieces of shit, he's clinging to life in a hospital bed behind a police protection detail." John ticked off a finger. "That woman, Ingra, she and her cooks are dead." He ticked off another. "Eric Brey is dead, and I was standing right fucking there, Ree, and I ran away!" The last words were a shout. Then John's shoulders slumped, and he took off the Cardinals cap and ran his fingers through his hair. "And now our only other lead is gone. I'm starting to understand why Gideon Moss blew his brains out rather than deal with these people."

"John—"

But John got out of the car and slammed the door.

Emery followed him inside. The smell of cinnamon and pastry dough met them, the house warm and quiet and dark. The only light came from the microwave above the stove, and it turned John into ink strokes as he moved across the kitchen, leaned over the sink, and stared out the window. The dark brushwork of his shoulders, his back, his hip. And then the gold leaf of his hair.

"Cassidy can't just disappear," Emery said. "He's not smart enough. He'll use a credit card, or he'll show up on a traffic camera, or he'll try to get on a flight. We'll find him."

John shook his head. The light foiled over his hair, caught the shell of his ear, gave a suggestion of his jaw.

"And when we do—"

"Ree, he's dead. How do you not understand that? You're right: Cassidy isn't smart. And somebody—this guy from Brey's house, somebody else, I don't know—somebody is cleaning house, and Cassidy is a loose end. He was useful. Now he's not. And he's dead. That's it, that's the end."

"It's not the end. We've still got Vermilya—"

John's shoulders moved in a way Emery found strange until he realized, with a shock, it was silent laughter. John put his hands over his face again, but they came down almost immediately to curl around the stainless-steel apron of the sink. "Can we please not?"

"He's a valuable lead. Besides, there are other things we haven't tried, other avenues—"

"Ree, for fuck's sake!" The shout echoed through the stillness of the house. When he spoke again, his voice was tempered. "Can you just not? Not right now."

Maybe it was the darkness of the house. Maybe his eyes were having trouble adjusting. The dimensions of the room seemed skewed, and Emery fought the desire to put out a hand, find a wall, stabilize himself. He barely heard John when he spoke again.

"It is just so fucking unfair."

Emery opened his mouth.

The front door opened, and heavy, staggering steps moved into the house.

John bent his head, and the movement carried him out of the light from the microwave. The gold fire of his hair went out, and he was just a shadow.

"A few more steps, bruh," Ashley said and grunted.

Colt made an inarticulate noise full of pain.

The sound galvanized Emery, and he moved into the living room as two shadowy shapes stumbled out of the entry hall. He found a light, flipped it on, and stared.

The boys were dressed for a night out, and a distant part of Emery recognized that no one had told him, that he had sent Colt to Ashley's house under the belief that they would stay home. Instead, Colt was dressed in a black button-up, black trousers, and the ridiculous velvet drivers that every teenage boy seemed determined to wear. He'd somehow managed to sneak John's camel-hair coat out of the closet without anyone noticing, and now something dark stained the fabric in a long smear. Ashley looked similarly done up, in a hunter green blazer that was, apparently, velvet, a white button-up, and gray trousers. His velvet drivers matched the blazer, of course. Food covered his shirt and blazer—a red sauce, a stray noodle, a gob of something that might have been ice cream. In spite of the mess, both boys looked strikingly adult, like young men instead of boys, and on another night, it probably would have simultaneously broken Emery's heart and made him unspeakably pleased to see.

Instead, he focused on his son: one eye swelling shut, blood caked around his nose, a split lip. Colt couldn't seem to stand up straight. He had one hand pressed to his ribs, and Ashley seemed to be bearing most of his weight.

"Mr. Hazard," Ashley said, his voice breaking.

Emery took Colt from him and helped his son to the sofa. Colt gasped in pain as Emery eased him down. He squeezed his eyes shut and let his head fall back.

"John!"

"Jesus," John said behind him. "We've got to get him to the ER."

Colt's eyes flew open. "No!" He struggled to sit up. "I'm fine!"

With one hand on Colt's chest, Emery forced him back down. "Pull the Odyssey out of the garage. It'll be easier to load him in from the driveway."

John nodded and went to grab the keys.

Biscuit slunk across the room; she looked like she'd just woken up, but she pressed herself against the sofa, trying to get as close to Colt as she could without actually climbing on top of him.

"Pops, no, please." Colt was still trying to sit up. He'd already come into his full height, and he was strong—a far cry from the half-starved boy who had appeared on their doorstep more than a year before. But right then, he might have been a child again, too hurt to dislodge Emery's hand and sit up. "I'm fine. Ash, tell him I'm fine."

Ashley was crying and wiping his cheeks.

"What happened?"

Colt closed his eyes.

"Colt," Emery barked.

The boy shook his head.

"What is that supposed to mean? Open your eyes and talk to me. This is serious, Colt. Someone hurt you. What in the world is going on?"

Colt's eyes opened a crack. Tears glimmered. His voice was thick but steady as he said, "Nobody hurt me. I fell."

"You fell? Are you out of your fucking mind?"

"Ree!" John's shocked cry came from the stairs.

"Are you listening to this?"

"Go outside."

Emery straightened. "What did you say to me?"

John met his gaze and tossed the van's keys. Emery caught them out of the air without breaking his glare.

"Go outside," John said, his voice low and hard. "Right now."

A wild noise caught in Emery's throat. He grabbed Ashley by the arm and towed the boy out of the house. The cold felt wild too, the wind slashing at them, pulling on Emery's hair, slicing at exposed skin. Ashley shrank inside his blazer. Some of his hair had fallen loose, and it hung in front of his face. In the weak light, the rich auburn color had been stripped to gray.

"Talk," Emery said.

"Mr. Hazard—"

"You're covered in food, you're scared out of your mind, and you brought my son home injured after I trusted you with him!" The shout echoed up and down the street. Ashley tried to pull away, but Emery tightened his grip. "What happened?"

"We went to Tucker's. You know, the steakhouse." Ashley started to cry. He wasn't fighting now, but Emery didn't relax his grip. He was aware, distantly, that his fingers were biting into Ashley's arm. That it must hurt. Good, that distant part of him thought. "We made reservations months ago so it would be special, and my parents said it would be ok if we went straight there and came back, and—and he's been so worried lately, and then everything with basketball, I just wanted him to have one good night."

Ashley wiped tears away with his free hand. He snuffled, sounding like he was on the verge of full-on sobs.

Emery released the boy's arm and flexed stiff fingers. "What happened?"

"There were some kids there. Some other kids, I mean. And I knew they wanted to start something with Colt, and Colt wanted to start something too, but the restaurant was busy, and I figured if we just ate and left, nothing would happen. Then Colt went to the bathroom, and after a while, when he didn't come back, I went to make sure he was ok. They were—they'd followed him."

It was strange, Emery thought, that on such a cold night, he could be sweating. That his cheeks could feel so hot. "Who were they?"

"Mr. Hazard, please. He made me promise not to tell."

"Do you know why?"

Ashley blinked. He ran his arm under his nose, sniffling.

"He is protecting them, Ashley, because they threatened to do the same thing to you if he told. Do you understand that? He is doing this for you. So, I'm going to ask you one more time who did this, and I want you to think long and hard about how you feel about my son."

Ashley was crying harder now, and when he finally spoke, the words were almost unintelligible.

But Emery recognized the names.

"Go inside," he said. "Help John get him to the hospital."

Sobbing, Ashley stumbled toward the front door.

Emery got in the van. He backed out of the driveway. He eased past the cars lined up on either side of the street, past the partygoers, past everyone living their safe, normal, happy lives. He drove out into the black of a dying day. And as he drove, he called Tucker's.

"Yes, that party is still here," the maître d' said when he came back to the phone. "Would you like me to give them a message?"

"Sure," Emery said. "Tell them I'm on my way."

16

John-Henry had learned a long time ago to trust his gut, and right then, as he raced to catch up with Emery, his gut told him something terrible was about to happen. Luck. Luck. Please, he thought, let me be lucky again. All the luck of his golden life, which had run dry over the last few months—maybe it had been saved up for tonight. Because tonight, he needed to be lucky, or Emery might literally kill someone.

He'd been lucky so far, or lucky enough, anyway. Lucky that Jem and Tean had gotten home when they had, and lucky that they'd been willing to take Colt and Ashley to the emergency room while he went after his husband. Lucky that the roads had been empty of traffic, clear of ice, that the Mustang had felt weightless as he'd dropped the accelerator.

And now here he was, the roadside steakhouse glowing like a beacon, windows warm with yellow light, and he might not be too late.

When John-Henry pulled into Tucker's parking lot, the Odyssey was parked at the curb, directly in front of the restaurant. Leave it to Emery to find a way to make even his parking dramatic. John-Henry pulled the Mustang behind the van and ran.

Inside, the restaurant was a pressure cooker: too hot, too loud, too many bodies crowding every available space. Men and women dressed for an evening out laughed over drinks as they spilled out into the vestibule. A crush of people surrounded the bar, hands outstretched as voices called out orders. The smell of seared meat mixed with the cutting sharpness of juniper, a hint of musky perfume, wool warmed by sweat and friction.

John-Henry pushed through the throng near the entrance, ignoring angry shouts and gasps of outrage as he forced a path into the restaurant. A man in a tux glared at him from behind a wooden stand and said, "Excuse me, sir—"

But John-Henry ignored him, turning in place, stretching up onto tiptoe to scan the dining room. So many people. A quartet was playing, the instruments competing with a mustachioed man who struggled to rise from his seat as he belted out the first words of "Auld Lang Syne." His companions, middle-aged women with matching mousey lobs of hair, stared up at him admiringly. A child who couldn't have been older than six darted past John-Henry, screaming as he dragged a tablecloth behind him, while a scrawny guy in a bow tie hurried after him saying, "Ian, stop. Ian, please stop!" At the bar, a glass broke, and a pair of women who had toned and tanned themselves to lizard-like perfection shrieked with laughter. And then John-Henry heard it: the growl, the rumble, the crack like thunder. He pushed past the maître d' and stepped into the next room.

Emery loomed over a table, talking in a low voice, but his tone carried. John-Henry knew some of the men and women at the table, but not all of them: Drew Klein, of course, who had been his friend back in high school, with a spare tire around his waist now and a double chin he'd tried to hide with a goatee; his wife, Katie, who apparently had opted for adult braces since the last time John-Henry had seen her; Redgie Moseby, big and bullnecked and red-faced, who hadn't said a word to John-Henry since Emery had first come back, since that day John-Henry had popped him one; his wife, Kenzi, with her narrow face and Phoebe-from-*Friends* haircut, which, as far as John-Henry knew, had never really taken off like the Rachel. The others he recognized from school events and from passing them in the Piggly-Wiggly, all of them white, all of them in their late thirties to early forties, all of them in that sneeringly middle-class niche of luxury vehicles and McMansions, all of them, of course, cishet couples.

Hearing those thoughts, how different he sounded from the person he'd been not so long ago, was like hearing someone in another room. Because if things had been different, he'd be sitting here with Cora, and he'd have a drink in his hand, and he'd be getting louder as Cora tried to shush him, and he'd be getting raunchier, and he'd be looking down Kenzi-from-*Friends*'s dress, and inside he'd be going at himself with a knife because he was living a lie, and drinking was one way to keep it all at arm's length.

"—fucking educate you," Emery was saying in that dead voice as John-Henry reached them. "Stand up."

Redgie's face got even redder. Drew had a shiny Rudolph nose. The other men at the table—there were four more of them—were torn between looking away, looking down, and trying to glare at Emery. If he noticed the glares, he didn't give any sign of it.

"Ree," John-Henry said, taking his arm at the elbow. "Let's step outside."

"I'm handling something." He slid his gaze from Drew to Redgie. "Are you going to make me drag your ass out of that chair?"

"Fuck off," Redgie said.

"Get the manager," Katie was stage-whispering, clawing at Drew. "Go get the manager."

"You can't come in here and ruin our night like this," Drew said. "You have to leave. They'll make you leave."

"You're afraid I'll ruin your night?" Emery pointed to a table farther back in the room, where a cluster of teens was watching the confrontation unfold. Among them, John-Henry recognized Allen Klein, Scotty Moseby, and plenty more little charmers from Wahredua High. "Then you should have kept your reprobate sons on a fucking leash."

John-Henry tightened his grip. "Ree, I want to talk to you."

Emery's gaze flicked to him and then back to the table. "Are you proud of this? That your boys act like a pack of wild dogs? That they have to gang up on my son because they're not brave enough to fight him like men."

"You're full of shit," Redgie said and took a long drink of his beer.

"I should have broken your jaw the first time we met," Emery said. "I never should have let John handle that."

"Outside," John-Henry said. He tried to pull, but it was like trying to uproot a tree. "Right now."

"Let go of me," Emery snapped.

One of the men at the table burst out laughing, and then several of the women joined in. Another man whispered something to a friend. Drew smirked, leaning back, and said to Katie in a voice meant to carry, "Trouble in paradise."

"I'm sure it must be a relief to you, Drew, to have someone else occupy everyone's attention for a moment, instead of this being yet another night when Katie's tits spill out and she pisses herself and you find her blowing the busboy behind a dumpster."

It was like someone had turned down the volume on the world. A cold draft moved through the room, and John-Henry would have sworn he could hear the candles gutter.

Emery turned his attention to Redgie. "And, of course, I imagine you're greatly relieved that, for a while anyway, people will be talking about how Scotty assaulted my son, instead of how he was caught masturbating to the stuffed animals in the preschool."

Redge's face was the color of wine, now, and he made a choked noise. Kenzi looked like she wanted to crawl under the table.

"That's enough," John-Henry said.

"Why are we just sitting here?" the man who had laughed asked. John-Henry had taken him in earlier, but now he studied him a little more closely: just the right hair, just the right scruff, a square jaw and a wide, amused mouth. "You're going to let him talk to you like that? He wants to start something, let's start something."

"Casey—" The woman next to him said.

"No, this'll be good. I've been hearing about this guy since I moved here." He pushed back his chair and tossed down his napkin. When he stood, he glanced at the men seated on either side of him. "Get up."

The other men stood with greater and lesser degrees of reluctance. Even through his escalating panic, John-Henry wanted to laugh. It was like high school all over again: the tough talk, the bravado, and then, when it came down to it, most guys didn't really want to take a swing. Most.

Redgie pushed back his chair. Drew was staring at Katie, who was draining a glass of wine, but he scrambled out of his seat a moment later.

Emery turned, and John-Henry held on to his arm and was towed toward the front door.

"Listen to me," he whispered. "Did you think about this? Did you think about what this might mean for Colt?"

"I'm doing this for Colt."

"No, you're doing this for you, because you're hurt and you want to punish someone. But this isn't going to solve anything, Ree. Leaving aside the lawsuits, the fact that you'll probably get yourself arrested, and the fact that we have been through enough as a family already, you're not even thinking about the reality of this. What are those boys going to do if you beat the shit out of their dads? Do you think they're going to shrug and say, 'Oh well,' and go on with their lives? They're going to go after Colt with everything they've got. This, up until now, has been bullying. After tonight, though, it'll be a vendetta."

"He's enrolled in a public school. He's entitled to his personal safety."

"Are you listening to yourself? We couldn't protect him at basketball practice, could we? We couldn't protect him tonight."

"Then we'll send him to another school, as you said."

"Ree!" They pushed through the front doors, and for a moment, the cold locked both of them in place. The world was silent and dark. "Stop this, please. Stop and think about what this means."

Then the doors opened again, heat and light and bodies pressing out into the dark, and Emery shook John-Henry's hand from his sleeve and moved forward.

All John-Henry could do was follow him around the side of the building. Emery stopped near the dumpster, where a pile of old pallets was moldering under a blanket of snow, a trail of footprints crisscrossing the concrete apron from Tucker's back door to the dumpster. A security light carved an orangish wedge out of the night, and it made Emery's profile alien.

"Please," John-Henry whispered. "I know you're upset. I know you're furious. But please think about Colt right now. There are other ways to handle this, the proper ways. Please think about what's best for your son."

The frozen amber of his eyes glittered in the security light. His expression didn't change. And then, without showing how much it might have cost him, he gave a tiny nod.

John-Henry let out a breath and put himself between Emery and the loose knot of men emerging from the darkness. Drew was in the lead with Redgie at his side. The instigator, Casey, stood a step behind them, and behind him, the other three men made an uneven line.

"Guys, let's stop this right here," John-Henry said. For a moment, it was like the last week had fallen away, and he was who he'd always been. He smiled, the right balance of apology and confidence, and held up a hand. He'd always been everyone's friend. People called it different things—good energy, charisma, animal magnetism. He could feel it, sometimes, the way people responded to him; it had always been that way, ever since he'd been a child. It had made him popular in high school. It had made him successful in college. It had, in ways he never would have expected, let him be a better police officer. And it had been like his own personal key to Emery Hazard, giving him access to the person he had wanted since he'd been a boy. He relaxed into it now, the strain in his muscles easing, his whole body loose. He felt young. Like high school, he thought. Most guys don't really want a fight. They just don't know how to back down. "It went too far in there, just like it went too far earlier with Colt. Let's not make it any worse."

"Do you hear that?" Casey asked. "He's afraid."

John-Henry began, "Redgie—"

Redgie spat. It missed John-Henry's sneakers, but only barely. The security light made little orange flames in his eyes. He'd been a big deal in high school; he'd been a wrestler. He'd been a big man around town. And one day, John-Henry had punched him in the face, and now, tonight, John-Henry realized he wanted payback.

"Drew," John-Henry said, taking a step closer, his voice softening because it was meant for one person. They went back, all the way back. All the dumbass nights. All the stupid parties. Lots of good memories—shooting bottle rockets off the dock at Drew's parents' place at Lake of the Ozarks, and sharing a limo to Prom, Drew pretending to jimmy the built-in liquor cabinet, and isolated memories of afternoons when they'd done nothing but shoot hoops in the driveway and eat way more pizza than anybody ever should. "Come on, man. You know this isn't the way to go."

"You heard what he said about Katie, man," Casey said.

"This doesn't have to happen. Nobody heard him say that stuff except you and your friends. This, what's about to happen out here, this is only going to make everything worse. For us and for you, Drew."

Drew shook his head. He wouldn't meet John-Henry's eyes. In the orange light, his split lip looked fat and swollen.

John-Henry took a step forward. "Drew—"

Drew stepped back, still not meeting John-Henry's gaze.

"Hey, Drew, come on. I mean, I know things have been tense this week, but we've been friends for thirty years."

Drew gave another shake of his head.

It was disbelief more than anger that made John-Henry step forward again. "Hey, look at me—"

Drew shoved him.

It wasn't much, but it rocked John-Henry back on his heels. He steadied himself and stared. Drew looked up now. His body was stiff, his shoulders locked. He looked like a kid again, and John-Henry realized with something like shock that Drew didn't know how to throw a punch. It was like they'd all gone back in time.

"Fine," John-Henry said when he recovered himself. He tried to relax back into that old John-Henry, the one who always knew what to say, always knew what to do. "Here's how this is going to go. You're going to walk back inside, and you're going to tell everybody you scared us off—"

Drew shoved him again. Harder this time. Hard enough to send John-Henry stumbling back.

Emery made a guttural noise and took a step, but John-Henry waved for him to stay where he was.

"This is your fault," Drew said. His voice was shaking. "You deserve it."

"Yeah," Casey said. He was smiling now, the expression big and open. "Tell him."

For a moment, John-Henry couldn't get the words out. "I deserve to have my son hurt and humiliated?"

"You're not my friend," Drew said. "I don't know who you are. The John-Henry I knew, he's gone. As soon as he—" Drew stabbed a finger at Emery. "—came back, you were different. I should have known something was wrong. As soon as you started letting him give it to you up the ass, I should have known. Fuck, man, you've been around Allen. I let you and Cora babysit him. And then I find out—I mean, Jesus Christ, Somers, little kids? What the fuck is wrong with you?"

Everything seemed to come undone. John-Henry felt like he was floating, like he was looking down from a great height. Something was wrong with his ears, maybe. Some sounds seemed too loud: the buzz of the security light, his breathing, the rustle of his coat. But everything else was silent, like he'd gone deaf. Your balance, he thought. The inner ear. Maybe that's why he felt like he was floating.

"Fucking pedophile," Casey added with a smile.

John-Henry barely heard him. Thoughts zipped through his head—*I never touched Allen* and *You know me* and then, like he was tuning in to a stronger signal that drowned out the rest, *How dare you?* He finally worked his jaw, heard something click, and said, "We're leaving. Tell your kids to stay away from our son."

John-Henry turned, took a step toward Emery, and stopped when Redgie spoke.

"He's not even your son," Redgie said. "He's some kid you picked up so you could diddle him. Everybody knows why you two wanted him." A wad of spit struck the back of John-Henry's coat. "Fucking groomers."

The piss-soaked jersey.

The ruined trophies.

The spray paint on the side of their house.

The night in jail, listening to its madhouse sounds.

The days of humiliation and frustration.

The years of watching everyone from his old life pull back, close ranks, shut him out.

Colt, beaten and bloody on the couch.

Emery's eyes, and the old, familiar pain.

John-Henry spun back toward the men and charged. Drew shrank back, tripped over his own feet, and fell flat on his ass. Casey drew back too, the smile falling off his face. Redgie, however, tried to set himself. When John-Henry crashed into him, they both went down. They hit the asphalt still locked together and rolled, Redgie hammering on John-Henry's ribs,

John-Henry pounding one fist against the side of Redgie's head. It wasn't martial arts. It wasn't even the basic grappling he'd learned as a police officer. This was down-and-dirty brawling, uncoordinated, an outlet for all John-Henry's rage, and he struck blindly and furiously, barely feeling the blows he took in return.

And then it all changed. Redgie got him into some kind of hold—all those years wrestling finally paying off—and he did something that made John-Henry's head feel like it was going to pop off his neck. He screamed, moving into the hold, trying to ease the pressure, and only saw Drew sneaking up, one fist raised, out of the corner of his eye. When the punch landed, his world flashed red, then black, and then it came back scrambled as fists and kicks rained down.

It went on for a long time. Moments of it crystallized like snapshots: Drew sneering through bloody lips, and John-Henry's distant, satisfied thought that he must have gotten a punch in somehow. Casey kicking him in the side, over and over again, laughing. Redgie pulling his hair to make him move as they dragged him toward the curb. One of the unnamed men wrapping a belt around his hand.

From far off came Emery's shouts, which quickly became cries of pain. And then John-Henry couldn't hear him anymore, and he didn't know what that meant. His world compacted into pain, cold air, the tang of blood, the rough solidity of asphalt.

And then someone was shouting, "What's going on out here?"

Steps raced away. Someone laughed. A man—a barely conscious part of John-Henry thought it was Redgie—roared in triumph.

John-Henry's vision was blurry no matter how many times he blinked to clear his eyes. All he could make out of the shape approaching him was black. Like night had taken form and was moving toward him. The man—it was a man—said something in Spanish, and then, "Don't move, ok?"

I won't, John-Henry tried to say, but the world was getting smaller and smaller, moving away from him. He felt like maybe it had been a joke, that he should laugh. The world was a marble now, small and frozen and just out of reach. And then it disappeared completely, and his last thought was, Where am I going to go?

17

John-Henry woke in another place, and for a moment, he didn't know where he was. Then it came back to him in flashes: the paramedics, the long ride in the ambulance, the fluorescents of the emergency room stabbing his eyes. Now it was morning, and he was in a hospital bed, and the sunlight that came through the window made him think of spiderwebs.

"You're awake," his father said and shook his newspaper for emphasis.

Pain crowded in on John-Henry's awareness, and when he tried to shift position, he stifled a groan.

"I thought you might feel that way," Glennworth Somerset said. The way he held the paper made it impossible to see his face. "I asked them not to give you anything for the pain until we had a chance to talk."

John-Henry lay there and considered that. In spite of the night's sleep, he felt wrung out. Scratch that, he was exhausted. He thought about trying to prop himself up. Then he decided to ask the most important thing first. "Emery?"

"Fine, of course." His father shut the paper with a snap. His cheeks were red. His eyes were bloodshot. "It seems one of your charming new friends borrowed a can of pepper spray from his wife. From what I can piece together, Emery was out before he was in." He was quiet for a long time. When he spoke again, all he managed was a strangled few words: "You, on the other hand."

"I feel fine, Father. Thanks for asking."

"Don't be smart." The sound of paper rubbing against paper came, and then John-Henry realized his father was trembling. "I know you're fine. No concussion, thank God. Some bruised ribs. I imagine you'll be eating soft foods for a while, but you've even kept all your teeth. Don't you feel lucky, son of mine?"

Somewhere nearby, a machine was beeping steadily. Rubber soles squeaked in the hallway. Something brushed the door, and it rattled softly in the frame.

"Do you have any idea," his father said, "how stupid you've been?"

John-Henry wanted to close his eyes. He was five years old again. Or ten. Or fifteen. Or twenty, telling them he'd changed his major. Maybe it had been the fight. Maybe it had been everything from the last few days. He listened to that steady beeping. It was weirdly soothing. And then he said, "You know what, Father? I honestly cannot give two fucks."

His father watched him for several empty seconds. Then he tossed the paper onto the bed next to John-Henry. The headline of the Wahredua *Courier* said, *CALLS FOR RESIGNATION MOUNT*, and it featured John-Henry's official photograph as chief of police.

"Allow me to disillusion you," his father said, "of whatever fantasy you may be under. Naomi sees this vulnerability as an opportunity, and she has been running around since the minute you got arrested, talking to anyone who would listen to her, trying to convince them that regardless of how the trial turns out, a suspension simply isn't enough. Even if you're found innocent, she says, no one will really believe it. You'll have gotten off because you're the chief of police. Or because you're my son. Or because for a time, this town thought you'd hung the moon. It would be to your benefit—" Amusement scorched his voice. "—for you to resign before the trial begins. And, if you won't resign, I should remove you. So that the trial will appear fair and impartial. And, of course, because the town needs strong law enforcement leadership during this crisis. So, tell me, John-Henry: can you give two fucks now?"

John-Henry picked up the paper. He tried to read the article, but the words swam together. He put it face down on the bed.

"Here's what we're going to do." And John-Henry could hear, in his father's voice, the years and years of these kinds of conversations. The resigned practicality. The hint of weariness at, over and over again, bailing his only son out of trouble. And always, the frank reality that John-Henry was not a participant in the conversation. He was simply there to hear what was going to be done. "We'll start by having you call a press conference. You're injured, which will garner some sympathy, or at the very least will assure people you're paying the price for your poor decisions. You'll give a public apology for brawling behind a steakhouse like a white trash drunk. You'll explain that you're enrolling in an anger management course and beginning therapy. Then you'll start making the rounds: city councilors, community leaders, the Lions Club. Pastor Saunders has been particularly vocal; let's keep him on the short list of people you'll need to visit."

"He's been vocal because he hates gay people. He's probably telling everyone this is proof of what half his congregation already believes, that gay people are—" He heard the word in Redgie's voice as memory flashed: *groomers*. "—recruiting kids or pedophiles or whatever the hell bullshit they think."

"And he's got not one but two of the city councilors in that congregation, John-Henry, and so you will meet with him, and you will tell him whatever he wants to hear. If he wants to hear that you've been reborn and will be baptized and have forsaken your sinning ways, you'll ask if you can go down to the Grand Rivere and do it right then."

John-Henry ran his hands down the bedding. He tried to push himself up into a sitting position, but his body ached, and he ended up gripping the sheet, his knuckles blanching as he tightened his hand around the fabric.

"In a few weeks, we'll make sure you get spotted quietly doing some charitable work during your suspension. Nothing gay. And nothing with children, of course."

It was the way he said it, the coolly disinterested reality of it. The beep of that nearby machine grew louder and louder until it felt like it was right next to his ear.

"No," John-Henry said.

His father looked at him. He seemed to be refocusing his gaze, as though he'd forgotten John-Henry was there. "What did you say?"

"No. I'm not doing any of that." In spite of protesting muscles, John-Henry managed to get himself upright, and a wave of dizziness rolled over him. He tried to hold his father in his gaze as the world rocked around him. "I'm done with that."

"If by *that* you mean your career, then yes, John-Henry, that may be correct. I am not going to let you—"

"Father, you're under some kind of—what did you call it? Some kind of fantasy here." A grin corkscrewed at the corner of John-Henry's mouth. "Allow me to disillusion you. I am not a child anymore. And what I do—or don't do—is not something you can control. I spent my entire life getting away with shit I did because of you and Mother. And I have to live with that, with the fact that I did those things, that I'm the person capable of doing those things, and nobody—" Nobody loved me enough to stop me, he almost said. But he managed to change it to "—stopped me, or made me pay for them. And that does something to you, Father. When you don't get to pay for what you did wrong. Because then you carry it around forever.

That's the best-case scenario. Or after a while, you stop carrying anything around, and you think that's how the world's supposed to be."

"Good God, John-Henry. You weren't always this naïve."

"Is that what you call it? I'd call it tired, Father. I feel very tired." He was clutching the bedding again. Out in the hallway, a woman laughed. He released the thin cotton, smoothed it out with one hand, his fingers throbbing from how tightly he'd been holding it. "If Drew wants to press charges, that's fine. I imagine he'll have a hard time making a case out of it, since he and his buddies beat the shit out of me. But that's why we have internal investigations. And if they find I did something wrong, I'll deal with it."

"And I suppose you'll 'deal with it'—" His father laid scorn on the words. "—when you're found guilty of possession of child pornography."

"I won't be found guilty. I'm innocent."

"There it is again, that charming naivete. Tell me, is he responsible for this newfound worldview? Emery has very few redeeming qualities, but I considered him practical, if nothing else."

"I didn't do anything wrong, Father. And I am not going to go back to being that person I was, the one who let you cover things up and make things go away. It's my problem. I'll deal with it."

"You have an affinity for that phrase, it seems. Tell, me, John-Henry, how will you 'deal with it?'"

John-Henry looked out the window. The sun was out, and what he could see of Wahredua glittered under a cap of frost, glass and brick and the glittering teeth of ice along the shores of the Grand Rivere. Like braces, he thought and smiled. Like Katie's adult braces.

"You're facing a felony charge, John-Henry. And from where I'm sitting, I think it's even odds that you'll be convicted. Tell me, how will this position of moral superiority help you in prison? How will it help you when you find yourself eventually released on parole and trying to find work? How will it help you when you're forced to identify yourself as a sex offender?"

The day was so bright everything seemed incandescent, and when he moved his head, afterimages glowed in his vision.

"Your job, gone. Your pension, gone. Your career, up in smoke."

"You're talking about a worst-case scenario—"

"Be silent." His father's breathing was suddenly ragged. "Don't speak. A worst-case scenario, John-Henry? Where have you been the last few days? As far as this town is concerned, you're already guilty. And let's say, by some miracle, you're found innocent. No one in this town will look you in the eye again. You will be removed from the force sooner or later—Lieutenant Peterson can't turn a blind eye anymore, not when Naomi has laid everything out like this, and even if you somehow escape criminal charges, she'll get rid of you when she inevitably wins the next election."

"There it is," John-Henry said, and the thickness of his voice surprised him. "That's what this is about."

"This is about our family, you idiot child. And about our future. And I have done what I could to—to insulate you while you lived out this fantasy with that man and turned your mother and me into a laughingstock in this town."

His throat was dry. He looked around for water and didn't see it, but that might have been because of the afterimages still drifting across his vision. "I think you should go."

"You didn't read that article, so I'll tell you what it says: quote after quote from Naomi, as she describes your efforts to, in her words, 'impede the course of justice.' Witness tampering. Obstruction. Abuse of power. Criminal interference from members of the police department still loyal to you. A history of working outside the law. You think it's an insult to your honor that I ask you to apologize?" His final words erupted in a shout. "I'm trying to save your fucking neck!"

When the shout died, John-Henry said, "Get out."

Instead, his father took several deep breaths. He perched on the edge of his seat, adjusted the jacket of his suit, touched his hair in an absent-minded gesture that was so familiar it snapped something deep inside John-Henry. "I imagine," he said, his voice compressed into a shade of normalcy again, "that you think those allegations are irrelevant. But consider, for a moment, their significance for Emery. They only have to make one of them stick, John-Henry, for him to lose his investigator's license."

"Get out."

"The two of you playing at this like it's a game, harassing people in town. Perhaps you're right, John-Henry. Perhaps I should have let you pay the price for your actions. You're certainly going to pay for them now."

Outside, the sky was a blue thinning to white, and the river looked like something drawn in gold. John-Henry's head was starting to ache. The woman in the hall was laughing again—laughing and laughing, a cackling kind of laugh. I'll have what she's having, John-Henry thought, and he wanted to burst out laughing. But he said, "I'd like you to leave."

His father stood. "I will remove you from the department if I have to, John-Henry. For your own sake."

The laugh tore its way free. He put a hand to his chest, and the pain of bruised muscles was strangely grounding. The sun was so bright outside, and he wanted to close his eyes. It was like those stadium lights all those years ago. He thought of the boy who'd been determined to be free. But that had been somebody else, somewhere else, and it had been a boy's dream. Naïve, that was the word. A boy's naïve dream. John-Henry laughed again, blinking against the brilliance of all that light. "You've never done anything for my sake, Father. I wouldn't expect you to start now."

18

The flash of cameras continued as the garage door rolled down behind them.

"Fucking bottom feeders," Emery said.

John didn't respond. He stared straight ahead, his face slack, like someone had cut the wires from his brain, clutching the newspaper to his chest. He'd been like that since Emery had gotten to the hospital to bring him home, answering in monosyllables, his body communicating only a kind of empty awareness stripped of emotion or affect.

Part of it, Emery knew, was because of the interview. Emery hadn't been present while Palomo talked to John, but he had a good idea what they'd discussed—among other things, the shooting of Jace Vermilya and the murder of Eric Brey. Palomo was a good detective, and she was just doing her job, and the Wahredua PD had reason to consider John a person of interest. None of that, however, softened the reality of John being interviewed by one of his own detectives. So, yes, part of it was the interview. But not all of it.

Representatives of what passed for the media had been waiting outside the hospital, but Emery had taken John out a side exit and managed to avoid them. They hadn't been so lucky with the vans and cameras at home. Faces and microphones pressing against the windows of the van. Shouted questions. Flash, flash, flash. All Emery could do was inch forward, trying not to crush some intrepid reporter's foot, until they managed to reach the safety of the garage.

And now, in the weak, indirect light, the familiar lines of John's face were blurred, as though someone had smudged them. John must have felt the weight of Emery's gaze because he glanced over, his expression still registering nothing, and stared at him. Say something, Emery thought. Say anything.

"Let's get you something to eat."

John stared at him for a moment longer, and then he opened the door and got out.

Emery sat in the van as his husband limped inside. He clutched the steering wheel, shoulders slumped, and his head was full of a pulsing nothingness. Then, after a while, he got out and went into the house.

Tean and Jem were at the stove, frozen in place, apparently in the middle of Jem trying to wrestle a can of pinto beans out of Tean's hand. Their gazes slid to him. Tean's face creased with sympathy. Jem grimaced and tucked the can of beans behind his back.

"We were going to make you something to eat," Tean said.

Jem glanced toward the stairs. "How's he doing?"

"Great, Jem," Emery said as he crossed the kitchen. "He's doing great."

It was unfair. It was small and mean and, maybe worse, unnecessary. But helplessness and frustration and hurt had been building in Emery for days now, and lashing out, even in such a petty way, provided a temporary release. It was a bad night, he told himself. We all had a bad night.

That was putting it mildly. He had spent the night after the fight at Tucker's shuttling between John and Colt. If you could call it a fight. A fucking disgrace was a better term for it—the pepper spray had caught him by surprise, and although he'd been trained not to let it incapacitate him, it had still interfered with his vision and compromised his effectiveness. A couple of the assholes had gotten in some good punches and then shoved him, and he'd fallen. On the ice, in the dark, he couldn't seem to regain his footing. All he could do was listen, and so he'd stopped shouting and tried to get to John. Tried and failed, he reminded himself. He had failed yet again.

Then, once John was being seen by a doctor—and undergoing what seemed to be the hospital's entire catalogue of scans and tests—he'd rushed to check on his son, who was in an emergency department cubicle with cotton plugs stuffed up his nose, his shirt off as a middle-aged Indian woman taped his ribs. And then, once he was sure Colt was ok, he'd rushed back to see if his husband had a cerebral edema, or internal bleeding, or a ruptured kidney. It had gone on and on like that, in and out of rooms, running endlessly under fluorescent lights, like one of those stupid movies John and Colt loved with "Yakety Sax" playing in the background. Until, finally, John had been admitted for the night and had told Emery to take Colt home.

And now, Emery thought, he was paying the price for it.

In their bedroom, John's newspaper lay on the floor, and the door to the bathroom was open. The shower was running. Water hissed and splashed. The familiar sound of John's morning routine came—the sound of his steps on the tile, the change in the sound of the water as the spray hit his back. Emery sat on the bed, and after a while, the water stopped. The whisper of the towel. Wet footsteps. John appeared in the doorway a moment later, his body flushed from the heat of the shower, toweling his hair. He looked at Emery for a long time, the towel slowing until he dropped his hand to his side. He still had that lean, swimmer's build, all that golden skin and dark ink and defined muscle, the kind of perfection that still, with shocking intensity, made Emery's mouth dry, made him wonder by what twist of fate he was allowed to touch, to care for, to love. Bruises purpled his chest and belly, muscles expanding and contracting with his breathing. His dick was soft, but it looked heavy and full.

It was like being caught, Emery's sudden awareness of John, of knowing that John was watching him watch John. A flush prickled up Emery's neck and into his face. For one disorienting moment, it was like they were in high school again, Emery's desire warring with his better judgment, his gaze coming back to John over and over again, even though he knew he was asking to get burned. And then the moment passed; they were partners and husbands and lovers, Emery reminded himself. They'd seen each other in the throes of passion. They'd seen each other sick. They'd seen each other in desperate need of a bathroom. Emery knew John, knew his mind and body, in a way that nobody else did. And there was no reason he ought to feel that adolescent discomfort at his own desire being exposed, at having the object of his desire fully present and bare to him.

But it lingered, a hint of it—a trace of sweat under his arms, the fresh itch of the Wildcats tee that usually was a comfort pick.

John watched him silently for another moment. And then something happened. It was like watching someone flick a switch. Light came on in his eyes. He twirled the towel against his leg, making a soft whump-whump sound as the cotton hit his calf, brushing the fine gold hairs there, a tiny smile curling his lips. When he spoke, his voice was soft. "Do you know how lucky I am?"

Emery watched him. His heart was beating faster. That prickle came again to the hollow of his throat. John's dick was filling out now, and there was no mistaking it for a side effect of the warmth of the shower.

Crossing to the bed, John said, "Do you have any idea how incredibly lucky I am?" He dropped the towel and straddled Emery's legs to sit in his lap. His dick was half-hard now, rubbing against Emery's stomach, and Emery felt the twist in his own gut, his body's automatic reaction—years of desire, decades of it, compounded by love.

John scooted up Emery's thighs, making a soft pained noise as bruised muscles stretched, until his dick was trapped between them. He brought his mouth to Emery's ear and rutted into him, continuing to harden. Emery was hard too, trapped under John's weight, fighting against the combination of warm skin, the smell of John's hair, the friction of bodies. John's breaths came in uneven bursts—hints of what it must have cost him to move like this, to act like this, in spite of everything he'd been through.

"Slow down," Emery said, settling a hand on John's flank. "Your ribs."

"Fuck my ribs. I need this. I need you." His mouth was still by Emery's ear, his breath hot and tickling, and now he leaned his head against Emery's. He pressed hard, until the contact almost hurt, with a kind of urgency and need that Emery couldn't unravel. "I am so fucking lucky. I love you so much. You are the most important thing in the world to me, do you know that?" He shuddered, breaking the rhythm of his hips, his dick grazing Emery's shirt. "Do you?"

"Of course. And I love you, but—John, stop. You're going to hurt yourself."

"I want you to fuck me. Do you remember the first time you fucked me?"

Emery remembered. The vulnerability that John had tried so hard to mask. The desire like a thing alive, hooking him in the guts. Finally, after all those years, the opportunity to see, to touch, to be present with, in a way that involved no shame, no hiding. Everything laid bare to the other. He remembered the sense of power, and all the years of powerlessness.

He clamped both hands on John's thighs and said, "Stop."

"I want it to be like that. You were so slow, so gentle, and you still fucked my brains out. The way you looked at me. I want you to look at me like that every day, like I'm Christmas morning and you've been waiting your whole life to open your present." He was still pressing against Emery, and now Emery was aware of the day's stubble on his jaw, the roughness of a fresh scab on his cheek. "Touch me."

"John."

But John reached down and took his hand, peeling it away from his thigh, and brought it to his dick. It was all so familiar. His hand tightened. He knew, because he'd wanted to know, how John liked it, and his hand moved. John let out a throaty noise. The rhythm of his hips broke again. One of his hands opened on Emery's shoulder and tightened again, clawing for a moment until he could get a handful of shirt. His breathing hitched. It sounded like he was crying.

"Could we slow down—" Emery said.

"Let's run away," John said, his voice clotted, the words almost unrecognizable. "Let's go somewhere, anywhere, together. We've got enough money. Let's go back to the Virgin Islands. Let's go to Tahiti, and we'll lie in a pool all day and eat fresh fruit and fuck our brains out and love each other."

Emery's hand still stroked John, the scent of his arousal mixing with the smell of the soap now. "A vacation? Or what are you talking about?"

"It doesn't matter. I just want to be away from here. Just want to be with you."

"We can't just run away. What about Colt and Evie?"

John's breath hitched again. Emery's free hand slid to the small of his back to steady him. He felt the dampness there, the first beginnings of sweat. It has to be hurting him, Emery thought. How much does this hurt him?

Then John laughed shakily. "You're such a good dad," he whispered. "I love that about you. I'd love to see you with a baby. What did Shaw say? I think my ovaries would explode."

Emery stopped moving his hand, but John continued to thrust into the circle of his fingers.

"We could do it," John whispered, clutching Emery to him. "We could do it. We could have a baby—I want a baby with you, oh God."

He came. Most of the orgasm went onto Emery's shirt, and the rest spilled onto his hand, running between his fingers, down his wrist. John's body stilled. And then Emery realized, not quite. He was trembling, his hands still twisted in Emery's shirt, face pressed against the side of Emery's head. His breathing was ragged, and when Emery eased his hand away from John's softening dick, John flinched and let out a low sound that was almost a moan.

Emery shushed him, one hand still bracing him at the small of his back. "Let's get you onto the bed, and then you need to lie down."

John made a slurred noise that wasn't quite a response.

It was an awkward, tortuous process, getting himself upright without letting John fall, and then shifting John to the mattress. Every movement elicited a grunt or a groan, and Emery wondered how John had managed his recent performance—how, and why. He had to help John straighten his legs on the bed, and then he got a washcloth from the bathroom and cleaned him up. The taped ribs looked like they'd survived the impromptu sex without further damage, but the abrasion on John's cheek had broken open again and now wept blood. Emery cleaned that up too. John's breathing was labored, his eyes half closed. Emery cleaned himself up next—he washed his hands, changed his shirt. The sound of the running water put his teeth on edge.

When he returned to sit on the edge of the mattress, John murmured, "You didn't get off."

"I'm alright."

Sounds from below filtered into their silence—Jem saying something, the words indistinct, and the clang of a pot, and a door opening and closing.

John's eyes opened to three-quarters.

"What?" Emery asked.

"What do you think?"

"I think we can manage a vacation, but not with the terms of your bail. We'll have to go after the trial." He tried to smile. "It'll be a celebration."

But John's gaze was strangely intent, and if the words registered, it didn't show on his face.

"What?" Emery asked again.

"What do you think, what? The baby."

Emery managed not to say, *Are you serious?* But what came out of his mouth was "A baby?"

It had been the wrong thing—the wrong tone, the wrong inflection, the rising note of disbelief. John closed his eyes. His face had a stiff, composed look that had nothing to do with rest. And then, after a moment, he rolled onto his side, his back to Emery—managing, in the process, to huff and puff and sound like he was giving himself a hernia.

"Is that really the best position?" Emery asked. "Your ribs—"

"I'm fine."

Downstairs, that door opened and closed again. Tean laughed. Biscuit began to bark. It was like being in a haunted house, Emery thought. The rule of a haunted house is you can't leave. You can never leave, not if you're one of the ghosts.

"John, I didn't mean to sound like—you caught me by surprise, that's all. We've talked about children, and we agreed—"

"You should check on Colt."

Emery put a hand on John's arm: golden skin, dark ink, firm muscle. It lasted about five seconds before John reached to adjust the pillow and, in the process, shook off Emery's touch.

He thought he should say something. He followed the lines of the tattoo with his eyes, but the lines became a maze across John's broad back. He reached out his hand, like he might trace the lines more easily that way, find his way to the end or the beginning. But he let his hand fall instead. The springs in the mattress made a small sound when he stood, and he walked as quietly as he could to let himself out of the room.

The hallway was lit only indirectly by the early afternoon: a trapezoid of shadow, an acute triangle of reflected light. He stared until they blurred, his hand still on the doorknob. His hand felt stiff when he finally released it, and he had the odd sensation that the floor wasn't level underfoot. Something with the foundation, he thought distantly. They'd have to mud jack it. Or have piering done.

Laughter drew him to the kitchen. Colt sat at the table, Biscuit crouched at his feet. He'd had his ribs taped too—you could tell from the slight hunch to how he sat—and a butterfly bandage winged across one cheekbone. Like father, like son, Emery thought with a kind of graveyard humor. No, not graveyard. Haunted house. Jem was picking pepperoni off a slice of pizza and popping them in his mouth, and for some reason, every time he did, Colt burst out laughing. Biscuit apparently didn't believe she was getting enough attention because she yapped at Colt; the boy, of course, ignored her.

The door to the backyard opened, and Tean stepped in, an empty stockpot hanging from one hand, saying, "My soup wasn't that bad—" But he cut off when he saw Emery. Jem froze, a slice of pepperoni in one hand. Colt's laughter cut off, and the light died in his face as he turned in his seat.

"How's J-H?" he asked.

"He's alright" was the first, automatic lie. And then Emery was committed, and he added, "Tired, and a little banged up."

"Does he need an ice pack?" Colt asked. "Did you get him an ice pack?"

It should have made Emery laugh because he remembered the sullen, angry boy who had come to him, the one who had worried so intently, the first time John had gotten hurt, about Pepsi and ice packs. Instead, his eyes stung, and he had to blink to keep them clear.

"Right now," he said, "he's going to rest. I wanted to check on you."

Colt shrugged and looked down at his pizza. "I'm fine."

"How's your head?"

Another shrug, one-shouldered.

Emery sat and brushed back some of that ridiculous hair. "Does it still hurt?"

Colt shook out a no.

"How about your ribs?"

"I'm fine, Pops. Jem, tell him."

But it was Tean who answered. "We've been keeping an eye on him. No physical exertion. Lots of rest. He and Jem are in a nap competition."

"Not to brag," Jem said, "but I'm winning."

"It doesn't count if you eat an extra plate of nachos," Colt mumbled, obviously fighting for normalcy. "I would have passed out too if I ate that many."

Tean smiled. "Also, if I have to watch them play War one more time, I'm going to lose my mind, so I'm putting in an official request for no more card games."

"You put in an official request for no more shows about megalodons," Jem protested. "You can't put in an official request about everything."

"I can and I will."

Colt was smiling again, his attention turned to the two men, and Emery studied his face in profile. And then he asked, "How's Ashley?"

It was like snuffing a candle, Colt's expression dark again, his face turned down once more. Tean's expression grew tight. Jem made a noise that suggested Emery had stepped in it.

"Did something happen?"

Colt shook his head. Then, in that same tone of forced evenness, "I guess his parents took away his phone because, um, he's not responding to any of my texts."

Emery brushed his hair away from his forehead again. Colt's amber eyes came up, wet and wide, and then he pulled back from Emery's touch. His shoulders curled in, and he pushed the slice of pizza around on his plate. A distant part of Emery thought, It's happening again. Because he knew what it felt like, to sit at home, alone, hurt, and to tell yourself lies and hope they were true.

"I was thinking," he said, "maybe it would be a good idea if you went on that service trip."

Colt's head snapped up. "For real?"

"You've worked hard to help them organize it. You've put in a lot of hours. You loaded the truck. It would look good on a college application."

"Ash and I did almost all of it ourselves," Colt said. "The girls didn't help at all. Well, except Trish, but she's way stronger than me or Ash. Pops, are you serious? That would be so dope."

"Don't say dope. And yes, I'm serious." Emery held up a hand to forestall Colt. "But I don't want you doing any of the manual labor, not while you're hurt. You're going to have to tell Koby you can help with anything else, but not the heavy stuff."

"I'm fine—"

Emery cut him off. "Promise."

"Pops!"

"Promise me."

The outrage in Colt's face threatened to make Emery smile, and he only barely managed to tamp it down. Finally, Colt said, "Fine! But that's the whole reason they need me! Koby's going to be so bummed."

"Koby is an adult, and I'm sure he'll understand that preventing you from injuring yourself further—and, as a result, being on the receiving end of a lawsuit from your overprotective father—is worth some small inconvenience. Also, I'm worried about you, and it's easier for me to let you go if I know that you're going to take practical measures to keep yourself safe."

Colt considered him for a moment. "You're kind of a bully, you know. Not just threatening to beat people up, but the emotional stuff."

"I had a very good teacher. Next time my mother 'needs help with some boxes'—" He drew the air quotes with his fingers. "—watch and learn."

A grin splashed across Colt's face, and he scrambled up from his seat—a slower scramble than usual, with some new twinges and winces, but still a scramble. "I've got to tell—" But he stopped, a blush rising in his cheeks.

"I'll talk to his parents," Emery said. "You'd better go pack." He checked the clock. "And call Koby to let him know; they're leaving in a few hours."

Colt sprinted off, grinning again.

"Do you see how that boy moves?" Jem asked. "I wish I were sixteen again. Busted ribs what?"

"If you were sixteen again, we'd have to take out a second mortgage to keep you in McDonald's," Tean said. "And can you imagine how many bags of chips I'd have to buy?"

"But, on the plus side, I'd be super horny all the time."

"Gee, what a change." As soon as the words left his mouth, Tean blushed and put his hand over his mouth. Jem burst out laughing and, in the process, almost choked to death on a piece of pepperoni. It flew from his mouth, and Biscuit immediately scooped it up and ate it.

"Maybe John's right," Emery said as he headed for the stairs. "Maybe we should just run away."

When he got to their bedroom, he was surprised to see the lights on under the door, and the sound of bare feet on the floorboards. He opened the door. John had pulled on a pair of sweats that left very little to the imagination—including the fact that he'd opted out of underwear. They rode low on his hips, exposing a band of pale skin below his faded tan lines and free of the dark ink of his tattoos. As Emery watched, John pulled something from the closet and threw it on the bed.

Emery stepped into the room and shut the door behind him.

He took the chair in the corner. John had already made a pile on the bed, and he folded a polo with the Wahredua PD logo on the breast. Farther down in the pile was the heavier navy fabric of John's dress uniform.

"I told Colt he could go on that service trip."

The light picked out the fine gold hairs on John's nape.

"I thought it would be good, you know. To get him out of town for a few days."

When John shifted his weight, his bare feet made a soft, sticking sound against the boards.

"Well?"

"Sure."

Emery dropped back into the chair and rubbed his eyes. "What's going on?"

John kept his attention on the shirt, drawing one hand across the fold, making it crisp and tight. Then he laid the shirt on top of the pile. He'd turned on every light in the room even though the afternoon light coming through the windows was white and sharp. It made it feel like it should have been dark. Like it was night. Night in the haunted house.

"My father stopped by the hospital."

That was all.

"And?"

"And—" John worked another Wahredua PD shirt off a hanger. "—he helped me understand some things."

"He did."

"Yes, Ree. He did."

"Like what?"

"Like the fact that, whatever happens, I'm out of a job."

Emery opened his mouth to respond, but John's phone made a familiar chirping noise—the sound of a notification from a social media app.

"I thought you turned those off."

John laid the shirt on the bed. He folded one side in. He straightened the sleeve.

"I thought you were going to delete those apps."

"They're talking about me. Why shouldn't I know what they're saying?"

"Because it's fucking toxic. Because they have no fucking idea what they're talking about, and because they're an internet mob, and because they don't deserve to occupy so much as a single brain cell's worth of attention. Because it's fucking hurting you. Should I go on?"

A tiny smile creased John's cheek. He laid the freshly folded shirt on top of the stack.

"Will you stop that and talk to me?"

John hesitated, another shirt hanging from his hand. He let it fall back onto the pile and turned to face Emery. His expression wasn't cool; it was disconnected, like someone else was behind the mask. He said nothing, and he said nothing, and all that saying nothing felt like a hand closing around Emery's throat.

Finally he managed, "What do you mean you're out of a job?"

John crooked a smile at him over one shoulder as he went back to the shirts. "Is there another meaning?"

Emery stood. He crossed the space to where John stood and reached out to draw him into an embrace. Before he could, though, John bent, picked up the pile of shirts, and moved them to the dresser.

"It's not a big deal," John said, straightening the edges of the shirts without looking up. "I don't want to make a whole thing out of it."

"In what way is it not a big deal?"

John didn't look up, but he was wearing that crooked smile again. His phone dinged, and he picked it up to glance at it.

"What did your father say exactly?"

"That either I resign, or he'll fire me because I'm too much of a liability. Sounds like my dad, doesn't it? I guess I can't really blame him. Everybody's got their priorities."

"What do you mean you can't blame him?" John opened a drawer and began rooting around in it. "Hey, I'm talking to you. Will you look at me?"

"In case you missed it, I'm in the middle of something."

"John, what is—" He wanted to ask, again, *What's going on?* But it was like smacking his head against a wall. He tried to think. Tried to work his way through the maze of his own thoughts. "You're not going to resign, are you?"

"Well, that's going to look better than getting fired, don't you think?"

"Who cares how it looks? You didn't do anything wrong. And on top of that, you're the best fucking chief of police this town has had—ever. Period. What the fuck does it matter how it looks?"

John shut the drawer hard. He turned and leaned hipshot against the dresser, the defined musculature of his torso in a sinuous curve. "It matters, Ree, because, depending on if I go to prison, I'm going to have to find another job sooner or later, and if I have to explain why my own father fired me, it's going to be a lot more difficult."

"He's not going to fire you."

"Of course he is. Naomi practically took out ad space in the *Courier* telling everyone what a disgrace I am—did you read that article, by the way? Just about every other sentence includes the phrase 'history of operating outside the law.' She blames me for the sheriff's death, just so you know. I mean, she's got me teed up for interference charges, witness tampering, everything you can imagine. Hell, Ree, I'd fire me at this point. So don't give me your moral high ground bullshit when I could use a little support!"

His voice rose into a shout, and when he cut off, the echo ran through their bedroom. Emery stared at him, at how his chest rose and fell, at ink gliding over muscle, bruises muddying the ink. The tape made a white blaze across his ribs. His heart must be racing, Emery thought. He's hurt. He's worn out.

Somehow, he managed to say, "I'm sorry."

John made a cutting motion with one hand. His phone dinged again, and he glanced at it. It was hard to read anything in his face. Like when Emery had first come back to this town. When every expression that crossed his features was a puzzle.

And because John was John, because even when he was hurting, he was so aware of other people, so tuned in, he must have known that Emery was struggling. He spoke again, his voice neutral now. "I know this isn't what we planned, Ree, but I think it's an opportunity. This could be a good thing."

A good thing, Emery thought. He didn't remember where he was standing, not really. He sat and, from some remote part of his brain, was grateful the bed was there to catch him. He caught himself nodding like this was all making sense.

"You know, I always thought about law school." John opened the next drawer, his back to Emery again. "I almost did it. I think now might be a good time."

"Law school."

"Lots of police officers go to law school."

"Yes."

The phone dinged again.

"I think I could do something good, Ree. You know how it is—when you're police, you're always cleaning up the mess after it happens. This is a chance for me to help fix problems, you know? Really get to the heart of things."

Emery cleared his throat. "Wroxall doesn't have a law school."

"Right, but wherever we move, there'll be a university."

In the winter sunlight, motes of dust hung motionless in the air.

"We're moving."

John glanced over his shoulder. He wore a tiny frown: the corners of his mouth, the furrow in his forehead, even a hint of it around his eyes. He was always good at lying, Emery thought. Always so good at it, especially when he was trying to protect himself.

"You want to stay?"

It was harder than Emery expected to swallow.

"Come on, Ree. From the minute you set foot in Wahredua again, you've wanted to leave. You hate this town. You told me the other week it was an infected genital wart, and that was because somebody cut you off on Market Street."

"This is our home."

"You hated it when you were growing up here. You only came back because of the job." John gave him a look like he was trying to see Emery more clearly, as though there were something confusing about this interaction, as though he were peering at him from a long way off. Always, Emery thought. He'd always been good at lying because he knew people. Because he'd always been so good at reading them. "Colt's not from here. Evie's too young to care. We'll have to work out something with Cora for custody, but honestly, I wouldn't be surprised if she wanted to move too. She'd love not to travel so much for work."

"John." He stopped because when he reached for the words, they weren't there. He heard himself saying again, "This is our home."

The phone dinged again.

"Will you turn that off?"

"I don't understand what the problem is. You want to stay? Is that what you're telling me? Because you love it here, and you want to raise our children here, and you think after everything that's happened, this is the best place for our family to be?"

"No—"

"So, what's the problem?"

"The problem is these small-minded assholes shouldn't get to run us out of town. That's the problem. The problem is we have a life here. I have a business here."

"Which you could do anywhere else. Hell, North would probably cry if you asked him if you could work at Borealis."

"We have friends here. Family. Our children have friends here."

"Remind me again about Colt's friends."

Emery rubbed his hands over his knees. The phone dinged again. It sounded like someone was ringing the doorbell, had their finger jammed on it. "You have a responsibility."

John straightened from the drawer. He turned around. His mouth hardened into a slash, and a hint of color came into his cheeks. "Say that again."

"You have a responsibility. To this town. To the people here." To our family, he wanted to say, but that ringing in his head made it impossible. "You took an oath."

"I took an oath."

"I don't understand—"

"What about you? You took an oath, Ree. And when you decided it was right, you quit. So much for your oath. And, in case you forgot, you didn't ask me. You didn't consult me. Do you remember that?"

"That was different."

"No, Ree. It wasn't. You were trying to do the right thing, what you thought was right. I'm trying to do the right thing."

"No, you're not! You're giving up, and I don't know why because never in my life have I known you to be a coward!" The phone dinged again. "And turn that fucking phone off!"

John stared at him, the seconds ticking past into minutes. And then he laughed. He pushed a hand through his hair, shook his head, and said, "I've always been a coward, Ree. You, of all people, ought to know."

He took a step toward the closet. Emery stood and moved into his path. He was shaking. His legs felt wet and rubbery.

"Move, please," John said. And then, "Move."

Emery stepped aside.

John opened the closet. He rifled through the clothes and emerged with a windbreaker with the Wahredua PD logo. As he worked it off the hanger, his phone began to ring. He looked at it, dismissed the call, and went back to the windbreaker.

A moment later, the phone began to ring again.

John dismissed the call.

The phone rang a third time. John's cheeks reddened, and after dismissing the call a third time, he fumbled with the phone for a moment. It didn't ring again.

Emery watched all of it. When his own phone buzzed, it felt like a nightmare, but he slowly worked it out of his pocket. Gray Dulac's name flashed on the screen. He slid his thumb across the screen to accept the call and placed it on speaker.

"He's gone," Dulac said. "He escaped. They found the deputy who was supposed to be guarding him in the fucking bathroom, a scalpel halfway through his throat."

Emery's head felt like it was packed with cotton, but his brain still managed to make the connection. "Vermilya."

"They've got no fucking clue how long ago he disappeared. He could be anywhere by this point." Frustration tightened Dulac's voice. "He had to have help."

And that was it, Emery knew. The end. The last thread snipped.

"There you go," John said as he picked up the stack of clothes. He shouldered past Emery to get to the door. "That's it, then."

19

Emery said something to Dulac—he wasn't sure what—and the call disconnected. The sound of John's fading footsteps moved away from him. The house was silent. We were yelling, Emery thought. They'll all have heard. They'll all feel uncomfortable. Colt will have heard. That last thought threatened to break a dam inside him, and so Emery started to move because if he moved, he had a chance of holding everything together.

He shut the drawers. He picked up the empty hangers and returned them to the closet, and then he shut the closet door. John's wet towel lay on the floor, so he hung it in the bathroom. His hands were still shaking, so he pressed them against his thighs. The last of the shower's humidity fogged an arc at the top of the mirror.

Leaving the bedroom, Emery made his way downstairs. When he passed through the living room, Colt sat on the couch, his eyes red. Jem sat next to him, rubbing his back, and he followed Emery with an unreadable look. Tean stood in the opening to the kitchen, a towel wrapped around one hand. His eyes followed Emery too. Emery ignored the silent questions. He grabbed his coat from the hall closet and let himself out into the garage.

The cold felt like a crack across the cheek, tightening flushed skin, sharp in his mouth and nostrils. The Mustang was still here, which meant John hadn't run away again. Emery hit the button to raise the garage door, and as it rattled up, he found the snow shovel and the ice melt. The driveway was already clear, but the sidewalks needed work. The ice melt would be last. He set to work the shovel and realized, a few seconds later, he'd forgotten gloves.

It didn't matter. He worked as the cold crept into him, shoveling until his face was numb, until his hands ached, until his knuckles felt arthritic and swollen, and the rest of his body was hot and covered in sweat. The snow had melted and refrozen into ice, and he thought the word was sintered. It broke under the shovel into chunks, and he flung them into the street. The only sound was the scrape of the shovel over concrete, and the shattering of ice against the pavement. Constellations of sound. Sometimes, when the ice broke, tiny crystals feathered against his face, and he could feel them melt.

When he got to the edge of their property, his back was killing him, and the pain in his hands had become something that belonged to someone else. He leaned on the shovel for a while, breathing hard and still, somehow, unable to catch his breath. Broken ribs. That was what broken ribs could feel like, that sharp pain when you tried to take a full breath. But his ribs were fine. It was John who was hurt. And Colt. His son, bruised and bloodied, refusing to speak.

He grabbed the shovel and slammed it against the ground, again and again, swinging it like a baseball bat, each blow flattening the aluminum blade, the shock traveling up his arms. The cold made everything feel like it was happening far off. He was aware of the sound he was making—choked, guttural, animal. And then it was over, his chest heaving, his body screaming at him, the world white and spinning as he caught himself and dragged himself upright.

Sometime later, when he looked up, Tean was sitting on the porch. The doctor was bundled in winter gear, and his glasses caught the afternoon sun and held wicks of yellow flame. Emery tried to think through his options, but he was too tired. He slogged to the porch, dragging the ruined shovel behind him, and dropped onto the step next to Tean. His breath was heavy and syncopated; he couldn't hear the doc's at all.

Without saying anything, Tean reached over and turned Emery's hands so that he could inspect them. A couple of blisters had formed and split, but the sting wasn't noticeable under the cold. Tean took a second set of gloves out of his pocket and held them out, and Emery dragged them on. A hat next, and he put that on too. Then Tean passed him a heat pack. Emery shook his head.

"Either you use that or we're going inside," Tean said.

"Are you going to make me?"

"Of course not. I'll call Shaw."

Emery snapped the heat pack to activate it, and then he held it between his hands. It didn't take long for the pack to warm, and as the heat worked its way through the gloves, Emery's hands began to throb with a bone-deep ache.

"I understand that he's upset," Emery said. "And that he's not thinking clearly. And that this isn't about me, not really. So I don't need to talk. And

I don't need your help." For some reason, he thought of what Colt might say if he heard that, and he added, "But thank you."

Tean nodded. Their breaths steamed in the air, the rhythm alternating, and it made Emery think of trains, the steady billowing of an engine. The day was already deepening toward dusk, the sun low in the sky, small and diffuse and distant, so pale it was almost the color of cream. Sunset, when it came, would be a nothing band of orange and yellow. And then night.

"Did you know I was raised Mormon?" Tean said.

"I thought you were supposed to say Latter-day Saint."

Tean smiled. His bushy eyebrows arched. "That's right. But growing up, everyone always said Mormon. I still think of it that way."

"No," Emery said. "I didn't know that. I wasn't sure—I mean, I knew it was a probability."

"My family still practices. Believes, I guess. That's a more generous word. I think they really do believe it."

The silence was like a crust of snow waiting to be broken.

"I imagine that makes it more difficult," Emery said.

"I knew I was gay when I was a teenager, but for a while, I thought I could balance things. That's not what I mean. Make things work, I guess. I went on a mission. And then I couldn't anymore."

"Why?"

"I loved someone. And for a while, he loved me."

Across the street, the fences were painted white with snow. More snow licked the leeward sides of the trees. A long apron of sunlight fell across part of the lawn, picking out the crystalline structure of the ice. A breeze lifted, and a tiny rosette of snow spun across the street.

"I appreciate you sharing this with me," Emery said, "but I'd like to be alone."

"Of course." But Tean didn't stand. He was staring out at the world through those chunky black glasses. His chest rose and fell so slowly he might have been sleeping. "When I came out, when I accepted it, I mean, I felt like my life was over. I'd lost everything—that's what I told myself, anyway. In a sense, it was true. I'd lost so much of what made me me. My family was devastated. The religious foundation of my life had crumbled, and along with it, my sense of purpose and place in the universe, my orientation toward good and evil, my knowledge of myself as a being of worth and dignity. That's putting it all in rather fanciful terms, but you know what I mean. I still had things I cared about. I had school, and then I had a career. I found friends, although believe it or not, not that many."

Emery couldn't repress the snort, and Tean chuckled.

"But for a long time, I was grieving. I think, in a way, I was grieving until Jem came into my life. I was grieving the relationships I'd lost. And I was grieving the self who was gone, who would never come back. And I was grieving the future I'd thought I was going to have. And I wish someone had told me back then that those griefs were real, and that they were valid, and that it was ok to mourn those losses."

That seemed to be the end because he fell silent. His clothing rustled as he adjusted his position on the porch, his gaze fixed on the middle distance. Maybe he was looking out at the tracks that had broken the crust of snow. Rabbits, Emery thought. Even in the snap-jaws of winter, life managed to go on.

"I'm sorry," he said. "About the shovel."

A laugh broke out of Tean, and he covered his mouth. But Emery heard his own words, and a chuckle escaped him, and they both looked at the shovel with its mangled aluminum blade, and the laughter came again. Emery laughed until his chest hurt. Tean laughed with him, pushing his glasses up to wipe his eyes. Their laughter died in fits. In the silence that came after, Emery was aware of the knots in his shoulders that had loosened, of the heat pack and the warmth easing the ache in his hands.

"It's really not funny, I know," Emery said. "It's a terrible example for Colt. He has enough anger already, and it's a miracle that it hasn't consumed him, as young as he is. Every time I do something like this, it's teaching him the wrong way to handle powerful emotions."

"Maybe not the best way," Tean said in his quiet way. "But not the worst either. He's a smart young man; I think he knows that."

"He knows I shouldn't yell at John. He's going to ride me about that, believe me."

Tean's smile was a quicksilver flash.

"How much did you hear?" Emery asked.

"The volume, mostly. Not what you were saying."

Maybe he hadn't noticed it until now. Or maybe it was new, something that had come about as the angle of the sun changed. Across the street, rainbows bent along the prisms of icicles hanging from the eaves of Mr. Johnson's house.

"For so much of my life, I've been angry at this town. Angry at John. Angry at the bigotry and intolerance, at all the injustice of it. It's been a weapon. And a shield. Growing up here, with people the way they were, I felt…"

"Powerless?"

Emery nodded. "Weak. Vulnerable. But when I was angry, I didn't feel any of those things." He adjusted the heat pack. He remembered the night he had understood the importance of his anger, lying alone in the dark in his childhood bedroom, with three fresh cuts on his belly, lines that made the crude beginnings of a G. Mikey Grames had caught him. And John had been there too, had held one of his arms as Mikey cut. And in the dark, smart enough to know what to worry about, he had envisioned nightmare scenarios of infection run rampant, flesh-eating bacteria, MRSA. He had lain there, watching the headlights move past his window like ships out on a vast, black sea, and his belly hot and itching and inflamed, and still he hadn't told his parents. And he had come to understand, during those long hours, that it felt so much better to be angry than to feel scared and hurting and alone. "I've tried to—to be better. With John, especially. With our children." Then his throat closed, and he couldn't say anymore.

Tean toed some of the snow off the step below them. His boot made a soft, scraping sound until it thunked against the wood. "Anger isn't always a bad emotion. It tells us where we've set our limits. It lets us protect ourselves and the people we care about. I think that's an important part of who you are. I think you love people deeply, and I think it must be difficult to know you can't protect them from everything, that even your anger can't keep them safe."

"It is fucking terrible," Emery said, his voice breaking in the middle, and he wiped his face on his shoulder. He wrestled to get control of himself. "I can't help John. I can't stop what's happening. God knows I can't protect my son; the minute he steps outside of the house, he's a moving target." He fought again for control and lost, his voice stretched thin as he said, "I am so fucking sick of feeling helpless."

Nodding, Tean rubbed Emery's back. Somewhere nearby, the voices of children rose, words mixed with laughter and screams of excitement. "It's none of my business, Emery, but I think right now, John-Henry doesn't need your anger. He's going to have plenty of his own."

"But that's what I don't get! That's my whole point! I would love for him to—to just go ballistic about this. Because it's killing him, and he's letting them do it, and I just want to tell him to be angry, to use that feeling, to stand up for himself and not let these sheepfuckers ruin every good thing he's done and destroy the person he's made himself." Emery's hands tightened around the heat pack. "Instead, he's acting like he's lost his mind."

"He's grieving. I think, in some ways, John-Henry understands the situation better than you, even though he hasn't been able to put it into words yet. And he needs you right now, even though he can't say it. Maybe even though he doesn't know it, or doesn't know how to tell himself what he needs. He needs you to be there for him, to help him understand that things are going to be ok. And he needs you to let him grieve all the things he's lost." Emery opened his mouth, and Tean spoke over him. "I'm not saying that we should all lie down and let these assholes get away with this, but that's separate, Emery. You need to distinguish between the two. And you need to help him distinguish between the two as well."

The wind picked up, spinning grains of snow to sting and melt against Emery's cheek. On the next street, or the next, or somewhere, children were laughing. His hands were hot inside the gloves, and he fought, now, to keep his head up, his breathing even, as he looked out at the small, pale sun.

Finally, when he was sure his voice wouldn't betray him, he said, "I believe Jem has a policy about the swear jar."

Tean slanted a smile at him. "Jem also believes strongly in the policy of 'what you don't know won't hurt you.'"

Nodding, Emery said, "I can live with that."

20

John-Henry was going through the boxes in the basement when the familiar sound of Emery's steps reached him. He opened the next box to discover a jumble of Easter decorations that, unless he was wrong, Cora had foisted on them when she decided she didn't want them anymore. He did a quick scan to make sure nothing valuable was hidden below the felt bunnies, and then he slid the box to the donate pile.

Behind him, he could feel Emery in the doorway, watching.

He reached for the next box, opened it, and stared. Inside were the Wahredua High clothes he'd tossed in the trash the other night—the newer stuff, the sweats and hoodies and jackets he'd bought once Colt started at the school, and the older stuff as well, the few pieces he'd kept. His letterman jacket. The faint smell of the leather mixed with the scent of the old cardboard box.

"I was hoping you wouldn't find those," Emery said.

John-Henry stared at the neatly folded clothing. Emery had rescued all of it, apparently. Gone out in the middle of the night, probably, when he should have been sleeping, because God knew he never got enough sleep, and especially not lately. And he'd folded it all, and he'd put it in this box, and he'd hidden the box at the back of the shelf. John closed the flaps on the box and slid it toward the donate pile.

"Could we talk?" Emery asked. "I'd like to apologize."

"You don't need to apologize; we both got a little heated."

"I'm going to anyway. I'm sorry, John."

John-Henry nodded. His face felt hot, and his eyes stung, and he kept his gaze on the next box, which apparently was full of old paint cans. Donate. "Thanks. I'm sorry too. I unloaded a lot on you, I guess. Hey, can we do this later? I'm—I'm not really in a good place right now." And then, in what—even to him—sounded like the most pathetic of all excuses, he added, "I've got to finish going through these boxes."

Emery's steps clipped against the bare concrete of the utility room. He moved into John-Henry's field of vision, crouched, and studied him. Then he reached out. His hands were warm, and his touch was surprisingly gentle as he eased John-Henry's hands off the next box. He turned them, adjusting them in his grip. John-Henry was surprised to feel the rawness of broken blisters as Emery's hands closed around his own.

"What did you—"

"You don't have to talk," Emery said. "But I'd like you to come with me. Because I want to tell you something. And then, when I've said what I want to say, we can come back, and I'll help you go through these boxes, or I'll stay out of your way, or I'll burn the goddamn house down, whatever you think is best." He adjusted his hands once more, and John-Henry realized, with a flash of surprise, that Emery was nervous. Not angry. Not tense. Not bristling for a fight. But scared. "Please?"

And that was how John-Henry found himself riding shotgun in the Odyssey as they drove out of their neighborhood. Day was falling into night, the sky purpling to black. No stars, not yet. Christmas lights shining on the old Arts and Crafts houses. A few other cars out and about, headlights splashing across the pavement. His breath fogged the glass, and he had the childlike urge to write his name in it and watch it disappear.

When they got to the high school, John-Henry said, "Ree."

But Emery just shook his head and kept driving. He parked out by the athletic fields and got out of the van and stood there, huddling with his back to the wind until John-Henry decided that dramatic husbands were perhaps even more unbearable than wrathful ones, and he got out of the van because apparently the other option was watching the only man he'd ever loved turn into a human popsicle.

Emery led them down a snow-covered slope toward the building. They approached a familiar pair of steel fire doors—generations of Wahredua High athletes had used these doors to go in and out from practice, to haul equipment out onto the fields, to hobble to the trainer after a bad tackle. When they reached the doors, Emery made a courtly, old-fashioned after-you gesture, and then he grinned. The grin was a surprise too, full of not only a kind of wry humor but also a vital energy that seemed like it belonged to another lifetime. But John-Henry found himself smiling too, and he did the little jump he'd perfected when he'd been seventeen, his palm slapping against the corner of the door. It popped open, and Emery caught it and held it so John-Henry could go first.

Inside, the warmth pushed back the evening's chill. Only the emergency lights were on, which meant the hallway was full of shadows. The faint hint of floor wax hung in the air. Emery took the lead again. As they made their way down the hall, something kicked on in the HVAC, and a soft humming noise began. It was strange, John-Henry thought, how time was also a place. Because he felt like he was walking back in time, like he was walking back twenty years, like it was just around the corner.

He made himself say, "Ree, I appreciate this, whatever it is, but if you've got some big reveal like you had my jersey cleaned or you fixed the spray paint—" He had to stop. "I'm not trying to be difficult, but I just don't think I can. Not tonight."

In answer, though, all Emery did was take his hand and keep walking. The raw spots where he'd broken the blisters must have stung, John-Henry thought, but his grip was tight and sure.

In retrospect, John-Henry should have expected it. But it was still a surprise when Emery stopped at the door to the boys' locker room. He frowned at the deadbolt and then, the corner of his mouth lifting, shrugged. "Ok, I have to admit I didn't think about the lock."

John-Henry's mouth was so dry he was amazed he could say anything, and even more amazed when the words sounded normal. "You might as well try it."

Emery gave the door a push, and it swung open, silent on its hinges. His smile was lopsided, and the thought came again: He's terrified. But he tugged on John-Henry's hand and led him into the locker room.

They'd updated the place since John-Henry and Emery had been in school, but locker rooms didn't change all that much. A handful of lights made pockets in the dark. The tile was different, but the walls were still painted cinderblock, and always—always—there was a leaky showerhead. It dripped now, a soft plonk in the distance. And in spite of a hint of bleach in the air, locker rooms apparently never smelled any better either: the mustiness of sweat and damp and gym shoes that never dried out. When they came around the curtain wall, a basketball rack was blocking the path, and its casters squeaked when Emery rolled it out of the way. In the mirrors above the sinks, their reflections were restless in the gloom, and it gave the sense that other people were here. Because, of course, there were. Because they were still here, even after all those years.

He broke the stillness and almost felt bad for doing so. "Ree."

But Emery shushed him. He looked around, orienting himself in the semidarkness, and then he steered John by the shoulders until he stood in the opening to the showers. He moved to stand near one of the metal benches. When he spoke, the tile caught his voice and bounced it, and John-Henry shivered.

"How's that?"

John-Henry didn't trust his voice, so he nodded.

Plonk. Plink. Even his breathing seemed to echo off the tile.

"We've never talked about that day, have we? Not really."

John-Henry shook his head. More seemed to be expected, though, so he whispered, "No."

In the dark, Emery's nod was more of a suggestion of movement than anything. "No, I didn't think so."

Something was building inside John-Henry—something that needed a release. Pressure building until it was a discomfort that bordered on pain. He wanted to touch his chest, fingers just below his breastbone, as though pressing there might make it better. But he couldn't move his arm. He couldn't do anything but stare at Emery, at the familiar shape of head and shoulders and hips, the way he stood, the hint, when he turned in profile, of scarecrow eyes.

"I wanted you so badly," Emery said. "I wanted you. I wanted to be you, too, I think. Happy, liked, at ease wherever you were. But mostly I wanted you. And I hated that I couldn't stop wanting you—that no matter what happened, it never went away."

No matter what I did, John-Henry amended. No matter what I did to you.

"We have a 'Gift of the Magi' situation, then," John-Henry said. "Because I wanted to be you."

Emery's soft exhalation sounded amused. "And that. I never expected you to be funny—not just clowning around, the way I saw you with your friends, but genuinely funny. I knew you were smart, but I didn't know you could make me laugh. Although I should have suspected you'd be drawn to something as mawkishly sentimental as an O. Henry story."

The tone, as much as the words themselves, broke the terrible solemnity of the moment, and whatever had been building inside John-Henry subsided. He laughed. "I'm serious, you know. About wanting to be you."

"Scrawny? Lonely?" That unexpected playfulness rose again in Emery's voice, and something thrilled inside John-Henry, like a golden wire stretched between them, that they were here, that they could be here, in this place, doing this—talking, joking, being. "Was it the frosted tips?"

Laughter burst from John-Henry again, and he was surprised, in the wake of the emotion, to find himself battling tears. He shook his head and gathered himself. "You were always…you." The first words were thick, but once he got his momentum, they cleared up. "You always knew who you were. You always knew what you wanted. You never let anyone or anything stop you. Do you know how attractive that was? Is, I guess. To be so totally, unswervingly committed to yourself, to your core, to what you know is true and right? God, Ree. I didn't know I was in love with you; I'm not going to say that. But I couldn't stay away from you. All I was doing was hiding, and there you were, bold and—and unbowed, I guess, although that sounds so old fashioned. Unafraid."

Emery shook his head, more a sound than a movement in the dark. "I was always afraid."

Machinery rumbled far off in the building. That pressure began to rise again in John-Henry's chest. He could hear his own breathing begin to accelerate.

"Do you have any idea how many hours I spent thinking about that kiss?" Emery asked.

The smile must have been lost in the dark, but John-Henry could feel the expression on his face, the cockeyed cut of it. "Not to be crass, but do you have any idea how many times I jerked off to it?"

His words startled a laugh out of Emery, and for a moment, amber gleamed again in the gloom. "That too," Emery said, and he sounded a little rueful. "I came up with every possible explanation. That it was a trap. That it was a test. That it was a joke. That it was, in some perverse way, some ultimate cruelty you had dreamed up."

"Not every possible explanation, then."

Emery was quiet for a long time before he said, "No."

Inside John-Henry, that sense of pressure increased until it felt like a knife, something sharp twisting just under his ribcage. "I didn't understand it for the longest time, why I was attracted to you. Maybe not until we were together."

"After it was too late, you might say."

"Something like that." The sound of every tiny movement echoed back from the tile. "I told myself it was because you were attracted to me. I told myself it was vanity. That I liked knowing I turned you on. Proof of my own hotness, stroking my ego, a kind of jerk-off satisfaction that didn't matter if you were a guy or a girl."

"Based on certain revelations this evening, that sounds true to form for teenage John."

"Oh, definitely. And after a while, when I wasn't so scared of it anymore, I could tell myself that it was validation. I hadn't done anything irredeemably awful to you—I was always trying to convince myself of that. A little bullying, sure. But maybe it wasn't as bad as it felt. Hell, maybe you even got off on it. You still liked me, after all. Or you wanted me, and that felt close enough. And sometimes I could almost convince myself it was true. But you know what? I never believed it, not really. Because I knew what I was doing. And I knew how awful it was. And I did it anyway because I was scared of you, and because I hated you because I couldn't be you." He drew a deep breath, surprised at the strength of the emotion sweeping through him. "And then you were here, and I was here, and I just…couldn't anymore. Couldn't keep fighting. Didn't want to keep fighting. It was a shitty thing I did, because I knew it was safe, and because I knew no one would ever believe you if you told. And, if I'm being honest, because I knew you wouldn't tell. So, I guess I'm apologizing. Again."

"Always so hard on yourself," Emery murmured. "That was another thing that surprised me, you know."

John-Henry was trembling, and he wiped away tears that hadn't fallen yet, but he managed a sound that might have been a laugh. "Overcorrecting, I guess."

"You did something that was brave and beautiful and that gave us each other, if only for a moment, John. You've got nothing to apologize for, even if you were scared at the time. Maybe because you were scared."

"Really?" He tried for that laugh again, and the first hot splash of a tear fell. "Because it doesn't feel like that."

In the silence that followed, the plonk-plink-plonk of dripping water seemed almost musical.

"I've done this all wrong," Emery said.

"No, it's ok." John-Henry's nose was a little snotty, but he dried his face on his sleeve. "I appreciate you bringing me here. You're the most important person in the world to me, and I hate when we fight. I fucking hate it. This was a good reminder. We've made so much progress. I love you. I told myself I'd never hurt you again."

"John."

"It's ironic, though, right? I mean, this whole town hates me now. Beyond hate. They despise me. And the irony is, they should hate me because I'm a piece of shit, but they hate me for the wrong reason." Another tear fell, stinging his cheek. "Hey, maybe it's karma."

"John."

But Emery stopped there. Because he knew John-Henry was right. Because there wasn't anything that anyone could say to that. John-Henry's face pulsed in time with his heartbeat. Sweat dampened his shirt under his arms. In the rush of strong emotions, he felt cored out, empty and exhausted in a way that went deeper than the body. His gaze wandered the locker room, found the blank faces of the mirrors. They covered mirrors, in some cultures, when they were mourning. Because mirrors were where you saw demons.

When Emery spoke again, his voice was rough. "When I was growing up, I knew what I wanted. I wanted to get away from here, away from the bigotry, the intolerance, the petty hates and small minds. I was going to go somewhere else, and I was going to be someone else. Even during the worst of it, I knew it was only a matter of time. If I could make it through high school, I told myself, I'd be free. College would be a whole other world. And then, after that, I'd have a job, I'd be independent, I'd find people who loved me and respected me for who I was. I was sure of it." For a long, silent moment he seemed to be wrestling with something. And then the strain in his body eased, and he gave a quiet laugh. "And then my life fell apart, and I lost everything."

John-Henry said nothing. He didn't think he could have said anything even if he'd known what to say.

"I came back here," Emery said, "because I'd lost everything. My career was in shambles. My relationship was over, even if I wasn't ready to admit it. The entire future I'd dreamed for myself—for years, John, years on years, the dream that had kept me going when it seemed like it would be so much easier to give up—it was gone. And I had nothing." John-Henry couldn't identify the note that entered Emery's voice when he added, "And then there was you."

"Insult to injury." John-Henry's jaw cracked as he worked it. "I know—"

"I don't think you do, John. Know, I mean. You're very intelligent, and you're sensitive, so I'm sure you have an idea. But I don't think you know, not completely. It was like I'd died. I'd lost everything I'd worked so hard for, and now I was back in the place I'd promised myself I'd never come back to. And even though I didn't know how to say it, even though I'd never put it to myself that way, I can look back now and see that a part of me—a part of me was ready to stop fighting. It would have been easier, I think. To find a way not to hurt so much, and let that escape become the sole purpose of my life."

"Easy for people like me. I don't think it would have been so easy for you."

"Maybe."

What happened next, John-Henry didn't have a name for. But he knew it: the way birds settled onto trees at dusk; the spin of iron filings drawn by a magnet; how he reached out at night, in the dark, to find him, to lay a hand on him, and then sleep again. It raised the hair on his arms. The skin across his chest tightened with goose bumps.

"You were here," Emery said, his voice buckling under that same emotion John-Henry couldn't name. "You were here, and everything changed. Everything, John. The life I have with you, I never could have imagined. Not in my wildest fantasies. Not even here, not even that first, singular moment when I thought maybe there was hope. I never could have imagined loving you the way I do, or the happiness of sharing your life, or the joy of raising children together. This wasn't in any of the plans. It wasn't the dream. It wasn't the future I'd built myself. It is so much more." He stopped, and the soft sounds he made suggested tears, but his voice was steadier when he spoke again. "I'm not saying that your situation is the same. I know it's different. What was done to you was unfair and unjust. It was cruel. It was evil. And I can't promise that what comes next will be better than the life you envisioned for yourself. All I can say is that I'll be here, John. With you. For you. And there will be a future. And things will get better."

John-Henry crossed the distance between them, the years falling away, Emery resolving out of shadow into the man John-Henry loved here, now—warm, solid, present. He was almost running because he didn't think his legs could hold him much longer; the walls were coming down, and everything he'd worked so hard to stave off threatened to wash over him. He crashed into Emery's chest, and Emery wrapped him in an embrace, and the last barrier fell, and John-Henry wept like a child.

21

It wasn't exactly like the fantasies. In the fantasies, John-Henry hadn't had to deal with the inconvenient realities of how cold the metal benches were, or how narrow, or the fact that—bottom line—the locker room was downright disgusting. But in some ways, it was better. He lay on the bench, his head in Emery's lap, and this Emery had a very nice lap, unlike the scrawny teenager John-Henry had known. And this Emery knew exactly how to run his fingers through John-Henry's hair, and he knew how John-Henry liked him to rub circles over his chest and stomach with the flat of his other hand, and he knew, most of all, how to be silent together.

In the aftermath of the tears, John-Henry felt wrung out, the emotional fatigue compounding the physical exhaustion of the strain of the last few days, his lack of sleep, and his injured body's efforts to heal itself. He ached all over. His joints throbbed. He remembered high school and how, by the end of a week of a two-a-days, after the double practices in the August heat, how he had felt like this. Back then, the solution had been eating an entire extra-large pizza and sleeping for most of the weekend.

But strangely, in its own way, the weariness was also pleasant. John-Henry could have done without the aches and pangs from the beating he'd taken, but otherwise he felt...purged. Cleansed. Like something festering inside him had been washed out, and the relief was in the knowledge that, no matter how he felt now, he could heal.

Emery's thumb traced his smile.

"Just thinking," John-Henry answered the unasked question. "About pizza."

Emery laughed quietly. "We can do that."

John-Henry took his hand and kissed it. "Thank you."

Fingers carded his hair once more, and Emery said, "This is what we do for each other." Then his voice shifted. "John, what you said about a baby—"

"I know. I'm sorry; I don't—I don't know. It just popped into my head, and then it seemed like the perfect solution, and God, I know, I must have sounded insane."

In the distance, the shower dripped.

"Is that something you want?" Emery asked.

"I don't know. Maybe. It's hard to think clearly right now. But it's not something I have to have. I think, more than anything, it felt like an outlet. Something else to fixate on, if that makes any sense."

Emery made a considering noise and stroked his hair. "In that case, perhaps now it'll be appropriate, as North suggested, to dick you down."

John-Henry burst out laughing.

"That wasn't a joke, John."

That only made him laugh harder.

"I didn't mean now as in this instant, you understand. I'm speaking in terms of your emotional state."

Now John-Henry had to wipe his eyes. Emery huffed and pushed his head out of his lap, but when John-Henry sat up, he wore one of those invisible Emery Hazard smiles.

"I honestly do not know," John-Henry said, "what I would do without you."

"Eat pizza and masturbate, apparently."

"Well, it's not the worst plan."

They drove home in silence, John-Henry's hand on Emery's thigh. The headlights carved hollows out of the dark and cold. The rumble of the tires. The rock and sway of bodies as the van's suspension adjusted to uneven pavement. The hiss of warm air in the vents.

The house was bright with lights when they got home. North's ridiculous new car—some black contraption from the '80s—was parked at the curb next to Tean and Jem's rental, and Theo and Auggie's Audi sat farther down the block. After the garage door had closed behind them, John-Henry could make out the sound of excited shouts from inside the house.

"At what point," Emery asked as he opened his door, "did we adopt six additional children?"

"Tean's more like your younger brother."

"Except that he's older than me."

"Trust me, I know."

When they stepped inside, John-Henry had to stop and stare at the scene in front of him. He had a clear line of sight across the kitchen and into the living room, where Tean—the younger brother in question—had a towel duct-taped around his head. Theo was holding a baseball bat out of North's reach and saying, "—really don't think this is a good idea."

"Let me guess," North said. "You've got a better way to teach him how to fight. Four-eyes, don't flinch, ok?"

Tean blinked. "Wait, what?"

"I can't believe you agreed to this," Theo said, moving the bat farther out of North's reach.

"I didn't agree to it! Jem just told me to wrap this towel around my head!"

"You'll be fine," Jem said. "The towel is like padding. It'll absorb the blows. Well, mostly."

"But not in the face," Shaw said.

"No, not in the face."

"The face is a big deal for me," Tean said, his voice rising.

North took Colt's hand—the one with the still-swollen knuckles from his encounter at the high school—and curled his fingers in. "Now, when you throw a punch, you want to make sure you keep your thumb out of there so it doesn't get broken, ok?"

Colt nodded, his face set in ferocious seriousness.

Auggie moved into a relaxed stance and demonstrated a punch. "And you don't generate the power from elbow or your shoulder. You generate it from your hips like this."

"Hey!" North barked. "Who's showing him?"

"I was helping—"

"No, you were interrupting because you had to be Suzy-on-top! So, shut your mouth and sit down."

"What is Suzy-on-top?" Jem asked, sounding like he was on the verge of a giggle.

"You're fucking looking at him."

"Oh, one time North was being Suzy-on-top," Shaw said. His voice grew even more excited. "And he wasn't generating any power from his hips. See, we were playing horse masseuse—"

"What is horse masseuse?" Tean asked. He was, as far as John-Henry could tell, discreetly trying to rip the duct tape that held the towel around his head.

"You're supposed to stand there and be quiet," North snapped.

Shaw, though, beamed. "Oh, it's so much fun. See, North was a beautiful but high-spirited sorrel called Applejack, and I was a lonely horse masseuse called Carl, and Applejack had pulled a muscle in his haunch, and

I was trying to massage it, only Applejack kept saying, 'A little higher, Shaw,' and I kept saying, 'No, it's Carl'—"

"Will you be quiet, you goddamn—" North seemed at a loss for a moment and finished with "—mooncalf?"

"Mooncalf?" Tean asked, yanking on the tape again.

"See?" Shaw looked around for validation. "That's Applejack talking."

North scowled at him, and the scowl drifted around the room until it settled on Colt, who was chewing on his collar in a failing attempt not to laugh. "Stand up straight. And show me your hand."

"You know," Theo said, "it's easy to mess up your hands even if you know how to punch. A lot safer to throw an elbow."

"Thanks, Grampsie," North said, and it sounded like he was gritting his teeth. "I'm sure you've got all sorts of nifty tricks the Doughboys taught you, but I'm handling this."

"Honestly," Jem said, "punching is kind of gay."

"You are gay," North said. "He's gay. We're all fucking gay."

"John's bi," Emery said.

Everyone looked at him.

"If that helps."

"I'm bi too," Shaw announced.

Auggie, who had been struggling to keep a straight face for most of the last few minutes, lost it at that point. He fell onto the couch and laughed into a cushion.

"I am," Shaw said. "I even went to a—what's the polite term for where you pay a lady to let you put your thingy on her thingy, and maybe both of you cry a little?"

"This is fucking fantastic," North said. "Thanks to you chowderheads, Colt's not going to know how to take care of those pieces of shit the next time they try something."

"Did he really just call us chowderheads?" Theo asked.

Jem shook his head. "I'm telling you, you don't need to punch them. You buy yourself some paracord and a hex nut as big as your thumb, and then you swing it really fast and—hold on, let me show you."

At that point, Tean backed into the kitchen.

"Babe!" Jem called.

"Ok," Emery said. "I think we've reached the end of this particular session of batshittery. Colt, ignore everything they told you. Do you understand me?"

Collar still between his teeth, Colt grinned and nodded.

"Are you packed?"

Another nod.

"Grab your bag. John and I are going to drop you off. What are the rest of you chowderheads doing in my house?"

"Giving that poor kid a male role model who won't make him want to jump off a roof when he's an adult," North said.

Shaw nodded. "And eating all that cheese you tried to hide at the back of the fridge."

North turned a wounded look on him.

"It was such a fun game," Shaw said. "It was like hide-and-seek. Only for a mouse. Oh! Mouse hide-and-seek! That's a new game we can play the next time we—"

"Go on," North said in a deadly voice. "Finish that sentence."

"Theo," Auggie wheezed from the couch. "Theo, I'm legit going to pee myself."

Theo rolled his eyes and then moved into the kitchen to help Tean free himself from the towel.

A few moments later, Colt was back with a duffel bag.

"What about Ashley?" John-Henry asked.

"He's already there," Colt said.

Emery took his bag and carried it out to the Mustang, and as they got into the car, he asked, "Are you two ok?"

Colt nodded.

"What's going on?" John-Henry asked.

Colt didn't answer as the garage door rolled up. He spoke as they backed out onto the driveway, and his voice was quiet. "It's his parents."

It shouldn't have been a surprise, but the flash of pain was still real. "What'd they say?"

"They're just worried, J-H. It's dumb. It's not a big deal."

"What did they say?"

"Pops."

But John-Henry heard the plea there, and he shook his head and said, "It's ok. You don't have to talk about it."

He knew, anyway, what it must have been. That Ashley wasn't allowed to come over to their house. That would be the bare minimum. The Boones were kind people, decent, and they'd handled it surprisingly well when their son had come out and started dating Colt. But everyone had their limit, and maybe they'd finally reached theirs.

They drove in silence to GLAM. The pride center was located in the corner unit of a strip mall in the northeast corner of town. It was one of the oldest parts of town, and the original buildings that hadn't been knocked down were tall and skinny and built on narrow lots. It had been dragged forward through time until approximately when Eisenhower had been president, and then it had settled there: squat brick buildings, asphalt lots patched with tar, a payday loan store with an inflatable Porky Pig tied outside. Every time the wind picked up, Porky would spin in place, scraping along the brick wall, which explained why half his face had been scratched away. It wouldn't be long, John-Henry figured, before the vinyl ripped, and Porky Pig would go to the great payday loan store in the sky.

A twenty-foot U-Haul was pulled up in front of GLAM, with a passenger van parked in front of it like a tugboat. A couple of kids were goofing off on the sidewalk—a long-haired boy chasing a boy with glitter threaded through his hair, while a girl tried to peg both of them with snowballs; another kid, who might have been nonbinary or agender, kicking the ornamental bushes free of snow; a girl in a lumpy sweater who was swinging her arms and legs rhythmically through the air, apparently performing a routine to music nobody else could hear. A boy who must have been the infamous Ty was trying to capture the routine on his phone and, in the process, was occasionally getting smacked with a snowball.

Ashley must have been watching for them because he exploded out of the van, a huge smile on his face, and jogged toward them.

"Oh my God," Colt said, but he was grinning. "He is such a dork."

"Have a good time," John-Henry said. "Be safe."

"Have a good time?" Emery said, reaching to unbuckle his seat belt. "That was a nice try, John, but we're not leaving him here until I've had all my questions answered to my satisfaction—"

"We already had all your questions answered. Weeks ago. When Colt first brought this up, and we spent forty-five minutes on the phone with these people."

"Exactly: by phone. Koby wouldn't even talk to us in person."

"And he answered all our questions." Emery opened his mouth, and John-Henry added, "To my satisfaction, if not to yours."

"Well, I'm sorry if 'We'll figure out dinner when we get there, Mr. Hazard,' doesn't inspire a robust confidence in their ability to plan this trip."

"There's Farah," John-Henry said as a dark-haired woman in a rainbow cardigan emerged from GLAM. He pulled Colt over, kissed him on the top of the head, and squeezed his neck. "Make good choices, bubs."

Emery gave Colt a hug, and Colt reached for the door. Then the boy stopped, and he looked back, and for a moment, he was a child again. "Are you guys ok?"

John-Henry smiled. "We're ok, bubs. Don't worry about us. Just have fun."

Colt opened the door as Ashley reached them. The boy was already talking. "Oh my God, bruh, I thought we were going to leave without you! What took so long? Hi, Mr. Hazard. Hi, Chief Somerset."

"Hi, Ash."

"Make sure nothing happens to my son, Ashley, or we'll revisit our conversation about the productive potential of power tools."

Ashley's face lost some color, and he stepped back so quickly that he slipped on a patch of ice. He would have fallen except Colt caught his arm and steadied him, and then the boy shot a furious look back at Emery. Without another word, he retrieved his duffel and led Ashley toward the van.

"Power tools?"

"Please," Emery said. "Colt lives for any opportunity to be annoyed with us. And honestly, I think Ashley likes it a little too. It must add a certain zest, don't you think?"

John-Henry shifted into drive as he said, "When Evie is old enough to date—"

"So, thirty."

"—I'm sending you somewhere else. Do they have study abroad opportunities for private investigators? Maybe you could spend years and years in the Amazon basin, hundreds of miles away from a computer or telephone."

"That's ridiculous, John. They have satellite phones and internet now."

"Maybe the International Space Station."

Emery rested a hand on the back of his neck and left it there as they drove home.

Their friends' cars were still parked on the street, and when they got inside, a familiar scene was playing out.

"Because if I'd wanted something healthy," North was saying, "I would have said, 'Hey, let's eat something that tastes like shit' not 'Hey, let's get pizza.'"

"Pizza can be healthy," Tean answered. "Have you ever had pizza with grape leaves?"

"Oh my God, there's this great Mediterranean place Theo and I love," Auggie said. "We could do that."

"Listen, Strawberry Shortcake, I'm sure it's nice that you finally found a place that will pre-chew Paw-Paw's food for him, but I want something that's actually good."

"How's their baba ganoush?" Shaw asked.

"I don't even like eggplant," Theo said, "and it's amazing."

"What don't you motherfuckers understand about pizza?" North demanded.

"Hey, how about tacos?" Jem asked. "Wait, hear me out: we DoorDash them."

"I'm changing the locks," Emery said to John-Henry. "Tonight."

John-Henry grinned as they passed through the kitchen into the living room.

"Will you please tell these shit-for-brains—" North began when he saw them.

"We're ordering pizza," Emery said. "Apparently that and masturbation were teenage John's only pursuits."

"That tracks," Tean murmured.

Jem gave a scandalized, "Tean!"

Tean blushed. "I'm so sorry. I didn't mean to say that out loud."

"No, it was amazing. I wish I'd said it. Also, it totally does track. I bet it was nonstop wang-a-rang from ages, like, twelve to—how old are you now?"

"I would have killed to meet teenage John," Auggie said. "Can you imagine if you'd had Twitter back then? He probably never would have left his bedroom."

Theo suddenly seemed to need to scratch his beard.

"Jesus Christ," John-Henry said, but it came out mixed with laughter. "I wasn't that bad."

"Get something good," Emery said as he passed a credit card to Theo. "And don't let him—" He spared a look for Jem. "—near that card."

"I was doing you a favor," Jem said. "They were slaughtering you with that interest rate."

"Where are you going?" Theo asked.

"We're going to pick up all the clothes that my husband decided to get rid of in perhaps the most dramatic way possible." Emery seemed to think about this and added, "Except maybe for burning them. John, did you consider burning them?"

"It wasn't that dramatic," John-Henry said.

"See, this is what I'm talking about." North made a face. "Bisexual my ass."

John-Henry felt like he might have needed to reply to that, but Emery herded him downstairs, and they set to work. The basement itself didn't take all that long—they returned most of the boxes to the shelves, and then they took John-Henry's Wahredua PD and Wahredua High clothing up to the bedroom. They worked together in silence to hang the clothes in the closet. John-Henry noticed when Emery hesitated over the letterman jacket.

He touched Emery's arm, and Emery glanced up. Then Emery smiled—not one of the tiny, invisible ones. But a real smile, full and open and vulnerable.

"Did I say thank you?" John-Henry asked.

"You did."

"Good. And I believe there was some mention of dicking me down."

Emery laughed quietly. "I do seem to recall that."

"You know, I wonder if that jacket still fits."

"You're more muscular than you were in high school."

"But maybe if I wore it without a shirt."

Emery's smile shaded toward uncertainty and a hint of color came into his cheeks.

"Unless that would be weird for you."

"No." The first word came quickly, and then Emery said more firmly, "No. I'd like that. I'm embarrassed by how much I'd like that."

John-Henry kissed him. He put a hand on Emery's cheek, and his skin was hot with the flush. He kissed him again, and Emery shivered.

When John-Henry pulled back, Emery whispered, "We have guests."

"They already think I'm a sex addict and a reprobate," John-Henry said with a shrug. "I don't think they'll be too disappointed."

"John, today has been a lot. If you don't feel—"

But John-Henry shushed him. He caught the hem of Emery's shirt and turned him out of it. Then he knelt and unfastened the button on Emery's jeans. He drew the zipper down, the slight stitch of resistance slowing him. Emery was hardening, the outline of his dick visible under the denim. John-Henry eased the jeans down. The black boxer briefs came next. Emery's lengthening dick swung out to brush his cheek, and the smell of Emery's arousal met him. He finished sliding the jeans down, and Emery's dick dragged along the side of his face, the faintest hint of wetness marking its passage. When he got the jeans around Emery's ankles, he laughed.

Emery twisted a hand in John-Henry's hair and, in a guttural voice, asked, "Something amusing down there?"

"I forgot about your boots."

Emery's answering noise was indeterminate.

"Leave them on," John-Henry said. "I want you like this."

In response, Emery caught more of John-Henry's hair and tugged him closer. John-Henry opened his mouth, taking the tip of Emery's dick, rolling it across his tongue. The noise Emery made in his chest was deep and feral, and his fingers tightened until the pull on John-Henry's hair bordered on pain. But it was the kind of discomfort that was arousing, too. It zigzagged like wildfire through John-Henry's chest, down to the pit of his belly, between his legs, and he was hard. He kept his hands on Emery's legs, stroking the massive thighs, following the curve of his ass. He took Emery deeper, and this time, Emery moaned.

John-Henry backed off. He stood and helped Emery to lie on the bed. It shouldn't have looked hot, with his jeans bunched around his ankles, with the boots, like this was the kind of quick fuck that didn't merit undressing completely. Or maybe it should have. John-Henry was past the point of knowing and way beyond the point of caring. He stripped, clothes and shoes, until he stood naked. Then he pulled on the letterman jacket. A little small, sure. But he caught a glimpse of himself in the mirror, of how the jacket looked hanging open over his developed chest to reveal the ripple of abdominal muscles, the way the jacket fell to hit him at the deep vee carved from hipbones to pelvis. His own dick was red with his arousal.

When he saw the look on Emery's face, a wave of fresh excitement washed over him. Emery was staring, his mouth slightly open, pupils dilated until the amber of his eyes was a dark gold. It was the raw, naked desire John-Henry remembered from the locker room. The desire that had lit a fire in him back then, that had made his skin feel electric, every inch of him alive with the energy ricocheting between them. He put a knee on the bed. Then he grinned and darted to the closet.

He put the Wahredua ball cap on backward and grinned, surprised that the goofiness didn't lessen his arousal—if anything, it amplified it. Because he could be this, too—silly and fun and relaxed—with Emery. Because he didn't have to be some porny stereotype of the ideal man. He certainly didn't have to be perfect, the town's golden boy. He could be himself. And being himself, right then, meant leaning into the fuckboy look a hundred and ten percent.

Emery lay propped against the headboard, his face unreadable. John-Henry crawled across the mattress to him. He straddled Emery's thighs and took his dick. The hard weight of it in his hand felt like resistance, but Emery's whole body responded to the touch, restless now, every part of him moving, reacting. Everything except his eyes. His eyes were fastened on John-Henry, and then John-Henry was aware of the ball cap on his head, of the leather and fabric against bare skin. Suddenly, he wanted this to be over.

He opened and closed his fingers. He slid his hand up and down Emery's dick. Emery made a low, pleased noise, almost like he was stretching. And then he caught John-Henry's hand and slowed him. Stopped him. He pulled John-Henry's hand away. He was still looking at him.

"Do you want me to take this stuff off?" John-Henry asked. His voice sounded too loud; he could hear himself trying to speak normally.

After a moment, Emery shook his head.

The wool was starting to chafe. The seams of the leather sleeves scratched sensitive skin above his arms. The hat. The hat had been such a stupid choice, putting it on backward. He probably looked like a badly aging Bart Simpson.

Emery slid his hands up under the jacket until he found John-Henry's hips. Then he sat up, and John-Henry had to shift to accommodate him. The new position still left him sitting higher than Emery. Their dicks brushed together, and John-Henry was surprised to realize he was soft. One of Emery's hands shifted to the small of his back. He looked up, and this time it was a question.

"I already got off, remember?" John-Henry tried for a smile.

Emery made a noise that could have meant anything.

"Why don't I suck you off?" John-Henry asked.

In answer, Emery leaned in and kissed John-Henry's collarbone. It was impossible to know if the kiss had been on ink or bare skin, but a part of John-Henry knew, without being told that, Emery had found one of the dark swirls. He kissed his way along the ridge of shoulder toward John-Henry's neck. He slowed and licked once at the hollow of John-Henry's throat.

"Why don't you fuck me?" John-Henry asked, the words gravelly. "I want you to fuck me like this."

That noise again, the one that could have meant anything. Emery kissed John-Henry's neck, and John-Henry shivered. It was too much, the jacket scratchy and rough, the hard length of Emery's dick poking John-Henry's belly, the way the hair on Emery's legs rubbed the sensitive backs of John-Henry's thighs. His hand at the small of John-Henry's back teased the cleft of his ass, and again, John-Henry thought, It's too much. He pulled away. The rasp of Emery's stubble lingered, lighting up the nerve endings of his neck. His breathing was raspy in the stillness of their bedroom. A detached observer inside his head noticed that it sounded like he was about to cry.

Nothing changed in Emery's face. The hand that was still on John-Henry's hip rubbed a circle. The hand at the small of his back seemed to be supporting him now.

"Let me lie down," John-Henry whispered, but it felt like begging. "And I want you to fuck me."

Instead, Emery leaned forward again. He didn't go for John-Henry's neck this time. He nuzzled aside the jacket and kissed a trail across John-Henry's chest. John-Henry's legs quivered. His brain catalogued the distance between what was going on inside his head and what was happening in his body: the awareness of attraction and desire, the touches and caresses of Emery slowly worshipping every inch of his body, his mouth latching on to John-Henry's nipple now, and the complete lack of response. It was this fucking jacket. It was the fucking Bart Simpson ball cap.

Emery released John-Henry's nipple and sat back. He was softening now too.

Cheeks hot, John-Henry couldn't quite meet his eyes. "Why are you—what's wrong?"

The silence lasted until John-Henry couldn't stand it anymore. He raised his head. Emery was staring at him, his gaze hooded, scarecrow eyes telling him nothing. The memory came without prompting: a childhood winter, the sunset filling the horizon with bands of gold, the stubble of a wheat field covered in hoarfrost that glinted with the last light of day. John-Henry didn't even remember why he'd been out there. His grandfather had taken him, he remembered that much, which meant it had been a long time ago. And he remembered the blackbirds taking flight, the dark scissors of their wings against the amber half-light.

Emery was still looking at him, but somehow, it was easier to speak now. "Sorry," John-Henry said. He forced himself to meet Emery's gaze. "I'm kind of a mess right now, in case you hadn't noticed. I wanted to do this, but I guess somebody has other ideas." He gave his dick a little shake. It was meant to be a joke, but Emery's expression remained unreadable. The weight and heat of his hands on John-Henry's body was grounding, though. The hand on his hip was still rubbing those little circles. John-Henry's voice trembled as he made himself say the rest of the words. "I wish I could have had this with you," he said. "God, we wasted so much time because of me. I wish I could have been this person for you when you needed me."

The corner of Emery's mouth slanted up, but he didn't say anything. He took John-Henry's face in his hands. He looked at him, and the seconds ticked past, but the frozen sunset of his eyes never wavered, never changed. He just looked. Tears prickled in John-Henry's eyes, and he wanted to turn his head, but Emery's fingers bit into his jawbone, holding him in place. He kept looking. It was like everything was being stripped away: the day's tragedies, the horrors of the last week and month, the strain and stress and despair. But more than that. He lost his armor piece by piece—the smile that, at one point in his life, had made him everyone's friend; the years he had spent as the town's golden boy, incapable of doing wrong; the clothes and fast car and big house. He was starting to tremble, and he tried to rear back, but Emery didn't let go. He felt naked—not just his body, but his mind or his soul or whatever you wanted to call it. They did this to prisoners, he thought. At the jail. The humiliation of being stripped of everything that made you a person. The dehumanization of having the trappings of civilization stripped away, of having another body invade yours, as you were reduced to meat.

"I love you," Emery whispered, and he laid the stress of the sentence on the final word. *You*. "I love you, John. I love you."

He released John-Henry, and John-Henry shifted his weight back in automatic retreat. But he managed to stop there, and he held himself stiffly, still trembling, as Emery eased the ball cap off his head. Emery scrubbed fingers through John-Henry's hair, smiling. Then he took hold of the jacket, and he paused, asking the question with his eyes. The trembling was coming harder now, but John-Henry managed a nod. Emery slid the jacket off his shoulders, pushed it down his arms, and tossed it to the side of the bed. The air in the room was cold against John-Henry's bare skin, and goose bumps broke out across his chest.

Emery was looking at him again, and John-Henry started to fold his arms, an automatic move to cover himself, the last line of defense. He remembered the jail. The harsh lights overhead. The vulnerability of being totally exposed.

And then he remembered the locker room. The heat from the shower still riding in his muscles, turning his skin pink where it wasn't dark from the sun. He remembered standing there, exposed to Emery's view, the way the boy had drunk him up with a desire that, decades later, John-Henry still found intoxicating. And now here he was, all these years later, with the man. Exposed again. Everything that had been his, everything that had made him John-Henry, taken away.

Naked. And, once again, being seen by Emery Hazard.

The goose bumps spread. His head felt packed with clouds, insulating him from the grief and pain he'd felt over the last few days. For a moment—for a few precious moments—he was here, safe, with someone who loved him. Someone who had seen him at his worst and at his best. Someone who loved him in spite of those things or because of them or both. He was getting hard again, trying to take deep breaths as his body demanded oxygen, urging him to breathe faster. To be seen. To be loved. To be known. That was one of the oldest euphemisms in the English language. To know someone. To have carnal knowledge. Only it wasn't a euphemism, John-Henry thought, dizzy as he scooted forward, his dick lengthening. This was it, or at least, it could be. Sex could be a lot of things. It could be casual. It could be fun. It could be demeaning and alienating. And it could be this: another way to know someone, and, in knowing them, to acknowledge them as human beings, to affirm their worth, to take a moment of ultimate vulnerability and use it as an expression of love.

He leaned down to kiss Emery.

"Well, hello," Emery murmured, his thumb rubbing the head of John-Henry's dick.

John-Henry laughed and whispered, "Shut up."

22

John-Henry must have slept because he woke to that strange clarity that sometimes came in the middle of the night. The clock said it was barely eleven. Ambient light drizzled through the blinds, streaking the room with gray. In bed next to him, Emery's breathing threatened to turn into a snore.

For a while, John-Henry lay there, enjoying the lingering glow of their lovemaking, his body loose and relaxed and reminding him, with a pleasant kind of discomfort, of what they'd been up to. Sleep seemed far away, but that was ok; his body's wakefulness seemed appropriate. And so he listened to the sounds of the old house, to Emery sleeping, to his body. He felt the kind of relief he used to feel after sobering up—a kind of lucidity that, in its stark contrast to the fogginess of the latest bender, told him how lost he'd been. Back when he'd been drinking, it had been a recrimination, yet another reason he'd promised himself he was done with beer and, more importantly, tequila. But now it was simply a marker. He could look back on the last few days and see that he'd been dysregulated, out of control. And now he was back in control. Or, at least, getting back there.

But after a while, he got out of bed. In the dark, he stepped on the letterman's jacket first. He picked it up. Then the ball cap. He picked that up too. Then his foot came down on something crinkly, and when he picked it up, he remembered the newspaper his father had brought to the hospital. It seemed like years ago. He laid the jacket and cap on the chair to be hung up later, dressed, and let himself out of the bedroom. Colt's room was dark of course, and at the far end of the hall, so was Evie's—she was still with Cora until things blew over. The guest room, which was normally the office, was dark as well. He wondered if Jem and Tean and the other guys were hanging out; a few months ago, they'd all been suffering a sleepless night, and it had turned into a strangely wonderful hour that had, in ways John-Henry couldn't put into words, cemented his love for those other men. Because ultimately, that's what it was, although he knew Emery would roll his eyes at it. What they'd been through together. What they'd shared. It was strange that, when everything else in his life seemed to be falling apart, he could see so clearly who he loved, could feel that love most powerfully. Or maybe not so strange, not really.

The blue-gray flicker of the television told him someone was still in the living room, and when he got to the bottom of the stairs, he saw that they had extra houseguests. North and Shaw were curled up on the sofa, North playing with Shaw's hair while he watched a spaghetti western—John-Henry thought it was *For a Few Dollars More*. Jem was in the armchair, one leg hanging over the side as he read a Goosebumps book—this one was *One Day at Horrorland*. Tean sat with his back against the chair, reading something on his laptop.

North noticed him first and whooped. The other men startled to various degrees, and while they were still recovering, North tried to sit up from under Shaw. "Where's my air horn? Where's my phone? Jem, pay the fuck up!"

"No," Jem said. "No!"

Shaw took one look at John-Henry and started giggling. Tean glanced up and then immediately turned his attention—with what seemed like an undue amount of earnestness—to his laptop.

"I don't even want to know," John-Henry said as he continued into the kitchen.

"Pay up, motherfucker," North said.

"Are you kidding me?" Jem said. "He's got bedhead. Big deal. He was tired. He fell asleep."

"He looks like he got well and truly fucked. Pay the fuck up."

"You said he wasn't going to be able to walk!"

"Did you see him shuffling his ancient ass through here? Jesus Christ, he looked like Theo."

"Because he got his ass handed to him last night, remember? He probably doesn't even feel like a man anymore. How's he going to get a boner after a bunch of dudes trashed him in front of his man?"

"Uh, Jem," Tean said, "you might be making your point a little too well."

"Thanks, babe."

"No, I meant—"

"It doesn't matter if he got his ass handed to him," North said. "He's a sex addict. It's a disease; he can't help himself. Did you see him when they went upstairs? You could have steered a frigate with that woody."

"Steered a—Tean, babe, settle the bet."

Tean's words were indistinct, but the tone was clearly a refusal.

"I think you both win the bet," Shaw announced. "Because John-Henry does look like a sex fiend who got his brains fucked out, and that was what North predicted, but Jem also predicted that they'd just go to bed because of their old and aged—" He gave the word two syllables. "—bodies, so I think you should call it a draw."

John-Henry made a line for the fridge.

The silence in the living room only lasted a moment before North and Jem both burst out at the same time.

"They totally fucked!" North shouted.

"Give me a break," Jem shouted at the same time, "anybody can see they fell asleep!"

"Maybe you should ask Emery," Shaw said. "He wouldn't even be mad if Tean was the one to do it."

"No!" Tean said quickly. "No, no. I think Shaw was right the first time. I think you should call it a draw."

John-Henry found a Diet Pepsi that had somehow escaped Shaw's raids on the soda stash. He opened it and considered his options for dinner, or his midnight snack, or whatever this meal was supposed to be called.

"Auggie," North said.

"Fuck yeah," Jem said. "Get Auggie over here. He'll tell you I'm right."

"I really don't think—" Tean tried.

But North and Jem's arguing moved toward the front of the house, fading—fortunately—until John-Henry couldn't hear them anymore. John-Henry tossed the newspaper on the counter and inspected a takeout container. He didn't remember ordering fried rice, so maybe this was ancient. Or maybe it was Colt's. Or maybe one of the other guys had ordered it. John-Henry dumped the food in a bowl, added a few drops of water, and put it in the microwave. There were probably better ways to reheat fried rice; Emery would know. He grinned, remembering the note of panic he'd heard in Tean's voice. Maybe he'd send Tean to wake him up.

As the microwave hummed, John-Henry's eyes fell on the newspaper. He picked it up to carry it to the recycling. Whatever Naomi was saying about him—whatever anyone was saying about him—he didn't need to know. He'd turn off his social media notifications again. He'd avoid the paper. He'd be civil in public, and in private, he'd find some healthy ways to cope and, as importantly, to help his husband and children as they made their way through this process together.

He was so caught up in his thoughts that he didn't notice the name until he was about to drop the paper in with the rest of the recycling. He stopped and brought the paper closer to make sure it wasn't a trick of the eye.

A SECOND CHANCE, the headline read, BUT NO SECOND MIRACLES. It was a short story at the bottom of the front page. He hadn't noticed it when he'd looked at the paper before because he'd been so focused on the call for his resignation.

He scanned the copy and located the name again: Marcie Fuentes. He knew that name. He'd been looking for Marcie Fuentes on and off for a couple of months. She was one of the women Dulac had saved from being trafficked.

John-Henry forced himself to read the article more slowly. It was spare on details, and it was clear that the double tragedies of Marcie's life were what had earned her a place in the news. *A hit-and-run incident Tuesday claimed Marcie Fuentes's life. Fuentes was rescued from a human trafficking operation in May of 2020 and had been living under the assumed name of Jessica Martinez. Police identified her from an expired driver's license she was carrying. Friends and neighbors were shocked to learn about her past, but one woman who asked not to be identified suggested Fuentes's experience was the reason she had been so passionate about her work at Wahredua's new GLAM Center. LGBTQ teens make up a large percentage of victims of trafficking...*

There was more, but his brain was moving too fast for him to read the rest of it.

Marcie Fuentes.

Human trafficking.

Assumed name.

GLAM Center.

Jessica.

And then, most forcefully: hit-and-run.

"John?"

John-Henry glanced up. Emery was standing there—when had he come into the kitchen?

"Are you ok?" Emery glanced at the paper. "Are you sure that's the best idea?"

"Marcie Fuentes."

A tiny furrow appeared between Emery's eyebrows. "What—"

"Ree, Marcie Fuentes."

John-Henry shoved the paper at Emery and sprinted to the stairs. He retrieved his phone from the room and placed a call on the way down. It went to voicemail, with a prerecorded message identifying the number he'd called. John-Henry sent a text, and a moment later, his phone rang.

"I know you said it's an emergency," Braxton said, "but I'm working—"

"The girl who died the other night. The carbon monoxide poisoning. What was her name?"

"Who?"

"What was her name, Braxton?"

The silence lasted a handful of seconds. "Just a minute."

John-Henry held the phone to his ear as he passed through the living room. Shaw was sitting up, worry darkening his face, and North frowned up at John-Henry. Tean had closed his laptop and was hugging it to his chest, while Jem ran the backs of his fingers over his beard.

"She was living here this whole time?" Emery asked. "The hit-and-run—do you think—"

But Braxton started to speak again, and John-Henry shook his head to stop Emery.

"Whitney Higgins," Braxton said. "Did you know her? Because we're having a hell of a time finding next of kin."

"Who found her?"

"What?"

"The call. Who called her in?"

"The landlord. Hey, what's going on?"

"Tell you later," John-Henry said as he moved his finger to disconnect. "Thanks, Braxton." When he looked up at Emery, he said, "Whitney Higgins."

Emery's eyes narrowed. And then he said, "Fuck."

"What's going on?" North asked from the opening to the living room.

Shaw stood behind him. "Is everything ok?"

"We're not sure—" John-Henry began.

"No," Emery said. "Everything is not ok. John, I'm willing to accept that one of these girls died suddenly. Maybe even two. They didn't have easy lives, and it's entirely possible, in the middle of the winter, for someone to die from exposure or carbon monoxide poisoning. But three of them? And one of them connected to GLAM?"

"Who was connected to GLAM?" Tean asked as he joined them. Jem bumped against him and slid an arm around his shoulders.

"We've been looking for the victims of a human trafficking organization," John-Henry said.

"The ones that boner cop rescued in the spring," North said. "Yeah, you've been talking about it for months."

"I found one of them in Kansas City just before the…events with John began," Emery said. "She had died from exposure. Or at least, that's what someone wanted us to think. God damn it—someone at the camp told me her friend had been there, or a friend was looking for her. No." He shook his head. "He asked about a friend. Like she'd been expecting someone. How much do you want to bet it was the same person who tracked down the rest of these girls?"

"Another of these girls was found dead from carbon monoxide poisoning in Auburn." John-Henry picked up the paper. "A third died last night. A hit-and-run right here in Wahredua. And she was working at GLAM."

Jem took the paper and began to read it, his mouth moving slowly as he parsed the words.

"You think someone's killing them," Shaw said, and it wasn't a question.

"Three of them?" Emery made a disgusted noise. "We haven't been able to find them for months, and now three of them turn up dead in, what? Less than a week?"

"It's like Brey," Jem said. "And that lady with the meth lab."

"Cleaning house," North said.

John-Henry shook his head. "Not just cleaning house. This is someone—this is someone cleaning up a mess."

"John-Henry," Tean said, clutching his laptop tighter against him. He seemed to struggle to find the right words, and then he blurted, "Were their names on your computer at work?"

No one said anything for a moment.

"Fuck me, Jesus," North breathed. "That's what this was about?"

"Part of it," Emery corrected automatically, but he sounded only half-aware of what he was saying. "Framing John, getting him out of the picture—God fucking damn it, why didn't I think of that possibility?"

"But these girls," Shaw said, "they didn't know anything, did they? I mean, they've been alive for months, and no one came after them. Someone had to break into your computer to get the records. Why go to so much trouble to kill them now?"

"Guys," Jem said slowly, lowering the paper. Blue-gray eyes crinkled with distress. "Who founded GLAM?"

"This guy named Koby—" John-Henry began.

"No." Emery's breathing sounded funny, and his color had dropped. "No, Koby's just—" He shook his head. "I never asked. It sounded like a non-profit. It sounded like something—" He cut off like he couldn't finish.

"What's the big deal who founded it?" North asked.

But Shaw looked bloodless. And Tean's eyes had gotten huge behind his glasses.

"Well, if I were looking to groom and traffic kids from the most vulnerable group possible," Jem said, "I might, you know, make a nice, safe space where they'd like to come hang out."

What came after wasn't silence. It was the vacuum that came after a thunderclap.

"Colt," John-Henry said as Emery lurched into a run toward their room.

"But that doesn't make any sense," North said. "Setting up something like that, it exposes you to a lot of risk. You're established in the community. People know who you are. There's a financial commitment."

"But it's a business," Shaw said. His hazel eyes looked glassy, and he sounded like he was speaking from a long way off. "It's an investment. And no one's going to ask questions if it's one kid who goes missing, or two, or five. LGBTQ kids run away from home all the time."

"Yeah, well, what if one of those kids escapes or survives and somehow they—"

"Somehow they recognize you," Tean whispered.

John-Henry felt the pieces falling into place. The victims of a trafficking operation, months old now, weren't a threat until one of them started volunteering at GLAM. And then something must have happened. Someone must have gotten worried. And then they were worried it wasn't just this one woman who might recognize them—anyone who had been rescued needed to be silenced. The risks were too high, and so whoever was behind this—Jace Vermilya, or the unnamed man John-Henry had fought in Eric Brey's house, or maybe someone else entirely—had decided to close up shop. Move somewhere else. Try again. And that meant getting rid of any connections here: your meth supplier, the local politician in your pocket—

The service trip.

One last haul. A vanload of kids who wouldn't make trouble, who were happy to follow whatever instructions you gave them, would do whatever you told them because they thought they were going on a service trip. He felt like he was reading one of those training packets again. Most victims of trafficking in the United States are U.S. citizens. LGBTQ teens are at a much higher risk—like other marginalized and vulnerable groups. Most victims know their trafficker and go along willingly because they've been deceived—fewer than ten percent of cases involve kidnapping or trafficking by force. Missouri has the fourteenth highest number of trafficking cases in the United States, most of those cases happening along I-70, and it was one of the FBI's top twenty destinations for trafficked victims.

For a moment, the sickening realization threatened to drag John-Henry down. He had put his son in that van. He had driven him to the pride center, and he had put him in the hands of those men. It was horror like nothing he'd ever felt before, knowing that he had delivered Colt to them, that he had done all the work for them. He wanted to close his eyes. He thought, for a moment, he might die from it.

"He's not answering his phone," Emery said, his voice rough. "It's off, and the parental app shows his last location at that fucking pride center."

John-Henry nodded and said, "They took their phones."

"Ashley isn't answering either. Should I call his parents?"

Another nod. "See if they know where they were taking the kids. Or if they have a tracking app. Tell them Colt's sick, whatever you have to tell them."

Emery left, floorboards creaking under his steps, a riptide pulling the air out of the room behind him.

Jem whispered, "I'll call Auggie."

The words sparked something. For what felt like long moments, John-Henry struggled with the weight of what he had done, of how stupid he'd been, how self-centered (as always), absorbed in his own petty drama (as usual), instead of worrying about his son. Why hadn't he tried harder to meet Koby? Why hadn't he ever insisted on accompanying Colt to the pride center? Why hadn't he done his due diligence? Because it had seemed like such a good cause was part of the answer. Because he'd met other adults there, Marcie—no, Jessica. And Farah. Because he'd been busy, and it had been easier to accept the truth at face value.

A hand gripped his arm, squeezing tight, and North said, "We're going to get him back."

"I'll call Jadon," Shaw said. "He's a detective with the Metropolitan Police."

"I'm going to see if I can pull any records or filings for GLAM," North said, squeezing John-Henry's arm again. "Tean?"

"We'll be ok," Tean said.

John-Henry was only distantly aware of North moving into the living room. I'm doing it again, he thought. I'm sitting here, wallowing, feeling sorry for myself, while God knows what is happening to my son, and all I can think about is me, and about how I fucked up. North is doing something. Shaw is doing something. Jem is doing something. Tean is doing something—babysitting me. Even Emery is doing something; he's not letting this paralyze him. I should be doing something. This is my job, I should be—

"John-Henry," Tean said in his gentle, firm way, "you need to take a deep breath."

The deep breath threatened to tip over into a sob. John-Henry took another breath, though, and he dug his thumbs into the corners of his eyes, and he took yet another. Think, he told himself. You've been trained to do this. Think. If North can find financial records, we might be able to get a hit off that—an address, something. If they took Colt's phone, they won't let him use his debit card either. Nothing that would leave a trail. That, John-Henry realized now in hindsight, was why Koby had been so ridiculously strict about the no-phones-or-photos rule at GLAM. It wasn't about protecting the privacy of the teens there; it had been about hiding himself. Maybe Auggie would be able to find something on GLAM's social media—

A possibility came like a lightning strike. John-Henry grabbed his phone.

"Farah's not answering," Emery said. "And the number I've got for Koby goes straight to voicemail. I want to call the Highway Patrol."

John-Henry nodded as he tapped his way through Instagram. He found Colt's account and did a quick check, but as he'd expected, Colt hadn't posted anything since being dropped off at GLAM. Koby—or whoever was in charge—had probably fed them a line about bonding, or about focus, or who knows what. The same kids who wouldn't give up their phones short of being murdered by their parents had probably willingly passed them over. Except—

John-Henry looked at Colt's profile and tapped on his Following. He scrolled down until he found butterfly.ty. The infamous Ty, who broke Koby's rules, who couldn't put his phone down for five seconds.

The most recent post showed a multistory hotel lit by fluorescents. It looked modern, with polished steel siding and long walls of glass. An illuminated sign proclaimed it The Laclede.

"Holy shit," Tean said.

From the other room, Jem called, "Swear jar."

"You guys, John-Henry found them."

Emery's familiar steps hammered toward them, and he appeared in the opening a moment later. "You did?"

But John-Henry didn't answer. He scrolled back in Ty's timeline, scanning each post for what he was looking for. There were several furtive shots from Ty's seat at the back of the bus. In a couple of them, Colt and Ashley were visible—laughing, their faces alight with happiness, having a great time on a trip that they knew was going to be fun. Those threatened to break him, so he scrolled past and kept looking.

He found what he wanted from almost a month back in Ty's extensive—and exhausting—feed.

A photo from inside GLAM.

A man with a nametag that said Koby.

And when John-Henry recognized him, the audacity of it all was staggering. He'd been here the whole time. In plain sight. If they'd only taken the time to look.

Koby was a little shorter than average, with a leanly muscled build. Dark hair in a buzz. Dark eyes. And a ridge of scar tissue on his neck. He was the man who had broken into John-Henry's computer. The man John-Henry had fought in Eric Brey's house. The man who had almost killed Theo and Jem and who had come close to killing North and Shaw.

And now he had Colt.

23

"No, I don't want to leave a message." Emery fought the urge to slam the phone on the dash as they drove through the night. The officer on the other end of the call started to say something, but Emery cut him off. "Because I've left half a dozen messages. I've spoken to two different sergeants, and I've gotten the runaround from ten or so pissants who can't seem to get it through their thick skulls that this is an emergency!"

Dead air met him on the other end of the call.

Disconnected.

Again.

Swallowing a scream, Emery pounded his fist against the Mustang's door.

"Try again," John-Henry said.

Emery had to count to ten before responding. "Try what? I've tried everything I can think of. I've asked to speak to their superior officer. I've explained the situation. I've talked to just about every fucking cop in the Metropolitan PD except the ones who can actually make a decision. So what, exactly, would you like me to try?"

The tires thrummed. When John-Henry spoke, his voice was flat. "Call them again."

Emery counted to twenty this time. Nothing he had tried so far had worked. The first call, to the St. Louis Metropolitan Police Department's emergency number, had garnered interest and a response. The dispatcher had said that she would send an officer to investigate. But when Emery had pressed, he had found himself transferred to a supervisor, asked to identify himself, and then placed on an interminable hold. He wasn't a fool; he knew that he had nothing concrete to offer them, that his panic might have made him sound deranged. This was a city with one of the highest murder rates in the country; they didn't have time to spend chasing rumors. Someone would be calling around, trying to corroborate his story. He also knew what that would mean. His own reputation in the Metropolitan PD, for those who remembered him, was tarnished by his departure. And whatever Peterson might believe personally about John, as acting chief of the Wahredua PD, he'd be obligated to tell the truth as he saw it: that he had no evidence of what they were claiming, and that John was out on bail and facing serious charges himself. North and Shaw hadn't been able to reach their friend in the department, and Emery didn't know what his other options were. It had been hours of this. Hours of being transferred and placed on hold and placated and ignored and accidentally disconnected. Hours of mounting frustration until he felt like he was choking on his rage.

He fought to reclaim the cold logic that had always been his refuge, battling the tide of his emotions—most of all, his fury at himself for not insisting on meeting every single staff member at that fucking pride center. Then he placed the call again.

They had been driving for almost two hours, and St. Louis was a bubble of light on the horizon. Everything had seemed to take too much time: getting Auggie and Theo up to speed, and then the inevitable argument about who would be coming, and putting together the gear they would need if things went bad, even the drive itself. A semi had overturned on I-70, backing up traffic for miles as emergency responders worked to clear a safe route for vehicles.

Through all of it, tension had ratcheted Emery's body tighter and tighter. Part of that was the general discomfort of the gear—the vest he was wearing, the gun holstered at his side, the tactical jacket. He should have removed some of the gear for the drive, instead of sweating his ass off, but he couldn't bring himself to do it. He needed to be prepared. He needed to be ready to help his son.

Another part of the tension, though, was manufactured by his imagination. He knew enough about trafficking, had read enough accounts from survivors, to understand what Colt might be going through. The best-case scenario was that, for the time being, Colt was still under the illusion that he was on a service trip. Koby—or whatever his real name was—might be continuing the farce in order to keep the kids compliant and manageable.

But the reality, Emery knew, was probably very different. If the kids were being taken for labor, violence would simply be used to ensure obedience. But if the trafficking were sexual in nature—he had read one story about a woman who had been taken to a resort community in Florida. She had been given her own villa. She had walked inside. And the minute she stepped through the door, three men were waiting for her. They had beaten her severely as a kind of foreplay. And then they had done worse.

"St. Louis Metropolitan Police—"

Emery launched into his explanation, and the struggle began again.

The city grew ahead of them, taking on height and depth, acquiring a granular density that was partly due to the scatter of sodium lights and partly due to the deep shadows that lay everywhere else. Across the water, Illinois's river cities glinted golden brown. Nearing four in the morning now, the highway was empty except for the occasional early commuter—men and women coming across the bridges for work. They were headed the opposite direction, passing fleets of light that left darkness behind them. Once, a Charger whipped past them, swerving across lanes to make an exit. In its wake, the city felt abandoned.

When the Maps app told them to exit, Emery disconnected the call.

"Try—" John-Henry said.

"We're past that," Emery said. After a taking a minute to figure it out, he placed another call.

"What's up?" Auggie asked.

"Emery?" Shaw said.

"Are Tean and Jem listening?"

A soft noise came, and then Auggie's voice came back, sounding different. "They can hear you now."

"We're almost there," Emery said. "I want to make sure everyone is clear about what we're going to do when we get to the hotel."

"We hang back and watch the exits," Tean said. "If anyone leaves, one of us follows."

"And for the record," North said, "that's a terrible plan. You haven't gone up against this guy—Koby, whatever you want to call him. You don't know what you're dealing with."

"John does," Emery said.

"Yeah? Well, what does he think about the two of you trying to do this alone?"

"I think this is a high-risk operation," John said, "and I want my friends to be safe."

"We know how to handle ourselves," Jem said. "Theo and I—"

"We have two stab vests," Emery said. "Two. John is wearing one. And I'm wearing the other."

John cut his eyes toward Emery at that comment, and something in his face suggested that, as usual, John's perceptiveness might pose a problem.

"We didn't have stab vests when we went up against him," Jem said. "Theo, back me up."

"Theo is going to agree with me—" Emery began.

"I think it's a bad idea," Theo said over him. "I understand your reasoning. We're not trained for these kinds of situations, and we don't know tactics. You're not wrong. But Emery, it's not just Koby. He's going to have other people with him. This woman, Farah, for example. And the kids are going to be confused. Some of them might take Koby's side, depending on what has happened so far. And what about this guy, Vermilya? We still don't know where he fits in all this. And we've got no idea how many other people he's got. He's transporting a lot of valuable merchandise, to put it bluntly. It's a mistake to assume he wouldn't protect it appropriately."

Air hissed through the Mustang's vents.

"See?" North asked.

"North," Shaw whispered.

John-Henry's face was tight, but when he met Emery's gaze, he shook his head.

"You're staying outside," Emery said. "End of discussion."

"Fuck that," North said, and in the last moment before the call disconnected, his engine roared.

A moment later, the black car shot past them like a dark star.

"God fucking damn it! John!"

John dropped his foot on the accelerator, and the Mustang sprang forward.

As Emery placed another call to Shaw—which rang and rang without being answered—John said in a tight voice, "It's interesting that we suddenly have two stab vests because I seem to recall you only purchased one for Astraea."

Fortunately, by that point, Emery was prepared. "I bought another when I hired Nico."

"Good thinking. Then you won't mind taking off that jacket when we get to the hotel so I can take a look at it."

"We don't have time—"

"We do have time, actually. We're dealing with a sadist who loves a close-up kill, Ree. If he's got a gun, we'll take cover and hold him down until the police get there. I'm not worried about him having a gun. I'm worried about that fucking sickle. I'm worried about that giant knife."

"I'm fairly sure it's a kama."

A beat passed. "What?"

"The weapon everyone keeps calling a sickle. I'm fairly sure, based on North's description of how he used it, it's a kama."

John opened his mouth. And then he scowled. "Don't do that. I want to see your vest when—is that the U-Haul?"

Ahead of them, the Laclede rose out of a large parking lot. Security lights smeared white along the building's steel cladding. Parked to one side of the lot was the U-Haul Emery had seen outside GLAM. The passenger van was nowhere in sight. What did that mean? Had Emery's first call, the one that the Metropolitan Police had seemed to take seriously—had it tipped off Koby and Vermilya? Had they already moved the kids somewhere else? Emery hadn't considered that possibility. In his panic, calling the police had seemed like the first and best option.

"Breathe, love," John-Henry said. "The U-Haul is still here. Colt is still here."

We don't know that, Emery wanted to say. But he fought the words down and tried to empty his mind, to fall into that reserve of cold and distance, where he was always at his best.

North and Shaw were already pulling into the lot—driving too fast, drawing attention to themselves, swerving across an aisle of spaces before they came to a stop parked across two stalls. For a moment, Emery thought maybe something was wrong—North had hurt himself, or he was experiencing some kind of emergency. Before he could try calling again, though, movement at the U-Haul drew his eye. A shadow moved inside the cab of the truck—a guard or sentry, his interest obviously drawn by North's erratic driving.

"Jesus Christ," John said as though speaking to himself. He slowed the Mustang as they approached the lot. "Are they actually that good, or do they just bumble into luck like this?"

Emery thought he'd been rendered speechless, but he heard himself say, "I honestly have no idea."

North got out of the car first. He'd ditched his jacket and wore nothing but a t-shirt in spite of the cold. In one hand, he held a bottle, and as he stumbled free of the car—his foot seeming to catch on something—he let out a drunken whoop.

Shaw emerged next, patting the air and saying something that must have been meant to be calming. Whatever it was, it didn't work because North whooped again. And then he lurched toward the U-Haul, fishing at his fly. To take a piss in the snow was the message. Shaw trotted after him, pulling on his arm and cajoling, which North ignored. They made their way across the asphalt like that as first John and Emery and then, behind them, the rest of the guys in Auggie's Audi, entered the lot. When North and Shaw reached the U-Haul, North leaned heavily against the front of the truck—he must have made the stagger real because the truck shifted on its suspension. He was still working on his fly.

The driver's door of the U-Haul opened, and a man in a heavy coat and a beanie dropped out of the cab.

A sentry, Emery thought with a kind of disconnected fury. Why didn't I think of a sentry? What else didn't I think of?

The man barked something at North and Shaw as he came around the front of the truck. North turned, the movement fumbling and slow—the way a surprised drunk might move—and liquid arced out from his body. Emery's first thought was that North had somehow managed to make the act completely real and that he was now pissing on the guard. The guard must have thought the same thing because he stumbled back, his outraged shouts carrying even over the sound of the Mustang.

Then Emery saw the bottle in North's hand, and Shaw launched into a blur of movement. Emery wasn't exactly sure what Shaw did—it was so fast, and it was over so quickly. Whatever it was, though, the guard dropped and didn't move again. Shaw stood over him, considering him. And then he humped the air.

After what felt like a long moment, John turned off the Mustang and said, "Fuck me."

"Precisely," Emery said. And then, "Let's not ever make him mad."

"Uh huh."

They got out of the car as Auggie, Theo, Jem, and Tean emerged from the Audi.

"Did you see that?" Auggie asked.

"Everyone saw it," Emery snapped and then jogged over to the U-Haul.

North had rolled the guard onto his stomach and was patting him down as he delivered a furiously whispered tirade. "Because, dumbass, I was going to take care of him. It was my idea with the bottle—"

"I know, and it was so cute that you found a way to turn your passion for watersports into—"

"My passion? My passion? Listen, fuck-twizzle, I'm not the one who kept asking that poor plumber if he knew how to quote 'install a golden shower'—"

"What the fuck was that?" Emery asked.

North glanced up and went back to his search. He tossed a wallet, a phone, and a walkie onto the ground. "That was me getting totally robbed. That was my takedown!"

"I meant—"

"How did you do that?" Auggie asked.

"Oh—" Shaw began.

"Easy," North snapped. "Wait for your boyfriend to do all the work and then take all the glory. Sound familiar, wundertwink?"

John stooped to recover the walkie. It was on, and as he picked it up, it crackled as a voice said, "Bobby? Bobby, you copy?"

Kneeling, Theo grabbed the wallet. He flipped it open and said, "Robert Jenkins."

"Shit," Jem said. "Did he call it in?"

A new voice came across the radio: "Somebody check it out."

Squabbling broke out on the radio as a game of hot potato began, everyone trying to toss the responsibility to someone else. It gave them a few moments, Emery knew. No more than that.

"We need to—" Emery began.

"I can get that padlock open," North said, tilting his head toward the U-Haul, "but I need time."

Emery didn't need to say—nobody needed to say—what North had left unsaid: that there might be kids in the truck too.

"I'll be your bodyguard," Shaw announced.

"Great. Perfect. Never mind. Somebody just blow me up the ass."

Nobody seemed to know what to say to that.

Even under the security lights, the color in North's face was obvious as he mumbled, "I meant with a gun or something."

"Uh huh," Jem said. But then he clapped Theo on the shoulder and said, "We'll take the back. If they send somebody out that way, we'll keep them busy."

Theo looked at Auggie.

"No—" Emery began.

"Go," Auggie said.

Nodding, Theo said, "Stay with Tean," and then he and Jem took off down the side of the hotel. Something was hanging from Jem's hand, swinging slightly as he ran. Emery hoped it was his imagination, but he thought he saw the grip of a gun under Theo's coat.

"So much for a fucking plan," Emery said.

"We're improvising, big boy," North said as he inspected the lock. "Otherwise, you'd have walked in there and gotten your pretty head blown open."

"Big boy?" Auggie said.

"I was more interested in the 'pretty head' thing," Tean admitted.

"I think it's romantic," Shaw said, "this whole I'm-perpetually-blue-balled-for-you—"

Shouts broke out near the back of the hotel. Under one of the security lights, a pair of men in dark winter gear were facing off with Jem and Theo. Jem danced back, and something whipped out from his hand. One of the men screamed. Emery expected Theo to go for the gun he was carrying, but instead, Theo lunged forward. He caught the second man by the coat, swung him around, and drove him face-first into the side of the hotel. The metal cladding rang like a gong, and there was a distinct crunch of bone. When Theo released the man, he fell and didn't get up.

"Good Christ," Emery said under his breath. "What kind of arm day does he do? I think that poor bastard's feet left the ground."

"We've got to move," John said, and he pulled Emery toward the hotel.

Emery caught Shaw's eye, and Shaw nodded.

It wasn't much of a backup plan, Emery thought. But it was the best he could do.

They were halfway to the building when he noticed Auggie and Tean running behind them. He waved for them to stay back, but Auggie shook his head. "We're covering the front."

Emery had a brief moment to wonder what Tean would do—the vet was extremely intelligent and knew a wide variety of important information about a range of topics, but he lost points in general argumentativeness and assholery, which were slightly more important at a moment like this. Before he could consider the question more, though, he and John reached the front doors to the hotel. They slid open, and a rush of cinnamon-laden air met them, warm enough to make his skin sting after the cold. John slowed to a walk, and Emery copied him as he scanned the lobby.

It was a large, open space done in creams and golds. Long, tufted banquettes and throne-like armchairs lined a pathway to the front desk, while wooden screens separated off additional seating areas and provided the illusion of privacy. A massive clock on one wall filled the silence with its ticking, the only sound until a tiny train appeared, winding a path through tiny snow-covered villages on a ledge above them, the train choo-chooing as it chugged along its tiny tracks. A red-cheeked Santa rode the back of the train, a bag slung over his shoulder. The only other person in the lobby was a skinny fortyish man. His suit looked like a polyester straitjacket, and he had opted for the traditional rat tail, a mark of concierges everywhere. He drooped over the desk, looking half asleep, but at the sound of the doors he straightened and tried for a smile. Then his face changed.

At the same time, the sound of a door opening came, and men's voices broke the quiet. "—gone out there when I told you to—"

Whatever the man had been about to say, he cut off as he passed one of the privacy screens and caught sight of Emery, John, Auggie, and Tean. He had his head shaved and was dressed in all black, and he had two other men with him. They were dressed in black too. One had a tattoo of an eagle climbing his neck, one wing stretching up across his cheek. The other had the too-thin look of a meth head. They all had guns.

Emery drew his revolver at the same time that the one with the shaved head reached for his gun. John tried to shout, "Get down!" but the other two were going for their guns as well. The Blackhawk bucked in Emery's hands, and the one with the shaved head went down.

The guy with the eagle tattoo screamed, his gun forgotten now, and spun to run back the way he'd come. The meth head, however, grabbed a strap hanging around his neck and brought up a submachine gun with a half-moon clip. Emery shouted wordlessly and dove to the floor. John landed next to him as bullets stitched the air above them. Foam padding exploded out of the tufted banquette where they'd taken cover, and as bullets hammered into it, the banquette rocked.

As abruptly as it had begun, the gunfire broke off. There was a strange gargling noise, and then the thump of a body hitting the floor.

"I'm sorry," Tean said. "I'm sorry. I'm sorry."

Emery scrambled to see past the banquette. Wires ran from the Taser in Tean's hands to the meth head, who was still jerking and jumping as the electric current ran through him.

"I'm sorry, I'm sorry, I'm sorry," Tean was saying as he squeezed the trigger—and, consequently, kept the shock going.

Eyes wide, Auggie looked like he was somewhere between a panic attack and an unstoppable case of the giggles. Then his face changed, and he sprinted toward the front desk. For a little guy, he threw on some serious gas. He practically flew across the room, and as he reached the front desk, he jumped and slid across the marble top. It was an annoyingly twentysomething move, flashy and risky and unbearably impressive. When Auggie landed on the other side, he wrenched the phone away from the skinny clerk. He turned and yanked the phone line from the wall.

Tean still looked like he was intent on cooking the meth head from the inside out, so Emery got to his feet. He took Tean gently by the wrists, lowering his hands, and said as calmly as he could, "You did a good job. That was very good. But I need you to relax your finger now, yep, just like that, and now take it off the trigger completely. Excellent."

"I'm sorry," Tean whispered. He looked like he was about to cry.

"You don't need to be sorry," Emery said, squeezing his wrists. "You saved our lives. If he moves again, even a little bit, give him the juice. Got it?"

Tean blinked to clear his eyes, but he nodded.

"Auggie?"

"We're good here," Auggie shouted back. "Hey Emery, get this. It's a landline!"

"Good fucking Lord," Emery muttered as he turned to find his husband.

John reappeared a moment later, holstering his Glock as he came around one of the screens. To the question he must have seen on Emery's face, he tilted his head in the direction he'd come from and said, "We had a runner."

Adrenaline still high, Emery nodded. A part of him knew, later, he would relive some of these moments in slow motion. The kick of the Blackhawk. The way the man with the shaved head had gone down. But for now, he had to stay here, like this. He passed the meth head's submachine gun to Tean. The meth head was taking labored breaths, his body still twitching in the aftermath of the electricity Tean had sent coursing through his body. Next, Emery checked the man with the shaved head. He was breathing, his color bad. Emery picked up his gun by the barrel in two fingers and carried it over to the front desk.

"Use this if you need it," Emery said. "Otherwise, don't touch it."

Auggie nodded. He jerked a thumb at a red box behind the desk that said FIRE.

With a tiny laugh, Emery glanced at John. John nodded.

"You're good here?" Emery asked.

"Good," Auggie said.

Tean nodded shakily. He gripped the Taser so tightly that the fine bones of his hands stood out against the skin.

"Hit it," Emery said.

Auggie pulled the fire alarm, and a klaxon began to blare as emergency lights flashed to life.

The volume bordered on painful, and as Emery and John made their way to the stairs, he asked himself how anyone could sleep through it. He had his answer soon enough: people began to stream out of doorways to clog the stairwell: a man in sailing boat boxers and a stained tank top; a woman in curlers and a terry cloth robe; barefooted children pursued by a harried-looking woman carrying a handful of tiny shoes. Everyone had the same expression, a mixture of confusion and worry, as they crowded the narrow stairs and pressed past Emery and John.

Auggie's idea presented an ideal opportunity to check the hotel. The alarm meant that the hotel would be evacuated. If Vermilya and Koby and whoever else was involved in this refused to let the kids leave, they'd immediately know something was wrong. On the other hand, if the traffickers tried to remove the children from the building, the men stationed outside the hotel would spot them and move to intercept—or, at a bare minimum, follow. Best of all, emergency services would respond.

As they reached each floor, Emery stuck his head out into the hallway to see if he could spot anything unusual. Depending on the traffickers' arrangement with the hotel, they might have booked anything from a handful of rooms to an entire floor—an entire floor would be ideal, of course, since it would reduce the number of people who saw and remembered the children being moved in and out. Also, that dark voice suggested, an entire floor would give them additional rooms for customers to use.

Checking the second floor was almost impossible because of the crush of people trying to escape into the stairwell. But Emery saw only frightened families and baggy-eyed road warriors, and he motioned for John to continue up. The flow of people was thinning at the third floor, and there too, Emery saw nothing out of the ordinary. By the time Emery and John reached the fourth floor, the flood of bodies had left them behind—a few people were still working their way down the stairs, but otherwise, Emery and John were alone.

Emery stepped out into the hallway and saw the man who called himself Jace Vermilya. He looked bad—his color awful, his hair lank, his action hero build wasted away over the last few days. But getting shot and almost killed would do that to anyone; the fact that Vermilya stood here, that he had possessed the strength and intelligence to murder the deputy guarding him and make his escape, suggested that even in an injured capacity, he was more dangerous than most people. He had a phone pressed to his ear and was talking, but when Emery stepped into the hallway, his head came up, and his eyes widened. He dropped the phone to his side and held up a hand.

"Hey," he said. "Hey! Hold on!"

Emery brought up the Blackhawk. He started down the hallway. His brain had gone into lockdown, acknowledging only the immediate realities: Vermilya currently wasn't holding a weapon, he was injured, he was afraid.

The doors lining the hallway were shut, and an alcove opened on Emery's left: ice and vending machines. His gaze fixed on Vermilya. "Where is he?"

"He's fine. They're all fine." Vermilya took a step back. It was hard to see the action hero now. Hard to see the guy who had conned men and women into believing he was a crusader. Inside a baggy hoodie and sweatpants, he looked old and tired and jaundiced. This was the man, Emery thought, who had tried to ruin John's life. This was the man who had taken Colt. "But you've got to stop right there, or I'm going to make another call, and he's not going to be fine."

Emery kept walking. Behind him, John was talking into his phone, requesting police at the hotel. That was smart, Emery thought. It was like a dream. That was the smart thing to do. He slipped his finger inside the trigger guard. "Where is he?"

"Stop!" Vermilya said, his voice cracking. "If I—"

Seeing him now, in person, awake and alive, Emery felt his last doubts fall away. This was the man. The one behind it all. Why else would he be here? Why else would his friends or accomplices or whatever they were—why else would they have risked so much to rescue him from the hospital? Anyone else, anyone except the mastermind, would have been left behind. Or eliminated. Emery thought of the ambush at the meth lab. Of the video of Vermilya cowing Brey. Of how he had, just now, threatened Colt. But it was more than that. Emery could see it in his face, and it wasn't anything that would hold up in court, it wasn't anything he could call proof or evidence. But he knew. Vermilya's boldness in putting himself forward as the witness was more proof, in its own way: it reeked of his contempt for them, his utter surety he could walk away after burning their lives to the ground. It was another mark of his spitefulness, his final attempts to twist the knife. Just like taking Colt and Ashley.

"You arranged for Missy Bennett to be killed. You arranged for Sheriff Dennis Engels to be killed. You arranged for Dalton Weber and Ambyr Hobbs to be killed. You arranged for Adam Ezell to be killed, and Deanna Vance, and Marcie Fuentes, and Whitney Higgins. And that's not getting into people like Eric Brey or Ingra Thomas. You destroyed my husband's life. And you took my son. Get on the fucking floor before I kill you right now."

"You'd better stop right there!"

"Where is he?"

"Ree, don't get too—"

John cut off with a grunt, and then bodies crashed to the floor. Emery glanced back, and in his peripheral vision, he was aware of Vermilya taking the opportunity to bolt toward the stairs at the end of the building. But Emery couldn't bring himself to go after him. All he could do was stare.

Koby—or whatever his real name was—and John were rolling across the floor. The kama lay on the floor a few feet away, and Koby was trying to drive a massive trench knife into John's throat, above the protection of the stab vest, while John fought to keep the blade at a distance. When the men rolled again, a long rip showed across the back of John's coat, and Emery knew what had happened: the kama had cut through the coat and been stopped by the stab vest underneath. The alcove, Emery realized. Koby had been hiding behind one of the machines. I walked right past him, Emery thought. I walked right the fuck past him.

He boxed up the self-recrimination and studied the men ahead of him. Koby's face was a mess from his previous encounter with John—skin split across the bridge of the nose John had broken, eyes black and puffy from the blow. But he had the element of surprise, he was younger, and he had the advantage of being on top, where he could use all his body weight to drive the blade down. Worse, John had hurt his shoulder; on an ordinary day, he might have been able to hold the knife off, but today, inch by inch, it was slowly coming down.

Emery brought up the Blackhawk, tried to decide on his shot. The closer he got to the men, the better his chance of disabling Koby without hurting John. But it also put him within reach of Koby and that big fucker of a knife. Emery weighed his options for a heartbeat and took a step forward.

A familiar sound came from behind him: a door opening.

He turned his head, the movement instinctive, checking the new threat.

Jonas Cassidy stood there: white-blond hair, a big smile. He'd traded the Auburn PD polo for a painted-on t-shirt and jeans. He'd always been a showoff.

That was probably why it seemed like it took so long for the gun in his hand to come up. Nice and slow and dramatic. Or that's what it seemed like, anyway, as Emery's brain tried to stop time. But the gun kept moving, drifting through the air like it was weightless, until it was aimed at Emery. Cassidy's smile brightened. And then he shot Emery in the back.

24

The gunshot tore through the hallway, loud enough to hurt John-Henry's ears even over the klaxon. If Koby noticed the loud clap, though, he gave no sign—his attention was fixed on John-Henry, on the knife he was trying to bury in John-Henry's throat. The smaller man was panting, obviously still struggling to breathe through his broken nose. His eyes were webbed with the red of broken blood vessels. And he was winning. By fractions of inches, for now, but it didn't matter.

"Ree?" John-Henry grunted. Nothing. He tried again, his ears still ringing from the shot, "Ree?"

Something twisted Koby's mouth, and it took a moment before John-Henry recognized it as a smile.

"He can't hear you now." The voice was amused—happy bordering on gleeful. And John-Henry recognized it as Jonas Cassidy's. "Big old dumb fuck. I should have shot you in that fucking garage. Would have made everything so much easier."

What the words suggested—what they meant—met a blank wall in John-Henry's head. No. No. Not that. The knife dipped toward him. "Ree?" The next time, it was a shout. "Ree!"

"Arrogant cock-sucking piece of shit." The muffled thud of a blow came. "All the bullshit I had to put up with from you. All that fucking work being nice to you. And then you turned around, you motherfucker—" Cassidy's voice rose into a scream. "—and told my dad!"

The words hammered against John-Henry's consciousness. He refused to let them in. The knife. Koby's battered face. The smug little knot of his mouth that could barely be called a smile. John-Henry's shoulder throbbed with the effort of holding back the blade. Worse, the mental energy of corralling his thoughts, of refusing to let those words inside himself, meant less energy and focus for the fight. The knife slid down another quarter inch. John-Henry's hands felt greasy on Koby's wrists, ready to slip.

Another of those muffled blows came again. "You told my dad!" Cassidy screamed, his voice unhinged now, the words distorted with fury. "And you ruined everything!"

Blackness speckled John-Henry's vision. A door at the back of his head opened, and raw, animal fury poured through him. He couldn't feel his shoulder. He couldn't feel anything except a wind blowing through his mind. He was screaming, a part of him noticed in a clinical voice. His spittle flecked Koby's face.

He bucked, dislodging Koby enough to begin to sit up. It took Koby by surprise, but the smaller man rolled with the force of John-Henry's movement and pulled John-Henry with him. John-Henry didn't mind. He didn't have anywhere else to be. It was just him and that black wind. It was just him and the cold.

With better leverage, now, John-Henry brought his weight to bear on the knife. He forced Koby's arms down. Somewhere, Cassidy was still talking, but the roar in John-Henry's head was too loud for him to hear anything else. He leaned forward, transferring as much of his weight to his arms as he could, pinning Koby and the knife. And then he released one hand from Koby's wrist and punched Koby in the broken nose.

Koby screamed.

John-Henry took the tiny opening. He scrambled back, trying to disengage. At the edge of his awareness, Cassidy was rolling Emery over. Emery flopped onto his back. Unconscious, John-Henry thought, the words barely on the horizon of the defenses he'd erected. Please, God, he's only unconscious. But the next thought was clearer as fear seeped through the barriers: a stab vest can't stop a bullet.

Still screaming, Koby got upright and scrambled across the floor. He was going for the kama, the trench knife still clutched in his other hand. John-Henry launched himself across the hall toward where the Glock had fallen when Koby had attacked him.

Koby reached the kama first. He came up onto his knees and slashed out with the trench knife. It felt like a whisper of cold air passing John-Henry. The kama spun so fast it blurred in his hands.

John-Henry landed on his bad shoulder. The world went white. His fingers closed around the Glock's polymer, and he brought the gun up and fired.

The sound was enormous in the hallway. John-Henry scooted backward as his vision cleared. In his mind, he could see the kama coming for him, the hiss of matte steel carving the air. But nothing. Nothing. And then he could see again.

Koby was still on his knees, slumped against the wall, the kama hanging from its strap in one hand. He'd lost the trench knife, and his other hand was pressed against his belly, where blood streamed between his fingers. The boy—he really was a boy, John-Henry realized—stared at him in disbelief, a hint of outrage forming on his lips, almost like a pout. The ridge of scar tissue on his neck was livid.

"Put that fucking gun down," Cassidy said.

John-Henry's gaze shifted to the Auburn chief of police. He was straddling Emery, the pose bizarrely sexual, and he held a pistol aimed at John-Henry. John-Henry knew he'd never be fast enough; if he moved, Cassidy would fire, and that would be the end.

"Drop it," Cassidy said.

John-Henry released the pistol.

Cassidy smirked. The fluorescent scattered rainbows over his white-blond hair. He turned his gaze down to Emery and said, "I've been dreaming about this for a long time—"

Emery's hand speared upwards: fingers rigid and pressed together, driving straight into Cassidy's throat. Cassidy reared back. His free hand went to his throat as he made a gagging noise. The hand with the gun went wide, John-Henry forgotten. Cassidy made another of those noises, this one deeper and longer. His color dropped as he scrambled backward, still clawing at his throat. Emery struggled into a sitting position, and John-Henry could tell from the way he moved that it was more than the bulky vest he was wearing, that he was hurting, probably badly. But he wrested the gun from Cassidy's hand without any trouble, and then he shoved Cassidy off him.

Legs scissoring across the carpet, Cassidy continued making those retching noises, raking his throat with his nails. Biscuit had once tried to eat a rock, and the sounds she had made trying to dislodge it from her throat had been similar to the ones Cassidy made now. John-Henry got to his feet and checked Koby again—his face was gray, and the steady pumping of blood between his fingers had slowed—before moving over to Emery.

"Motherfucker shot me in the back," Emery said, wincing as he rolled onto his hands and knees. "I suppose it wasn't enough for him to have stabbed me in the back once already. Jesus Christ, John, you're going to have to help me up."

"I guess I was correct about our family only owning one stab vest."

Emery's answering smile was surprisingly boyish as he held up a hand.

John-Henry helped his husband to his feet. Emery's face tightened with pain, and he grunted as he leaned heavily on John-Henry. They stayed like that a moment. Cassidy's choking gurgles alternated with Koby's shallow breaths. The smell of blood filled the air, mixing with the stink of gunpowder and loose bowels. The stink clung to skin, and John-Henry was aware of sweat and body oil and the new, urgent desire for fresh air and hot water and, piercing with its intensity, a beer.

Then Emery set his forehead against John-Henry's, and his hand curled around John-Henry's nape. For a heartbeat, it was just the two of them. And then sirens sang in the distance, and Emery whispered, "Colt."

"Go on," John-Henry said. "I'll keep an eye on them." Cassidy's face was ashy, his eyes peppered with red. "Is he going to die?"

"Most likely," Emery said. "I doubt the paramedics will arrive in time to administer an emergency tracheotomy."

"But."

"But," Emery said grudgingly, "I'll see what I can do." He appraised the fallen man for a moment. Cassidy's sneakers scraped across the carpet. "After I find our son."

John-Henry nodded, pulled the cuffs from his belt, and turned his attention to Koby. Once he had the smaller man secure, he made a makeshift bandage out of his shirt and used it to compress the gunshot wound in an attempt to slow the bleeding. Koby screamed as John-Henry bore down on the bullet hole, and then his eyes rolled up in his head and he passed out.

Emery made his way down the hall, hammering on doors, calling, "Colt! Colt!"

A door at the end of the hall opened, and Colt stuck his head out. His eyes were wide, and even from a distance, his terror had an almost physical presence. His gaze fell on Emery, and then he sprinted into the hall and crashed into his dad. He wrapped Emery in an embrace, and Emery's pained grunt suggested the strength of his hold. But Emery didn't pull back. He hugged Colt to him, and he didn't let go. More kids began to emerge from their rooms, faces teary and frightened. Ashley crept out of the same room where Colt had been. He was dressed in pajama pants printed with reindeer, and his sleep shirt showed a stylized Santa face with sunglasses. Emery looped him into the hug too, and a shudder ran through Ashley as he started to cry. And John-Henry realized, as Koby's blood soaked through his t-shirt, warm and staining his hands, that it was Christmas Eve.

25

The day that followed was long. The interviews, which were really more like interrogations. The unending hours in impersonal, institutional settings: the back of an ambulance, the hospital, and then the Metropolitan police station.

The most important thing Emery learned was that the kids were fine. Until the fire alarm and the shooting, they'd all thought it had just been a fun trip made slightly inconvenient because Koby had taken their phones.

The second most important thing was that both Koby and Cassidy were going to survive. John had kept Koby from bleeding out, and Emery had administered an emergency tracheotomy (pocketknife and the empty tube of a ballpoint pen), which meant Cassidy would make a total, albeit uncomfortable, recovery. He took that as good news. Emery didn't know much about this Koby character, but he knew Jonas Cassidy, and Cassidy was a coward. He'd flip as soon as anyone so much as breathed the word *deal*. If they were lucky, Koby might flip too. Farah, the woman who had helped coordinate the trip, was also under arrest. It was unclear to Emery what her role in all of it had been, but he guessed that she, like the kids at GLAM, had been headed for a terrible fate.

Vermilya had escaped. For now. But he'd been hospitalized and fingerprinted. He was in the system now, and that meant he couldn't stay invisible forever. Or at least, that's what Emery hoped.

It was midafternoon before they drove home. And then, in the wake of everything that had happened, total exhaustion caught up with all three of them. Biscuit, of course, was oblivious, but after her first spurt of zoomies, she seemed content to climb on Colt, and Colt practically had a death grip on the dog. Too tired for anything else, they ate frozen pizzas and stayed close to one another, and they didn't say much. The TV droned in the background. That was enough.

For the first time in Emery didn't know how many years, John-Henry Somerset didn't celebrate his birthday with a brunch. No friends filled their home. No one called, as far as he knew. He watched the dark settle like snow. And when he turned on the lights on the Christmas tree, he discovered that his son and husband both had fallen asleep on the couch.

He covered them with blankets. And then he made a call and got into the minivan.

A little less than an hour later, he passed a truck stop called The Big Muddy. It was a massive operation: dozens of fuel pumps, a meandering convenience store-slash-restaurant with a timber veneer and picture windows, and a flashing sign near the interstate that said THE BIG MUDDY – CHEAP GAS – HOT SHOWERS – CLEAN ROOMS – DINA'S GRUB. Even on Christmas Eve, the truck stop had steady traffic. He slowed and eased onto the shoulder of the road a quarter mile later and walked back. Because you never knew about cameras.

He started at the back of the lot, where one wing of the truck stop offered rooms for rent, and walked slowly down the lot. He stopped when he found the passenger van. The plates were different, but he recognized it anyway. He bent and removed the tracker that Shaw had placed beneath the trailer hitch, wiped the spot with his sleeve to remove any incidental prints, and moved up the walk to wait. He produced a vape pen confiscated from Colt and turned it on. The pen glowed, and from time to time, Emery raised it to his mouth and blew out a stream of breath to create the illusion that he'd stepped outside to vape. Like smoking, it was one of those simple things that gave you an excuse to wait anywhere.

Emery didn't have to wait long. He stood there, listening to the sound of cars whipping past on the interstate, to Christmas music playing on the fuel island speakers, to a girl calling for her mom to wait up, to life—because that's what it was. All these people going about their lives. The cold stung his cheeks. Judy Garland came on, and she sang about the promise of next year, and muddling through. After about fifteen minutes, his phone buzzed. He checked the message and resumed his waiting.

The unsteady slap of feet was the first sign, and then a darkened shape came around the corner of the Big Muddy. The shape resolved itself into a man. His blond hair was now a brown so dark it was almost black, and he wore a ball cap and a bulky coat that made it hard to tell his build. He'd even added glasses—wire frames that changed the shape of his face. Jace Vermilya, or whatever his real name was, didn't look good. But that was the risk you took when you left the hospital early.

He didn't even look at Emery as he stumbled to one of the motel room doors. He wobbled and braced himself with one hand on the jamb as he produced a key, and then he began the process of trying to unlock the door. As he tried to line up the key, another shadow appeared from around the corner of the building. It resolved itself into Shaw: black jeans, an unremarkable jacket hanging open over a t-shirt that said THE BIG MUDDY, only a hint of his auburn hair showing under the dark beanie. His face was pale, his eyes bruised. But clear, Emery thought. No hint of doubt or wavering. He pocketed the vape and walked down the sidewalk toward Vermilya.

Shaw met him, and they both looked at Vermilya, who was still fumbling with his key.

"He has enough oxy in him to put down a horse," Shaw said. "And that's not even taking into consideration the beers."

Emery nodded. "Did anyone see you?"

"Of course." Shaw pointed at the t-shirt and shrugged. "They saw helpful wait staff bringing someone a fresh beer while he was in the bathroom."

"The cameras—"

"I knew what we were doing when I said yes, Emery." Shaw considered him and something softened in his face. "If this is too much, I can handle the rest of it."

Emery let the words fade away into the darkness. He couldn't hear the music anymore, and he wasn't sure if it had ended or if that was him, and the rush of his own thoughts. But he shook his head.

Vermilya mumbled something, and the door opened. He made his way inside, pushing the door shut behind him as he went, and Emery sprinted to catch it. He grabbed the knob before the door could shut completely, and he held it so that the door was almost closed. He counted to a hundred in his head. And then he inched the door open.

Facedown on the bed, Vermilya was still bundled in his coat. Emery stepped inside. He spotted the laptop and phone right away, handed them to Shaw, and shut the door. It was like any motel room anywhere—the smell of bleach on the bedding, the carpet that felt slimy under his boots, the chipped furniture and speckled mirror. He took off his winter gloves and pulled on a disposable pair. Then he took out the hard plastic case from his back pocket. He'd prepared the solution in advance, made from crushed-up pills prescribed to John after the fight at Tucker's. He set out the syringe and the hypo. Then he moved over to Vermilya.

He rolled the man onto his side and caught a whiff of yeasty breath. The man was heavier than Emery had expected, and he made a faint sound of discomfort as the rough movement jarred his injuries. His eyes flickered, but they didn't open. Emery slid one arm out of the coat. Then he let Vermilya fall onto his back, eliciting another groan. He freed the man's other arm and pushed the coat across the bed. Then he pushed up one sleeve of Vermilya's Henley. The story would be simple. He got drunk. He came back to his room to get high. He overdid it, the way so many people did every day.

Emery went back to his kit. He opened the two unlubricated condoms and pressed the wrapper for each against the pads of Vermilya's fingers. Then he left the wrappers on the nightstand. He didn't expect anyone to check, but it was often the little things that came back to get you. He tied the condoms together and then used them as an impromptu tourniquet, tying it off above Vermilya's elbow. He squeezed Vermilya's hand a few times until a vein emerged, blue against the pale skin of his inner arm.

The needle went in easily, and Emery depressed the plunger. When the syringe was empty, he repeated the process of pressing the syringe and plunger against Vermilya's fingers. Then he set the syringe on the mattress, where it would look like it had fallen after Vermilya shot up. He passed the next five minutes walking himself through what he could remember of the general pharmacology of opioids, including adverse effects. Nausea and vomiting. Itching. Constipation. Respiratory depression.

After one minute, he couldn't hear Vermilya breathing, but he waited the full five before he checked for a pulse. Nothing. He finished setting the scene by pouring the dregs of the solution into a plastic cup from the bathroom. He transferred fingerprints to the cup too. He left a plastic baggy, used to crush the pills and still lined with their residue, and he got Vermilya's prints on it as well. The smell of piss began to rise, a sign that Vermilya's sphincters had relaxed. Emery gave the room one last look and let himself outside.

He walked down the interstate, the wind at his back, the sky black with stars. He got into the Odyssey. When he reached an emergency pullout, he turned around and headed back toward Wahredua. His phone buzzed, and he answered by saying, "It's done."

Shaw's breathing came across the line. Then he said, "Good."

"Did you get what you needed?"

"I got something," Shaw said.

He was looking for someone, he had told Emery. A boy named Nik.

"We'll see if it gets us anywhere," Shaw added. "I put the phone and laptop back when I was done."

Silence made him aware of a white hiss on the call.

"Even if we'd turned him in," Emery said, "there's no guarantee he would have gone to prison."

More silence.

"Even if Koby and Cassidy turn on him, there's no guarantee."

The silence met him like a held breath.

"He arranged for murder inside a secure facility before. Koby and Cassidy might both be dead before they had a chance to testify. He ruined John's life with these fucking allegations, and he managed to make it happen in a town where John has friends, where his dad is the fucking mayor."

Ahead of him, the Big Muddy huddled under a canopy of silver light.

"He was simply too dangerous," Emery said, and he thought his voice might break. "We didn't have any other choice."

"We did the right thing, Emery," Shaw said gently.

Emery swallowed against the knot in his throat and disconnected. He drove another mile, and then, at a cloverleaf interchange, he pulled off again and sat on the side of the road. Cars passed him, lights moving in the dark. Air displaced by a semi rocked the minivan. He told himself to drive home. He told himself to signal, to merge onto the highway, to go back to his family. But he didn't. He sat there under a map of stars. And he remembered reading somewhere, a long time ago, that all our mourning, we do for ourselves.

26

"No," John-Henry said, "absolutely not."

Colt perked up with indignation to peer at him over the back of the sofa. "J-H!"

"The last time I let you and Ash order level four kung pao, the two of you laid on the floor and moaned after you were finished."

"Because it was so good!"

"Because you made yourselves sick. I'm not joking, Colt, I think Ash was crying."

"Pops!"

Emery scruffed a hand through Colt's hair as he passed him to join John-Henry in the kitchen. "If it burns going down, my son."

Indecision twisted Colt's face. "Fine. Level three."

John-Henry wrote the order down. "What about you? Besides the dumplings."

Emery grabbed the takeout menu from the fridge and said, "They should start printing the sodium content on these things."

Biscuit must have had a dog's intuition because she trotted over to rub against Emery's leg.

"Mind your own business," Emery told her.

It was Christmas, even if it didn't feel like it. From the beginning of the day, everything had been off. Emery had slept late and been distant throughout the morning, although he'd warmed up as the day went on. John-Henry hadn't slept much either, in part because the couch wasn't all that comfortable, and in part because he'd stayed there anyway, unwilling to send Colt to bed, and thus had been woken again and again by Colt's nightmares. The boy's fears, from what he could tell, were less about the fact that he had, in essence, been abducted and more about the fight he'd overheard at the hotel—and, of course, its aftermath. John-Henry himself had dreamed of the fight—that first instant of surprise, when Koby had emerged from the alcove and John-Henry had seen the kama scything through the air toward him. And then the blind, helpless fury at the end, when the Glock had kicked in his hands. He'd woken to the kind of exhaustion that sleep couldn't wipe away. Even though it seemed like things might finally be moving in the right direction, with both Cassidy and the man they called Koby trying to cut a deal, the weight of the last week—hell, the weight of the last year—was still crushing.

But since it was Christmas, and since they hadn't planned or prepared or done anything Christmas-y, not since the charges had been brought against John-Henry, they were going to round out the day with takeout from China Village, and that was going to be that. Definitely not the best Christmas ever, but maybe the one they needed.

"Ree, come on. You want the General Tso's. Just tell me you want the General Tso's so I can call this in."

"I might not want the General Tso's. I might want the moo goo gai pan."

"Uh huh."

"I might want the pork egg foo young."

"I'm calling in the order, love."

Grumbling, Emery returned the menu to the side of the fridge, and John-Henry placed the call. Emery returned to his book—something on forensic entomology that John-Henry had banned from the kitchen—and Colt went back to *Die Hard*. The original, of course. John-Henry joined him because that's what good dads did.

When the doorbell rang, John-Henry said, "That was fast."

"Colt," Emery said without looking up from his book.

John-Henry was still fighting against the aches and stiffness of the last few days, trying to get to his feet, when Colt rolled off the couch and padded toward the front door. Biscuit raced to catch up with him.

"We're getting old," John-Henry told Emery.

Emery snorted and turned a page.

Colt sprinted back through the living room and charged up the stairs. Biscuit darted back and forth, obviously torn between inspecting the strangers at the front door and following the person she loved most in the entire universe.

"What the hell?" Emery asked.

"Bubs—" John-Henry tried.

"I've got to change!" Colt screamed back at them.

"Why would he—" Emery stopped and said, "Good God, no."

John-Henry was still trying to get up from the couch—maybe the springs had gone bad, and that's why it felt so sinky and difficult to escape—when the front door opened.

"—because that's why people have doors, jerkweed," North was saying.

"But the door was unlocked," Shaw said, his voice moving toward the living room. "And, on account of my natural soulmatedness with Emery—"

"What are you doing here?" Emery asked as North and Shaw stepped into the room.

Shaw was dressed in what John-Henry was sure had been billed as a sexy Santa's elf leotard that he'd upgraded with candy-cane-striped thigh-high socks. The knee-high suede boots matched the deep green of the leotard. It looked like he might be wearing garters. Biscuit immediately began to growl at him.

North, of course, had on a Carhartt jacket, a hideous sweater with real, flashing Christmas lights on it—the old-fashioned kind with the big bulbs—jeans, and the Red Wings. He was also, John-Henry noticed, wearing a Christmas bow hair clip.

"Does that sweater have a battery pack?" Emery asked, book forgotten.

"Merry fucking Christmas to you too." He displayed the takeout bags he was carrying. "And go fuck yourself. Where do you want these?"

"What is it?" John-Henry asked.

North stared at him as though there might, somewhere, have been a genetic blip in John-Henry's past. Then, slowly, he said, "Food."

"Where do you think we want it?" Emery snapped, getting to his feet to herd North into the kitchen. The bickering began almost immediately.

"Uh, thank you," John-Henry said after them.

"You're welcome," Shaw as he pranced into the kitchen, apparently choosing to ignore that Biscuit was biting one of the suede boots and being dragged along with him.

Another knock came at the door, and as John-Henry went to answer it, Colt appeared on the stairs. He wore a quilted red pullover and dark jeans, and his hair was freshly styled and dark with water. When he noticed John-Henry's attention, he looked off into the middle distance and hurried toward the kitchen.

"Maybe Emery wasn't wrong about boarding school," John-Henry said to himself.

When he opened the door, Tean and Jem stood there. Tean held a large paper bag stamped with the Wahredua Family Bakery's logo. His hair was less wild than usual—clearly Jem's handiwork—and he looked comfortable in a cardigan and khakis. Jem wore a sweater that somehow managed to look even uglier than North's—it featured an extremely muscular and shirtless Santa who had the head of a cat, and he appeared to be riding a surfboard. Extensive use had been made of a reflective silver fabric, so that it looked like streamers of tinsel had been woven into the sweater. He was holding a McDonald's bag.

"There's enough to share," he said, "but Tean said I could be in charge of rationing the fries."

"He told the girls about it for fifteen minutes," Tean said.

"I wanted them to be proud of me."

"Oh God, you're here on Christmas," John-Henry said.

"It's okay," Tean said. "We couldn't have gotten a flight home anyway. We talked to the girls for a long time this morning, and we're going to celebrate again when we get home."

"More importantly," Jem said, "we got Emery his own fudge cake."

"But don't tell him it's just for him," Tean said, pressing the bag into John-Henry's hands. "He'll feel self-conscious."

They shook snow from their shoes and headed into the house, and John-Henry was reaching to close the door when the black Audi zipped up and parked across the driveway, blocking North in. When Auggie got out, he was laughing. Theo was shaking his head and saying, "—going to kill you if he sees where you parked."

"Duh," Auggie said as he helped Lana out of the car. "That's what makes it so fun."

"Uncle John," Lana screamed as she bowled into him, unhindered by the brace, the snow, or the stairs.

Laughing, John-Henry hugged her, stroked her hair, and let her go as she raced into the house, screaming, "Evie?"

"She's with her mom," John-Henry called after her, but Lana was gone by then.

Auggie and Theo were carrying covered glass dishes as they came onto the porch.

"Did we miss a text?" John-Henry asked. "Did somebody send up the Bat Signal?"

Theo smiled. "I told them they should ask."

"To be fair, Tean thought we should ask too," Auggie said. "But we decided we wanted it to be a surprise. Mashed potatoes." He nodded at the dish in Theo's hands and then to his own. "Green bean casserole."

"Auggie's family recipes."

For some reason, Auggie blushed and shrugged.

At that moment, an old Dodge Durango with an illuminated China Village sign on its roof pulled up next to the Audi.

"Takeout on Christmas?" Auggie said in a disapproving voice.

"We were tired," John-Henry said with a laugh.

Theo kissed the side of Auggie's head. "Let's get these in the oven."

"Thanks, Mel," John-Henry said as the girl waded through the snow, laden down with bags of takeout. Melanie Wong had delivered their food more times than he could count, and her younger sister was in Colt's grade at school.

She flashed him a grin, and the crystal on her tooth sparkled in the porch light. "Full house, Chief Somerset. You sure this is going to be enough?"

"It's more of potluck, it turns out." He dug cash out of his wallet and handed it over. "Thanks again, happy holidays."

"Merry Christmas, Chief."

"It's not chief, Mel."

The crystal sparkled again as snow crunched under her steps. "Sure, it is."

John-Henry carried the food inside, but he'd barely made it to the kitchen before the front door opened again. Familiar footsteps sprinted down the hall, and Evie appeared in the living room, cheeks red from the cold.

"Hi, baby," John-Henry said as he handed the bags to Emery, who was organizing the expanding spread on the counter, while North, at the same time, tried to tell him where to put everything. "Merry—"

"Where's Lana?" And then Evie turned and raced for the stairs. "Lana!"

"—Christmas, baby."

"A little help?" Cora called from the front of the house.

"Colt, do you—"

"I'll help!" Colt said, shooting a quick look at North before hurrying toward the front of the house.

A huge smile slanted across Auggie's face. Jem's eyes were bright. Shaw made a soft, cooing noise.

"One of you motherfuckers say something." North's face was red as he opened one of the takeout containers he and Shaw had brought, revealing a mound of nachos. "Go right ahead."

John-Henry was trying not to laugh as he went back to give Cora a hand.

But apparently, his help wasn't needed, because Colt was carrying two insulated bags and talking a mile a minute to Nico, who was holding a brown paper bag in his arms, his face politely interested as Colt began a rundown of "the dopest shit ever," which apparently referred to the last couple of days.

"Language," John-Henry said.

"Merry Christmas," Nico said as he passed him. "And happy birthday. Hope you're ready."

"Ready for what?"

"And then Pops broke his neck with his bare hands," Colt said.

"No," Emery called from the kitchen, "I didn't."

John-Henry leaned out the storm door and saw Cora still at her car, passing more bags to, of all people, Noah and Rebeca. Their oldest daughter, Raquel, was toting another insulated cooler toward the house, while Robbie, the next oldest, screamed orders at Ricky and Roman, who were chasing each other through the snow. Rafe was helping Rocio up the steps, and Rocio, who was Evie's age, was carrying a wrapped present.

"It's for Evie," Rafe said, reaching to take the present from Rocio.

Rocio screeched, "I'm carrying it!"

So, John-Henry opened the door and got out of the way.

By that point, Cora, Noah, and Rebeca were working their way toward the house. Noah barked a command, and the rest of the kids zipped inside.

"Is there more?" John-Henry asked as he accepted a kiss on the cheek first from Cora and then from Rebeca.

"This is it," Cora said. "Happy birthday, merry Christmas. Also, we need to have a talk because Evie told my mom, 'Merry fucking Christmas'." And without missing a beat, she drifted inside.

Noah had a huge grin on his face.

"You realize that's not my fault, right?" John-Henry said.

"Happy birthday," Rebeca said with a smile.

"And merry fucking Christmas," Noah said.

John-Henry waved them inside. "Maybe this is what Emery's always complaining about. Everyone wants to be a comedian."

He was about to shut the door when a truck came grumbling up the street, followed by a small, silver sedan. The truck parked first, and Ashley dropped out of the back of the cab, followed a moment later by his parents. Brendon and Anais Boone hadn't always been thrilled with Ashley's relationship to Colt, but they'd been supportive, and the fact that they were here said more than John-Henry could put into words. The silver sedan found a spot, and Emery's mom got out and began to rummage around in the trunk.

"We've officially got a full house," Emery said as he joined John-Henry at the door. "What are you—hello, Ashley. Why are you inside my house?"

John-Henry opened his mouth to say something, but before he could, Ashley wrapped Emery in a hug and started to cry. Not big tears, but the boy was shaking as he tried, over and over again, to say, "Thank you."

The look on Emery's face was priceless. After a moment, though, his eyes softened, and he rubbed Ashley's back. "You don't need to thank me," he said quietly. "Everything's ok."

John-Henry got a hug from Ash too—a noticeably damp one—and then Colt said from the opening to the living room, "Everybody's hungry. Can we—Ash!"

Emery responding to Ashley's hug had been cute, John-Henry decided as he revised his opinion. Emery's thundercloud of an expression when Colt kissed Ashley, however, was priceless.

"All right," Emery snapped. "Enough."

For whatever reason, that made both boys laugh, and when Colt said, "Bruh, they brought cheese fries," it apparently made everything better. They darted toward the kitchen.

Anais tapped lightly on the storm door as she opened it, and she and Brendon stepped inside. Unlike their son, Ash's parents seemed to have difficulty meeting Emery and John-Henry's gazes. Then Anais seemed to brace herself and offered a smile. "I can't believe I'm saying this again, but thank you for saving our son's life."

Brendon was getting teary-eyed, and John-Henry thought maybe he, like Ashley, was a crier.

"I'm sorry," John-Henry said. "We had no idea GLAM—"

"Nobody did." Brendon shook his head. "And we're sorry, John-Henry. We knew those stories about you were lies. We should have—we should have done more."

For a moment, John-Henry didn't know what to say.

"There was nothing anyone could do," Emery said gruffly.

And John-Henry wondered if they knew how hard he was trying, for Colt's sake.

"We heard those men are trying to make a deal," Anais said. "Everyone knows you were framed."

John-Henry managed a smile. "I'll be happy when it's all behind us."

If they heard what he didn't say, they gave no sign of it. Brendon wanted to shake their hands, and then they moved toward the happy voices in the kitchen.

Aileen Hazard came through the door. She set a big bag on the floor and was already smiling as she took Emery into a hug. "Merry Christmas, muffin."

"Merry Christmas. Why are you here?"

"John-Henry, do you hear this?" she asked as she hugged John-Henry in turn. "He's terrible to his mother." She squeezed him extra tight, and John-Henry's eyes stung. "You sweet, sweet boy," she whispered. "Are you ok?"

"He's not particularly sweet," Emery said. "Shall I remind you of the time he gutted my rock-collecting budget? His exact words were 'But you don't even do anything with them.'"

Aileen's gaze was fixed on John-Henry, though, and he managed a nod to her question. She squeezed his hands in hers and then looked at Emery and said, "Don't be awful. I'm here because it's Christmas."

"I think asking why you chose to drive over a hundred miles on icy roads in the dark without letting anyone know where you were or what you were doing—Mother, come back here." As she moved into the living room, he called after her, "It's a perfectly legitimate question."

John-Henry was wiping his eyes when Emery glanced over at him. He dredged up a smile, and it felt a little closer to real when Emery put an arm around him and pulled John-Henry against him. After a few moments, John-Henry said, "I'm good."

Emery kissed his hair.

"And we'd better get in there before Colt, Ash, North, and Jem eat everything in sight."

It turned out, that wasn't really a possibility. In addition to the range of takeout that everyone had contributed, Cora had brought all the food from John-Henry's birthday meal. More importantly, she'd also brought champagne and prosecco. The options ran the gamut from Emery's General Tso's—which he was guarding from Jem—to the McDonald's french fries—which Jem was guarding from everyone—to the birthday quiches. Auggie and Theo handled the drinks after Noah and Rebeca produced plastic champagne flutes, and Colt put some music on. Not the rap that sometimes threatened to shake the house down, but a Christmas playlist that hummed quietly in the background.

John-Henry slipped into host mode without even really thinking about it; it was something he did, something he knew how to do without even needing to put it into words. Theo was still in the kitchen after the drinks had been served, John-Henry noticed, reading on his phone. North was also reading on his phone as he picked over the nachos.

John-Henry got a glimpse of North's phone and said, "We'd be doing better if Tarasenko hadn't gotten injured."

North snorted. "We'd be doing better if we weren't eating shit."

Grinning, John-Henry said, "Theo, want to weigh in on that?"

"He's not wrong," Theo said, lowering his phone. "One player shouldn't make or break a team like this."

"It's still early in the season. We're not doing that badly."

"Are you kidding me?" North said.

At the same time, Theo said, "You've got to be joking."

"We're the defending champs."

"We just won the Stanley Cup."

John-Henry smiled and held his hands up in surrender. "I expected you guys to say it was all Binnington's fault."

North's look was flat disbelief. "Do you have any fucking clue what you're talking about? Theo, for fuck's sake, help me out."

After they had both—thoroughly—told him how wrong he was, John-Henry found a way to slip out of the conversation and leave them to hash out every mistake the Blues had made so far this season.

In the living room, Shaw and Auggie were on all fours, crawling around on top of blankets that had clearly been brought down from Evie's room. Evie and Lana were giggling and throwing potato chips at the two men, while Tean was trying to make himself as small as possible in an armchair, his nose in a book.

"What in the world—" John-Henry began with a laugh.

"Daddy!" Evie screamed. "You're ruining their house!"

He dutifully straightened the blanket he'd messed up.

"We're playing magical zoo," Shaw said.

A grin streaked across Auggie's face. "I'm a rhinocerwhompophant."

Biscuit sprinted into the room and chose that moment to bite Shaw's elf leotard, or whatever it was called, and try to drag him down to the floor. The girls laughed even harder as Shaw said, "Oh no, it's the vicious woolly fangtangler! Help! Help!"

It was hard to tell, as Shaw continued to be mauled by Biscuit, how many of the cries for help were real and how many were pretend.

Perching on the arm of Tean's chair, John-Henry said, "I bet you have to play games like this with your girls all the time."

Tean looked up, blinked, and adjusted his glasses. Then he glanced at Shaw, who was being thoroughly dominated by Biscuit, and smiled. "Jem always has to be the tigerocious maximus."

"I bet you could tell these girls how to wrangle a vicious woolly fangtangler."

Smile widening, Tean set aside his book. "The woolly fangtangler's only weakness is when little girls—"

"Princesses!" Lana corrected him.

"When princesses call her name and distract her with treats."

The girls dutifully jumped down from the couch and began calling Biscuit's name, holding out broken pieces of potato chips. Biscuit lost interest in Shaw, who was red-faced and giggling now, and went over to the girls.

"But," Tean said, his voice rising dramatically, "the rhincerwhompophant loves to charge at little princesses!"

Auggie made a roaring noise that also incorporated some elephant-like trumpeting. He pretended to paw the ground, and then he charged, lightly headbutting first Lana and then Evie. It immediately turned into a melee, with the girls climbing all over Auggie and Biscuit circling around to nip at his legs. Shaw tried to crawl away, but Biscuit took that as a sign of weakness and went after him.

John-Henry left them and chose to believe that the screams—even Shaw's—were expressions of excitement and fun.

He found Colt, Ashley, Brendon, Anais, Noah, and Rebeca in the dining room. Colt and Ashley were obviously in their own world, and as the adults chatted, they spared them looks that ranged from amused to thoughtful.

"J-H," Colt said, "Ash brought you and Pops gifts for, you know, helping us out."

"Saving our lives," Ashley said with a gentle smile.

"He got Pops a tactical pen."

"Bruh!"

"What? He's not here. Isn't that fire, J-H?"

John-Henry smiled as he sat at the table. "He's going to love it."

Ashley rolled one shoulder, obviously caught between a moment of shyness and his pleasure at John-Henry's response. Anais took a gift out of her bag and handed it to Ashley, who passed it to John-Henry. The paper had torn in a couple of places, and it was thoroughly—and unevenly—taped at every seam, all the signs that a teenage boy had been in charge of wrapping it. John-Henry opened it.

"Cologne," he said, with a smile for Ashley. "I always need a new fragrance. Thank you, Ashley."

"Bruh," Colt said, dissolving into laughter.

"What?" Ashley said. He poked Colt. "Hey!"

Colt laughed harder, but he managed to drag himself upright long enough to say, "Night Thrust?"

"Oh my God," Brendon said under his breath, and Anais's eyes got huge.

"That's not—" Ashley's face flooded with color. "I didn't—" He looked pleadingly at John-Henry. "It's just the name!"

"It's perfect, Ashley," John-Henry said. "Colt's just giving you grief; don't listen to him. It's a very thoughtful gift."

"I wear Night Thrust," Noah said.

With an unmistakable trace of horror, Rebeca said, "You do?"

After a few more thank-yous to make sure Ashley's feelings weren't hurt, John-Henry excused himself. He knew he was lucky in many regards, and one was that his son was an inveterate thief, which meant that in a few days or weeks, Night Thrust would end up safely in Colt's bathroom, and John-Henry could conveniently forget about the well-intentioned but disastrously executed gift.

Emery was in the front room, with his mom, Cora, Jem, and Nico. After a glance at the cologne, Emery raised his eyebrows and said, "Would you like to share something with the class?"

"Ha ha. It's a long story. Actually, not that long—it's a gift from Ash."

"Why am I not surprised?"

"You'll be pleased to learn you're getting the companion fragrance: Black Hole."

Emery stared for a full second. "You're shitting me."

"Bunny!"

"He thinks he's got jokes, Mom. What did he really get me?"

John-Henry did what he knew would drive his husband crazy: he smiled.

"I'm serious, John. I need to be prepared so that I can react appropriately."

"What are we talking about?" John-Henry asked, catching Cora's eye. Lots of things had changed between them over the years, but one thing that hadn't was Cora's ability to read him—and she was hiding a smile now.

"Nothing," Nico said. "In fact—"

"We're giving Nico dating advice," Aileen said. "It's so much fun."

"I don't know about fun," Nico muttered.

"He's in a long-distance thing," Jem said. And then, sourness edging the next words: "With a cop."

John-Henry laughed in spite of himself. "I didn't know it was officially a thing, Nico."

"It's not! It's—it's whatever." But color rose in Nico's face, and after a moment of wavering, he said, "Jem!"

"What?" Jem asked with a laugh. "You can't keep it secret forever."

"Keep what secret?" John-Henry asked.

"Why would you keep anything secret from us?" Emery asked. "That's counterproductive to my efforts to manage your life for you."

Nico's eyes got very wide, and he looked at Aileen and said, "See?"

"I know, sweetheart," Aileen said and patted his knee. "But to be fair, you do seem like a bit of a mess."

"Fine," Nico said. "Yes. It's a thing. We're dating."

"That's lovely," Cora said.

John-Henry nodded. "Congratulations."

"Don't congratulate me yet. It's long-distance, and—" Nico gave a despairing shake of his shaggy hair. "I mean, I screw up every relationship when it's in person, and now I'm supposed to do it long distance?"

"Maybe it'll be a help," Emery said. "Maybe the distance will mitigate your—"

Nico's head came up.

"Uh," Emery said. "John, what were you saying?"

John-Henry rolled his eyes, but he said, "I was saying, again, congratulations. And don't freak out. Long-distance is hard, but it's not a death sentence."

"You need to look at the positives," Cora said. "Think about how this gives you opportunities to be creative about how you're going to strengthen your relationship. When I was dating this guy in Kansas City—" She cut off, color flooding her face, her gaze rigidly fixed away from John-Henry.

"I didn't know—" John-Henry began. Then he stopped and said, "Was?"

Some of the tension went out of Cora, and she threw him a smile. "Was. Is officially over. But when I was, we had to work hard to build trust and feel close to each other, which meant coming up with movie nights while we talked on the phone, or reading a book together, that kind of thing." Then she laughed. "It didn't work out, obviously, so I'm not the expert."

"Dude," Jem said, "it's all about taking advantage of the time you're together, and then working hard when you're not. Touch. Lots and lots of touch when you're together. Hold hands. Kiss. Smush naughty bits."

"Jeremiah!" Emery barked.

But Aileen burst out laughing, and after a moment, so did everyone else.

"And when you're not together, find ways to open up. Come up with questions you can discuss. Or tell him one thing about yourself every night before bed, and ask him to do the same." Jem shrugged. "Every relationship is about building trust and making yourself vulnerable. You've just got to work a little harder."

"In the '80s," Aileen said, "we came up with something called phone sex."

For a moment, John-Henry thought he'd blown an eardrum.

Aileen frowned at Nico. "Can't you do that with FaceTime?"

"Who," Emery asked like a man staring into the abyss, "is the 'we' in that sentence?"

That was when Jem officially died from laughing.

Before too long, Noah and Rebeca started packing up their kids. John-Henry and Emery walked them to the door.

"I'm sorry," Rebeca said. "I'm sorry for everything that happened. I'm sorry we couldn't help."

"You weren't even in town," Emery said.

"But we're still sorry," Noah said.

"Thank you," John-Henry said. "Things are going to work out. And thank you for tonight."

Cora was next, with Nico on her heels. "You're sure she can stay tonight? I can wake her up."

"She and Lana are totally zonked. She's fine."

She kissed his cheek and said, "Happy birthday a day late."

"I love you."

"I love you too. And don't forget we're going to have a talk about Evie's comment to my mom."

"What's that about?" Emery asked.

"Just wait," John-Henry said.

Nico's hug took him by surprise, and his hug with Emery lasted even longer.

"Next time he comes to town," John-Henry said, "let's double."

Tears glittered in Nico's lashes, but he smiled. "Yeah. Ok."

"Better idea," Emery said. "I'd love to have coffee with him."

They could still hear Nico laughing as he walked down the sidewalk.

The Boones left next—after a lot of pleading from Ashley that he be allowed to spend the night. He brightened, though, when Emery told him again how much he liked the tactical pen.

"You're such a softy," John-Henry said as they trooped toward the truck.

"I have no idea what you're talking about." And then he caught his mother's arm as she tried to sneak past. "Absolutely not."

Aileen laughed as she put on her scarf. "I'm staying with June Louise tonight, bunny. We're going to watch *Dr. Zhivago* and drink mulled wine."

"One glass. More than that isn't good for your heart."

She kissed his cheek, kissed John-Henry's cheek, and slipped out into the night.

As Emery and John-Henry started toward the living room, a knock came at the door.

"If Noah and Rebeca forgot a child, I'm donating it," Emery said.

"I'll get it," John-Henry said with a laugh, and he reversed course.

When he opened the door, his father stood there. Glenn Somerset wore a suit, even though it was late, even though it was Christmas. His scarf was the perfect Christmas red. His tie was green and stitched with Christmas trees. The porch light threw deep shadows in the sockets of his eyes.

"I didn't realize you were having a party," he said.

"It just sort of happened." The cold began to soak through John-Henry's clothes. He adjusted his hand on the storm door.

His father waited and then shook his head. "I just spoke with a…friend. The prosecutor's office is putting together a plea deal. Cassidy has confessed, among other things, to helping that man Vermilya fabricate the recording. According to him, Vermilya is behind all of it, the entire operation. You'll be cleared of all charges."

After what felt like a long time, John-Henry nodded.

"I see that you're going to make this difficult." His father's smile crooked across his mouth. "Very well, I suppose I owe you that much. I'd like you to resume your duties as chief of police. Immediately."

The wind picked up. A spindrift of snow glittered for a moment, rainbow-like, under the streetlight. And then the wind dropped again, and the silence was like a drumbeat.

"I need to think about it," John-Henry said.

Maybe it was the cold. Or maybe the red in Glenn Somerset's face was from something else. "What do you mean, you need to think about it?"

"Excuse me, Father," John-Henry said. And as he shut the door, he remembered something his son had said not so long ago. "I'm going to spend tonight with my family."

He joined the others in the living room: Jem and Tean curled up together in the armchair; Theo on the sofa, with Auggie sitting on the floor between his legs; Shaw draped over North, the two of them taking up the rest of the sofa. Colt lay on the floor, playing on his phone. Biscuit had fallen asleep with her head across his legs.

"Everything okay?" Emery asked.

John-Henry nodded.

"We should go," Theo said. "Let me help you clean up."

Auggie leaned into Theo's knee. That was all.

Theo threaded fingers through the dark crew cut, cleared his throat, and said, "But we don't have to go."

Emery looked at John-Henry, and John-Henry wondered what his husband had overheard, how much he had understood. Enough was probably the answer. And then Emery smiled and took his hand.

"No," John-Henry said, surprised at the thickness of his voice. "Please. Stay."

Mystery Magnet

Keep reading for a sneak preview of *Mystery Magnet,* the first book in The Last Picks, a new cozy mystery series from Gregory Ashe.

CHAPTER 1

"Do you like puzzles?"

"Um, yes?"

Okay, maybe not the strongest answer in what was technically a job interview. But cut me some slack; I had a lot going against me. In the first place, I was talking to Vivienne Carver. The Vivienne Carver. In the second place, I was operating on zero sleep because my cross-country drive had taken longer than I expected, and I'd covered the last hundred miles this morning in a bleary-eyed sprint. And third, in spite of everything that had happened, I was still (apparently) the same old Dash.

Which was why the next words out of my mouth were "Actually, yes. I mean, definitely." The words were like a freight train; I couldn't stop them as I blurted, "In fact, I love puzzles."

Vivienne's eyebrows went up. She looked like she does on TV, in case you're wondering. And in the author photo on her dust jackets. She was blond, like a lot of women of a certain age, her hair a medium length and layered and curled and styled until it was the size of a basketball. A red sweater—classic Vivienne. A pair of cheaters hung on a chain around her neck, but it was hard to imagine she needed them, because her eyes were a startlingly intense blue. She had great skin. Wrinkles, sure, but she could have passed for twenty years younger.

Okay, ten.

"I think puzzles are the heart of a mystery," she said. "Don't you?"

"Well," I said, "yes."

Vivienne opened her mouth.

I tried to stop myself, I really did. But it was another blurt: "And no."

Vivienne closed her mouth.

"But mostly yes," I said. "I mean, yes. Absolutely. The heart of a mystery novel."

She opened her mouth again.

Sometimes, being Dashiell Dawson Dane was like being in a horror movie: you knew you weren't supposed to go down into the basement alone to check the circuit breaker, or you knew you weren't supposed to get freaky with the rude but cute jock in the backseat of his car at Make-out Point, or (just for the sake of example) you knew you weren't supposed to keep talking. But you just. couldn't. help yourself.

"It's just—the puzzle," I said, "and the human element."

Vivienne closed her mouth again. Her eyes really were stunning. That was, apparently, the kind of thing I could think while I was having an out-of-body experience.

But then she smiled and said, "Quite right, Dashiell. That's well put. The puzzle and the human element. Very well put. Not that I would expect any less from you. I read 'Murder on the Emerald Express.' It was very clever. Quite the send-up of Christie, I think."

"Thank you."

"And your parents, of course."

And there it was. The whole reason I was here. Not because I'd written a couple of short stories that had eventually landed in *Black Mask* and *Flying Aces*. But because I was the son of Patricia Lockwood (*Mommy's Sleeping* and *Blind Furies* and *What the Laundress Saw*) and Jonny Dane (the Talon Maverick series). Because, to put it bluntly, Vivienne was doing her colleagues a favor.

Not that I cared. Well, not too much. I needed to get away from Providence, and here I was—about as far as you could get.

"How are your parents?" Vivienne asked. "I haven't seen them in ages."

"They're all right."

"And what are they doing these days?"

"Oh, you know. Mom stays busy with the chickens, and Dad has his guns."

Vivienne laughed, and I tried to smile, fighting the familiar tightness in my chest.

"Portsmouth really is so charming," Vivienne murmured. "I've only been once, and your parents were such wonderful hosts. I'd love to see them again."

"I'm sure they'd love to have you visit." I dredged up another smile. "I hope you like skeet shooting."

That made her laugh again. She settled back into her chair—it was so massive that it was really more of a throne—and examined me more carefully. After a moment of that long, considering stare, I looked away. Her study, where we were having this interview, was exactly what a famous author's study should look like: a cavernous fireplace, built-in bookcases (filled with her own titles, of course—all the books in the Matron of Murder series, and translations into dozens of languages), a massive cherrywood desk. She had a laptop, a sleek little aluminum thing, but the typewriter that featured so prominently in the *Matron of Murder* TV adaptation had pride of place on the desk. Posters from the show lined the walls. The actor they'd picked looked remarkably like Vivienne, even though the protagonist in the books, Genevieve Webster, was nominally fictional; I wondered if she'd had any say in the casting. Interspersed with the posters were photos of Vivienne. Vivienne with politicians. Vivienne with celebrities. Vivienne accepting honorary degrees and keys to various cities. Pictures of Vivienne when she'd been younger—glamorous, but not quite beautiful. Apparently, she owned (or had owned) a yacht.

"Tell me, Dashiell—"

"Just Dash." I rushed to add, "Unless you prefer Dashiell, that is."

She was silent for a beat. "Tell me about your writing, Dashiell."

"Well," I said. And that was as far as I got. That sense of tightness in my chest worsened. Vivienne's beautiful study got a little blurry around the edges. "I'm very passionate—"

"Your ideas, Dashiell." She waved a hand. "Your plans. Yes, I understand that your position here will be as my administrative assistant. But we both know it's a bit more than that. You're a talented writer." She gestured to the desk, even though it was bare aside from the laptop and typewriter. "Your resume is impressive. You've attended top writing workshops. You've done some teaching yourself."

"Just as an adjunct."

"And you have publications."

"Two short stories."

"But good, Dashiell." She leaned forward. Her glasses swung on their chain. Her gaze seemed to spear me to my chair. "They're good stories. They're smart. Even better, they're true. I don't need to ask you about your references. I don't need to know that you can type and use a word processor and answer phone calls. I want to know who you are, and I think you know, Dashiell, that the way to know a writer, truly know them, is to know their stories. People lie all the time. But every story is an act of disclosure, no matter how hard we try otherwise." She waited, as though I might say something, and then sat back again. "So, let's hear them."

"Well," I said. I almost mentioned Will Gower. Vivienne genuinely seemed to want to know, and I'd lived with Will Gower for so long, in all his various incarnations. But Phil, Mom and Dad's agent, had said no more Will Gower. He'd said I needed something high concept. Something with a hook. "I guess one of them is—have you seen *21 Jump Street*?" The silence grew until I said, "Like that. Only gayer."

Vivienne blinked. "That sounds…timely."

The words loosened something in my chest, and I sat forward, talking more easily now. "Oh, and do you know *Veronica Mars*? That's another idea. But make it, like, super gay."

"I see."

Excitement made me speak faster. "Or *Riverdale*. And I know what you're going to say, but yes, we can go gayer."

"Uh huh." For a moment, her face was blank. And then she gave a rueful grin. "Are you going to be terribly disappointed if I tell you I have no idea what you're talking about?"

Then she started to laugh, and for some reason, I burst out laughing too.

"I'm sorry," I said. "I can explain—"

"You'll explain later," she said, waving the words away. "I want to hear all about these ideas. I'm very impressed with what you've done, Dashiell. Very impressed. And I want to see more of it. You're very talented, and you're going to go on to do great things." She gave me a droll little smile. "And if I can offer a spot of advice here and there, well, I'd be happy to help however I can."

"Oh my God, that would be incredible. I—I've been struggling lately. With writing. Struggling to finish things. Struggling, um, to write anything, actually."

It was impossible to read her expression, but her voice was kind when she finally said, "I know a little something about that myself, believe it or not. We'll see if we can't shake something loose."

"That would be amazing."

"It would be friendly, Dashiell. This is a small town; being friendly is our way of life."

"I don't want you to think I expect you to, I don't know, do anything. You're busy, I understand that. And this is a job. I'm not asking for special treatment or favors or anything."

"I understand," she said gently. "And I'm telling you that I want to help you. I'm looking forward to it, actually. Believe it or not, life does get a little stale every once in a while. I believe you're going to be a breath of fresh air." Her pause had an unexpected quality to it—something I thought might be another kindness. "Your mother was distressed when she called me. I understand you made the decision to move rather suddenly."

"It might have seemed sudden to other people," I said. I fought to keep my voice easy and relaxed. "But I'd needed a change for a long time."

"I understand you've had some…difficulties lately."

Shaking my head, I said, "I'm fine. My parents are being dramatic."

Vivienne said nothing, but the raw intelligence of those blue of her eyes told me she didn't buy it. I waited for the thing I couldn't handle: questions about Hugo. Questions about why. The questions my parents had been asking for weeks.

"I promise, Mrs. Carver: I'm fine. The chance to work with you is an incredible opportunity. I'm excited to be here, and I promise, I'm not—" I almost said, *I'm not running away from anything*, but that would have been a lie. "—going to let you down."

In the distance, the surf crashed restlessly.

Then Vivienne nodded. "So, you'll take the job?"

A beat passed as I processed the words. "Yes, definitely, absolutely."

"Wonderful. We'll have some paperwork for you to sign later, of course. Non-disclosure agreements, tax forms, that kind of thing. Writing is a craft and an art, I don't need to tell you that, but it's also a business—most people are terribly disappointed when they learn that, but I'm sure it's something you learned growing up with your parents."

"I don't know if *they've* ever learned it," I said. The surge of relief at her offer—a job, a place to live, stability—was so great that the words slipped out before I could stop them. My face heated as I added, "They let their agent handle everything. And their accountant, I suppose."

"Then I see we have some work to do," Vivienne said as she came around the desk and took my arm. "If there's one thing I can teach you, it's business. Now, let me give you a quick tour, and we'll get you settled. I bet you want to rest after your early start this morning."

"How did you—" I cut myself off and grinned. This was, after all, Vivienne Carver. "Okay, how did you know?"

"A hint of stubble; you don't have a heavy beard, but it's there. And you missed a button on your shirt."

I fumbled at my placket.

"And you did seem a bit flustered as you came up the drive, dear."

Groaning, I shook my head. A bit flustered was putting it mildly.

Vivienne patted my arm and laughed gently. "It's all right. We'll get you squared away in no time."

She hadn't been joking when she'd called it a quick tour. Hemlock House—Vivienne's cliffside manor (there really wasn't any other word for it)—was massive, and it was old, too. Fireplaces in every room, damask wallpaper in deep hues of red and green and blue, wainscotting, polished wood floors covered by thick rugs. And God, so many crystal chandeliers. Heavy drapes framed the windows, and as we walked, I caught glimpses of the sea cliffs and, below them, the slate-green waters of the Pacific. The briny smell of the ocean was familiar and not at the same time. I'd grown up in a seaside town, but in a very different part of the world.

"Hemlock House was built by Nathaniel Blackwood," Vivienne said as we walked, her arm in mine. "He made a fortune in the late nineteenth century, fur and timber and agriculture, and—this will be your room, dear—" She opened a door, and I caught a glimpse of an enormous canopy bed, a secretary desk, an oil painting of a horse, and what looked like a very expensive clock. Then we moved on. "—and he retired here with his much, much younger bride."

"Some things never change," I said.

Vivienne laughed. "No, they don't. And I'm sure it won't surprise you to learn that Nathaniel Blackwood was, to put it mildly, an eccentric."

"The Howard Hughes of beaver pelts."

"Something like that. He spent years working on the plans for Hemlock House. Years, dear. And he was unbelievably exacting in the construction. Spent an absolute fortune building it, making sure everything was exactly as he'd dreamed, and then died shortly after it was finished. He fell from the balcony and died on the cliffs. His bride, as you might imagine, went on to live a long, happy life with a parade of lovers."

"He fell," I said. "Right."

Vivienne gave me that droll little smile again, but it faded as she said, "She died the same way, strangely enough. A fall from the balcony."

"So, no going out on the balconies. Check."

"She was pushed by a younger man. He claimed he didn't do it, of course, but everyone knew—there'd been fights about money, fights about other women. The bride never had any children, and the estate was a legal morass for decades. Finally, the house was sold to a private investor who went to great lengths to preserve the historic aspects. Most of the furniture is original, although there have been updates for modern conveniences." In a guilty whisper, she added, "I couldn't live without cable."

"I couldn't live without coffee."

A grand central staircase led down to the main floor, and when I say grand, I mean grand. Think, Disney castle grand: a sweeping spiral of polished marble, with a crystal chandelier hanging in the open well at the center. I'd come this way when I'd arrived, of course, but I'd been so nervous about the interview—if that conversation, in hindsight, could even be called an interview—that the details had registered only peripherally. Now I took it all in: the oil paintings in gilded frames (more horses), the black-and-white checkerboard tile (more marble), the unmistakable spaciousness of it all, as though the house had been built for giants. And, now, I noticed the person lying on the floor, splayed out like a body at a crime scene.

"Uh—"

"That's Fox," Vivienne said. "Fox, this is Dashiell."

"Just Dash," I said apologetically.

Vivienne studied Fox for a moment and said, "They're doing something with the wallpaper. I have to admit I don't really understand it. How's it going Fox?"

Fox was stocky, their dark hair buzzed and sprinkled with silver; I put them somewhere in their forties. In their ankle boots and paisley vest, they looked like they were striking a balance between hipster and steampunk. Without raising their head, they said, "Terrible. It's a disaster, and everything's the worst, and I'm dead."

"They're very dramatic," Vivienne confided.

"I'm not being dramatic. This design was a huge mistake. I'll never be able to replicate it. I'm a fraud and a sham. My life is over."

"They're an artist," Vivienne said, and then, a bit more loudly, "And an artiste."

Fox moaned.

"Something with sea-glass," Vivienne said as we continued down the stairs. For a lady in her sixties, she was spry—I'd read an interview she'd done in *Ellery Queen,* and she'd talked about running and bicycling and, I kid you not, her beloved mini trampoline. "Fox is very successful."

"Not anymore," Fox said from the floor. "I'm a huckster. I'm done."

"Dashiell is going to be joining us at Hemlock House, Fox. Do you have any words of wisdom for him as he settles in at Hastings Rock?"

"Never love or cherish or hope for anything," Fox said in a broken voice. "Life is a trap."

"And they're ever so much fun at parties," Vivienne murmured as she led me across the hall. We passed through a pair of pocket doors into the living room. It had the biggest fireplace I'd seen yet, with a pristine marble surround, a tarnished overmantel mirror, and a decorative tile-work hearth. Shiny brass fireplace tools and a matching screen. Maybe it sounds like I'm spending too much time on this fireplace, but it was enormous. You could have driven a hearse through it.

Like the rest of the house, this room had those lovely details and decorative elements that marked it as a product of another time (and another socioeconomic class). Cornicing, ceiling roses, more of those dramatic crystal chandeliers. Tufted sofas in brocade and velvet flanked by wingback chairs of cracked leather. Mahogany tables cluttered with brass and glass curios (a telescope, a miniature globe, a bowl). Tall windows, their curtains held open with tasseled tiebacks to let in more of the day's cloudy light. And, of course, bookcases. These weren't Vivienne's books. These looked like they'd come with the house, with beautiful bindings that had weathered the perpetual seaside damp surprisingly well. Interspersed with the books were botanical prints and porcelain figurines and glass cloches that held taxidermy birds.

"I know, dear," Vivienne said. "Barbaric. I couldn't sleep for a week the first time I saw them staring down at me. The dining room is through here."

Another set of doors carried us through the dining room (a ginormous table, paneled walls, and yes, a fireplace). Vivienne pointed to a door across from us and said, "That's the sun parlor." Then she headed for a second, smaller door that looked like it was designed to be unobtrusive. "And the kitchen is through here."

As she opened the door, a woman's voice rang out behind us: "Mrs. Carver!"

I turned to look, of course. Just like Vivienne. But before I did, I caught a glimpse of a butler's pantry immediately behind the door and, through the open doorway on the far side, the kitchen: patterned tile, cabinets with slate countertops, big sash windows, an island covered with butcher block. It looked updated in a way the rest of the house didn't, with the Thermador fridge and the Viking stove and the LED lights. But that was probably for the best—most people wouldn't enjoy actually working in a Victorian kitchen, with a table and a wood stove and a "kitchen dresser" (yes, I put it in quotes on purpose) instead of, well, modern conveniences.

All of that passed through my mind in an instant, though, because what caught my attention was the boy and the woman.

The boy was a teenager, with long, dark hair that had clearly been lightened by the sun and a deep tan. He was small, swallowed up in board shorts and a baggy tee that showed a crab riding a surfboard, but he had a wiry build that said he was stronger than he looked. His features suggested he might have Native American ancestry. He was staring at me with a look that straddled the line between startled and panicked.

The woman was older; she might have been close to Vivienne's age, maybe a few years younger. She had dark eyes and generous laugh lines, and her mane of thick hair had a shock of white in it that made me think of a witch. Her hand was on the boy's shoulder, and I couldn't tell if the pose was possessive or defensive. Her expression had a grim, locked-down quality like a woman ready for a fight. She met my gaze for a long moment, and I was distantly aware of Vivienne saying something to whoever had called her name. And then, without a word, the woman gave the boy a push, and he darted through a door.

"—is Dashiell," Vivienne was saying. "He'll be working with me at Hemlock House." I turned around in time for her to say, "Dashiell, this is Millie."

I had a single instant to take in the woman in front of me: early twenties, blond, a wide mouth and a scattering of freckles. She looked like five feet of flyaways and what Hugo had once called *manic pixie energy*.

"Oh my God," she squealed as she hugged me. "It's so nice to meet you!"

I tried to disentangle myself. "Um, yes, hi." The hug was ongoing, and she was surprisingly tenacious. "I'm Dash. Nice to, uh, meet you."

After one final squeeze, she released me and stepped back. "You are going to *love* Hemlock House. Isn't it amazing? You're going to love it!" And then, just for good measure, she bounced on her toes and clapped her hands. "It's amazing!"

"So amazing," I said because I honestly had no idea what to say.

"I do all sorts of things for Vivienne," Millie said. "I bring her coffee. Oh! I work at Chipper. And I bring her sandwiches sometimes, only she doesn't always like how they make the sandwiches, so then she writes down a HUGE LIST—" I'm using capital letters because at that point, Millie got very loud and also used her hands to show me how big the list was. "—of how she wants them to make it, and then I take them the list, and then they make the sandwich exactly how she wants it, and it is *so good*, like better than any sandwich I've ever had. Oh! And the sandwich place is called The Mermaid's Gill, only it was supposed to be Grill, but they didn't make the sign right, and then Fred didn't have to pay for it." She stopped for breath and added, "Or not all of it, I don't think. Oh! And—"

"Millie, I'm giving Dashiell a tour—"

"Just Dash," I put in.

Vivienne powered on. "—so you'll have to excuse us."

"Of course!" Millie hugged me again and darted toward the kitchen, shouting back, "It was so nice to meet you!"

I wondered, as the silence settled back down, if this was how people felt after they got picked up by a tornado.

"She's very…" Vivienne began doubtfully.

Then Millie's voice carried from the kitchen. "Oh my God, Indira, have you met Dash yet? He's so cute. So, so, so, cute! Oh my God, he's dreamy! I think I'm in love!"

"…enthusiastic," Vivienne finished.

"Oh!" That was Millie again. Apparently, solid-wood doors and inches of lath and plaster weren't up to the task of quieting her. "Unless he's gay! Oh my God, that would be even BETTER!"

(The capitalization doesn't fully convey the experience.)

"Uh," I said.

Vivienne made a tutting noise and pushed open the kitchen door. "Nothing to worry about, dear. Hastings Rock is very accepting."

"That's not what I was worried about—" I tried, but Vivienne had already pressed on without me, so I followed her into the kitchen.

"This is Indira," Vivienne said, gesturing to the woman with the witch-streak of white hair. "Indira, this is Dashiell."

"Actually, it's—"

"It's nice to meet you," Indira said over me. She had a lovely, low voice. "Do you have any dietary restrictions?"

"No."

"What about preferences? Things you won't eat?"

"Uh, no?"

She smiled. "Don't worry; we aren't too adventurous, and I'll let you know if I'm planning something I think you might not like. I keep snacks in the refrigerator, so please help yourself. I do ask, however, that you not use the kitchen to cook. As I explain to all of Vivienne's guests, this is my workspace, and I hope you'll respect it the same way I respect your personal space."

There didn't seem to be anything I could say to that except: "Of course."

"If you have any special requests," Vivienne said, "Indira will be happy to accommodate you."

"Another thing I explain to all of Vivienne's guests," Indira said in that same, hello-we're-friends-but-don't-screw-around voice, "is that, although I live on the property, I am not an on-call employee. I have contracted hours when I work for Vivienne. The rest of the time is my own, so if you have a midnight craving, I suggest helping yourself to snacks and leftovers, or you're always free to bike into town." Another polite, no-nonsense smile. "I promise I won't be offended if you choose to eat out, but I do like to know, if possible, so we can avoid food waste."

"Sure," I said—because again, what else was I going to say? "Of course." And then, because it felt like I had to say something, I asked, "Was that your son?"

The sudden silence was suffocating. Vivienne turned her head slowly toward Indira, and one eyebrow came up.

Indira's expression was flat and unreadable.

"I thought we talked about this," Vivienne said.

"We did," Indira said.

"I thought the issue was resolved."

"It is."

"Wonderful," Vivienne said the way people say it when they mean a word you can't print in the newspaper.

Indira tried to keep up her end of the staring match. And then she turned and chopped an onion in half. One strong, swift *schick* of the knife. It sounded like the last thing Marie Antoinette ever heard.

Maybe Vivienne saw something on my face because her expression relaxed, and she motioned for me to follow her. She said in a low voice, "I'm sorry. A bit of an ongoing disagreement. Indira can be a bit…stormy, but you wouldn't believe what she can do in a kitchen."

Build a gingerbread house to lure children in, I thought as I followed Vivienne through another door. Roast them at 425 for about an hour, and the meat falls right off the bone.

We passed through what must have been, in the olden days, the servants' dining room. It was still set up with a table and chairs, gingham curtains in the windows. They looked out on the sea cliffs. The boy I'd seen in the kitchen had come this way, but I didn't see him here. Vivienne pointed to a door and said, "That's the rear entrance. There's also a side entrance just around the stairs. The Blackwoods had strong opinions, like other wealthy people at the time, about servants not using the same spaces as decent people. The cellar's down there—I don't suppose you have a lot to store? We could make room."

"Not really," I said. "But thank you."

"Then I'll show you the billiards room and the den," she said, pushing through another door, which carried us back into the main hall. We had made a full loop of the ground floor, I realized, and Fox now lay on the tile directly ahead of us, snoring lightly. Vivienne chuffed a laugh as she indicated another pair of pocket doors.

Before I could open them, though, footsteps rang out in the vestibule, and a door closed a little too hard. Hasty steps moved toward us, and a moment later, a man entered the hall. He was white, with the comfortable padding of a man in middle-age, his receding hair clipped almost to the scalp. His suit looked like something out of a mortician's supply catalogue. He started for the stairs, glanced at Fox, and continued—obviously unfazed, which really said something.

"Mr. Huggins," Vivienne said, "perfect timing. This is Dashiell—"

"Dash is fine," I said.

"—and we've just about finished the tour. Why don't you get set up in my study, and we'll complete the necessary paperwork?" In an aside to me, Vivienne said with a smile, "Mr. Huggins is a fiend for forms."

Huggins stared at me, as though he weren't really seeing me. Little beads of sweat dotted his forehead, I could now see, and he had an unhealthy cast to his complexion. "Vivienne, we need to talk."

Something changed in Vivienne's face—I wanted to call it surprise, but it wasn't quite that. Then it was gone. She squeezed my arm and said, "Dashiell, why don't you bring in your luggage and make yourself at home? I'm going to have a quick chat with Mr. Huggins."

"Oh, right. Sure. I, uh—I didn't know where to park, actually, so I left my car down on the road."

"Of course. Come right up the drive and follow it to the back. The coach house is technically the motor house, now, I suppose. You can let yourself in through the side and open the overhead door. We'll find you one of those remote thingies. Oh, please don't go poking around—Indira lives on the second floor, and she's protective of her space."

Why wouldn't she be, I thought. She's got all those children she's fattening up.

"That was your car?" Huggins asked, dabbing at his forehead with a handkerchief. He finally seemed to have realized I was there. "Parked on the shoulder?"

"The Jeep," I said.

"You'd better get down there. We've got an overzealous deputy on the local force, and he looked like he was about to have it towed away."

I looked at Vivienne with what I hoped was an apology, and then I ran.

Acknowledgments

My deepest thanks go out to the following people (in reverse alphabetical order):

Wendy Wickett, for help with so many things, but most importantly, for three wonderful insights into these characters: Tean and Jem's daughters; Emery beating himself up; and John-Henry reclaiming his power.

Mark Wallace, for helping me find the soul of this book, for his wonderful insights into Colt and Emery and John, and his red pen edits to make it even better!

Tray Stephenson, for catching my sentence fragments, for spotting my typos, and for his kind words about these guys, particularly Shaw!

Nichole Reeder, for her help with missing letters and words, for help with my continuity errors (John's phone!), and for asking that critical question about Cassidy.

Pepe, for thinking of the Mosses and their church, for helping me clarify awkward sentences, and for the wonderful suggestion about Kitty/Cat (I can't wait to find a place to use that).

Cheryl Oakley, for asking about Cassidy's past, for helping me fix the shootout at the trailer, and for catching so many continuity errors.

Raj Mangat, for remembering the Christmas decorations, keeping track of Auggie's search history, and the wonderful suggestion about Colt making the call (even though that didn't end up making it into the story).

Steve Leonard, for his feedback about Emery's decision at the end, the inability of the other characters to read the room, and the parts of the story he enjoyed.

Marie Lenglet, for helping me make this book better in so many ways—to name only a few, by helping solidify Vermilya as the "big bad," amping up the pressure with the Wahredua PD, and suggesting the threat of Child

Services intervening. (And an extra thanks for the final read-through corrections!)

Austin Gwin, for his thoughtful comments about the final reveal, about the threat posed to John and Emery's relationship, and most of all for helping me think more carefully about Emery in the final chapter.

Fritz, for asking about the timeline in the final chapters, for (among other things), help with the Ford Airstream, and for one of my favorite edits of all time (like taking sixth-grade health all over again).

Savannah Cordle, for asking very important questions about Jace's motivation in being the witness, for her insight into the progression of the final act, and all her reactions to the story that reminded me there was some good stuff happening in here.

A special thanks to Raye, Crystal, Alyssa, and Alicia for catching errors in the ARC.

And finally, a tremendous thank you to everyone who supported the Iron on Iron Kickstarter (in no particular order): Tobi F., Hazel, Diane Crew, Rebecca Kopf, Cheryl, Gerie Jones, Roberta Vitale, Alyssa, Kristina L., Jamie B., Elanore, Piper, Nicoleta M., Chiara, Emma Macadie, Mimi Cirik, Russ Sadd, Nikki Simpson, David Bedwell, Ela @ TheQueerBookish, Connie Kendall, Darrel M Wood, Silvia P., Jason R., MtSnow, Bev Sutherland, Brittney Hooker, Donald Proffit, Courtney Bassett, Lloyd Dodd, Nancy L. Fulton, Urban Andenius Skeppstedt, Kerri Hinkel, Rochelle Selwyn, Jacs, ML Quackenbush, Emma de Boer, Julie Whitehead, Yaara Aloni, Åsa F, Dri Gomez, Andi Byassee, Ruth Johnson, Liz Kruse, Jolanta Benal, Mary Dolphin, LiLe Upp, Marti, Joseph D. Carriker, Jr., Susanne Werner, Laura Tobin, Olivia, Kelly Johnson, Nick Miano-Kegg, Amy Zontek-Carney, Dayle B., Babette B., Nakaji, Kristin Noone, EWC, Emery, Dan Leonard, Mich Cahl, Caroline Simon, Nica Flor, Yvonne Jones, Jessamyn Donovan, Devon Monk, Cristov Russell, Abraham Josep, Kurt Granzow, Francisca, Tracey L., J. Abrams, Amanda B., C. Peters, Emily Pfeifer, Christine Rost, Ravyn Bryce, Elizabeth R., L Tran, LenaBelle, Saranna Riley, Emily, Rhys Everly-Lawless, Addie M., Eirinelli, Julie Ashmead, Marcy Velte, DKauffman, Wardy, Maegan Richards, Nicolas Maurand-Garet, Sheila Vance, Jessicapybara, Cathy Lechien, Mandy A., Colette, Bob Turnure, Mark Wallace, Caroline Nelson, Carol Higgins, Maya Bretzius, Aude, Elizabeth Rasic, Robyn, Hank Edwards, Annery, Laurene, Murphy-Ann Craig, Ruth Cannon, Vinh Ho, Alan Weaver, Kylie, Raye, Michael of Deserts, Mody Bossy Canada, Debra Edwards, Juli Hincks, Chloe Smith, Tricia Bowden, Steve Leonard, Sandra Kirchner, Chloe T., Melissa Hensley, Megan Dansie, DK, Lisa Sullivan, Megan Tarbett, Kelly Rayson, Q, Kate Child, S.Y., Stacy Sirkel, Christina

Lovette, Caroline Nelson, Jessica Wynne, Crystal Jackson-Kaloz, Caroline, Antara Chowdhury, Savannah Cordle, Molli B., Kat Shenton, Shannon, Alyssa Ma, Crystal, Laura Jordan, Deb Sutton, Miriam Brodbeck, Melissa Brus, Nichole Reeder, Ellen McManus, Connie Munoz, Meredith Sweeney, Cristina Nieves, Mitchel Walters, Bec Lasky, Kirby Yount, Carlene McLaughlin, Christine Fredrickson, Emily Dye, Kate Collopy, Dawn Cutler-Tran, Amanda K., Cyndi Reynolds, Marleen Martinez, Justin Trimboli, Jill Kirkland, Sierra Anaya, Debbie J., Sarah Sutton, KarenABQ, Carey Eldridge, Kevin Craig, Eri, Eli H, Aethena, Chris Hasala, Michael Carter, Ulrike Fischer, Zyn Marlin, Ida Sue Umphers, Tara Greene, Ron Trucks, and Randall Gilchrist.

I may have missed a backer because of a miscommunication, an incomplete survey, or a mistake on my part – in that case, please accept my sincere apology (and let me know so I can correct it).

Thank you again for making these books possible!

About the Author

For advanced access, exclusive content, limited-time promotions, and insider information, please sign up for my mailing list at **www.gregoryashe.com**.

www.ingramcontent.com/pod-product-compliance
Lightning Source LLC
Chambersburg PA
CBHW052034240626
47153CB00006B/2084

* 9 7 8 1 6 3 6 2 1 0 7 1 1 *